International P

'Bruising, beautiful and u... ...per-
fect thought on sport, hu... ...out
every page' Mar... ...hief

'Absorbing on many levels. A book about violence, youth, mythology, history, guilt and love – all set to the agonizing rhythm of an inhuman bike race. Some achievement!'
Ned Boulting, cycling broadcaster and author

'A wonderfully colourful and attentive novel that subtly combines the tangible pains of the race with the echoes of war. It isn't myth-making or playing true events like puppets. Coventry commendably creates his own legend and pays homage to our ancestral competitors in doing so . . . Bursts of brilliance . . .'
Sunday Express

'An important and impressive debut'
Sunday Star Times, New Zealand

'Beautifully and brutally poetic . . . A truly extraordinary first novel'
New Zealand Listener

'The year's most interesting New Zealand novel is a dream to read, in all senses of the word . . . The writing is fierce, a bravura mix of narcissism, masochism and lyricism, grounded in the honesty of the unnamed rider's journey into his self'
New Zealand Metro

'It's such an accomplished and beautifully refined novel. It almost makes other writers look like they're just mucking around'
New Zealand Herald

THE INVISIBLE MILE

David Coventry received his MA in 2010 from the International Institute of Modern Letters at Victoria University. *The Invisible Mile*, based on the true story of the first English-speaking team in the Tour de France, is his first novel.

THE INVISIBLE MILE

David Coventry

PICADOR

First published 2015 by Victoria University Press
Victoria University of Wellington
PO Box 600 Wellington
vup.victoria.ac.nz

First published in the UK 2016 by Picador

This is edition published 2017 by Picador
an imprint of Pan Macmillan
20 New Wharf Road, London N1 9RR
Associated companies throughout the world
www.panmacmillan.com

ISBN 978-1-5098-2293-5

1 3 5 7 9 8 6 4 2

A CIP catalogue record for this book is available from the British Library.

Printed and bound by CPI Group (UK) Ltd, Croydon, CR0 4YY

Visit **www.picador.com** to read more about all our books
and to buy them. You will also find features, author interviews and
news of any author events, and you can sign up for e-newsletters
so that you're always first to hear about our new releases.

for Laura

We suffer, from start to finish we suffer.
You want to know how we keep going?

– Henri Pélissier to Albert Londres
in Café de la Gare, Coutances

Prologue

I arrived in Canterbury, the flat lands and the unerring sky. It was 1921 and the sun bore holes in my eyes and shrank the lakes to salt and mineral. At Timaru I borrowed a bike in borrowed shoes and raced in the dust storm ripping from the tips of the Alps across those dry plains to the side of the sea. The road was planted in the centre of the wind. The air shaped into a tunnel, at times narrowing to draw us towards the edge of speed, at others to wreck us in a swift twist of dirt and heat. It was a brute summer that could only be imagined.

For 100 miles I paced beside men and older men, each of them breathing hard and some in the throes of a cough, rough patches of voice when they called out. We ran across creeks where there were no bridges, we scrambled in the dust as it rose around us, searching for the road, and when there was no road we ran in the mud, our bicycles held high above our heads. No man was free until he quit. And many quit. The first run of the Classic since that rail car on the outskirts of Compiègne. I knew nothing of the men I rode beside.

My brother Thomas and his wife drove behind. He shouted anything to keep me going on. Thomas and Katherine leaning from the car in the rush. Men tried to

talk to me, to harangue me, to encourage me, but I just rode on in silence. For an hour rain buckled in the wind-hit and the blood was washed straight from our wounds. Then the sun, and I stared up the road. Silence and the red buttons on her sleeves as Katherine waved from the window, a Butchers Carbine balanced in her hands. Her pale arms and the arch of her neck.

In a scramble for the line I placed fourth behind Phil O'Shea – a man from before the war, a hero after – and he gave me congratulations. Somebody took my bike from my hands and I stood wondering what it all meant. O'Shea carried flowers in a bouquet like somebody else's baby. He put an arm about me, congratulated me and welcomed me to this religion of suffering and dirt. His words, my misery. I didn't know his name till after. By then any memory I had of his face was gone, but I shall make sure he was handsome.

This was the first race in which I'd worn a numbered shirt, the first not around the mountain with my pals from the club taking turns to race me in relay. In truth, I should have been last. A squalid 19-year-old, I could not gain muscle, I was a rake with fast-moving tendons between its tines. I had a beard, but the hair shot out like actors' fake bristles. All my thoughts were life and this damned speed I wanted like the train that barrels on rails towards the moment where they narrow near the horizon and collide. Life, speed and a future I couldn't adequately imagine, that was my constitution. I placed in front of named riders, riders of solid years' pacing. I had my back patted by men of uncertain intentions. I was smiling like lipstick on a glass still warm from wine. I whistled between my teeth when congratulated. Still, I struggled with the belief I'd got through, and Katherine, she said as much.

In the night, my brother and I were drunk. Singing and high and I imagine smelling rank. We parked the car at the rough waters of the Waimakariri and drank in the light of the Ford's headlamps. I told him what others had said. I had none of my own phrases, they were still out there under the bridge. I told him about the wind and mud. I had twigs in my hair and grass down my shirt front. My brother with his beaten face nodding as several wethers wandered through. He smiled and cursed. He shouted beside the car as we drank our beer. It seems sad I can't recall what I smelt of, what taint was in my clothes and deeper in my skin. It's the most personal of the senses: the hardest to dismiss, the hardest to diminish. That memory is absent, as if exchanged for some fate I was suddenly a part of.

Indeed, I should never have finished. I should have been last. I should not have made my fine sprint into the aerodrome in which four riders slipped behind as if I had paused time for them and made my own out of another curiously quicker rate. A bridge over the Rangitata and the race was split: those who passed the span prior to the truck's entrance, and those who scrambled in its path as it lost control and wheels slid and the smell of brakes forced the air to close itself. I rode somewhere between disaster and triumph, a pair of half-blinked eyes racing amongst dung and dust. I avoided its path through luck and blind reaction. I should have been sitting in a ditch, nursing my bad pride, building a cairn in tribute to past things: my sister Marya and all I saw in the moment when the truck came and I rushed forth out of death's way. Instead I stood leaning on the Ford with Thomas and the night and things that get said in the night.

He socked me, eventually. His hit took out a tooth which I picked up from the dirt and placed in my pocket. He's a short man, powerful shoulders with strong arms and a look

that betrayed the violence he had been guilty of in certain pasts. Indeed, he'd had a calm since the war passed through him, as if suited to a life on a farm, or nearby so he could walk in pastures and brush the hindquarters of a calf, fix the hinge of a gate that rattles against the night. All as if he has no fear of memory. An impression that quite disappeared in those few moments. For all that had been done to him in the sand south of Middelkerke – the pitiless maimed proprium, the war's death wash and stain – it showed out.

We stood with blood on ourselves. I couldn't see the water but for occasional flashes of white where it broke and tore. He sat on a log and his face disappeared out of the light.

'What did you say?' I asked. 'To Marya?'

'What did I say?'

'What did you say to her? What did you say to Marya?'

'What did I say?'

'What did you say?'

He stood and came to me. He lurked. Leaned on the darkness and stood over me. He began talking, mumbling and cursing. He said my name, my sister's name. He said all our names as if we were there. As if Marya and I were there ready to listen to what he had to say. He gestured and mouthed, stared and spat. But Marya and I, we heard nothing, nothing but the throttling run of the river, the hustle and speed of the river as it slowly made mountains into rocks and rocks into sand.

Part 1

1

I suspect none of us have ever foreseen the gaze of so many thousands, these faces and the bodies behind. These 50,000 eyes, brown, blue and hazel, all staring. I sit on the seat as Harry steadies the bicycle. He's tall and he stands at my handlebars, looking past my shoulder. His own eyes are quite distant, their whites bloodshot with coffee and sugar and a hundred varying queries. The cobblestones make the wait awkward; I fear my bike is going to topple before we set off, a fool before the Paris thousands. I ask the time but no one will answer me. It is within the hour in which the Tour starts and that is all we know. 9:20 is our due; when it'll arrive I can't say. Harry nods at me but then his jaw stiffens as a draft of noise comes off the crowd. He blinks and this sound flattens for an instant, the faces and mouths and all the brilliant eyes dim, fold and brighten again. I adjust the brake lever. I make the change in racing position. Then I change it back.

It should be warm but pockets of night still sit in the shadows, its air running over our arms, over the run of nerves which have pimpled the skin. A pretty girl leans out of the crowd on the balcony above trying to get a rider's, any rider's, attention. She's wearing a coat but pleasantly all the buttons that matter are undone. One of our team

says, 'Phew.' It's Percy and his accent's rough, so rough the French look at their shoes when he speaks. He's nervous and slaps Harry on the back. Nobody looks him in the eye. At least not Harry, because I know what he's contemplating as he looks back at the crowd, what half the men are asking as they ready themselves.

'What's –' Harry starts.

'What's what?' I say back.

'Do we know –' But he stops again as he's drowned out. All the noise, the cathedral sound of le Tour. Another team has left the line. We each wait out our turn, suspended on the rattling noise of the city.

I doff my hat the girl's way. She seems to shout something out. I smile at all of us. Harry asks me what her name is, but then the crowd begins again. It surges, the sound seems to move and gather, setting a high point in its tide. He twists his neck and elbows my side. I nod and see what he is looking at. We all sense the dense weight of the eight touristes-routiers standing in the rear about to set off on a warm-up. Some I recognise. François Louvière is amongst them. I go quiet. As does the crowd. I watch him stretch his legs.

Harry's squinting once more. I watch him because I believe I know what he is thinking, what he is doing: he's asking how the dark has fallen outside his house, he's asking what might be on the table inside the house at the end of the road at the start of the plains, for it is that approximate time back far in the south. He's thinking of the room where his wife stands beside the quiet boil of the pot. I know how comforting these thoughts can be to one who fears the noise, the cauldron sound of murmurs growing to calls and shouts and moans. It surrounds us, crawls under our shirts and runs along our skin. The sudden loneliness hits and you turn and look around and think back to the things of food and drink, of love and quietness. I know because everyone fears the noise.

8

'Hey,' Percy calls out to the girl. She winces but grins. Three Australians and two New Zealanders, we can't know what we sound like this deep in Paris. And I say Paris but we are really in the outskirts at Le Vésinet, but still, the city is here.

Ernie Bainbridge yawns. He starts humming a song, but Percy interrupts, or is already interrupting as he had never really stopped talking. It's a nervous monologue, joking and serious and uncertain. Words he's said before, said before we left for Brussels, said when we flowed out of Perth that March dawn. Something about mornings and Percy Osborne.

'We're gunna sink,' he says.

'You're a nervous nelly,' Ernie says.

'A bridge'll be out and you jokers'll go down. I won't be there, I'll have quit.'

Harry smiles and opens his mouth.

'You're nervous,' I say.

'Damned right, I'm nervous,' Percy says. 'I'm nervous. I'm filthy. I'm filthy nervous.' The repetition seems to help, seems to summon up some new pluck I hadn't noticed previously because he whistles to the girl, doffs his hat and waits as she blows a kiss across all of us. She beams but this time I can't say if her smile is a secret gift for Harry, Percy, Ernie, me, or indeed for Opperman who's happily listening in and keeping quiet, or if it's a gift for the broad sweep of the scene she must be seeing from up there; tens of thousands bright.

'Do we know,' Harry says, 'what –'

'What signal we get?' I ask, and Harry nods.

'Who?' asks Percy.

'Us. What signal do we get to start?'

'Hubert?' Harry says, and turns to find Opperman, who is concentrating on his handlebar tape.

'How do we know the race has begun?' Percy asks.

Opperman puts out his bottom lip and shrugs. 'I dunno, Percy. When we've started racing, I'll let you know.'

Percy mumbles something, says in half a voice not quite his own: 'Asked for a captain and they send us young sonny cadet here.' His brow is furrowed and he's thinking, surprised at where this voice came from: some butcher in the lane, a broken digger at the station selling stamps and newspapers, perhaps a relative who's been here before. It's all as if he's taken aback by the sudden need to be another to be himself.

'It's not the Sinai,' I say.

'You mean the Somme.'

'Fuck the Somme.'

'Do we go to the Somme?' Harry asks.

'Oppy?'

Our leader jerks his head at Ernie Bainbridge, who nods. 'Not really,' he says.

'Somebody do some more star jumps,' Percy says, and Opperman laughs as he bends to adjust his toe clips which do not need adjusting. An official waves for us to move up another place towards the line and the crowd sounds out like the inside of a wave tearing itself apart; we know a favourite has left the line. We look at one another and wonder which of the darlings has made their start. Monsieur France shouts to us from up ahead. He's our manager and speaks without uttering a word of English. Mister France. We take bets on his first name. 'What's he saying?' Percy asks – but we know it doesn't matter, what he says, not in this noise. It's the look in his eyes that tells us what we need to know, and it is saying we are up next, the next to ride into the howl this city makes when men are set free.

✺

We were hosted by Le Vallois Cycling Club at Les Loges-en-Josas. We lived in an attic as the chalets were overrun by the French Olympic team. They too were there to train, man machines. Much to admire in their movements on the track. We watched them in the misted mornings, before our training had us on the roads covering anything from 40 to 60 to 95 kilometres. They streamed around the track like the chains between their sprockets, they seemed effortless, a calm fury in their speed. We mimicked their hunched stance over the handlebars. Monsieur France manhandling us in our saddles to get our arses in place.

Calm fury. Harry said those two words on one wet morning at Versailles and they made me smile as we walked those grounds, not so far distant from our lodgings.

We burnt the effects of the sea in weeks of endless concentration and blind application. We boiled water in the room with eucalyptus leaves Percy Osborne had stuffed in his pack and placed towels over our heads and breathed in the steam. Our sinuses were thick from colds and everything else we picked up on arrival. Bainbridge was particularly affected. He had a stomach complaint and we stopped often to allow him to vomit the breakfasts we received in the early morning. A sight often seen: Ernie Bainbridge with his fingers in his mouth coughing and hacking beside a culvert away from the side of the road. He wished to be alone as he went through these moments. Privacy was hard fought.

They drank coffee by the pot and stared at their shaking hands. I read letters from London sent by a family member of such a distance it burns to think whether she is related at all; I have seen her name written a few dozen times, the men we see competing, hundreds.

We watched races, the Bordeaux–Paris Classic, we watched the track. Extraordinary riders, the shape of them as a group. We tried to imitate cycling as one, each pump

of the leg in tune with the man in front, the man behind. Our bodies pitched forward, la cadence. We found a smooth speed. I purchased clothes from a shop in the lane. I bought a beret. My teammates laughed at me, but soon had the same urge to melt in when crowds became too much. Yes, we mimic the French, but that is what we must do to survive. Seat position, head position. At a six-day event we were introduced to the crowd. We did a circuit of the indoor track and waved and men and women yelled. Opperman said we're a boon for French racing, foreigners of a truly foreign kind.

We had our lights turned out at 9:30pm. At night I could hear Bainbridge talk in his sleep.

At six we'd arise to ride again, to be laughed at once more by Frenchmen who believed our presence to be an amusement of some cruel kind. They pointed at our outdated machines and our tyres and soon we were forced to buy them anew. Thin, road-quick tyres we hadn't seen before arriving on the continent. We bought new handlebars so we could align our backs as we imitated the French. We found new pace, and while training with the Olympic team we could match them for speed on the longer days: Harry and Opperman stretching out leads once they passed the 100-kilometre mark. We rode with intent. Fitness made us machines to match the new bikes we were later given for the Tour by the organisers. Cycles that took weeks to get used to, to fine-tune into something that fitted our bodies and their complexity of shape and form.

I did not trust my new machine at first, none of us trusted them. The fittings came loose, the handlebars shifted, the seat twisted when I made an effort on the pedals. It took us two weeks to make the bikes roadworthy. And when finally we did, they flew. Harry wrote home making complaints. He wrote to O'Shea, the former champion

who'd taken him under his wing since Harry first won the Timaru—Christchurch, two years after my first compete, who'd become his mechanic and made his machines fast. He complained in letters. Read them out loud in the attic before sending them on. We'd murmur our agreement.

We walked in Paris and I wondered how it was just as my brother said it would be: grand avenues and shrunken alleys, horse-borne heroes unmoving in statue and a million shuttered windows shaken by the tremor of perfect light, all of which we rode through in the long evening as we became one with the bicycles.

We fought our first battle racing from Paris to Rennes. It was still May, Spring, a season laced with winter hailstorms and sleet. At 2am we rode. We hunched over and pedalled outside the peloton. We were not there to win, just to practise and compete, though we found the five of us in the lead. After five minutes we were looking over our shoulders. The Frenchmen were lazing, just drifting at a pace akin to an outing in the heat of summer down shaded lanes. A sluggish education.

We slowed and felt the pack swallow us. We rejoined at their pace, and we listened as they chatted. These powerhouses, with their immaculate bodies and fine-tuned machines just talking as if on their way to a village tavern. They talked. I watched Harry listen, his eyes flicking from racer to racer as laughs were had and stories shared. Opperman, he wanted to run ahead but somehow knew this was just a ruse, some pretend waiting game. We cycled beside greats, André Leducq, the Algerian François Louvière, Nicolas Frantz from Luxembourg and current champion of the Tour. They were mere men until one of them, Leducq, the French road champion, punctured and the 31 other riders went mad and bit their lower lips and powered away. We went with them. It was a race suddenly. Men turned to

sweat as muscles unwound, tightened and convulsed. The conversations disappeared, all went hard at the road. The leaders swapping out, letting others take their slipstreams for a few minutes before peeling off and letting another head the pack in the vanguard. We kept pace. After 40 minutes Leducq had rejoined the peloton and the pace once more fell away and the conversations started up again. Hands off the handlebars as men gestured and protested or agreed. A fraternity of riders heading south-west towards Brittany. I heard Louvière speaking Arabic and it felt familiar.

I came 19th, one place behind Harry, 11 behind Oppy. He rode beautifully and was in the papers. The owners of le Tour, *L'Auto*, mentioned our names.

We raced to Brussels with the flu deep in my body. Harry's cones became loose and he had to leave the race to have them fixed. By the time he had rejoined me, Oppy had disappeared. He'd latched on to Nicolas Frantz and gone with him. I was lost, coughing out mucus. Harry was a pacer. The erratic speed of the continentals wasn't to his liking or technique and we lingered near the back until I cried off before the borderlands. I returned to Versailles by train. During the journey I drifted in relief, the train rocking me through to a state I hadn't experienced since being merged with these men to a group, a calm. A calm, for I wasn't ready to ride so far north, not yet. I arrived at the club late in the evening to find news that Opperman had come third.

L'Auto took his photo. We were complimented and applauded in the strangest ways.

On the team's return we came together and fêted him. We bought the best meal we could afford. Many of the French riders joined us and we drank wine, something that made my heart stand and salute. The French who took our company made conversation in fractured English. It was

amusement for both sides and in exchange Harry and Oppy tried their poor French. We talked until dawn when the wine took us all out onto the streets. We asked ourselves if we were ready. No one had an answer.

That was all in May. Now it's June. June 17, 1928, and I tell myself to wake up.

Harry checks the spare tubes he has wrapped around his body like strange eels. We carry four of the things. Any more punctures than four and we will be forced to unstitch the inner tube from the canvas bag it resides within, then use glue and a patch before stitching it up once more. We've heard tales of men bribing local seamstresses to do their work, begging them not to tell the officials who linger about the race hoping to add hours to a rider's total, to shove him back in the pack with a bad wish. I recall stories told that night after Brussels. Battles between riders and officials. I think of them and look around searching for their protagonists amongst the riders, believing that they must all be here somewhere, even if they aren't racing. I realise I have no idea what they look like, though I have formed faces for their heads. So I ask: these men of fame, whose memories are they made of? For surely they aren't real. They all seem an eternity away, though I understand that they are not, they are at the distance of that flag fall, or whatever signal we shall receive to begin this thing. For at that moment we will all be in this race together, its pasts and this moment, each suddenly unveiled to each other. We wear matching deep blue shirts with a green band. Who or what these colours represent no one has said.

I start concentrating, shift the periphery out of focus and think about the shape of my body draped over the frame, the

adjustment of each angle of joint and limb – each so vital, more so than the organs within. Indeed, all we need is a heart for blood and lungs for air, all the rest are extra weight. We are soon to be engines. Soon to be flyers, eagles, bats, whatever kind you like. White caps and goggles, a mouthful of bugs and dust.

We depart 10 minutes before the gaggle of routiers, 40 minutes after Alcyon-Dunlop. The official starter nods, counts down and points the five of us on our way. We push off. We have, it seems, finally left New Zealand.

Despite this, my legs won't work. I'm coasting with limp limbs rotating with the wheels. Ernie looks behind him and sees me struggling. He mouths at me, I hear him perfectly as if his mouth were beside my ear. I shrug and he yells. There's nothing but the slow glide from the push Monsieur France had given my behind. A sensation like butterflies in my thighs as they slowly turn. Harry looks back, then the others. A cry from the crowd. There is nothing, and it seems there will forever be nothing. I am a skiff pushed out into the wash, surrounded by surf sound and drowning men. I am a failed tide. I move, but it's a strange powerless movement amongst the shapeless noise, the volume of rows and rows of shouting mouths. Whose faces do I see? I look for them, family, and friends. Of course I see no one, not until I see a scarf around the neck of a woman. It is yellow, bright. Harry sways outwards, his bike following his gaze back over his shoulder. I see our manager shouting at me, he's running alongside shouting. I grin at him. Slowly, with a curious returning, my legs begin to move, migrating energy from my thighs to the road. Harry says something and I find myself following him as I have time and again.

Someone. Someone deep in the crowd laughs and I join in for a moment.

Hallelujah, as the angels say.

Now we flow down the street, the dawn light bouncing off green steel. We are beneath the stare of thousands. I struggle to deal with their dimensions and I do calculations in my head. A habit of a habitual amateur mathematician; I struggle to resist giving numbers to things. The air remains hard with sound. We are within a shell. Children scream, though I doubt they know who we are or what it is we are doing; they are screaming for the sake of the scream, the facial contortion that lets their air join the others' (their parents, their siblings, their friends, and so on until each person on the end of each held hand is a part of this sound). It's immense and I know we all do it, we all fear the noise. It's everywhere, all about us, so we don't listen. We ride into a silence only we know how to make.

2

Then we are in the countryside. Wide green pastures and the run of a smooth road. Paris has gone, not even an echo of its noise hangs in the air. An hour, two hours. We have joined other riders. Individuals riding on their own: isolés, provincial and trade teams. The pack smells of coffee and skin and leather. I look over my shoulder and expect to see evidence of the capital, but there is nothing, just the country.

Opperman sits behind Osborne's wheel and turns and gives me a wink and I go. I ride to the front and try to get a sense of the mood. I listen to them breathe, watch the pack twitch at the movements of others. For the moment there is a lazy breathy air about us. No one is talking, no one is willing to think out loud and nobody makes a break. I sweat and feel the drips fall onto my thighs. I watch my fellow riders and I'm amazed by some men's ability not to lose water as they blaze through the sun.

Farmland and trees hanging their greenery over the road. The paving alternates between gravel and concrete. In the villages the cobblestones begin once more and our bodies jar as if shaken by a distant hand. The French wave to the crowds lining the streets and eventually we do the same.

We jump from our bikes beside a river and run to tables

18

strewn with foods. Bananas and bread, apples and coffee. There's chops and they taste muttony, but we swallow them down anyway. Twenty or thirty grown men with fat glistening on their chins. Monsieur France is there, he's saying: 'You must hurry. Hurry and hurry.'

Soon we are back in the race and France rides in the car behind us with Bruce Small (Hubert's friend from Melbourne) and our interpretor, René. Placed on the bonnet is a Union Jack and strapped to the back a kangaroo. Toys for tourists. This is our support as we chew off the day's kilometres, 207 in total. They unravel, distinctly, as if words spoken between two cities. We trade positions, shift places in that long missive, amazed at the people we have become.

Rain flattens the dust.

The format is a time trial, a team time trial. We race the clock, though we don't know what it says. Any riders that come alongside are potentially quite some time behind us, or ahead. The lot of us make a clattering sound when we hit a crossroad made of cobblestones. We forget who is where and it is only when Bruce Small comes alongside that we have information. He shouts with one hand on the steering wheel and the other holding a cone, a hailer that supposedly amplifies his voice but to my ear makes it thin and inaudible. Percy seems to understand the fragments and relays time and distance.

We find ourselves passing stragglers: one from Alcyon, two out of Alleluia, riders who have fallen behind their packs. We overtake them as they dawdle. Slow like campers. I hear Ernie shout out, 'Pitch a tent, ya filthy frogs.' I barely understand him but enjoy the titter that runs through our group. Riders and groups of riders jockey for position, elbows and hips bang. People swear in their own sweet voices and riders threaten to break away. There are grunts, noises of animals as one rider makes gestures and feints, puts on a fake rush to lure riders out. And some go. Most stay, waiting.

Outside of Lisieux the Louvet team ride straight through us and Percy shouts and Hubert goes with them and I try to follow. I pace him for an hour until my legs start to lose rhythm and I fall off to the rear. At Caen I come in five minutes behind him, 300 yards ahead of Percy and Harry. 19th. There are still 150 others on the clock behind me. Opperman receives flowers and kisses. We come together in the evening to discuss and unwrap the day. We talk of tactics, of our bodies. There is the burning sensation and a sharp smell in small successes.

'You know what I'm doing?' Percy says. 'You know what I'm thinking? I'm thinking 'bout Louvet.' He's got a mouthful and stops to swallow. He's heavy set for a cyclist, jokes that he got lost on the way to footy training and ended in these strange levels of hell. 'How close they get to each other. I'm thinking –'

'They're French, they don't care about the smell,' Ernie says. 'They'll ride up their own arses.' There's mud under his eye, has been there for hours.

'I'm being serious. I'm gunna ask if they take passengers next time they come through. "Excuse me dear sir, would you mind awfully –"'

'Use your elbows,' Ernie says. 'Just get in there.'

'Just the way they went through us,' Percy says. I look over at him and see that he is thinking, perhaps thinking over what we know. The facts of energy. The fact of our effort and how the effort we expend on poor technique is the effort they expel riding at a rate faster than we can summon. We are aware of this: we make a rattle in our ride which could be a fraction of a horsepower pulling us through. He won't blame his build for his slow pace, but seems certain about the French, how they understand form in a way we couldn't hope to know.

Harry taps me on my shoulder as I tear bread with

my teeth. It is rubbery and I squint at him as he speaks. 'Tomorrow, we go together. If he goes,' and he nods at Opperman, 'we make sure of it. All right?'

I nod and drink water. 'I'm happy with that.'

'The way they went through us,' Percy repeats. 'I just, I just – I'd hate to know the place that kind of discipline leads to.'

'Mate, they're starting their own monastery,' Ernie says. 'Them and Alcyon. You're their first –' and Ernie has his old mate in a headlock for a second. They do this: rough-housing the love out of the late evening.

'But the thing is,' Harry says, 'if he goes and I'm not there, you go, right?' I watch him for a long time and realise he is being serious. His expression some kind of rule of measurement against my slowness to respond. I nod and lightly punch his shoulder. A friendly punch. The act of a young man too close to caring to have anything intelligent to say about it.

After eating I leave the men and walk.

3

On this first night I find myself watching down at the street from three storeys up, in a room recently decorated. The length of the road below is full of men in cars making their presence known, honking and yells. I watch and try to get the names of these vehicles in my head. For the last month Harry has had me repeat words hoping they will stick, but most often they fade instantly, like a cheap sherry spilt in the sun — an aroma briefly hazes and then vanishes and who knows what it ever tasted like or cost. The woman whose hotel room this is watches me by the curtains, the way I lean, or perhaps the way my head keeps looking from side to side out the window and down the street, I'm not sure, but she calls out and says for me to stop doing what I am doing.

'I'm watching for rain,' I say.

'Not going to come yet,' she says. 'Due in the morning.'

'So I understand. I'm watching for it. I'm not looking forward to it, so I watch for it.'

'Wait for it tomorrow,' she says. She speaks a fine English, though the accent leaves its trace like a snail's trail over glass. Some province in this country making a blur in her voice.

'What colour is it?' I ask. 'The car, what colour is the car?'

'Blue. Come back here.'

I go to her on the bed and sit and she touches the hem of my trousers as I tuck a leg under the other. She reaches into her bag. She doesn't have a name yet, not one she wishes to offer and that is fine as long as she doesn't expect me to remember if I see her tomorrow at the start and she leans out and shouts.

'More of this?' she says. I look at the bottle in her hand, then back at her face. She is at least ten years my senior, though she retains a distinctly youthful aspect. She smiles and hides a small scar at the edge of her mouth.

I call her Miss Mademoiselle. She says: 'How do you know?'

'How do I know what?'

'To call me that. Here.' She leans close to me and puts the topette in my hand, a small ornate bottle. 'Put a little on your handkerchief and wear it like, erm. Wear it like this.' She takes her own handkerchief and places it over her nose so a triangle of white falls over her mouth. She looks like a bandit, though one used to finery and the feel of lace.

'You look ready for a robbery. Ready for a hold-up.'

'Yes, I am a thief. Now —' And she looks at me for a moment and then gets up and goes to the window. She's waiting for a car. Earlier in the evening I had come across her outside the Abbey of Saint-Étienne as I walked looking for architecture of interest. My neck ached and caused a limp somehow. She said my name and looked shy, as if she had made a mistake and I wasn't the rider she thought she recognised from my profile in L'Auto. But I was that rider, I still am in fact, despite the effect of the ether she gave me when I came to her hotel room. I am slightly awash.

'Do you have family?'

'Me?'

'Do you have family? Children?' She speaks quietly, as if hushed by the presence of other sounds she would prefer to hear.

'No children. Though I am likely to work on that. One day I will work on it. How about yourself?'

'At home?' she asks. 'At home in New Zealand?' I can't tell if she is biding time here or interested. She keeps looking toward the window. A car is due. She says she needs to get in it. That's all I've been told.

'At home,' I say. 'A brother.'

'A sister?'

'Once. She's –' I put my hand up, I wave goodbye to the thought.

'Mmm. I'm sorry. So, and – what about here? Out here: these old countries? Extended family. If I see a man or woman from the colonies I can't help but wonder, where are they from? Their family, I mean. What stock, if I may?'

'Yes,' I say, and laugh lightly. 'Family in England. Margate. My mother emigrated back in the 90s with her sister and brother. She has family back in England, another sister. My father, I'm not sure. But yes. Family. Family are everywhere.'

'Aren't they?' she says. 'Aren't they always somewhere? So uncles and aunts. Then cousins. I have cousins in South America. Lord knows.'

'Quite so.'

She lies down on the bed and says nothing for a moment, as if concentrating on something, a pure sensation of the sort I don't expect to be privy to, but then she says, 'God. My feet. My feet feel so perfect. Do you ever have that sensation – they are. It's like I have never noticed them before.' She looks at me.

'They're nice feet; nothing fancy but nice,' I say, then look up at her. 'Don't take me seriously,' I say in recompense.

'Nothing fancy. Well, I'll tell you something,' she says. She laughs quietly. 'England. Any intention of travelling there once this is done?'

I shake my head. 'Not so much. They are coming to me,' I say, and look at her. I feel the secret parts of me fade: the loose connections I have to this place, things I've told few about. Harry tells me I'm too easy to con out of my own ideas, and by the smell of this woman, I fear he's right. 'At least it seems so. I have a cousin. She's nearby apparently.'

'A cousin?'

'From Margate. I'm likely to meet her in the next few days if things go to plan. We made plans over the months.'

'A plan?'

'If our correspondence matches up.'

She doesn't reply, but rather stands on her tiptoes and looks down at the road. 'Mmm —' she says.

'They here?'

'I go now,' she says and signals for me to stand.

'Who are they?'

'Men and the kind of men who aren't family. Part of this thing.'

'The Tour.'

'Mmm. The Tour. In June, in July, everyone's part of the Tour. Now,' she says and hurries me up. I wave the topette at her and she looks at it for a few moments as if weighing the contents. 'No. You carry on with it. There's pain to come.'

Outside I bid farewell and head in the opposite direction as she walks towards a car parked across the road. I flick my eyes towards her as I walk away. She circles the car in a slow motion ponder before opening a door and disappearing into the leather interior. I want to name the car as a Ford, but then all cars are Fords to me at first glance. My father's first car was a Model T. He bought it in February 1914. I, my brother, and Marya my sister, we each stood staring as it came up the drive interrupting our tennis match. Thomas the eldest at one end and we younger ones at the other.

We walked about it as he came out of the driver's door. We walked around and around, watching our reflections in the black that wasn't splattered in the mud from the ride, from the docks where he'd received the vehicle and a lesson in its functions and particulars.

Half an hour had passed in the woman's room: one day's pain was reduced to a hum. Now I walk towards the end of the street thinking about how easily she had slipped inside the car. I think this because of how impossible it was for either Marya, Thomas, or me to get into my father's new machine. We each stood there as he rushed inside to relieve himself. The car, the way it sang and we all stood around.

'You do it,' Marya said. 'You're the boy.'

'What're you afraid of?' I asked.

'I'm not afraid. I'm being polite.' How old was she? Nine, ten. Something like that. She knew nothing of being polite, no one at that age knows anything of manners. She sidled up beside me and put her arm into the crook of my elbow. 'Yours to drive,' she said.

'Thomas?' I called out to my brother. 'You drive the thing. We'll watch.'

'No, not Thomas,' Marya said. 'He's so much more the handsome of the brothers. If one of you needs to be maimed, well –' She had a wonderful ability not to qualify jokes with laughter. She stared at my brother, squeezing my arm. Such were her directions for her siblings to act. Thomas put his arm around me and we both went and sat in the front seat. We looked at each other and the levers and the steering wheel, the pedals and the horn. Nothing was as I thought it would be, nothing was quite as simple as the one lever I imagined which would take you forward. Our father came out and told us to get out and get the hose. It needed cleaning, it needed the distance of 25 miles washed off. We sprayed the vehicle. He told us it was the 3,000th Model T

26

sold in New Zealand. We all nodded in a kind of trance. For years, even all the years my father no longer spoke to me, I was in the trance of truth, that this was true, a fact. The 3,000th car. But as I jump to the side of the road and watch the woman and the car come towards me, I know it was a lie, a bluff and puff. But such are the things of lies, their harmlessness and play, it was a fine story to tell my friends. I could tell it to anyone and it made a hush in the mouths of young men.

A rattle and the car coughs on the street. The woman passes a look my way from the window as they go by, and hints at smiling. I nod with the shy eagerness of an uncourted man.

4

The dawn is serene and Harry rides out of the morning, a pacer through the plains and gentle undulation. We are under a grey sky graduating the deepest imaginable blacks to white. We ride out of it into the day – the rain gone, the woman from the hotel in some other time, reduced to memory and the things we forget. Our small train, we hustle until we ride in unison and our pace is tied to Harry's, then Percy's, then mine and so on as we head east and slightly to the north. The Cotentin Peninsula, Cherbourg. I try to remember all skies, a marker of place and the time spent beside them. I watch the clouds and say to myself that I must remember.

For weeks we have prepared for this. Worked our bodies into a shape that would allow them to survive the rigour. Harry made complaints that we would never get fit for the mountains taking jaunts across the farmland outside of Paris. Of course he was right, but we had little choice but to ride and ride on to prime ourselves the best we could. And riding in the plains helped prepare us for this, this long scoot to the hills. Still Harry stammers his disquiet.

Mr France last week decided we were all, excepting Hubert and myself, sitting too far forward on our saddles. Inefficient, he'd said through a translator. Now I watch my

28

fellow riders and notice how they have inclined to move forward once again. I tap Harry and point to his rump and he shifts without engaging my eyes. He finds pace, though I suspect it is not an effect of his alteration that speeds him, rather a reflex against my observation. Nobody wants to be told anything at this hour.

We ride. The five of us cross the land. Though, and I am not certain why, it seems in some moments it is only Harry and myself. We are used to each other, used to habits of acceleration and deceleration, of powering up hills or pulling back that small amount when the rise becomes precipitous. Our bodies are oddly intimate with the signals they send: I know the way his bike tilts to the right side minutely when he decides to add extra revolutions to his wheels and gain pace on the pack. I know his sounds, the quickening of his breath when something seems ready to happen amongst a clutch of riders setting to break. And I expect he knows things similar about me. Though we have never been on the same team, we have raced beside each other for many hundreds of hours, within which things became familiar, strong and necessary. This only became obvious to me the first day we set out on our initial practice ride in Paris, the morning after our arrival. We were each feeling as well as a slept-on limb, pathetic and unworthy. And though slowly the rhythm returned, I found myself in an old pattern sitting on Harry's rear wheel and watching his long legs for signs of change, as if he were talking and telling. I realised I knew him in ways intimate, as if there were a love between us never before signalled.

It is from Caen we ride, the plains ahead. Harry takes us forward. Few riders catch us, and we too overtake only a clutch. 140 kilometres, not much more than a training ride and Opperman leaves us with 20 to go as we each seem to puncture in a row. Harry's pump falls out of its bracket

29

and catches in the wheel causing further delay. He rides as though a steep anger has taken him and laid on him strength to beat them all. We watch and sweat in the afternoon sun. My promise to him unfulfilled.

Without Opperman we make our own runs and feel the distance he puts on us, the strength and power he can summon. Hubert Ferdinand Opperman, we found out that second name when stealing glances at one another's passports. Percy always ready with a guffaw. He used to be Oppermann with an extra 'n', as his parents remain. When he changed the spelling no one is sure, but Percy takes bets that it was during the war, that he rubbed it out as if erasing that particular limb on his father's family tree which connected his ancestors to old Prussia. An utterly Australian act, Percy claimed, but I'm sure an act repeated the world over in those crushing years. So a mystery, his name, no mystery as to his brilliance. But on the long straights on the outskirts of Cherbourg we are caught by ten riders barely panting. We watch ahead, Hubert's outline slowly being dragged in. He is out there close to the horizon and still they catch him, still they swallow his ride.

Half an hour later, Harry and I hit the entrance to the stadium and feel the sound of thousands. It wells around us, starting in one section then running through the rest as recognition spreads. Half the souls can't see past the person in front and I sense something. I sense the point is not to see but to be amongst it, to feel the movement of the crowd, to sense the race through the movements of others, tiny movements, to hear with hands, to see with skin. The trading of senses: that is what makes it all seem so holy. I want desperately to leap from my seat and jostle my way into the centre and hear what they are hearing, for it isn't spoken in French, not in English. It's a voice wholly other. Muscles rolling through a snake.

We sprint against one another almost in jest. We coast across the line 11 minutes behind, but still they call for us in our mock duel. A giant call, a hum of multitudes asking for a prayer. They'd almost got it in Opperman. He'd fought those ten men with just a bicycle and a hard nerve. He came within six minutes of their shadows.

I sit myself down on the track. We watch André Leducq, Nicolas Frantz and Jan Mertens spray the crowd with a hose. Nearby men are quaffing fortified wine and the rich smell of it drifts to where we sit. I recall the sensation of communion bread, the way it would crumple on my tongue. Harry sits beside me and I ask the whereabouts of Opperman. He shakes his head but points towards the stage. I search about for him, the kid whose first job was as a courier, a kid who cycled all over Melbourne with missives and parcels. He did it every day after school until he was racing for money. Now he owns records too many to repeat. I can't see him anywhere, though I suspect he is amongst the champions, charming with his lack of real French.

People say our names over the fence. I can't but laugh and wave.

Harry pulls out a postcard. A picture of the city we'd ridden through before we hit this stadium. He reads his words slowly as he puts them onto the card. I know what they say before they are said. He writes to his wife, he writes dearly. I write to my brother and his wife. I place accents atop random vowels within their names to make my English seem French and the French seem nearer.

Some of the crowd yell our whole names, then say our home towns as if they are in charge of something we can't name.

'There's one or two riders who are going to win this thing,' Harry says. 'One, two, three, four or five.'

'Four or five,' I say.

31

'And they know our names. Is that something to be concerned about?'

I laugh.

'I'm not serious, obviously,' he says. 'But maybe I am. Maybe I'm being serious. When it becomes every town.'

'Then I'll worry with you.'

'People have more important things to remember,' he says, 'wouldn't you think?'

'Than Harry Watson of Christchurch?' I say. 'I believe they have more important things to remember, yes.'

'Such and such of Dingo City, New South Wales. If we get to Charleville and they are saying our names and towns.'

'I was talking to a woman last night. Last night? Some night. She asked if I thought we'd make it up that far.'

'To the north?'

'The old borders in the north. I improvised. I told her we would make it to the end.'

'Of course you did. Let me finish writing this. Did you sound convincing?'

'Yes, maybe.'

'What else would you say? I mean – anyway. You seeing her? When you seeing her?'

'This woman?'

'No. Your cousin.'

'Brest.'

'What a name for a town. Let me write this.'

Harry reads to me what he writes and I think of my brother. I write to Thomas and Katherine in the mornings before we ride. Thómãs and Kãthérinë. It is a long letter I will not send until this is over. There are parts of him I sense in the race, I hear voices and turn expecting my brother's face, but he is far from here. I write to him of the race. I write telling him I'm due to meet our cousin in a few days. Such a thing, to be meeting someone so distant. I think

32

to create space on the page to include my memory of our father's first car, that hard machine in the entrance to the home where horses used to ride and stand blinking at flies in the sun, the car which I eventually ruined on a bright morning of fence posts and mud. But there isn't room for that, just the spread of words describing this race. This race and the sense there is nothing beyond it.

"'I miss the early hours,'" Harry says, quoting himself. "'Mornings and the sun with you in it. Love and all thoughts.'"

'Amen.'

Harry and I, we share things, the things we love and doubt, we share how to ride against the tide of Frenchmen who pour down these roads leaving us wanting. We share memories of this place we have borrowed from others, memories and expressions we practise with our faces. All of it adds to questions we have of this land and of this race. We are unsure if we have an answer, so we share silences too.

The first time we raced, Harry was behind from the beginning, right up until we entered Pukekura Park in New Plymouth. I was started 30 minutes ahead of the scratch bunch due to bad form during the early summer, I had 11 miles' advantage when he set off. And, I swear oaths, even with those 11 miles I heard each of his breaths at my back. The crowds that leant from farm fences for a glimpse of the race barely saw me, did not recognise me, though they cheered me on. No, they were looking for the Cantabrian.

I rode under the cone of Egmont, mapping its slopes with my widening eyes, the slopes of white snows and volcanic black. We circled the national park, the centre of which belongs to Marya and me. The place where we climbed, the place where we made stories and laughed. The air under the shadow of the great peak was cool and the legs struggled all

33

the harder as they exported blood to drive the muscles and force the cranks hard and pull the chain and caress the axle. There the earth smelt different, the vegetation was close, the dirt close, the run-off stink was close, the dung and shepherd's tea was close and I sucked in the air and pumped it out again. I rode through riders who'd set off an hour before me. Overtaking riders and riders and riders, each of them in a deep ritual of breathing and pain and ecstasy as they headed for New Plymouth. We chatted, each asked about the southerner.

'He's behind me,' I'd say. 'He's coming.'

Then, the group I was looking for, men from my club. I sat on each of their wheels and listened to them speak as my body recuperated and I drank from my bottle in their slipstreams as they paced me, used up all their energy repairing my shaky limbs. They spoke of their own tiredness. My clubmates, my teammates who had planned to meet me there, to help me rest while keeping my pace. We sailed through Stratford singing songs. I left them soon after and they dropped off. I said cheerio, leaving them to their eternal conversation and awaited the Priest's arrival at my rear wheel. They sang handsome words behind me.

The Priest. I am not the only one to name Harry as such and you will later see why.

Another hour. Another hour. Soon the city. Soon the sunset. I took out riders barely crawling, as if their bodies had finally given up. I hunted them all down.

I was expecting a hurricane, a tornado of sweat and limb to catch me and tear me up. But there was only the soothing chime of my chain against the growing crowds shouting. Eventually, though, I turned. Harry was 60 yards back, a serene silhouette pouring down Vivian Street like the sun did behind him. In the last invisible mile he came alongside, his cap discarded, his hair the only exclamation and he was at pace.

We burst at the gates of Pukekura Park, sweat, thighs and cries, and entered the dense surround of green. Two thousand in the terraces and we raced. He was suddenly 10, 15 yards ahead. I doubled over to make a shell to thwart the wind and hide me from the winter ills, though it was summer and it was I who made the wind.

He was inelegant when he walked, a vulture stumbling about a corpse, but on his bike he flowed, a river long and smooth. I dug my thighs into the pedals and forced my lungs to the edge of breathing. My heart and veins fought. I thought of broken things, the things that had cracked through time and landed their sharp pieces on my life. I needed anger to break the limit my legs placed on progress. My body built to a scream. I shouted. The throng shouted back, their daydreams beginning to unfold.

Harry must have heard my noise but still he didn't stand on his pedals, and still he maintained that pace. My body raged and hustle came into my blood, ligaments stretched and barely held the muscle to bone. I watched his back wheel come towards me, I went outwards and felt my wheels spinning as the pain was overcome, the knowledge that I had him, that I was passing him with 30 yards to go. I felt him stand on his wheels beside me and give one last push, but it was too late. I took him by half a bike length and suddenly the whole length of the race was counted; in an instant I was no longer racing. I had raced and a story was made of it.

My lungs punched out.

Of course I hadn't won, Harry had won. I was merely a man in front. Time is what mattered. He had beaten me by half an hour and we sat together after the race in a rotunda. We didn't speak, only breathed like horses kneeling at the trough, ragged but for the desire to drink. But I felt a calm in him, a sense that neither placing mattered, it was the way

we had crossed the line that gave strength to the fact of our duel. If he had a complication in his personality it was a set of understandings that allowed him to think beyond his time to the instant of the finish. It was how one finished, he seemed to be saying.

'Two exclamation marks,' he said. He told me to come south where we could ride again. And a week later, maybe more, I took the boat across and down the coast. He met me at the harbour and from the Port of Lyttelton we cycled through the old volcano hills to Christchurch. I met his wife and his two sisters. I stayed with them as we both prepared to do battle once more. A slow rivalry that, from then on, always saw me behind.

We sit on the track watching all the men mill. I see men, I see women open their mouths and shout for the winners still on the podium. Sailors merge with the girls and I make a guess as to their conversations. Sailors are everywhere as once soldiers were. They move in circles of striped sleeves and short trousers. They seem unfit for the land, uncomfortable and diffident. I watch as the sweet wine washes on their mouths and down their shirt fronts. The crowd stammers as the officials move off the makeshift stage and the riders cast weary grins to teammates and to each other. In the morning we will ride again, but I don't think of that. Instead I find myself thinking of Harry's wife as he writes to her of our day. Back home she is so pregnant we get shy when her name is mentioned.

5

As we hit the low hills of Collines de Normandie any conversation is halted. Opperman signals to me, his great ears sticking out, and I take the front. With my head down I force a pace upwards. I stand and feel the four men behind me hold the imaginary rope that hangs from the small of my back and I take each of us forward into the slope.

These hills, hillocks really, are nothing in comparison to the visions we anticipate. Things that will define the race, end it in some ways. But they must be ridden at hard. In moments, distracted moments, I look up and scan the southern sky for hints of what is to come. The insanity of such a gesture doesn't escape me but I look nonetheless, trying to span the 700 kilometres with my eyes, eyes that believe they can penetrate the dust in the atmosphere, and defeat the curve of the earth. If there is a farce about me it is that I am a man whose actions seek cracks in science. For this reason, my sister once said, it is best that I am hidden from view.

It was O'Shea who taught me about hills and their importance. He taught me this amongst many things, but this most of all — air pressure: it is why we force the pace when we climb. In the open all ride at close to the same speed, kept there by the force of the air in our faces. To make

any significant distance on the flat means a superhuman effort. Though, believe me, I am seeing superhumans. The Algerian, for one, has collided with our pack and ridden off without us several times. He is a monster, but the time he gains is small compared to that which the mountain climbers will make. A mile's gain in the Pyrénées or the Alps is 10 miles on the flat. This is the rumour I spread.

I remember him as tall, O'Shea, but in reality he is short, small like Opperman. What is it about pocket-men that makes them fit to fire themselves across the land like cannon shot?

I take us up, pull us through gravity's yank. Our breathing is heavy though not so much it weighs us down. On the plateau we look out beyond the farmland to a brief lake of mist over fields where the sun has yet to make itself welcome. Harry takes my place and I drift back to rest a small amount and the pace is quickened. Opperman rides in front of me, telling me to take it easy. The unison of our pedalling is hypnotising and the wake of another's shape moving through the air is something.

We begin a descent, my legs being pulled by the cranks, and this is the closest one gets to coasting in these gears we have chosen for the day. The conversation stops, as it does often for long periods. I sense concentration, that something is happening. Percy heads to the front and pushes. We follow as our small pack ducks into the coming valley. The sun falls away and the cool is at us. We are near sprinting as we fall. The chronic beauty of speed while time is forgotten as if drunk long ago. My colleagues form into a snake.

I become a hollow in the wind as it rushes over Percy's hunched frame, over Bainbridge, over Harry, over Oppy, and I am like sound racing to your ears. This is why we do this. I'll speak for the others because I believe it is true. Speed doesn't need kilometres, it doesn't need time, it only needs the will to take it faster.

A hum in my ears as we fall. A ring, and then they pop.

Percy grunts in the rush. 'I've a dog,' Percy is saying to Ernie.

'What's its name?'

'I haven't given it a name. Not yet, anyway.'

'Good–looking dog? I like a handsome dog,' Ernie says. 'A dog with a good set of knackers. You know a joker's got pedigree behind it, with a good set of knackers.'

Percy says, 'Uh huh, he's no ugly brute. Pig dog.'

'Pig dog.'

'What kinda dog takes on a pig?' Hubert Opperman says.

'The lad's a city boy,' Percy says, turning our leader into a subject for slight derision. 'Any dog with eyes wider than there is to see. That's your pig dog.'

'Whatcha gunna call him,' Ernie says.

'I haven't got a name.'

'Pig dog, huh,' Ernie sighs.

'He'll get amongst it,' Percy says.

'What about them other kind?' Ernie says. 'Them other pigs? Get amongst them?'

'Uh huh,' Percy says. 'Damned snitcher.'

'The two–legged kind.'

'Those boys in black cars,' Percy confirms to himself.

'The two–legged kind in black cars with a siren. Bumbling down St Kilda.'

'Hope not. Need them to keep the shearers off my sister. Dog only bites so hard.'

And the boys are laughing. Though they speak this way, it is not always their mode of conversation and I can't say whether it is this or the more formal garb they occasionally dress their sentences in which belongs to them most utterly; one is the mimicked voice and one is their own. 'He'll muck them up,' Ernie says and I think for a moment how some men are actors and some just act. Whatever the case for the

next 10, 15 minutes I'm thinking about an imaginary doe-eyed killer of a pig dog resting his head on Percy's lap out at his parents' farm, a snarl for the approach of a cruising police officer, the lift of a lip and a sudden bark. I list in my thinking and daydream, imagining the bite of these teeth, the sinking and settling of salivating tooth into muscle.

I daydream out of day into night. A habit and it seems I have had it forever. I listen to these men and their talk and I drift into a world of daydreams. I drift and inhabit the world and all its stories. I let them all down with my witless fumbling. I say words never spoken, become a thief of friends, family and more famous ones. I become the prince of unlikely persuasions. It seems to me that I know too little, that there have been large amounts of time I afforded to other things, to daydreams and more. Large farcical amounts of time, amounts of time that were slow and eager. Time that might have contained better actions, reading, watching, seeing. Readings that contain the history of things, of revolution, of war; the last war and the future of war. Centuries of it sitting in libraries as I rode my cycle about the town hunting out visions of women I'd seen sometime, somewhere earlier, and had to spy again. The cut of a dress, the flow of hair, the hint of rose in the skin, the sound of stockings against cotton, the way a glance is taken – all of these I had to see repeated. I reduced all humanity, women and men, to these simple things. I rode over and again to street corners believing this action would produce the vision once more. Sadness lingers in each longing you take with you. Jenny Fisher, her friend, Janice Adamson. How could I not love them when they grinned at the curve I made in the road, arcing around corners just to see them again? Sharon Fuller, Deirdre Learner, Katherine Frier. What is it about the shapes bone and muscle make under skin? Why does it reduce me to the grand-king-waster-of-time?

Hanker and want; for such things we could go to war, but we are always told it is something else. We were told it was another largely abstract kind of love: The King. The Country. Those marvellous ideas whose scope I have barely considered.

I ride the plains and search out eyes and mouths. I whisper my strange English towards the eyes and mouths of faces I can't know the names of. That is where time has gone; vanished into the eyes of women I gaze at with such solemn hankering. So much history wasted on faces and the hunt for their names and their smile. I try for new thoughts to replace the time I have wasted. Thoughts bold and grand. And during this exercise I find these thoughts have a landlord, every emotion seems to belong to another. The effect is I don't have to feel so involved in the certainty I fear; that time is the one fundamental that is true without physics to prop it up. In fact, it doesn't even need numbers, it just happens.

See me glide past the small shelter as we climb once more where two young women in aprons are stalled waiting with a boy for us to pass, waiting so they might cross back to the other side of the road where a farm gate is open and a set of goats are threatening to walk right through. I take my hands from the handlebars and raise the wide white peak of my hat and smile. Percy does something similar though he is behind me and I don't see what it is he offers. It is something, though, as I hear the women speak. They sound like birds waking in the dawn. I chuckle and I hear stern Ernie do the same. Percy is as married as the other boys, but he can't but look. I heard him one evening talk with Mavys back in Paris, admitting his sins. Young Mrs Mavys Opperman, who had come with her husband this far, was quiet and shaking her head, perhaps at wonder as to why he

would feel the need to admit to such shallow misdeeds. But I understand it. As soon as we admit to things, a part of us disappears.

This reminds me, I should really name my bicycle.

I feel something, a person. A breathing chest full of air and heart. The sound of the chain of another, another chime, a crystalline tune running smooth. I slowly turn and catch a glimpse of the Algerian again on our tail: 10 yards back and gaining. A strange speed about him as he pushes through the air and comes alongside. He's bald and hatless, a dark head in the sun.

'Good day,' I say. I assume he has no English except for a few scant words, as I do French.

'You ride,' he says.

'Very good,' I say, and tip the peak of my cap his way.

And that's what we do.

Now, the impressions of an amateur: speed is a thing. Though its measure is ratio, all else about it is malleable; remove your hand from the bars as you drop off a hillside and feel the thickness of the air, open your mouth and chew on its rubbery substance. The sky, the hills, the trees – they become rumours, then the whole world is a blur and you're the only stationary thing. That is speed. And here we reach for it. All, each of the five riders. I bury my forehead into the space between my hands and sprint. I say something and I ride out from the train we make and head for the apex of a distant corner, the point of which is calculated by some magic in the brain. Beyond the bend is a stream, a stand of trees, the first one there wins. It doesn't need discussion. Louvière tears out from my shadow and comes alongside once more; he is hardly pedalling. I look down at his gearing and see a huge cog at the front of his machine turning with his cranks. I blurt a word, quickly forgotten for

it did not need a language, and feel him pull away. He looks a champion steed and the bend comes and he is through it. Soon enough I am only watching his dark form reduce down in the morning light so he is merely a smear in the vanishing distance. I ride at the front for a good 20 minutes. I feel like a shadow, the wind's shadow itself as he goes. Something powerful, and simple. I find it hard to believe I am in the same race as him. There are spectacular stories and I'm not sure I belong to any of them.

An hour passes by. Two, three. No other riders approach. Then Louvière is beside a tree. He has his tackle out and is pissing. I feel us all slow and come to a stop beside his bike. It seems we are set to join him. It is the first time I have seen him standing alone without a bicycle leaning on him or astride its wheels. He is at least six-foot-four and I finally notice this fact. His nose is long and shaped like the Matterhorn. We all flop out of our shorts and begin the long exercise of easing off four hours of tight bladder. The splash and tinkle in the grass and wood.

'You caught me?' Louvière says. He taps me on the shoulder.

'Sorry?' I blurt, not expecting this English.

'You caught me?' he says again.

'You must have slowed,' I say in a kind of stutter that comes directly out of the belief no conversation was ever likely to form between the two of us. Rumour was he worked as a metal worker in Marseille before he came to cycling. That he was deaf. That he was illiterate. I heard all sorts of things and believed them all because that's what you do in foreign countries, you believe everything because these places, even small places are vast for the things you don't know. Every step of the way you wish to fill the void, just to bring them down to size so you might fit them in

43

your head. 'Did you slow?' I ask. Indeed, we had made no real effort to catch him, he was just found there on the side of the road. So that's what I say next: 'We found you.'

He grins, an unexpected expression that ranges up as he scratches the back of his neck.

'We found you here,' I say.

'Okay,' he says and nods. 'Okay. No matter. Can you?'

'Sorry, sir,' I say. It's the first time I have said sir to anyone without volition since I left university in that odd funk five years ago.

'Take a look,' he says. And then I realise my eyes are following his hand as it descends from his neck where the edges of his beard begin, that I can see a grimace in his features. The hand falls down his chest and over the slight convex mound of his belly to his thigh. Sticking out of the muscle is a thin splinter of stone. It's buried deep, it bulges and seems to thicken in the muscle. His hand hovers over the pain as if feeling for the hurt, as if the pain has an aura, its own halo perhaps, that he can touch and rub, or even hold if need be. 'Can you?'

'You want me to pull it out?'

'After the hill I went into a fence. Here,' he says.

'And this —'

'This went in. Yes.'

'You want me —'

'Yes.'

I get on my hands and knees and look at the sliver of slate. It gleams, the silicon or quartz catching the sun. I touch it and feel a vibration, a lingering nerve twitch coming out from his leg.

'Come on,' Harry says behind me, and I realise everyone is watching.

I touch it again and this time he makes a noise. An utterance attached to the same nerve endings I'd just triggered. 'Just pull,' he says.

44

In the end there is a tiny piece of rock lying on the ground and blood on my handlebars as I ride off. Louvière is back behind us pushing that huge cog around as we make to disappear into the distance where towns and food and bandages await. Eventually all I will recall of the day is his blood, the fact of his blood and the thought of how blood becomes memory.

6

I have seen riders drinking in the minutes before the race, and some during. Taking wine when they pause at the side of the road. Red wine, cognac, various spirits I don't recognise the names of. Brandies and liqueurs. I have smelt it on them at the cafés into which we find ourselves falling after the stage for soup, bread and coffee. I find the effects of coffee quickly debilitating and avoid it. Harry and the others cannot stop themselves, feeding on the black substance they serve in small cups. I drink wine instead and the French riders raise their glasses to me.

This is a grand adventure.

The regional teams have their local specialties. Red wine from Beaujolais, white from Alsace. Burgundy from Burgundy. I could be making this up; I enjoy symmetry, a god in the inclination of things to pattern. Whatever the case, most try to hide it: from themselves, from those around them, I'm not sure. It was a Spanish lad from the Discuter team who told me he drinks most of the day, wine in his bidon. Then he sleeps straight after the race before rising, eating and sleeping again. He's 20, he's a domestique and spends half the day sprinting until his lungs are jumping out of his ribs, the other half just struggling to make it to the next control. He says he rides this race and others and sends

his earnings back to Catalonia to his family, his father who works in a factory and his mother who is bedridden, her back broken by a fall from a horse. He says he won't make it back to Paris, that the Pyrénées are likely to kill him, or if not that, the Alps. I tried his cognac last night. It threatens the nostrils then lights up your eyes.

Harry finds me on the stairs of our lodging and pulls me up by the arm. He's a strong one. Built like a fence, all wire and struts, could stop a bull if needed. I tell him that and he shakes his head down at me. I take up my satchel and walk with him to the street where Oppy is standing.

The French had started with the name a month back, Oppy. Calling out to him as we trained. If we were on the track the Olympic team would shout out to him, 'Oppy.' He is easy with people, quiet but with a brow that inclines you to know that you are being listened to. His eyes glisten, separate emeralds as if from far beneath terra firma, which, let me say, adds an eager depth to his demeanour. There is volume to his quietness; people wish to be near when he speaks, and when he rides. Harry lurks when he is beside the man, and though he has told me he enjoys his company he appears to me to exhibit an unease when they are stood at each other's side. It could be a tall man uncertain in the presence of the small. Either way, they don't fit in the same box.

We walk upwards towards the keep of Château de Dinan. Opperman narrates for me and Harry, or perhaps just for himself. He tells us the history of the area, the keep and the ramparts that encircle the old town, closing it off in a grey hedge of stone. I take peeks at my companions as I walk behind. There's no reason for secrets, other than one's shame. And I'm not sure I have such a thing, but I hide the bottle anyway.

Harry came in 7th fastest. Opperman 8th. And Percy,

47

Percy was there too in 9th. I was number 10, 30 yards back. I'd shouted as I had in New Plymouth, but not for any feeling other than being overcome by elation as those three powered to the finish. I had caught them, to a degree, running off Louvet – who'd earlier come though us – with a sprint that was forced out of me by annoyance at a crash 60 kilometres out which tore my shin and knee so blood was everywhere, in my shoes, in my shorts. I lost two minutes picking myself out of the rocks and bending my seat and handlebars back into position. I came at the extremely picturesque finish a bloodied fool and drank with a small elation for the placing. Indeed, from Cherbourg we had set out first, in Dinan we had arrived first. And though I was 11th fastest there was a certain rapid thrill in hitting the end with the entire field behind us. More inches in the papers, our names coming from the mouths of radios. At control I'd signed my name as 'Bit Knackered'.

So we didn't rest. After eating a huge amount of food for dinner we sang and astounded our hosts with the lack of harmony in our voices. Then we left the hotel for a walk. Ernie and Percy absent on their own stiff-legged dawdle.

Now, I watch the castle come near.

I try to imagine the men who built it, those who took the stone in carts and those who lifted and swung it into position using extraordinary cranes made from pinewood and rope. A remarkable edifice, one that seems older than the mathematics that hold it in place. The castle's donjon, 100 feet high, projects out of the ramparts, almost beckoning an enemy from the surrounding woodlands to upset its balance and topple it into the river. We walk onward to where a moat and drawbridge divides the interior from the world beyond the ramparts, a stronghold against both outsiders and townspeople disturbed by rumour and plague. Harry walks with his left hand in his pocket, the other rubbing his fingers

48

together in an indication of thought. He and Opperman both seem half-hearted about their placing and walk at a pace that suggests bickering minds. We walk on for some minutes in the sun that pours bright upon the surrounds. Oppy stops before the donjon. Harry trots ahead to search for a way into the tower. He is heavy on his feet, proving a rider shouldn't run.. Opperman squints at the strange sight of Harry jogging towards the donjon as if he were that lone soldier destined to infiltrate by trick of deed the hard stone of the Duke's redoubt.

Hubert starts talking about Melbourne, the months and the lead-up to this, all this. Opperman is 23, four years my junior, but often it seems youth is merely something his body enjoys. The preparations, the communications and letters and how the strange fact of our participation slowly became truth. He tells me he had seen a list of names Ravat had organised to ride with our team. Jean-Luc Maron was one, he says, so was François Louvière. Only a couple of days ago we found out we weren't going to get our other riders. Opperman and Bruce Small attempted to get us transferred into the JB Louvet Company, but nothing transpired there.

'This whole thing −'

'It's like playing footy, fifteen against five,' I say.

'That's it,' he says.

I look at him and know he is disappointed, not just having had his time beaten, but by something else. With the race being run as a time trial many of the subtleties of road racing have been lost. The complexity of racing as a pack, the chess play of feints and attacks proper, of defence and fake drama and true fatality. All this is replaced by guesswork, brute force and numbers on your side. We are few and any tactics we might hold up our sleeve are useless when racing against ourselves. 46 have left the race already, but we remain. I say this.

He nods and scowls, a face of lines marking out a sadness born, quite possibly, back in Melbourne in the still moments of a hot night when all about you doubts hang heavy like the bats we saw in the trees at the oasis springs of Egypt and Alexandria. I think for a moment he is likely to shout. But he just puts that face in his hands and lets a lot of air out through his fingers. I offer him the bottle when he shows his eyes again. He shakes his head. I take a long drink and feel the depth of the burn. He looks at me. 'You're used to it? The booze?' he asks, nodding at the bottle.

I shake my head. 'No,' I say.

He laughs and takes the bottle from me and reads the label. 'Do you know what it's like,' he asks, 'when you believe you've been told something that will change your life. And it slowly becomes apparent over time this fact has changed. That no one believed that you – the one whom it would affect the most – would be concerned?' He hands me back the bottle. 'Do you ever get that sense that things are not true at all. That others take it for granted that what they tell you is a fabrication and only a fabrication to protect themselves from attack until after it matters?'

'Of course.'

He nods. 'Christ,' he says. 'And it's eighteen players. Eighteen in a footy team. Eighteen against five.'

I rough up his hair as Percy and Bainbridge come back around with Harry. Three riders whose shapes look embarrassingly lean against the stone of the keep, their hard thighs and absent calves. Three riders who don't have a chance.

7

I puncture twice within 10 minutes of Brest. At the second rupture I throw my bike on the side of the road and kick at it, pull the tubes from my shoulders and get the wheel off. I had been within sight of the broken conical roof of Tour de la Motte Tanguy and was watching it come near as metal pierced the tyre and ruined the inner tube. I yell at children who close in and they run shouting. I've lost time already and sit for a moment cursing, a sacrifice of base words. I soon realise I know something about the tower. I have never seen an image before, but have fashioned it in my head. I sit with the wheel between my legs and the tyre irons between the wood of the rim and the rubber and recall this: from the tower one can see over the port and down the Penfold River to the harbour. It was once the seat of justice for the lords of Le Châtel, once in the keep of the French royal family. My cousin Alice somehow knew these things, and now, as I observe the edifice, so do I. And I know this much as it is the stage-end where I am due to meet her. Alice Sévellec of Margate. A cousin whose face I have never seen, or at least never identified – though in my mind she looks almost precisely like my Marya. Compact and light, a set of smiles she saves for the times I make her humour twitch.

There was once a photograph sent from England of her

51

family beside a river where willows draped their branches to the water. Out of the fifteen pictured, eight were young women. I remain ignorant of her looks, her demeanour, her voice. Though I know well the tone of her hand. For years she had given to me many hours reading, describing in her letters the cities of Europe, the towns and villages she travelled through from a young age. Her family journey regular summers in the south, west, east or indeed the centre of the continent. She wrote long explications of their travels in the kind of longhand that swept the page like sails running on a breeze. I wrote back, a hurried excitement. After a number of years her letters began to change, they became more personal and eventually were addressed to just myself, though I still read them to my family in the lounge and they laughed and commented on the luck of that side of the family. I left out the parts where she responded to my questions, the independent queries I had of her life up here in the north. In December of '27, when it was confirmed that I would be the fifth member of the team, I wrote to her and expressed my surprise and delight. In Paris I received a missive thirty pages long filled with encyclopedic entries describing the towns through which we now ride. She appeared to have had knowledge of the route before I did, a description of the towns, the highlights, the food, the best hotels. Indeed, she had described this odd tower, fallen into disrepair, almost leaning on old memories of how it once was.

Though I'm due to meet her in the evening, I lose the hurry to right my ruined tyre. For much of the ride from Dinan I was anticipating my arrival at the café on rue de Siam; it is there I am to meet her, it is there I am due to lay eyes on her and know her face for the first time. Seven hours ago we were the last to leave that little town and I found myself deep in undulating countryside with my

teammates. There we found a rhythm and tracked down the teams who'd set forth before us. We sat on their tails for an hour and then Harry led the way out, he paced us across the countryside. It flashed, it blurred. Green and blue. Tall trees and farm gates and the sun in my eyes, all this only made the ride more serene as tears made rivers in the dusted sweat that clung on to my face. Even another crash into a sudden hedge could not dull the ride. All a beautiful postcard to return to the family, a beautiful thought to hand over to my cousin when I finally saw her. Eventually we spread out, Percy and Ernie dropping off as the three of us reached for extra speed. Then this, a disappointment to match yesterday's ill-timed crash. I pause here taking in the outskirts to the city, the ruined hump of a tower, the way things survive centuries to become artefacts and proof of an idea we have of the past: history and all its failings.

I lean into the embankment as Ernie rides by. He nods an old man's nod. Though he is less than 40, there's an age to him I can't touch. I left him behind some two hours ago. Now I spit on the road and watch it juice in the dust. Ernie, whose speed is failing, whose legs aren't what they once were. The veteran of France and of the road, though none of us knows, with the exception of perhaps Percy Osborne, where he served. They might have discussed this return of sorts sometime in the past, or even on the boat on the way over. Possibly when we sat poised in the Suez awaiting Alexandria and the mouth to the Mediterranean. I have no idea where he served, what front or what company. I also have no clear idea if he knows our proximity to the sites of his service. At the end of our days he rides at the back where he has long hours to himself; I imagine him gauging his place on this continent by a centre once forged in fields far north 10, 11, 12 years ago. I see him ride smoothly on and think that in

these two months together we have rarely spoken.

A car slows to watch me and I don't look up, I don't want to connect eyes with any other soul. Annoyance is making my spirit foul. And, as if to damn myself with my own arrogant will, I'd looked forward to riding into the velodrome where thousands would stand and applaud and scream as the three of us hit the track and put on a sprint. I've thought for months how Alice would be there amongst them and how she'd see the shine on my head, my concentration, the deliberate power and easy manoeuvre. Instead, I will ride in alone.

I wipe the blood from the graze on my shin across my cheek and set off. I am a Red Indian.

As I walk towards our meeting place I wonder what she saw when I finally came into the velodrome. I had been able to catch Ernie, once I had got my tyre back on. He was struggling to get his bike about the turns and tight streets. We shouted as I went past. When the velodrome rose in front of me I felt the grip of my abdomen squeeze at my stomach. All the organs on the inside clenched. I took a group of four as I bounced into the stadium. Two more in the home stretch. I bellowed, saliva fell from my mouth and hung off my chin as I grimaced almost dying for the crowd. The triumph was corporeal, thick. The stuff you breathe through a pipe and feel deep within. And they screamed out, the crowd, they yelled as they do time and again.

Harry and Opperman finished seven minutes in front of me, the amount of time I had lost to bad luck and children's pranks. I found the two of them. Their faces were blurs. My legs were shaking. Harry said something. Even when he is happy he looks serious. I heard a group yelling, 'Oppy!' They'd come in close to the leaders, places 12 and 13. They were within 10 minutes of Alcyon. Harry shook his head

and he poured two bidons of water over my crown. I was on my knees. I only heard sounds. I didn't know if my eyes were open or closed. Things were black. It'd all come back, I remember thinking. Opperman poured his water down the back of my neck. I looked up at Harry though he had no outline. 'Wait till the mountains,' he said.

Bodies walking around like meat too hard for the oven, too hard to make taste. The outline of genitals clear for all to see in our tight shorts.

I laugh as I walk, ducking into small alleys. I look up at the names of these streets and wonder how long these places have had names, how long they have existed. On and on. I walk, I walk. I lose north, I lose east and south and west. I give up and head for a main street. I step past a cart of vegetables that appear to have been abandoned. It is from this kind of predicament I might be rescued if I am indeed lost, Bruce Small – Hubert's mentor from Melbourne – jogging about the streets making enquiries. The man does an incredible job. The job Ravat are supposed to do but don't. Some nights he is up until the morning making provisions for the next day, correcting our bicycles, repairing any relations undone by poor translation on my or anyone's part.

I fear I am late for my cousin and break into a trot as clouds shut out the light. I watch them briefly gauging wind shift and direction, recalling the breeze that came off the Atlantic an hour or so earlier and hope for bearings. All they seem to do is expand over the sun. I recall how Alice once described a sky-borne thing she and her sisters saw coming across the countryside on their way to London during the war: an airship imitating a cloud. It was summer in the south, the sun ripe as Europe plundered its men. She wrote of a young aeronaut at the rear manning a set of large guns, that he waved as the gargantuan thing flew on by as

if a cloud and things of the sky were controlled by a man wearing a jacket festooned with bright brass buttons.

Soon I find a group of people but notice how I veer away as they turn to look at me. I am obvious, a rider out of uniform, which is surely another uniform itself. I feel the proximity of language, of words forming about myself, my presence audible in their voices. It's an odd loneliness, your name amongst words you can't say.

I sit outside away from the other riders who have found this eatery and made it their resting spot for the evening. They drink and shout. I hope not to be recognised. I hope the girl who wants to take my order does not, despite her charms and simple beauty, return until I am acquainted with my cousin. I fear, in this immediate moment, that I will stumble in the attention my strange accent attracts, for I am not British, and I make this clear. No, it seems I am something quite foreign.

I enjoy the fact the tablecloth is chequered red and white. I have seen pictures of scenes such as this. They were black and white but I knew the colour was red.

The waitress flashes me looks. Eventually she brings me a wine bottle full of water. She lingers as she pours the liquid into the tall glass. Her perfume is blue and there is a hint of her own smell and I want to touch her hand, to taste her fingers. But all this I put aside as I feel Alice watching me. Feel that she is near and this is perhaps some test. For half an hour I wait, then an hour. Time echoes time. It seems my paranoia is just that and she is not in the vicinity and never was.

I think about my brother, or I think about how I think about my brother each time I sit at such a table in such a street, how I assume he has been here before me. It is an assumption guided by long hours of imagining, of seeing his face in the crowds and not feeling startled, but rather

somehow relieved. In my youth I imagined him in such places, that angry face and his lack of recognisable words. I imagined how women knew he was a flyer and remembered how jealous I was that I wasn't, that I wasn't a flyer and never would be, despite the speed I managed on the rather poor cycle I owned as an adolescent. Jealousy is a poor motivator, it's a motivator that only leads to harm. Though oddly, I believe the only harm he caused me was not born from such a thing, but another, stranger, but no less violent contagion: the stories he told and the infection they spread.

I watch a woman wearing a yellow scarf jog across the road to a blue car. She puts her head into the window and talks to its occupants. It takes a few seconds for me to realise it is her, the woman from the hotel. The movement of a body is a fascination hard to ignore when you slow it down and start to imagine bones and muscle. I think to call out but the waitress comes back. She starts to speak but soon stops. A look of confusion and regret crosses her face. I know, suddenly, that she knows I am a mute, and possibly dumb with it. She points at a wine glass on another table and I nod and smile and nod again.

'Have you seen a young woman?' I ask. I realise I am indicating towards her. She jabs at her solar plexus and raises her brow. 'Yes, yes,' I say. 'But no. Erm. La femme est plus âgée que vous.'

She angles her head at me, picks up a wine bottle and pretends to swallow its contents.

'Drink?'

'Mmm,' she says. She totters as if truly full of alcohol and grins for me.

'Certainly,' I say and laugh. I look away thinking what to say, then look back but her attention is taken by the arrival of François Louvière. Bodies seem to shift as the rider walks through. The ripple effect of fame and the illusions of rapport that cling to it.

'Louvière,' she says and smiles more. She points at me. 'Mmm, Ernie Bainbridge,' she says, and she raises her impressively even eyebrow so I see the smooth of her pale skin rumble below her hairline.

'Huh?' I laugh.

'Le Tour,' she says and points at me as I had earlier at her. 'Monsieur Bainbridge.'

I grin. She touches her mouth, puts her head to the side. I reach for her hip. She moves her hand up my forearm. Then, the sound. We hear it coming across the court. Patrons scamper inside where drunk men stand and stare from the tall windows: the rain. I stand under a sun umbrella watching and the girl hops back into the café. I'm there for 20 minutes before I decide I must get wet. I step into the rain. It does not stop.

Before I return to my rooms I look about for the woman, but I see her nowhere and notice the car she ran to has gone also. Washed away in the rain. At our hotel I go to the bikes and remove my back wheel and chain. I take them up the stairs into the room I share with Harry. He has his wheel on the floor, a cog in his hand and a set of tools on the small table.

'Did you have a nice evening?' Harry asks.

'No,' I say. I am dripping on the floor. I tell him how I got lost and was late to the café. I tell him how I sat admiring the waitress. I tell him about Louvière's entrance and he laughs. We are getting used to the stars, the way they alter the gravity of any given situation and drag eyes in their wake.

'But she wasn't there?'

'Sadly not.'

'How long since you last had communication?'

It's six weeks since I last heard from her, but instead

of saying this I lie. 'Five days before the race. I received a postcard. I showed you. You saw it.'

Harry shrugs. 'Possibly.' He wipes his hands on a cloth. 'I see everyone's postcards. Everyone gets a postcard and everyone shows it around. Have you noticed?'

'I'd never shared a postcard before I got here.'

'It's something they do. They share the scents of their girlfriends.'

'Habit from the war?' I ask.

'They share the scents of their girlfriends. They share postcards.'

'Perfumes?'

'Some Belgian put a photo of his girlfriend under my nose yesterday,' Harry says. 'It had writing on the back. It smelt of rose water.' He laughs or sighs, I'm not sure which, and looks out the window.

'Silly words, silly lies,' I say.

'You remember getting lollies when you were a kid with the change for the cheese and tobacco for Dad, and you lied to your mother about what you did with the money? That is this race.'

'In a thousand postcards.'

'Eight thousand, a hundred.'

'You counting?' I ask. 'What's that smell?'

He nods to the front pocket of his satchel where I see several cards poking through. He murmurs to himself, a half-laughter, a common cough at the end, as if all things are finished by a common cough.

'What's that smell?' I ask again. The room smells of mustard as if in a sandwich with corned beef and butter.

'Here,' he says and leans over and passes a small box. 'It's for you.' I look at the label, 'Mustard Plasters', it reads. 'Put them on your legs,' Harry says, 'put them anywhere. Anywhere that hurts.'

'Where'd they come from?'

'No idea. Opperman was given them. He gave them to me. Told me to pass them on.' He lifts up his shirt and displays an array of the items on his side where his liver resides under his skin. 'They're some kind of cure. We'll see.'

I say little and paste them on my calves and thighs as Harry suggests. 'Gears?' I ask.

'Here,' he says. He tosses me a piece of paper with ratios written in handwriting I don't recognise. Indeed, at the top of the page the words are written in French.

'Alcyon?' I ask.

He nods. 'Ludo came by,' he says and slowly twists his neck and several vertebrae click in or out of place. Ludo Feuillet, Alcyon's manager. The man has befriended Opperman, offering advice to the rider. They lent equipment and words. 'They know we're nothing,' Harry says.

'Come on now,' I say. I laugh for him, trying to stir his heart. But he says nothing more, just uses his rag on the bike, clearing away dust caught in the oil. The bike is a beautiful thing when pulled apart and its constituent parts are lined up on a table. It is so simple, each part finely machined, factory-born, lingered over by mechanics with breath that smells hairy, then sent our way. Each bike the same, a copy of the last.

'Did you get the towns mixed up?' he asks and I'm reminded we are talking about Alice. Harry has an ability to change subjects without saying anything.

'I don't believe so,' I say. I go to my tool bag and take out the items I want. Crescent, pliers and oil. We work in silence. I inspect my chain for fatigue.

8

We exit Brest in that still-falling rain and ride forward. We ride in pursuit through the tight dark streets. Always hungry men; our bodies feeding on muscle tissue, fat found in unsuspected places and the things that make our organs. A chain of always hungry men in the wet. I feel us looking for things to occupy ourselves. The road is a grey stretch, dust and shingle settled by the rain. Our tyres throw up a thin veil of water and spray our legs. I watch the arrival of road and road and road and road, a clay streak through endless provinces, through gangs of animals barely looking up to see us pass, through country divided by fence and hedge, beside the unending trough that separates road from farm where water collects and runs off to streams, to rivers, past hamlets where a woman watches from her door, under the shadows of great trees thick with summer leaves (how I'd hate to see this land once winter hits and they are barren, how skeletal and cruel it must be), over bridges built by what seems to be the same hand for centuries and years, under the eyes of the same officials who watch us pass again and again as their cars rumble at the side of the road waiting to take them on so they might watch us again as we aggregate the miles. Concentration, stamina, cold, trust, rain, belief, wind, endurance, pain, skin, heat, urine, blood, scabbing, stench,

faith, filth, food, water, wine, blister, drug. The undoing of men is this repetition: the everyday agonies we can take; it's the boredom that kills us off one by one.

And I have seen them. They finish and make some protest and raise their hands above their heads saying some words and walk right on past control where poor Ernie is leaning over some poor Frenchman signing his poor signature. Then he goes to bed where he coughs and lets his body shake with the flu. The others celebrate their departure from the race raising glasses. I feel black and want to lash out. Instead I step outside and take a cigarette from a passerby and smoke it leaning on the back of a car I can't name the make of and wait for someone to tell me not to.

Everything an education.

And each day I learn something new. Weather and words, names. I find myself writing mean humidity percentages on the map I am slowly drawing in my head. Toulouse, 83 percent. Montpellier, 79 percent. Dinan, 55 percent. I join the numbers with shaky lines and recall how the woman in Caen told me the Tour had given a map to the average Frenchman's idea of this country. Before 1903, she claimed, people didn't have a precise notion of its outline. Before the turn of the century 80 percent of Frenchmen did not speak French, so descriptions were no use either. Now, every July since that year, it is printed in the newspaper and pinned to walls and glued to windows. The regions named, the cities circled, the riders handed aliases and fantastical reputations by Henri Desgrange. Hippolyte Aucouturier: the Terrible. Ottavio Bottecchia: the Bricklayer of Friuli. Cyrille Van Hauwaert: the Lion of Flanders. Maurice Garin: the Little Chimney Sweep. Lucien Pothier: the Butcher of Sens. François Louvière: the Assassin of Algiers. As Desgrange had phrased it: 'Those reckless and uncouth sowers of energy who are the great professional riders of the world.'

I remember that from Harry's own memory. (And today's 23rd placegetter: 'the Monk'. Antonin Magne, so taciturn I am yet to hear him speak. A man to love well.)

At 8am Brest's temperature was 18 degrees Celsius, by midday it was 25. In Vannes it was 35. Tonight it will be 14 degrees and in five days there will be no numbers, just elevation, feet and metres, yards and the faces of Hieronymus Bosch chiselled into men. The Butcher, the Terrible, the Assassin. Whether Louvière ever killed a man is a matter for the war to tell.

<center>❖</center>

In Vannes I find myself ambling towards the cathedral. The centre of the city accented by the church. Close alleys and streets complicate and merge and narrow and open into the square where the church awaits. You walk, everything moves backward through years and days and centuries towards the mark in time when the basilica was the centre of all idea. Things are so narrow the shadow of the spire has no room to move or stretch. There's a sense of compression, shops and goods, the calls of the keepers and their patrons becoming small and hard, everyone needs each other, everyone needs their need for the centre. I pass a shop from whose frontage, as if carved from rock, protrude the upper torsos and faces of two amused men looking down at the passersby from above. I watch them as if expecting them to change expression as I walk; I expect the sound of leering amusement. A man holds up a fish and murmurs its qualities. He watches me walk. My gait is that of a tourist and nothing more.

I enter the basilica through a small entrance cut into the larger, 15-foot main doors, which are pink and strangely so. The entry is colossal, the arches render the intruder insignificant to the owner of the house. You are welcome,

<center>63</center>

these doors gesture and suggest, but know how slight you appear before the Almighty. That is how I feel about it. Also, I feel the urge to do something stupid, something vulgar and loud. Though as soon as I step inside this urge is replaced by an urgency to be naked, to be still and recorded in some great mind as a soul unburdened by fact or cloth. It's an unusual request my mind makes. I am as sober as a goat.

I find myself shifting my eyes towards two young woman. This glance hopes one might reveal herself to be my kin. Since Brest I've watched the movements of women hoping one will step forward and announce herself as my cousin Alice. I am lonely, I admit. It is a strange lonesomeness, one that contains a proximity to things I know well, and things I cannot explain, which is at once beautiful and unkind.

I stare upwards.

I walk towards the main aisle that leads to the altar. The wood of the pews rubbed smooth by 600 years of touching as each parishioner moves in to pray palming the wood and reducing it to the true shape of the common hand. Christ posed on the cross. We stand and stare, we don't turn away. Above me the arches. I look to where the two sides meet, a vanishing point. I'm surrounded by the absolute well of human silence. I close my eyes and put my hands out as I feel the sensation of a long fall. There are no walls, only the sense that I will be caught before the foundations arrive and crush me. A promise that marks eternity. It is a silence one can't replicate by means of architecture other than this.

A priest joins another at the altar. They bless themselves and the air about them. Incense and Latin. Nobody is a part of the service. The two men eat and drink on their own.

I head for the small alcove where I believe no one is sitting, nobody needs to bother the saint who resides there. I look about for signs of artefacts. The strange loot of bygone days

when the holy strode the earth making gestures that soon gathered momentum and became impossible deeds, then legend, then myth. Some of my favourite things, so do not suppose I think ill of them. We must recycle stories or we would not know what for.

Beatification.

There are more than 3,000 saints. I heard that recently.

A painting sits in the corner. It's in the process of being shifted from one part of the church to another. I make this assumption because I see no space for it on the walls which are rich with the icons attached to the saint to whom it is dedicated. I sit and look close at the piece. A saint and his left eye slightly closed over, his right hand holding fire. In his left is the bible, at what page it is open I do not know. But his fingers are clenched and the pages are rippled by his grasp. He looks quite unwell, as if on the verge of something, the turning point of an illness perhaps, or at the instant of revelation. It could be anything. But I suspect he is at the end.

The silence amplifies the smallest sound.

There's the sound of shoes as another enters the alcove, but I don't look up, instead I look closer at the bible held in place by the saint. I'm hoping to understand the numbers written on the page so I might someday inspect the verse. I find myself squinting and feel a large difficult lump halting my breath. I stand and walk to the back where I feel faint. I put out my hands to steady myself and I am swung by my forward motion into a pew where my head falls into the palms of my hands. I'm not breathing. I seem to be choking and I soon realise I am crying, my body hugging itself as it softly heaves. I cough and it sounds out around the church, echoes of an unknown source as I can't anchor this moment to anything I recall.

A woman sits two rows in front of me. I imagine her touching her beads, running them through her fingers like

a chain. I imagined the feel of them on her skin, the smooth nubs and the way they made such a soft sound. I close my eyes when I see her stand and turn towards me. It is her, the same woman from Caen but I don't look up, not for the moment. My head between the palms of my hands. The slight echo of sandals. Her voice starts and I watch her speak.

We drive in the dark, her at the wheel and my body snug in the small seats of her Citroën. The breeze catches. It's cool, dry, and I wear only the cotton shirt I purchased in Colombo back in late March against the hit of air. She gives no inclination of the direction into which we drive. I sense it to be north but have no true gauge to measure against my assumption; the stars are shrouded by distant stratiform as if flour flicked there by a waitress's finger on dark cloth. She stays silent, whether to keep me ill-informed or because she knows whatever words she might share are likely to be whipped to our wake, I can't say. All I know is I followed her to her car; I liked the smell of her and quickly was able to imagine her naked. I said nothing as she drove us out of the city. I thought perhaps we would arrive at a small country house and once inside we would pull the curtains.

Instead I find myself sleeping and when I awake it is still dark and the air immobile, as if tranquillised by a secret dart. The woman is sleeping, a soft murmur in her mouth. It is the first time I have had a chance to look at her without the influence of her eyes looking back at me.

We'd spoken for an hour quietly amongst the pews. She asked about New Plymouth and I told her about my city there beneath the volcano. It's hard not to be impressed by a city beneath such a mount; all one needs do is mention Vesuvius and suddenly you are a stout-hearted survivor. She smiled at the idea and touched my hand.

'Your family?' she asked. 'You have a brother. You told me you had a brother.'

'He's a farmer nowadays. My dad's a doctor.'

'Wealthy?'

'Not poor.'

'You don't need to ride?' she asked. She watched me shake my head. 'And yet you ride. Nicolas Frantz has a wealthy family. You know he used to enter races under false names so they wouldn't find out. You should be on his team.' Her smile was sad.

I nodded for her. 'I'm sorry you found me like this,' I said. I was still sitting. My hands salty, the smell of me like a handkerchief.

'It's fine,' she said. 'If there's a place to weep, here it is. Look around.'

But I didn't have to, I knew precisely the contents of the walls. I couldn't name the paintings, but I knew what they were saying to me. The sculptures too. Leaning rows of suffering. I felt guilty I wasn't weeping out in sympathy, in sympathy with the general arrangement of grief that filled this place. 'This is your church?'

'I'm part of the congregation,' she said.

'This is your city? You're from Vannes?'

'Currently. I come from other places too, but today, this year, this is where I am from.'

'And you come here for mass.'

'Sometimes, yes. Otherwise I come to mingle. You have been to France before? I understand one of you came before. One of you, during the war. I'm not being rude, I hope I am not being rude.' She sounded as though she were commanding rather than questioning and I felt my shoulders shrug in deliberation.

'I have never been to a service in a cathedral, at least not like this,' I said.

She looked at me, the calm of her voice settled with her wide mouth. That was an answer to a different question and she seemed patient, waiting. But I'm still thinking about it now. The question of the war. And I think about it often: this journey and the places it is likely to take us. I'm not the only one. Harry made mention of it last night. We both reminisced how we were once kids waiting to be old enough. It was just around the corner. It beckoned. That was the war, a beckoning. And Harry and I, we both realised we'd been thinking about it since we got here. We arrived in Toulon and started looking. We'd been here before, that was the sensation.

She rubbed my arm. Her hands weren't so much soft but firm, skin youthful and kept that way by the application of creams and ointments I couldn't possibly name. 'You'd want to be here on a Sunday then,' she said. 'What day is it? Thursday. You ride tomorrow?'

'Tomorrow, yes, for Les Sables d'Olonne.'

'I will be following. I sometimes follow.'

'You can give me a ride, if you like,' I said and she laughed. 'How many people come here on a Sunday? I'm guessing, maybe, how many? A thousand, twelve hundred, they come in and sing?'

'Mmm, yes. I haven't ever counted.' She smiled for me, but it wasn't one that stated anything more than restless politeness. 'Do you explore churches? Is this something you do?'

I didn't answer. Instead I stood, finally, with my legs heavy and the strange taste of dry mucus in the back of my mouth. I put my hand in front of my lips, afraid of my breath. It had been a short ride, barely six hours from Brest. I had bathed before I went walking to the basilica, but I feared I still smelt. All of me. She put her hand on my shoulder, she has wide eyes, pupils surrounded completely in white.

They are the kind of eyes one shies away from because if you look too long you'll become in love with something. 'I come to churches, yes. I like to see, watch, listen. I'm a poor parishioner,' I said. 'I like it empty, or I like it full to the brim. When there are people like me around I get antsy.'

'Antsy?'

'I get frustrated.'

'Is that why you were crying?'

I laughed. 'No. God, I cried.'

'It's okay. It makes you warm inside to cry.' She had her eyebrows up as if she were suggesting something succinct and inside the moment.

I nodded and that was all I had in the instant. If I thought why I had cried it would have set me off again, making me vulnerable to her questions, and though I had known her for a bare few minutes, I expect she would have had a great deal to say on the matter.

'If I show you something, will you tell me why you were crying?'

'How far do we have to go?'

'Mmm,' she said. 'I have a car.'

And we drove.

Now I have no idea where I am. I've no idea what time it is, at least not outside of this car. A car deals with time in different ways, it makes it out of miles instead of minutes. I sense something and I am reminded of the glow off the land in the Taranaki, the rise of a bruise from the volcanic plateau in the centre of the island, I know then the direction I am looking is east, the hint in an otherwise dark sky is the hump of colour slowly emerging across France. I love the coming of dawn, the impossibility of retreat, as if a thought in a crowd spreading out forever. We are parked in a field and that is all I can say.

The surrounds slowly reveal themselves as low hills, trees on the near horizon in silhouette, thick morning skies waiting to be burnt off by the heat of the sun. The woman stirs. A weight in the air, movement perhaps. My back stiffens. I sense the volume of my breathing, as if in a silent hoar frost and the ghost of my breath hangs for all to see. Someone is watching. I look around for eyes and hands and what they might hold and threaten. I flash my head left and right. A man, I believe it to be a man, standing not five feet from where I sit. 'Christ,' I say and flinch, as if a fist is in the air. I feel my lungs and my heart beat. I pant. Slowly another figure appears out of the purple. 'Hey,' I hear myself say and retreat to the back of the seat. I watch for movement. I doubt any sound has exited my mouth, though I feel like I have been speaking. I have the idea that the woman has steered us onto the paddock of a farm, that a shotgun-ready farmer stands before us.

'Hey,' I say. They stay still, as if my voice is empty, as if something outside of thought. I look hard; I try to see their eyes; I want to know why they are staring so intently at me. I look to the woman who appears to still be sleeping. Beyond her I can see at least a dozen more men and I choke on the phlegm in the back of my throat. I push her shoulder and try to rouse her.

She touches my hand, takes my fingers in her own and whispers. 'You see them?'

'What do they want?'

She says, almost inaudibly: 'I can never quite decide.'

'What?' The purple crinkles and lets pink shine onto the land and it becomes clear that there aren't a mere dozen surrounding us, but hundreds. 'Good God,' I hear myself whispering. They move slowly as the light comes, closer. Shadows leaning towards us. I cough again. Nothing moves. Nothing is moving, only my heart and eyes. My head and

hands are still. So many hundreds. How quickly my heart is racing. I am fit, but it never runs this fast. They seem an army at least. I turn back to the farmer and see his shape is not that of a farmer but a hooded man.

'I wonder, sometimes,' she says so quietly her breath is barely breaking.

'What −' I start and realise what I am about to say. Or, what it is I am seeing. I feel a red shame in my cheeks. Stones. Standing stones. Everywhere I look, rows upon rows of stones, each neatly lined up equidistant from the other, grey rock standing staring into the sudden reign of the new day.

'You see them now, don't you? You see.'

I nod and whisper, 'What are they?'

'Stones. Menhirs. You amazed? Be amazed. I wonder sometimes,' she says, 'whether they are permanent or just visiting.'

'God. My heart. Put your hand here.' She touches my chest and keeps her hand there. 'What are they −'

'They are, they're anything, really. No one knows. Not to guess at least. I imagine they are stand-ins,' she says. 'For who, I can't be sure. I come here and look. They've been waiting five thousand years, more. Just waiting for us to come and look.'

'Five thousand? How many?' I ask. 'How far do they go?' and I point back behind us where the lines reach a low ridge and it seems they go on and on. I stare, gawk. Ancient stone, silent; always ever silent. I look for eyes in their form, I look for mouths, but most of all I listen for sound.

'So,' she says. Her eyes are wide also, large eyes whose globes seem twin planets in orbit of her thoughts.

'So,' I say.

'Well,' she says, and I see her smiling. 'This is something, no?'

71

I'm nodding like an idiot and I realise my mouth is open and that the word 'gape' has precedence, it's not just a word in fiction. And I realise, too, why we are here. She has brought me to another kind of church, another cathedral, but in the open for all to see. Standing stones, inscrutable and ancient. Ancient and dead but for the moss that has spread over their faces. A strange congregation, like stand-ins for those who couldn't wait out time.

'I know they are mute, but –' she says. She murmurs to herself for a moment. She takes my elbow in her hand. 'I expect them to have mouths, to make them move.'

'You got an idea about what they'd say?'

She shrugs. 'Mmm. Now you can laugh. Now you can find me funny. But let's –'

I step out of the car in time with the woman and walk amongst them. I step slowly, making as little noise as possible. Even so, a fox is startled from its sleep at the foot of the first stone. My first fox. I look and see a sweetness in its eye. Its brush is red. I feel an ease with the animal. It is what I had always believed it to be from books and tales. The woman takes my arm again. 'Those things bite,' she says. 'So–' And she grimaces. I walk and touch what I'd believed to be faces. I put my arm about the stones like old friends, lost and now returned. I laugh and look at the woman and she follows me. We amble about the exact lines standing in a precise array. Hundreds, thousands, and thousands of years old. Measured in what numbers – form, standard and length? It's the result of this order, the manner of their arrangement, their harmonious arrangement, the gaps, the distance between each weighted rock, that has me think they must speak, they must say something.

'All I can think,' the woman tells me, 'is a great violence happened here. That's all I can think. Markers? Look at them. Memorials? Do you think? Some, some great thing.

72

I walk, and –'

'Stand-ins. You said stand-ins,' I say. 'Stand-ins for what?'

'I do not know,' she says. 'But sometimes I wonder, I wonder if at some point they became the actual thing. They no longer had a past and became the real thing. Look at them.'

I stand. I look. Hard stone, their shadows in the grass where the fox hurries through.

9

Each day we ride. Each day the experience begins to mould on the road: 110, 120 kilometres pass, the four of us stay with Hubert Opperman. We stay linked in the run south towards the mountains, a five-man chain fastened by the slipstream that starts at my front wheel pushing through the air and over my head bent forward into the breeze. Harry sits behind, a foot to the left off my rear wheel in the displaced air, Osborne in the same approximate position, and then Bainbridge, then Oppy. I peel from the head of our strange snake and let Harry go forward. Eventually Ernie will drop off, then Percy, then Harry and myself. Opperman will ride alone, the sole signifier of the urge to break away. Such is the pattern; he will ride alone.

For now we are a chain.

Then others join the chain, two groups from the lesser teams. The road is straight for many miles and flanked by plane trees marking the borders of farms to our left and right. We ride as if on a dreamt river towards a never-nearing hillock out of which these trees ride up and over; from the centre of the road they appear to border a canal through the farmland. I think of the people who take such things, shepherding their barges to the cities and towns, never settling, a life on thin strips of water. I imagine a life

as such for us, that we may never leave the road, just take its purpose to its towns and there share what we have from the saddlebags of our bikes. Meagre lives on meagre land.

Our feet are cooled by fords. The raw skin blanched.

At each low hillock I expect another army of stones to be waiting, their impossible stare. An unnamed woman standing amongst them. Their glare demanding we stop and watch their motionless jaunt across time. But I have yet to see them again, nor the woman. Instead everywhere we go we are greeted with kind words and kisses. Percy and I make jokes, Harry too. Oppy has his smile, a gift for everyone. Children come up to us with shy smiles, holding their mothers' skirts and saying incomprehensible things. Harry and Oppy seem to understand and chat with the mothers, offer nods and courteous words. Crowds cheer when we wave from our bike seats, sometimes they are ten men deep, but mostly it is the countryside and green fields. Green fields and green fields and it seems I am thwarted each time I search for their presence, a disappointment which prompts me to search all the more for the long shadows, the staring stones watching us ride.

Another thing I search for. And I can't help it, and nor — as I discovered — can Harry. Though we are hundreds of miles south of the front, we search for signs of trench and battlement. When the sun gets behind the lip of a hill and the grass turns black and the fences and gates silhouette against a reddening sky, then they turn into broken men and their machines. Now, to add to this, I also search for stone men staring out of the past, looking for men to set them free. That's what I imagine.

And what Harry says — Harry claims France is just another kind of Holy Land. He said this to me in Dinan as we admired the surrounds. We laughed and he went on in

the kind of voice that knows the weight of its own mirth. But he might've been right.

We watch and search and we are watched. We're watched from windows and awnings, we're watched from verandas and balconies, we're watched from gaps in the hedgerows, from the steeples by bellringers and their pets, we're watched from the sky when small planes loop in from the blue, we're watched from balloons, we're watched from cars paused at the side of the road, their drivers in purple scarves and goggles, we're watched from school gates where 500 children shout names hoping for faces to turn, we're watched by police and clergy, teachers and butchers and carpenters and masons and thieves and rapists and killers and heroes of the war, amputees and the blind holding handfuls of flowers at their chests, we're watched from the edge of the road. We're watched by all. So we ride and make our song.

And it seems quite barmy. 'I'm going mad by the sun,' I hear Percy say one night. 'Shit in the air. I'll tell you I've got inner visions marking me out for the mad house.'

'Come on,' Ernie says.

'Aha.'

'I'll tell you about mad people,' Ernie says.

'What then?'

'Aha.'

'You're gunna say something?'

'That's right.'

So we ride, and each day we start 10 minutes ahead of JB Louvet, each day they catch us. We are made fools by their strength. These days are long, longer than I know how to ride, longer than Percy and Ernie's bodies can deal with, longer than Harry's sick body will let him. Opperman drags us into the countryside. Disappointment is rich and though he says nothing I understand he longs to be a part of the French tide of racers who pour down these roads. I see him

talking to Bruce Small. They don't share their words for they are made of frustrations.

We are sponsored in this race by fools. Ravat and their idiot ideas, or lack of them.

So many miles for such disappointment.

Then, as if the sail cracks and awakes him, Hubert sets off with only 40 kilometres between our formation and the velodrome at Les Sables d'Olonne. He takes the front, I go with him. Harry goes. Osborne goes. Bainbridge has done his day's work and retreats to the rear. Slowly Oppy leaves us behind and for two hours I ride alone.

And a word, a word on being alone, on the loneliness. A pit, a hole, a place to which we fall when no one is around to see how wretched we have become. These are my brother's words; I have no fear in telling that. From Egypt, from Cairo where the army had him in its hospital waiting on his recovery so he might join the rest at Gallipoli, in the Dardanelles where men clung to the hillsides like burnt rope with ships just a few miles out to sea in the Mediterranean wash magnificent and sullen, Thomas wrote to me. He'd had to look up the Dardanelles in the atlas when he was well enough to venture out beyond the confines of the hospital. Not I: a stone's throw from Troy, I knew its place beyond the Bosporus and the strange site of Constantinople on the crack between the Black Sea and the Sea of Marmara. A crack between the worlds as we have defined them. Despite what I knew and what he didn't, he had reason to know loneliness. He had months in hospital waiting on a queer illness that had neither name nor fever, waiting on limbs that were broken then repaired. Months walking in the streets and bazaars once a recovery was upon him, walking amongst the Islamic and descendants of men who built pyramids and stone armies to stand guard over the city. He walked until

the English took pity on him and put him to the air. He wrote and now I ride again over the land of his eventual education, if I may call it that. That was loneliness.

I kissed both her cheeks when we departed, that woman and I. Now I expect her at every turn, the woman standing there ready to listen.

We ride. I note that direction is hard to determine. We look to the peripheries. We look within: I touch my thigh and remind myself of the muscles operating, the mechanics of limb and bone, the hard twitch as they undulate and turn, as they produce wattage and heat. Energy transferred from bread and water and wine to blood, speed and words as we shout out. We see riders stop at the sight of an orange grove where they jump from their saddles and gorge themselves momentarily. We yell at them and they hear nothing. We see a rider brake at the sight of a girl and pause to pull her close, hand about her waist. We shout. We see riders stop at the sight of a church and run inside to find the silent solitude to replace that of the road, the strange noise we all make as we go forth. We see men stop to piss in the hedges. We see men crying. We see their knees wrecked and torn, their bikes twisted. We leave them, we don't stop. This race, it goes on. A sentence unwinding in the hills.

10

Les Sables d'Olonne, France. Bordeaux, France.

I murmur the word to myself, France.

Hills like teeth. People in their midst.

I remove my goggles, pale circles where the grey and sun hasn't got to my eyes. At night we lie in salted baths. Some pour vinegar into the water and claim it soothes their muscles. Dirt and dung gets everywhere. Infection finds places to hide and bloom. At night Harry shows me his back. Boils have taken hold.

11

My body is still, I ride from the hips. Handlebars bang off the men beside me. Hips and wheels collide. I am still. I am in the sunset, the breeze that runs from its heart. I'm just rhythm and the world has no sound but the chains wrapped about our gearing.

My eyes shut and I drift.

I hear the close voice of each man's breath. The mind's eye makes their mouths. The life of their mouths, their jaws' clatter: men who say such things as the names of their children; who say such words as the rivers that mark their towns; who say the shape of smoke is a sign of things to come; who say the things to come can't be trusted because these are the sorts of things men say. I keep the light out of my eyes until I sense I'm falling, slipping from the road. I open them to see a mass of yellow nodding heads: sunflowers just outside of an unnamed town like a soft sea on the surface of the sun. Nodding heads like the cawing crowds that line the streets, that yell at us and summon us forward, nodding like they know something that we can't possibly know.

I ride beside Harry, but it is for Opperman that we keep the pace taut.

In Bordeaux they shout, 'Long live the Australians!' We keep the pace taut.

Bodies beside me. Blood and power. I close my eyes and drift onwards. For a moment I'm out of the race. I depart this odd exodus and float in a short, manmade darkness.

I open them again, I always open them again and I ride, the ether-soaked kerchief fastened about my chin and over my nose. Vapour running through my sinuses, nausea thick in my body.

You hear them from a kilometre out, the populations of four villages congregating in a hamlet. They have gathered at a street corner chosen by an urge to come and see, to scream us onwards. We near and feel the ache in our limbs dissipate; the shouting burrows into our spines and makes us grand machines. We flow, we are the blood in one another's veins. The shout of a single face. A desire for our speed, for the rapid turn of our wheels rotating quicker and ever faster. They scream for everyone. A boy jumps and jumps again as we come close. Those around him jump. A woman throws flowers in our path and she jumps so her scarf falls from her head and black and grey hair descends her shoulders. There is a single noise arising out of the racket. A chant, a sound. Mesmerised, as if touched by a virus, I become a shell and all around me falls quiet.

Cameramen stand on verandas and watch our pass. I suspect them to be the same two individuals in each town. Men with a curious eye for our ride; who knows what they see? I don't believe, after all the mud, after all the rain and heat and salt and hunger, my image will stick to the nitrate that winds through the cameraman's apparatus. Why should it? Why would my image last in prosperity? I see no reason for it to last. The crowd knows our names, that is surely enough. They call to us as we try to make the evening ours.

I begin by dragging the front of the pack forward until we

are strung out along the flats, prayer beads in the rough dust heat, my silhouette daring the rest to follow. Opperman sits in my slipstream and I pull him headlong into the evening. He lets go and peels off as planned. The crowds shout us forward, a screaming mass of Frenchmen running at our side. Australians too, men with flags. He will ride until the wind screams at his ears and the day will be crimson as it completes its hours with him standing on the podium, a blue-eyed specimen of old martyrdoms re-enacted each day in the waning dusk.

Such was the idea.

There seemed a conspiracy amongst the teams on this last day before the mountains. That there would be no big fight for time, that bodies were to be rested. Teams rode sedately, easy against the weight of expectation. So I took the lead as the pack lazed. We headed out and flung Opperman forward like a stone from the mitt of a slingshot, just as Harry had suggested. No one expected us to rush, and only panic halted our victory. That and the fact we are five versus ten, the unmerciful team of Alcyon–Dunlop, the unstoppable Alcyon–Dunlop. Frantz of Luxembourg, André Leducq of France, Maurice De Waele of Belgium. They're all champions in one way or another. The fuckers.

We rode hard, in tune; we have for the last three days. Opperman saying slogans, that we were a true team riding. The fight was keen, graphic. We pushed. Jammed out of the scramble of riders and faced the wind only leaders can feel. For 60 miles we led and breathed. Five fingers in a fist punching through the plains. Alcyon's general manager put his car alongside and watched our pace. We did not divert our eyes, just rode at the road and on and harder until he relayed our pace to his team. Alcyon put all ten men into the task of chasing us, dragging us back behind their time.

Opperman came 9th, Harry 10th, Ernie 20th. As a team we were 3rd. And if not for being knocked from their machines by a motorcyclist veering out of the road they might have won the stage. It was close. Small minutes the time it took to check their bones.

I longed to be amongst them. Instead, I was vomiting in the roses on the outskirts of Hendaye. The woman on her haunches asking if I was all right. At least I assume that is what she was asking, she spoke all in French, whispering my name in goggles tinted to keep out bright light. She held me up as I coughed and wiped my mouth and face. She looked at me closely then stepped to her car and quickly returned. She had colour in her face, something I hadn't noticed in the cool of the cathedral and the dawn amongst the standing stones. I flashed a look over her shoulder as she squatted and her knees inside her trousers clicked in unison. I hoped again for the strange stones, that congregation. Instead I saw the arrival of François Louvière to the town. I realised he must have been behind me the entire stage, I was used to seeing him overtake us in the late of the afternoon as he chased Frantz. Today he was struggling in the heat. He slowed as he came near, watching me as I drank from the bottle the woman held to my mouth as I took down the pills. He spoke, but the words were just the words of a cyclist fading as his wheels took him past. The woman looked up and took those goggles from her face, she squinted an eye. Soon I was finishing with the stragglers, a burning sensation in the back of my mouth. She knows my name, I know her face.

I search for her in the café. We've come here to have a single drink. A celebration of the day's small victory. A man with a clipboard is talking seriously to a number of the Alcyon team and I manage a smile to the racers. Despite still feeling sick from ether, my heart is racing. Ephedrine, that's the

word she used and it's in a race of its own. I take a seat and feel the flicker of candlelight on my face. They nod and one winks and I sense they are happily impressed with our effort. I see the eyes of Louvière flash across the room. He does not see me but I hide my face in the crook of my elbow anyway to keep it that way, pretending I have a cough. Why I think the woman would be here, I do not know. It's a night of emptying out and nerves.

Five men I recognise as soloists sit and salute one another with wine. I ask a local man what they are saying. He shakes his head and says, 'Démissionner.' His bottom lip is out. 'Erm,' he sounds, 'quitter.' One of his eyes stays still as he looks around. A dead eye.

I nod and he nods back vigorously. I take it the men are leaving the race. I reach for his shoulder as he walks away so I might ask something more. So I might ask him why. But I know why. I know what the day after tomorrow's rest day brings, or at least I believe I do. He steps out of reach and I'm alone as I wait for my boys to return from the stalls out on the street.

Tomorrow is a rest day if one looks at the schedule, however we are due to begin the next stage at midnight: at the fall of the first minute of the next day. The threat of this is with everyone. When Harry returns, he is alone. He tells me he is going to the hotel with the others. I turn and see Ernie wave from the door. He is bandaged and smiling, the motorcyclist having made a mess of his arms. I inform him I am staying. I'm shouting to have myself heard. 'He's all right?' I say, nodding to where Ernie just disappeared.

'He'll do, he's fine,' Harry says. 'But I need sleep.'

'You can sleep at any time,' I say. He smiles and turns. He leaves by the front door and I am alone for a moment. I stand still waiting for something, someone. The air is thick with the things of men: their smell and the smell of wine,

smoke, shouts and small crimes as liberties are taken on the waitress's behind. She slaps at hands and cringes and moves quickly.

'Hola.' It is the young Spaniard from Discuter. I eye him and he smiles. I hear myself say, 'I'm amazed anyone sleeps, if you consider it.'

'Si?' he says and steps back as he comes forward.

'You close your eyes,' I say. 'It happens, dust settling; it's like that. Birds coming in to roost. Amazing.'

'You close your eyes, and what is it?'

'That's my question,' I say. 'What actually happens?'

'I – I have no –' the lad stammers.

'But something happens. Something always happens.'

'Sleep?' the boy says.

'That's right,' I say. I look at him, he has a kind face, young and unhurt. 'How are you, my señor?'

'Mmm. Tired. I am tired and broken,' he says.

'Tired and broken?'

'Si.'

'It's nice to see you again,' I say.

'Mmm, yes.' He raises his eyebrows. Barely five-foot-something but with a set of moustaches that flow down past his chin. I like him very much for this. We stand smiling at each other.

'I fear I'm going to lose it,' I say and feel my brow tighten. 'I sit around asking myself where it is, so I know how to look for it if it disappears. Sleep, I'm talking about sleep.'

'Like breathing.'

'Perhaps.'

'I don't know where it is,' the Spaniard says. He's looking past me. 'Excusas, I'm going to bed. I'm going to have a big sleep. Something my old people, they would've sung songs to. Ha!'

I laugh and take his hand. 'Sounds terrifying,' I say.

'Sleep?'

I nod. I look around. He kisses my cheek and is gone. I smile into his wake. All around – young men and the old: somehow this race takes us all.

Earlier we walked past churches and stood beside the cross at Saint Vincent's. Hubert had sought that site out, telling us it was supposed to portend the imminent end of the world. A purifying fire to engulf us all. We stood, watched and waited before we moved on. For hundreds of years the cross has stood by that church quietly inert, but its prediction written on the stone has remained quick, waiting. We walked beside the sea and watched the breakers smash on the sand. We walked amongst palms, old and disconcerting. We ate bread, cheese and tomatoes in a café looking across the estuary. At each one of these way stations I had hoped to see her, hoped the lines we walked somehow connected the two of us to a meeting point. I had hoped she would be able to explain to me the stones, as much as anything. In Bordeaux I had asked anyone who looked like they might speak English; I asked if they knew what it was I had seen that night. Nobody seemed to have anything to offer. I thought of telling the team, of admitting to Hubert that I had been out an entire night, driving in the countryside with a woman whose name I couldn't confess. There seemed no good reason to excuse my behaviour, for that is how I suspect my absence in the night would be interpreted, behaviour. And not something appreciated. Instead, I walked the town and stared up at the buildings and wondered what they knew. Everything attached to age seems to know something. But then at times I look at the world and realise I quite fear the tissue that links things, the connective tissue. I fear the stuff it is made of, I fear how it explains itself when we put together words. And perhaps that's why I desired to see her, that she might

speak English once more and tell me some truth about those old rocks staring across the fields in such colossal dedication. How she might have done that I'm not sure. I hoped too that she'd then offer me an antidote to the drug I had ingested just a few hours earlier: I wanted confirmation of my inner eye. I also wanted to be able to sleep.

I use the toilet stall and begin to leave. I am halted by my name. It is Louvière.

'Kiwi,' he says across the room. 'Nouvelle Zélande.' His voice is neither deep nor resonant, but it cuts through the conversations and reaches my ears in a way that I know it is him. I have the choice not to turn, not to look him in the eye, but I do. I find myself walking, eyes flashing from candle to candle, towards him. I didn't know until this moment that the odd temporal sense I have of the Algerian is, in fact, fear. I had previously taken it to be admiration.

'I hear you, err,' he says and indicates to his mouth and points at his tongue. He nods to the vacant seat beside him.

'Vomited. Yes. Not so unusual,' I say.

'You might have had,' he looks at the ceiling waiting on the word, 'erm. Victory.'

'I never win,' I say.

He laughs and nods. 'Your team, I mean your team. Yes? Ravat. Third is good for five. For five of you racing. It's good, no?'

'Yes, no.'

'Ha ha.'

'Second is good. But as I say, I never win.'

'Domestique,' he says. I nod, though I hadn't thought of myself as such, but supposed I was, that he was right. A word which if either of my parents were to hear would cause upset and pointing. The son of a doctor and a town councillor does not belong on the road hunting miles and rough agony. He certainly should not be doing it for the

glory of another. Despite this I nod. For that is what I am. I am Opperman's domestique, though it has never been said, and I am happy to be that way. I stand there for a while and he says nothing more, he is drinking water and I nod and he pours one for me also. I sit. 'Some say they le moine,' he says. 'Some, domestiques. I: le moine.'

'Le moine?'

'Slow, like. Erm, concentrated,' he says. 'How do you say? Frier?'

'Oh. Friar. A monk.'

He nods. Pauses and looks concerned for a moment and I suspect he is working through a sentence he has never said before, in English or French. 'They not real thing. Though – though without le moine, the race would be –' and he looks up and puts out his hands. 'They. True devote.'

'Really?'

'Happy sacrifice.' He shakes his head. 'Not really. I not really know. I never one.' We both laugh, though in truth it doesn't somehow feel consensual. As if I have been dragged into the joke without quite knowing its full purpose.

'Your leg? How's your leg?' I ask.

'My leg? It is fit,' he says. 'You did good job.'

'I haven't seen you on the road.'

'I pass you in your sleep.'

'You're a brave man,' I say, 'to approach me in my sleep.'

'Yes. Yes. I pass you as you dream.'

I give off a laugh, put my hands through my hair and look at him.

'You dream?' he asks. 'Of her? Celia.'

'Who?'

'Her name – Celia. You want. Want ask me her name.'

I laugh. 'Ah,' I say. 'That's her name?'

'Yes, and you dream of her. Am I right?' He pulls a pipe from his pocket.

'Perhaps.' Until now I haven't thought such a thing but now it is true. I have dreamed of her. I look at him and feel myself play the part of a man asking a name, the name of a woman who's recalled in my memory only by a wide thin mouth and eyes that meet at her nose from slightly different angles. It is all I can think of for the moments that go by. Louvière seems to understand what rushes through my mind, for he looks at me with an eyebrow raised. He has strong eyebrows and they rise up as he packs the bowl and puts a flame to the tobacco, seemingly knowing the precise nature of the word I was looking for. Sex. Or if not that word, another that speaks to it.

'Who is she?' I ask.

'Those men are quitting,' he says and nods to the touristes-routiers. Five men chatting to the Discuter team.

'Not unreasonable,' I say.

'I do not,' he starts and stops. 'I do not think. I detester. Erm, the idea. Hate.'

I look at him and wait for more. I'm not certain what he means. I assume he wishes to say he despises the idea of these men quitting. I approach my response with this as its kindling. 'Of course. We all do, don't we? At least, so do I,' I say. 'But it's not unreasonable.' It had never been an option until I saw these men celebrating their demise. I couldn't name the specific frustration I felt looking at them so I look back at the Algerian.

He raises his eyebrows. 'My old team,' he says, and nods at the men from the young Spaniard's team.

'Discuter?'

'Mmm,' he says. 'Now run by – what? Bad quality men. Old team.'

'You quit two years ago. I know that much.'

'Men with hard attitude. Don't go near them. After war, I ride with them. No more. Now, no more.'

I squint at him.

'Old story,' he says. 'People know my story. If they have read a newspaper. Bad attitude men. Six-foot-four of them. Ready with sticks. I ride on my own. You know my story.'

'She's a friend?' I ask.

'I don't answer for her. Not something I do.'

'Who is she?'

'She is from nearby I grew up. Not France.'

'North Africa? When did you come to France?'

'Mmhm. We buried my father when he die. Sail to Corsica, to Nice. The first time I see France. Sunrise. City red. Boomed, it almost –' and he puts two hands up in front of me and shakes them '– it shook.'

'It is one of the cities –' I say, waiting for something. Something, and I realise I believe there is something he is going to tell me. Or I wait on what it is I am going to say because I realise fame has the power to extract something from me. I feel like a sentence spelt long ago, that its shape resides inside me but has yet to be traced and made extant.

'I hope you make it,' he says.

'I have no choice.'

'No. There is little choice.' He blows smoke out from beside the pipe resting between his teeth. 'You have a brother?'

I nod and Louvière leans forward, his face wrinkled by the flicker of a candle's wandering. I pause but he squints and I take it as a signal to continue on. 'He went to the front in '17,' I say. 'He flew. Quite something. I ride. In New Zealand my name is known in circles, nationally, though I am no star. But my brother – he flew, and that's got to be something.'

'He died? Most brothers seem to die.'

'No. But he did get taken out.'

'He was shot down?'

'That's right.'

He nods. 'My brothers – they're all gone. We need something to drink.' He stands and gestures to the man at the bar. 'I saw flyers go down,' he says. 'I saw the ways men could die. Out of nowhere they would come screaming. Battles so high above you weren't aware it was happening.'

'How could you not be aware?'

'There is a lot of noise. Men would suddenly stop moving. One moment talking or walking and next, they fall to ground.'

Again I sense I know the moment he is arriving at, that it is a part of me I am yet to speak.

'The earth shattered and limbs and stomachs and lungs were thrown about. You heard those coming. God and Mary. Noise everywhere. Whistles. Din and blare. It's black and thick and it is full of holes. He survive?'

'He survived.'

'I was lucky enough,' he says and coughs and hacks. 'I'm from Bagnères-de-Luchon, now I'm from Bagnères-de-Luchon. Wasn't always from there. The mountains teach you how to ride. You'll find out about that tomorrow. If the skies are clear you get to see them all. Every last star and they sing, they have song all to themselves. I returned there after war, everything was a surprise.'

I watch him for long time, waiting for something else.

He nods.

'I look for it everywhere,' I say.

'This is the south. Nothing happened here.'

'I know,' I say. 'But I hunt it out. I look for it everywhere.'

'You hunt out what? Wait. Wait for the north. I was in Wallonia when it started. Cruel. Go there if you want to remember cruel things.' He looks composed, waiting. I have the sense that I am supposed to leave all of a sudden, that my time with the man is up. I am readying myself. But he

says: 'I remember boys falling, like struck by sleep. But you don't remember, no one remember. Every day. Every day. There's no memory, just, erm. Just experience. Experience. Experience because it is always, always happening; it hasn't ever stopped. And to say it, to make imitate of it; that is a cruel violence in itself. How was your brother?'

'My brother coming home?'

'What of him?'

'He took over the house. He walked the house. Stalked it. Walked the halls. Silent vigils. We couldn't escape him. He was everywhere. Silent. Wanting nothing of us. Except from our sister. I remember how he and my sister walked the rooms of the house.'

'Her name?'

'She is a sleepwalker. They would follow each other about the house.'

'Her name?'

I say nothing for a moment. I'm not sure how true to his definition of memory and experience I have been here. I fear I don't want to argue against it, just as one doesn't argue against a man's definition of God. When there is no science, there is nothing but the whim of personality. 'Marya,' I say finally. 'That's her name. I think about it often enough. I think my mother liked the virgin birth, but not quite enough to go the whole way. The whole solemn nature of the ordeal. Such an occasion, imagine it.'

A smile starts in the small places of his face and rises up so it is in his eyes. This is something that makes my blood warm, though its source isn't such a true statement; my sister's oddly exotic name is as much a mistake as a gift. My father gave her name as Mary to the registrar, I am told he paused between the giving of the first and the second. He said, 'and – Annette. Mary Annette.' Thinking he was saying Maryanne, the registrar placed an 'a' to the rear of

the 'y' and lifted her pen and waited until something was forgotten and it was the fact of the 'a'. The intruding article wasn't noticed until days after my baby sister was brought home and Thomas made attempts to read the document, left in the top drawer of the bureau in the dining room. He saw the word Marya and read it as such. So did the family gather around and ponder. And so did the name stay pinned to her, much like the brooch handed down and glinting in such a way to set off her dark blue eyes with the light of generations; it took no leave. So my brother gave her the name. And he blamed me years later for taking it away from her. When that Model T hit the fence and was torn apart, he said in the after that I had broken her. But that wasn't ever quite true, never quite able to be made truth.

'Here,' Louvière says with his brow raised. He passes a crumpled piece of paper into my hand.

I nod at him. He leaves. The room is emptying.

I finally arrive back at the hotel and find my bed. I let the breeze in through the window. It comes off the Atlantic. A word I struggle to mouth. It seems unlikely, foreign despite being so near at this southern moment of the Bay of Biscay. I remove my shoes and hear Harry shuffle his limbs in the opposite bed. I catch myself in the mirror. My face thin, a beard arising I have never seen before, yet it is very familiar. I lie on the bed and practise breathing. In and out, a smooth rise and fall as my lungs fill and depress. I breathe as I do when I ride and listen only to my wheels and chain. I look past my chest as something takes my attention. I see my feet and know that they belong to me, though they seem quite distant, the horizon of the body. They seem a memory, one from home, one quite in front of us.

I remember the piece of paper and retrieve it from my pocket. It is a list of gear inches for each stage.

12

My Marya, see her sleepwalking in the hours after midnight. Wandering the halls of the house and making detours into rooms she had no right to enter, even taking a book from my hands as I sat up reading and placing it on the shelf in its proper place. I'd whisper her name and she'd speak unintelligible things to whoever it was she believed was listening. If I managed to wake her she'd make that noise so sharp, so loud it seemed an animal breaking.

I think of her to pass the time. The soft sound of her feet moving through the hall and how I knew she was near. She trod rugs my father brought back from Persia during the time he spent travelling with his brother through Europe and Turkey, Afghanistan and Syria, Arabia and Egypt. Nostalgias they spoke of when beer was drunk. Rich rugs, colour and feel, fibres soft between toes like a heavy velvet. I often wondered if she could name the sensation as she strolled. She walked quite upright and only occasionally held out her hand to feel the space in front of her. On a summer's evening I followed her into the garden and towards the fountain in the centre of the lines of roses that ran to the border of the property. She sat on the fountain's edge and looked at the sky. What shapes she saw in the stars as she dreamed, I can't say, but in the morning after each of these excursions she

would be composed and tranquil as if she had been given a glimpse of something simple and whole, something unseen to the wakeful, as if love finally had a shape and she had seen it move and talk. She poured tea and watched how milk made the dark tannin turn tan, she'd dip in a teaspoon of honey and taste how it went sweet.

Of these excursion's origins, I have no true idea. They began in her adolescence not long after I had begun riding. Driven by what, I couldn't find an answer. I sought out the word for her condition and found she suffered from somnambulism. I thought it a beautiful word, and I would say it to myself in class, or at the dinner table. It ran clearly in a smooth rise, then tumbled, as if the letters had come to an unseen staircase and fallen. I kept the word secret from her, and her condition felt as much mine as hers. Her night walks continued until the late Spring of 1918, several months after my brother returned. Marya was 15 years old. Thomas came home from the air corps, Europe and the hospital, and stalked the house. I have often thought how they ran into each other in the hall, how there they shared whatever sights they saw behind their shut eyes. My brother too could be found walking in the night, though he was quite awake. He would pause on the way to the lavatory or the kitchen and stand stock-still in the hall, his eyes closed, his hands clenched. He'd whisper, say words near her ear.

I watched. I did. A voyeur for the two of them – strange the melt of love.

And now, what do I do? I search out stand-ins at the side of the road, spectral stand-ins. I'm reminded of how I miss them by men and women I see being young. Their eyes latching on to the things each other say and become so wide. I want to blow them kisses when I ride by. But I don't; instead I seek out the eyes of the woman, Celia, as Louvière has named her, and hope they are wide awake, and willing.

We are a deluge in the night of the lowlands, a hundred riders in flood. It's hot before the mountains and I feel a wetness inside my jersey, but it isn't sweat. My nose has begun to bleed and it's only the first hour. I put my hand into the V of the garment and bring it up to smell; it has the odour of iron as when your gum is damaged and you taste blood. It's dark and I know nobody will see the stain until morning. I am certain too that by then I will have crashed from the bike five, six times. We ride blind, as if in the centre of another man's thoughts, guided by events never experienced, never heard. Direction is guesswork, a question like the feathers of a crow flying in the night. No one will notice where the blood has come from. By then it will be everywhere.

I look for Louvière on the road, for a hint of last night's conversation to return via a glance or a finger lifted from the handlebars. I see nothing of him. I have his ratios set in my chain ring and rear sprockets. I sport a 46-inch for the day.

I find a rhythm. I feel the road vanish as the miles turn to vapour behind us. The throng of riders streaming in the darkness. Take away the rattle and a low hum emanates from this great bunch, the bottomless sound of a male choir. The whole of the peloton sniffing as if an influenza had passed through the village during the brief sleep we managed before the start. Our pupils swollen so they are as large as the moon hidden behind the highest peaks clambering at 10,000 feet. The mountains, the Pyrénées – risen ruptures as if some stern god has taken Spain and thrust it into France, forcing the earth up and up until the plains buckled and cracked and became violent ridges and peaks, until they were impassable except by goat. And indeed, they are. Henri Desgrange, the inventor and spector, the father and director, absent, unseen and everywhere, paid some thousands of francs to have their

tracks cleared of rubble and snow for the Tour. That was 20 years ago. Now we ride in the black beneath the peaks.

Here, I list them:

Aneto

Pico Posets

Monte Perdido

Pic Maudit

Cilindro de Marboré

Pic de la Maladeta

Pico de Aneto. There she is somewhere hidden in the dark: 11,168 feet and no more. The granite lump that lurks highest, peaked by a Christian cross ported to the summit by zealous souls some years ago and wedged in place by rocks and gravel. I've seen photographic proof of this thing, this oversized crucifix lurking in the formations, the glacier below melting into an eventual sea. Percy offered it to me after a woman put it in his hand outside that café in Paris before the race to Rennes. She had seen him on one knee as if in prayer. There was sleet falling with the hail. She brought it to him, handling it with great care. And without poetry or precision, Percy thanked her. We'd stared at each other, fascinated, as she walked away. Now I wonder what they see, those mighty alps, as they stare down at us, a river of men riding so close.

My knees flick the petals of flowers pushing out from a near garden; its house a hundred yards distant amongst its farm where the sleeping are rustled in their slumber by our chains and wheels, the charge of a hundred men as if dispatched into the night with a message for kings and their court, the footmen, the generals, the parliamentarians, the suitors of the queen. Though, sadly, all we have to offer is the sponsors' names. The scent of the petals linger in my shorts, the stigmas staining my skin yellow with the colour of the

sun still to break the horizon, a yolk behind the shell.

My other knee is bleeding. I have fallen twice into the wall of the road. The second time two others tumbled with me and I heard a sound so familiar, a tone so distinct. I was then recalled to her in the dark, my sister quiet and alone, the sudden noise she made as she awoke standing in the hall. The sound of metal tearing itself from metal running through the hills. Her mouth open like a tunnel into some province untamed.

Will me on, Marya, I say to myself. Stand me on my pedals. Today I must climb.

The cars follow behind, their lights making long shadows of our wheels, queer ellipsoids and the spokes like darts into the rough of the road. I lose the others spread out around the hillside. Dim shapes come and recede as we struggle by the moon. Darkness blooms and becomes hard. Darkness, like coal for a furnace. It retreats, then grows. Fear is close. I plummet into valleys not knowing their depth. I fear the bottom for I do not know if I will still be on my wheels when it hits, or if I will be airborne like a stone hurled from above. The support vehicles slowly disappear, their lights on more famous sons than we southern urchins. Bruce Small lost amongst the riders. I manifest questions like regrets:

How long do I climb?

How long until the sun?

How long until I find them?

And then, inevitably: When will I fall?

This last question, it is answered time and again.

The effort is to keep this machine in the smooth slot of the tracks made by the leaders. The handlebars almost wrenched from my hands, my body off the seat. I feel myself heading for the darkness beyond that of the night. Somehow I right myself and I'm back on my seat. I'm sweating like old dynamite. I'm ready to be thrown the far and ultimate distance by a lack of concentration. I shout at myself.

I say no words.

I seem to be slowing. Slowing.

And then, a voice: 'Fiche moi le paix.'

I hadn't noticed the rider beside me until the sound broke the rustle of tyres and gravel. He's a shadow rider in the dark. All is shadow. I call back, a phrase learnt and kept for a time like this: 'Est-ce que vous pouvez l'écrire?'

No answer though I feel him breathing. I try again: 'Je ne comprends pas.'

Again nothing. We ride on. An hour, maybe more. Creeks of dark water make sound nearby as they head into the valleys we once saw on a map but whose shape I cannot describe. Valleys whose walls we climb but know nothing of. There are moments when I shut my eyes. I have said it before, but I say it again, because in this morning the sky is that exact darkness, the road at one with the trees and ravines. We pass by figures pissing beside their bikes in a hollow where the streams run, a man holding his cock to the road and spraying the gravel. Later: a man bent over his wheel with the tube in his hands like the innards of some failed creature. Then back to the lone darkness where creeks run with the endless blood of a shadow land inhabited by hunched men seeking the end of Desgrange's nightmare. It was his idea and it makes me think all madness is his, every inch of it. I call to my companion once more, one other question for this silent Frenchman (it is a question, I believe, regarding the freshness of milk).

A cough, then he calls out: 'Bonjour you French fuck. Sit in ya piss.'

'Ha,' I blurt. I know the voice, the tide of profanities like profundities. It's Ernie. Ernie with his anger rolled up like a sleeping mat and unfurled at the lowliest passerby. He is the sweariest of us, the foulest-toothed and I love him for it like an old dog whose stink stays in the clothes of its angel-eyed owner. 'Ernie.' I say. 'Thank God.'

'What?' His voice vexed by the sudden English. 'Who's that?'

'Come on.' Our voices sound like wounds, or the words of old men spoken long before. It's hard to pin anything on us.

'It's you. Thank fuck,' he half-stammers, each word calling out for its own full stop so it might rest a while. We'd been riding beside each other for over an hour without any idea.

'You didn't recognise me?'

'Digger, I am done.'

'Digger, digger, digger,' I say. He rides on quietly, not speaking for a few hundred yards. I realise he is likely doing what I'm doing, gauging the distance between us, the necessary span needed to keep us from crashing into each other. I listen to the sound of his bike, the light tyre crunch through the gravel. That, I understand, is how each of us knows the space we reserve to avoid putting our pedals into our spokes and send us into the wall or over the cliff. I can't remember if I'd caught him or if he'd found me. Either way we're a congregation awaiting the sun and its teachings. Things will be better when it comes. It is a promise we need.

'You seen the others?' he asks.

'Percy is dead,' I say.

'You're an idiot. Watson?'

'I don't know.'

'Someone must have seen him.'

'Why?'

'I saw his back –'

I had seen it too. The hurt: the boils ranging up under the skin, the fibrous anger of deep infection. Bearings of pus.

'He's coming up behind,' I say.

'Truth?'

'Truth.'

His breathing seems to relax.

'He'll find us soon,' I say, though I fear I am lying. I haven't seen Harry in hours. It's rare for him to lapse into the distance. I ride on with Ernie, that aging veteran, and I long for a sight of my friend. I long for him to be out in front where I always had the best view of his will to keep on. But I'm frightened at the idea of him. I imagine him amongst the stones standing in those fields. That uncertain congregation. I find myself in shivers. I have a sudden fear the night won't stop. In truth, I fear everything.

We ride under the dome of the dark, hunting out the dawn.

I ride looking in the rear of my mind for things to recall succinctly. People come and go, days, events. Summers and girls and women. My sister fills in long hours of darkness. Her mind's eye so clear as she walked the halls. There is a comparison to be made of her darkness and the one through which we ride. Though, in truth, I do not know what it is, how they match. I look for her amongst the women in night gowns who stand at the gate to some farm. Sisters, five of them, and Ernie makes a noise.

I want to ask her questions, my Marya.

Ernie shouts at me and I veer. Two bikes linked in the

road, their owners nowhere near we can see. We seem to be heading downward but I am uncertain. Ernie shouts again, but there is nothing but a dark road. I see lights in the sky above, or if not the sky, on the side of the mountain. I'm perplexed that I cannot make a decision, which further terrifies me. I hunt out the shape of the alps but my eyes cannot make contact with the rock. The rest of our team must be somewhere in the night and I just hope they are on that hillside, for surely they are riders we see, support vehicles glinting their lights off the spokes and frame. I can't help but wonder through other things though: Perhaps these are planes. Perhaps balloons or other contrivances I can't think into my mind's eye? I watch them like they are fireflies and imagine my sister and me driving upwards, a final ride in a moonless dawn. And then I must ask, is Harry one of them? Opperman, Osborne?

<div align="center">❖</div>

Nobody dies, yet the sun comes to save us. The belligerent surge of pinks and yellows, a day as if blown from the palm of a child's hand. I feel the peloton push as one towards a common speed some rate quicker. The mountains rise up before us and we begin our climb. We near the foot of Col d'Aubisque. A group of 20 or 30 arrived before us and removed their rear wheels, spun them around then slipped them back into place with the lowest of the gears attached to the chain. Then more riders, and again more. The entire peloton arrives out of the shadows. They ride off in silence as we pause to make the adjustment. I take a pill from the bottle and let it dissolve in my mouth. I feel the light explode.

Marya, did you ever see such a thing?

Part 2

13

Sometime before noon, François Louvière exited the road where the rains had cut the track so it resembled a funnel and a yellow slew of clay dripped to the valley. With his bicycle beneath him he sidled through and felt his wheels leave the road, a road that always seemed built just for him; but it failed, he fell. He fell at open grave, the pace at which your very own tomb creaks open to show you its environs. And if you fall. Tumble and lurch.

He lay in the trench of the valley where the creeks ride together, a long moan echoing off the rock. It appeared he had fallen in silence, for I heard nothing from his mouth until that groan, that bassoon sound from out beyond. A sound so precarious I knew life was near and Louvière, despite his extraordinary legend, despite the way we held our breath, was near to a certain kind of end.

I watched the French doctor scamper down the hillside with a syringe between his teeth in order to fill Louvière's pipes with morphine. I stood on my pedals, balancing on the gearing and thanked the rays of the slanting sun for catching my goggles and blinding me and pushing me back behind the wheels of the breakaway pack. Five bikes had gone down that temporary ravine; I might have been the sixth but for fear of the dark. That is what you get when you

are staring right at the sun: a darkness like the deepest cave, like no other kind of light. I stood, balanced with my feet shifting the cranks back and forth minutely. Still moving, still in the race, still a verb in this sentence.

We circled in the dirt waiting for a sign of the living to arise from the valley so the race might go on. Solemn-eyed men on the verges, not knowing whether to follow him down or to stay on the road. That bald legend who, as his legs broke and muscles were torn from ligament, became confined to that mythical status for time onwards and on, for all the truth about him seemed to fall away as he went down.

Here's one for a start: if he'd ever carried a whip, we would have felt its crack on our skins.

I waited and hoped for a sign of Osborne and Harry.

Sometime earlier, perhaps an hour after the sun had risen, with Ernie Bainbridge and I still a pair talking through the dawn, our team had come together. We rode more or less in the middle of the peloton which had formed at Col d'Aubisque, as if all the riders had been summoned by the coming demand, the Pyrénées and the animal tracks barely roads. Louvière had led a breakaway group trying to catch Fontan who had torn out from the pack into the valley after Saint-Jean-Pied-de-Port. Chased the group that followed. I went forward and sat on Louvière's wheel until just below the first climb of Tourmalet when the light caught me and I fell back.

Camille Van de Casteele had taken the lead some 40 minutes earlier and would not relinquish it. The first to the top of this cursed piece of road was afforded a grand prize: lungs burst for this. I couldn't catch them, hence it would not be mine. I shouted at myself as I climbed. My bones felt the terror of my muscles as they stretched and shrank. Trying to

take me up and up, they seemed to bend in the effort. I say this, but we were barely pedalling. And it's a heavy agony. I thought only to cry when we hit the snowline. The pain was exquisite and I could not comprehend how my body kept working me onwards. It was deep, it was everywhere, surrounding every part of me. I felt myself become damaged; I felt every muscle disintegrating, lungs and heart turning to bloody pulp in my chest. But I went on, and it's not a case of knowing how, rather it is the case that we did. It's a miracle that we overcome such pain and no surprise some are chosen as gods. I was amongst five Belgians and a pair of Italians. Frantz just to the rear. We each made queer noises as we sought to hold on to Louvière's wheel who sought to hold on to de Casteele. The Belgian got to the summit some 10 minutes before us. He stood and watched the rest straining at the pass before changing his gearing and diving into the valley. He would not win the stage, Victor Fontan has that honour, though I suspect he would not have had a chance had Louvière not come such a cropper.

At the height of the col the group as one leapt from their bikes and flipped their back wheels and hitched the chain to the smallest cog there and set off into the afternoon in a blaze of light and speed. In less than five minutes Louvière had fallen into the valley. We were travelling at over 60 kilometres an hour, according to the chase car. A withered man with driver's gloves in his shoulder tabs told how he had been falling behind.

Eventually I took myself from the bike and sat beside the road. Harry arrived a quarter of an hour after the accident and skidded his bike to a stop beside the car that would be Louvière's ambulance. I went to the Cantabrian and pointed. He looked at me and without any interpretation of my expressions jumped from the track into the clay and scrambled down the 40 or so yards to where the Algerian

lay bleeding, a doctor and a stretcher bearer-hunched over his broken body. Signs of bleeding in the discarded towels beside the stream.

Blood sport.

Now other teams have become passersby. Discuter slow and watch. I call out to the Spanish lad. Only he looks my way. The rest ride through the scene saying nothing, a car behind them at low revs. A familiar machine, the car I saw Celia approach back in Caen, jutting smoke in Pyrenean air. Though men at the side of the road shout to them Louvière's name, there's not a glance from the car nor the riders. Men calling and pointing into the gully.

Hours later Percy made the statement that he'd known his name, not his face. Though I knew his face well enough, I understood. You never see the face of such a man, just the air that seems thicker about their being. His crash described the end of a legend, it also voiced the beginning of another, more respectful, set of lies:

The white of the bone stuck through his thigh (read in *L'Auto*).

He moaned like dying mutton, blood rendered the dirt red, the grass purple (*Le Figaro*).

The sky was black in cloud, the river red with the slither of sunset (*L'Auto* again), despite it being midday.

An old man died at the exact moment in a village nearby of a swollen heart, his daughter's hand in his.

The riders of the Tour found they rode more freely once his body had been taken from his machine.

On and on. Shadows to the truth. In the end we all fell: Opperman three times, Harry twice. Harry broke his brakes, sat at the side of the road for almost half an hour fixing them at the snow line. Ernie cracked a wheel. Percy's

head is bandaged and bloodied. Only when your bones splinter do you stop for good.

Of course Opperman and Harry had discussed Louvière during our planning meetings, but it was Frantz that took most of their talk. They analysed and sought advice. They knew the man would start in the yellow jersey and could be trusted to keep it as long as he or his body could hold out. By the time they were finished with Frantz, there was nobody else to think about. The man was unbeatable, such were the statistics and his team. He had been that way for some time. In Luxembourg he was champion before he was 20, came to the Tour four years later and came second, then fourth behind Ottavio Bottecchia before utterly dominating the race. He never broke down, his body was seemingly resistant to all sour things.

But I, I had studied Louvière. I had studied him from New Zealand, letters sent via spies. English spies. Nimble-fingered, judging by their elegant missives. Envelopes sealed with lipstick and looped signatures.

A lie and the amour of distance. Cousin Alice.

I think of those letters and imagine binoculars focused from a mile out. I imagine spy stuff. Men in long coats, great coats, cologne-wearing shadows in the shadows themselves peering out of cracks in the light. But no, you see I call them my spies but they were merely family, cousins holidaying in the south; Marseille during a summer two years passed. I had asked that she send me descriptions of the race as they followed it east from Perpignan to Nice. My dear cousin Alice sent perfumed letters and told me of the 'piston thighs' of Louvière. Did I laugh at that? Of course I laughed at that.

The proposal that I might one day see this man, ride beside him always seemed impossible; even by arriving here in May

it seemed impossible. But Henri Desgrange, he had allowed us a chance at divinity, and I have now heard Louvière's chain, seen those legs like a pacer's, so metronomic it half seemed he hypnotised challengers into lagging.

He did not win the previous year, that was the provenance of Frantz. But Frantz is no Louvière.

Louvière had never won: 3rd to Ottavio Bottecchia in '26; 20th to Frantz in '27; 18th in '25; 4th in '24. In 1919 he was unable to finish. In 1920 he came 3rd. Luck and destiny. The next year he was hauled from his bike in Malo-les-Bains by five drinking Belgians as he rode into the town's tentative outskirts. They were there to welcome Philippe Thys, their countryman, the unrelinquishing leader. They saw Louvière in the colours of his home town, they came to the road shouting, their beer frothing. One threw the ale to his face when they saw his swarthy looks. Louvière went crooked on the road and his tyres caught the cobblestones and he went sideways and over the bars. His arm broken, the race finished without him three days hence. He tried to ride with his arm in a sling. He came off again and again and was ordered not to go on.

Eighth the next year. He has won 15 stages but never worn the yellow shirt. Never stood in the centre of a podium. But, in spite of this, he is the greatest. My cousin whispered she had never seen a man more beautiful to behold as he stood on his pedals and shifted speed so the pack seemed to flounder and shimmer and slow. The way he never smiled, just peered out from blue deep eyes. And from her writing, all this effortless expenditure of immense energies appeared to be made so he could look my cousin in the eye, that he eased across the front of the pack merely to make her stammer.

I understand her crush, I understand the newspapers' lust for victory, I understand the men from that border

town. He instils spontaneous action in the limbs of those easy to fall in love with beauty, and, it seems, to see its death. Indeed, a victory will never come now, and the man, it seems, will never return to the road. Since we spoke in Hendaye, I have tried to ignore his interest in our presence. We were, I suspect, some oddity. Just as our presence in the war was peculiar to any who thought of it. We were there with Indians, with Africans, with the English and Scots and Welsh. Who knows why.

Earlier this evening I left my rooms and went to visit the man. I intended to see him in his bedroom to say commiserating words. To see those eyes one last time. Perhaps I was thinking of cousin Alice, perhaps I wanted to have a story for her once I finally met her and knew what she looked like. Whatever the case it never happened. Happily, the will of another diverted me here to this calm room, downy cheeks who would share the topette I have in my top pocket. This girl, she found me returning from the river and whispered my name as if it were a secret; though it was the only word we could share for I speak only English, and only a few words at a time. They told us to learn as much French as we could leading to the start. I learnt to point and stare. I am a puppet of cloth and straw.

We lie looking at the ceiling, the girl in the crook of my arm. Quite beautiful, half-naked like in dreams. I have the sense that I should be feeling lucky, as if gifted the moment by strange circumstance or fortune. But I don't, I feel only a proximity to shame. She kisses me, her tongue and mine. I fear the hole in my row of teeth, that she might feel revolt if she finds it with her soft wet mouth. But perhaps it is only I who can feel it, who is aware of what was there previously.

111

I drift into long flights of dream. The girl does the same, she caresses the back of my head as if it is bruised in a fall. Indeed, it might well be, it might be with her fingers she can sense this kind of hurt, the kind that happens when you crash and collect stray agonies but forget them soon after with a fresh fall. Pain is multi-limbed and forgetful. I lie there and I wonder what parts of Louvière's body are being ignored for the fact of his truly bad injury. That shattered tibia and the flakes of hard bone in his muscle.

Louvière, I say to myself, almost believing I had gone there to his room. I am sorry for your fall. I'm sorry I can't take this bone from your thigh.

He might have replied, he might have said: Go back to your boys and stop pricking me with your apologies. His face bloodless from morphine and pain.

I am a weakling with a weakling's inclinations to fail, I say.

There are no weaklings in the mountains.

Only me, I reply.

And he says, I'm sure he says in his morphine gaze, eyes like ice: All fools on the road! All men who pretend; the road will shake you from its course and my God if you aren't in my way!

And I say nothing back because I do not speak to him. I didn't venture into the room with the four-poster bed where they laid him to shake my head at his forlorn figure. Instead I took wine and sat beside the bridge where the stream gurgles its waters like a throat cut towards the valley floor, to the conjoining river that spans and rushes towards the Iberian plains or the Pyrénées-Orientales and then the sea and how many years does it take until it is run through the gates of Gibraltar to the ocean and the shores of countries that come here to spend their men in war and this insane race itself. I drank to kill the pain, to make my thighs sane

112

once more. She came and sat, a seamstress, a milkmaid, a comely one who knew what rested in my top pocket. The thing Celia (Celia, I am yet to say the name aloud) had given in Caen. The girl and I came to this room and we lay still, we finished the bottle and I brought forth the handkerchief and produced the topette.

We take breaths deep. Her pretty hands.

'Do you know Louvière?' I say.

Her pretty smile.

'He is the king. In America they would make a dollar in his image, a line of cars in his name.'

'New York?' she says.

'New York?' I say.

'New York, New York?!'

Soon I realise, soon I surmise: she believes I am American. I laugh and she looks at me with long, long eyelashes that beat like the wings of the languid hawk that scours the mountain walls looking for blooded carrion or an updraft to transport her far away. A beauty indeed, and I place next to her an undeserving simile: that hawk's pursuit is for necessity and life, she is here only for the hit of this wet rag, and I for certain admire this honesty and precision.

'Oh yes,' I say. You see, I'll borrow the Yankee formula if it means I will not have to look Louvière in the eye and see the broken sneer of a man who mocks the fact he rides a machine. He flies whilst we crawl in the shallows of his wake, and he knows, he knows not one of us will ever truly win without him behind our shadow. Indeed, tomorrow people will write that the concatenated effects of fate and element have broken the only man worthy of the yellow jersey (despite him never having worn it). They will be lying, of course – but they will sell newspapers, and boys will make paper planes from their pages and we will watch them float and sway and pray for their safe passage away

from our spokes and gearing. So to the girl I feel a gratitude, and I wonder if I owe her greater sums than the waking ether dreams I have offered.

Lie close, I say. Be near.

I am an Antipodean. No Yank team has ridden this race, no English, no Welsh. This I'm told. We are New Zealand, we are Australia. But I shall be American, I shall be anything.

14

Ten days before she died, my sister went white. Her face damp and her legs giving out in the hall. I watched her fall, her hands reaching out for the walls and touching air. The hollow of her cheeks the kind of pale one barely associates with the living. Now we stand waiting for the race to head out from the town and the faces I see by candlelight in the rain flicker thoughts of her. Candle flames unsteady in the hands of the sisters, the habited who floated in from the convent that watches us all from the mountainside. These are the lights by which we see, by which we ride in the cavern, by which our shadows play on medieval constructions, the chapels and homes and barns and businesses. Midnight suns, shadow faces gifting us light to ride by, the white of their skin matching that of my own stricken sister. This is the way we connect things: colour, light, sound.

Our number is 78. We cram into the street. Some have slept, some are in mourning for the lost hours that await them; it seems fear smells of liniment and coffee and milk. Each looks a kind of puppet, barely brave and foolhardy. Fooled by the promise of glory. Though, at times, it is the fool who has the clearest view. Marya once said that as we sat atop Egmont, the world we knew spread out in front of us. When men were here on the continent fighting, Marya and

I climbed the mountain twice with our father. Clambered over the fields of volcanic rock and broad patches of snow and watched the world and pretended we knew all about it. She had a habit, my sister, of getting into my head with such words. She stays there still, unmoving, and now I feel her watching as we prepare to move out into the snow-capped hills. I want to reach for one of the nuns and pull her in near and ask why it is we have come here to fight. I'd expect no answer, just the sound of surprise and delight.

I try to recall the surrounds of the town from the day before. I know the place is hedged in, I know mountains range overhead, but so it is for all towns in the Pyrénées. I only remember that the road out was lined with trees separating the footpath and traffic. The shape of the mountains, the burden of snow and their precise proximity, I cannot recall. I look around and if there are a thousand people in this town, they are all out of bed awaiting our grim departure.

Percy and Bainbridge play leapfrog to keep warm until Bruce shouts out and the men return to their bikes. Monsieur France is somewhere. 3:30 and we are ready in the dark, between the walls of the dark.

We go. Stopwatches are set whirring as the torque of the mainspring is let loose and cogs fly unseen. We crawl out with the pack, a funeral run of shivering men. Yes, it is cold and the children who have gathered with the parents are draped in blankets. Morning faces. No play, no smart remarks. This is a solemn beginning.

I hear Opperman say quiet words. He intends to take to the front early and stay there as long as possible. The same tactic as two days ago out of Hendaye. Which worked until elbow-tight corners and the speed at which his pursuers took them sent him into the dirt: he crashed and crashed again, unused to the speed, unacquainted with the manoeuvres

116

needed to survive on the course. He is determined to fight them off, all the men who wish to ride at him, to unseat him and see him fail before their lesser desires.

We ride, we pass through into the countryside. The sisters quiet in the wake.

⬚

The climb sees the peloton fall to pieces and spread out across the hill. I pick riders off one by one. The first climb is steep. One in six gradient, many walk. Harry walks, Ernie and Osborne. I ride past a man pissing in his shorts, the smell and sight of it. I'll soon do the same, I'm sure. The gradient tilts towards the sky and I find myself at the front of fragmented teams split by the confusion of the start. It's dark, still and cold. As with the Tuesday when we set off as one from Hendaye, we ride from Luchon en masse. These days are no time trials, they are the place we ride as a true peloton and show our frailties as our bodies buckle and strain.

We lose one another as the long length of the peloton stretches so it's inevitable it will snap. Minutes don't pass in the dark, nor do seconds. We can't gauge speed, nor can we mark distance. But then it seems we have merged once more, as if drawn back together by the inevitable fact of us. I ride with Harry, but he doesn't talk. He's sullen. As if his temper was bruised, knocked about in the lead-up to the stage. We sit behind Percy and Opperman. We are riding in a bleak half-light as if half blinded and I find my thoughts drift to a night. Another night and a colder night in a winter hard with the presence of men near the brink. A hotel public bar and the sight of my brother throwing haymakers at the black air in the lightless space out the back used by the brewery truck to deliver the beer.

117

It was a quarter past six in early August, I know that for it was the time I had told him I would be outside to fetch him for dinner. He might have been home for a week, two. Whichever, in that time he'd obviously lost his ability to hit well and flung drunk arms at whoever wanted a piece of his story. I know this because I learnt by observation that this was how these fights came about. Questions of time and place, they quickly turned to questions of valour. I was a boy when I threw my first punch, twelve. It came from my legs, my hips, then through my shoulders so force was at the end of my knuckle. My brother took the punch and looked stunned for a moment and quickly put me in a headlock and roughed up my hair. He said over and over, 'Where'd you learn that, boy? Where'd you learn that?' I'd learnt it from him of course and, hence, as I put the car to a stop with the headlamps pushing their way into the melange, I was a small bit deflated. Though he was short, a half-back for the seniors in his short career, he could wallop and do it with timing and performed none of this floundering, none of this flapping about.

I asked him as we drove towards home who he was fighting. He didn't say a word. Truth: he hadn't said a word in the time since he'd arrived from Scotland. Barely a word. The talk would come later. At that point I assumed he didn't know who he was hitting, just as he didn't know what words he could state. I think this as wheels bang against my own, as handlebars bruise my hips, and I see no faces. I wonder if it is easier to fight when you don't know who surrounds you. Blackness and the edges of darkness. Silence there and the willingness to hit out at whatever comes near; the honesty of silence and how it bridges everything, lives everywhere there aren't words. My brother before he learnt to speak again with blood on his face, swinging. Violence a remedy against the stillness of solitude. I discover it is near

118

morning when the puncture comes, many pass and I am alone.

❖

It is the unstated hour of dawn when I squat beside a brook with tools in my hands and speak with an elderly farmer and his son, who have arrived with the faint sun. That bright globe broke out of the shackle of the mountains and filled the valley with a silver pink. They came from the field adjacent to watch me correct my tyre and offer water from a gourd he carries over his shoulder and the light from his lantern. It tastes sweet, as sweet as water can taste without an additive of honey or juice squeezed from a fruit. He speaks through his son. The man, my age at a guess, though I am wary of comparison, explains that he works in Toulouse as a teacher. His English is stuttered but that seems not to matter. I glance at his left hand; the skin is folded over several times and where I expect to see fingers there is only a red twist of scar. I gather, then, that he is more likely my brother's age than mine. The old man speaks quickly, knowing the lack of time I have to offer as I undo the bolts holding my wheel to the frame and remove the tube from around my shoulder. His son translates rapidly and thoughtfully. I'm asked where I am from. I tell him. 'Nouvelle-Zélande.'

The farmer confers with his son. They speak, one with his head down, the other looking up at the sky. There is a softness, as if they speak what is under their skin. They swap their gaze, one up, one down. The farmer stammers out a word several times until I understand. He is asking if I am Ernie. There isn't time for corrections so I smile and hold the name a moment. 'Ernie Bainbridge, that is right,' I say.

'The priest!' the old farmer says.

'That's right!' I say. Though how one might confuse Harry and Ernie, I can't say.

The old man puts out both his hands and I briefly offer him mine to shake and he holds it, his skin improbably rough. He talks to his son as I work.

'When the first race came here,' the son says, 'my father had never saw a bicycle, he had never hear a bicycle. He poor. His mother did no speak French, you know? And when my grandpapa died she want to leave this valley and he was almost forced out to beg. She wanted to travel to her family in the north.'

I look at the farmer. 'What language did his mother speak, then?'

The young man coughs out a rough noise. He tells me he doesn't know. Then the farmer speaks, an atavistic rattle from his mouth, talking to his son who looks down at me nodding. I dig my tyre irons into the space between the rubber and the wooden rim where I lever them apart, that old air smell of rust and water. Eventually the son says, 'My father. He want to know. He want,' the young man says, 'he want to know if you come here before.'

'To these mountains?'

'No. No, to France. You were made to fight? This is what he ask.'

'Did I come here during the war?'

'Yes. He want to ask you.'

I put down the tyre irons and wipe my hands and stand and cough to clear my throat. 'I was too young.' I indicate something small by placing one hand above the other, pushing them closer as if compacting the air into a balloon. I put out my bottom lip and shake my head. 'Too small,' I say.

'Yes, I understand,' the son says. He speaks more with his father and I go back on my knees and begin laying the tube on the tape protecting the rubber from the ends of the spokes where they met the rim. The young man taps

my shoulder. 'He also want know if you saw north. Hell of North. You know Hell of the North?'

'Sorry? Did I ride there?' I look at him waiting on something. I shake my head.

He shakes his head. 'He say you here before. You here and you fought.'

Sweat becomes cold on my face and in my clothes. I can feel my blood start to slow. Seconds make their presence known as water comes down the creek by which we stand. Apart from the gases we breathe, it sometimes seems everything in this world is in a race to the sea. I look around, to make sure no one who knows better is listening. 'I was here,' I say. 'I flew RE8s.' I make my arms into the shape of an aircraft's wings and push air through my lips so they flutter and fart. 'Aeroplanes in the north. Flew in the north. I flew RE8s. Rubbish aircraft, really. Slow, poor manoeuvrability.'

'And you live through,' the young man says.

I laugh. 'Well, I did. I fell out of the sky, eventually. But I got through. Crashed near the sea. That was my war.'

'But you live. I happy to hear. I first spoke English with Australians, men at front. They taught me to say, "My helmet, my head." The rest come easy for me. I learn the rest off sisters at monastery. Then I teach.'

'You do well enough.' I cough on the cool air. I'm telling my brother's story. Seems simple enough. My brother, he was as poor as I at the exchange of languages. He crashed into a dune on the wrong side of the line. We are amongst pasture lining a valley deep within mountains which loom and offer little resistance to the slight but overbearing fear that sometimes stuns logic when the path seems to offer no route out. Fear has a phantom's face. Fear operates by its own rules, as though it is just and reasonable. 'I lived,' I say. 'Well enough to ride again. But I have never flown again.'

The old man is speaking once more as I struggle with the

tube. He puts his hand on his son's shoulder and they both laugh. I notice for the first time they are holding hands. The young man's hands bigger and wider than his father's. With his free hand the farmer points upwards but I don't follow his gesture. I put the wheel back into place and loosely tighten the nuts.

'My father, he say,' the young man says, 'he once saw flying machine. He call it flying machine. He once thought he saw aeroplane. He, up on the ridge,' he says, and he points with his stump to where his father pointed moments earlier. I have to look over my shoulder. There I see a col where two ridges come together some thousands of feet above where the sun glints off the rocks. 'He thought he saw an aeroplane. This is what he say, he say he found two dead goat up on ridge and was angry and sad and sat trying to think what to do and he saw it.'

'Dead goats? That sounds, what? That sounds ominous.'

'Yes. They bloody, gored. Fresh. This what he say in his story. He might carry back down the mountain but they too heavy and wasn't leaving hill for week. He repairing fences which had fallen to the winter. He wonder about the weather and look up. Up high near sun, he saw shape, a heavy shape like cross and he steady himself. He think he seeing an aeroplane. Flying machine. He listen for engine and hear nothing. He not know what aeroplane might sound like but he think because it was in the sky the noise of its engine just flew away. He didn't know because he had never seen one. Perhaps sound rose softly away. Mmm: steam. Smoke. That what he thought. He jump and he wave to machine, hoping to catch the attention of flyer. Then machine seem to turn and slowly fall, it started – err. Like a boat collapses?'

I nod for him as I make a final adjustment of my wheel so it is lined up straight. 'List?'

'List, okay. Good. List. Good,' he says. 'And my father,

he watch and the speed of thing got faster and faster until it must have been screaming but it not, it just fall towards him and so he ran and ran to pile of stones and there he hid expecting a great explosion but there was nothing and he looked and saw what he saw all time. Eagle two metres over the ground.'

'An eagle?' I say. I laugh and pull the canister of compressed air from my bag. 'There are eagles?'

'And you know, he sat, my father, and watched this eagle, something he has seen many times before. But the idea, the idea of the aeroplane, such a strong thing to think, but he watched this eagle as it stood beside two dead goat on guard. It was size of a hog, he like to say. And then came the foxes, and then came the cats, the lynx. You know them?'

'And then after two days. After two days those goats were picked clean,' I say, finishing his story. 'Talons like clawed fists.'

'Yes. That right. You know story?' They are still holding hands, the young man's fingers wrapped about his father's, the other hand gesticulating at his side, ghost fingers somewhere saying something.

I affix the nozzle to the valve and smile back at him. I release the air and in seconds the tyre is full once more, and hard enough to support my weight. I tighten the bolts one last time. I wave as I push off and begin my descent towards the floor of the valley from which I see the first big climb ahead under the new sun. I will catch my team by rising quickly, that is my plan. But before that I will crash and crash again and I will search the sky for shapes, and for clues as to what those shapes might be. I look back and wish I'd said what I think now, that I have in my head now: all stories are rhythm, and all rhythms return.

We come down the zigzag below Portet d'Aspet. I push ahead through the village as it follows the curve of the valley in pursuit of faster men, Opperman amongst them. A boy stands looking at me, a boy standing on the track, the way lit by candles, more candles, but this time in the hands of children cuddled in their parents' wind shadows. The boy stands calm and expectant, as if for a rider who isn't me, nor anyone else I have seen on the path. I imagine my face is without inspiration or heroism. It is sagging, banging as I run over the ruts.

The village is set on a curve and I run through as if chased by something violent and heavy. And I am, the entire peloton sits on my heels. But it isn't them I imagine, rather it's a creature with black wings diving from the roof of the sky. I'd thanked the farmer for his story, thanked him for the water and his time. But all his tale offered me was this: black wings and the black air to fly upon. Heavy air, fear in its folds. It was his question in the main, and not the question itself, but the repetition of the question. And now what? What response comes? How close are we to being another, to being ourselves? I feel no guilt for stealing his story. A bout of alert words had stretched out from inside, touched things I shouldn't touch. Being someone, anyone, it seems, is merely a habit we don't wish to halt. In moments like these I suspect skin is the only real thing we know. I feel a need to tell someone afresh this idea. If my cousin makes an approach, I shall admit my sin and these thoughts and wait for her to tell me how mad I have become. As if that will resolve everything.

The light slowly becomes more apparent, surrounds reveal themselves to be green, an uplifted forest. Above us trees hang their limbs and drag their leaves across the path. My cheeks are grazed as branches burst and cut against my face. I jostle with riders I don't know the name of. I

shove and hug low into the hairpins. I pull the brakes and slow my legs then sprint out again like a Belgian on a short course race up in Wallonia. The villages come and I hit their cobblestones on my own, 100 metres to the riders in front and 50 to those behind. I am alone in the valley that I believe takes us to Saint-Girons. No one approaches and the leaders do not slow. I flash glances behind, always expecting Louvière to follow and get in my shadow.

I am angling south-east to the last of the mountains. My team somewhere on the track ahead or behind. I can't tell. I shout out in the middle of a valley where mountains converge. I yell Harry's name. I shout it many times, and Hubert's, and Ernie's, and Percy's. I shout my own as those hills close in around me and I have a sudden thought that I am no longer in France. That the mountains are no longer of France but of Catalonia. I am in Spain. Though I know, according to the map I have a habit to memorise before the stages begin, I am not to leave these borders. I have a fright that I've missed a turn. I slow and speed up. I find a group of riders. They try to speak to me but I have nothing to say back. We ride together in a deep valley until we turn to face the mountains, winding up the massif through switchbacks and hard mud.

One by one the riders fall away. I pass men on the side of the path, faces exchanged for crumpled paper. The sun's breaking the sky open and the heat is rising out of the earth. I recognise one of the teammates of the Spanish youth I'd met in Cherbourg sitting with his bidon open above his head and streaming down his face. For a moment I fear I am following that lad, that the Spaniard has disappeared into the hills to make his way home. I call out to the lone rider. 'Bonjour,' I say. I have no idea what country he is from,

where he rides out of. Everyone uses French, even if they know no proper words. The man's face is ruined by an open mouth and a dozen black teeth. All the muscles stretched, a pain somewhere deep deafening all else so nothing gets through but this grimace.

And my God, if I don't come to the realisation that something is peculiar about my ride. In my attitude, my demeanour, I'm not sure. But it is this: I somehow find the agony acceptable. It's as though it rides beside me and I see it and ignore its demand that I kiss its hand. I don't go near. And it *is* agony, it is nothing else. My face would paint its picture, I am sure. The utter rude elementary pain that runs from toes to legs to lungs. Lungs shaped like hard flat river stones. Pain that runs the whole circuit of your body, an agony harder than iron and deeper than love. Deeper than love. I'll never kiss anything whose eyes I can't see.

I reach the col and pause to drink and flip my back wheel to the highest gear. Two men run at me. They come carrying newspapers. I say, 'What?' They lift my shirt and place the papers against my skin.

'Contre le froid. Le froid,' one says. Then they run towards the sun and slip away. I call my thanks and search below amongst the riders climbing slowly towards me. I see not one I recognise. No one whom I could ride on with and talk with. I hope that the Spanish lad might show, that we could ride together. I have seen him ride previously. He was tough, one expression for the road. It seemed he would make good company in the stead of my friends. I climb back on my ride, I'm reminded to think of the farmer who shared his water, who shared his story through his son and I think of those two goats on the ridge, their eyes picked clean away by the hard beak of the eagle, curved like its own talons whose sharp puncture the animal's flank each time it moves to step. I think how unruly this land is, these mountains and

126

the rude rules we attempt to make as we describe it with our ride and our demand for better roads, for roads at least.

I think how much a memory is like the eagle swooping in my mind, hunting for carrion amongst the cracks in the massif to keep it alive so it might at some moment swoop on hardier prey and claim meat from the bone. It is always hungry, always looking to be made full. I look up for the bird and imagine what it might do to a lone rider, how it might aid in his escape from this torture. My, how you hide in your own thoughts when the day seems unending. I realise that memories are never quite finished with you because again I think of that day in August ten years ago which nearly ended with my brother throwing bad punches at the air but didn't and instead finished at a dance with him in a heap and Katherine looking on. But the memory's not for their sake recalled, rather it's for my sister and something she said with her arm in mine against the cold.

I played my school game that morning. Then I stood and watched on the sidelines as the remains of our club's senior team were beaten in a match organised to raise funds. A thousand of us in the crowd. My Marya and Thomas stood beside me unmoving. Every weekend of peacetime winter I went to watch that team play. Its ranks obliterated by the war but I still believed, each week, each Saturday, that the moment would come and the grit and pain and rain for each one of us in the hundreds shouting from the sidelines would somehow evaporate, that blood would be stolen from our veins and be suddenly replaced by a kind of gold. The grunt and grind, the heave, the placement of the ball over a line. How it amounted to such a thing I didn't know, but we believed that that moment would come and all those rain-soaked days of tribulation would pass. All things would be erased from memory, forgotten. We put our hearts in the hands of young men, ageless giants. Thomas walked with

me about the field in the rain. We stood at Hawera's dead-ball line with time nearly up. Our team were behind by two when a bomb went astray. The ball hung in the air, its shadow shot across the earth against the low sun. Our fullback caught it on his 25-yard line and started to run. Thomas muttered something in his gumboots. I didn't hear him, I said, 'What, Tom?' He replied, but again it was inaudible. All around us men were mumbling.

Marya was holding my hand. She slipped so often I was always in the process of pulling her up. She kicked my knee. 'What?' I said.

'He said,' she said, '"Just kick it. For fuck's sake, just kick it."'

'Don't use that word,' I said and went on my tiptoes to see over the players. The fullback got it to a winger who went around his man and hit the 10-yard line.

'That's what he said.' She was 14 with something about her that wished to be a young woman. Childhood clothes had given way to hand-me-downs from our other sister. Her hair was somehow different, though perhaps it was the angles of her face changing. But more than this her voice had changed, not in timbre, but rather within its timbre. Was it girlish that she wanted to hold my hand? I hope not, I hope she always felt love, an uncomplicated love.

The winger beat two, was scragged on the 25-yard line. The ball went to ground and the boys were kicking at it, the forwards rushing with the ball at their feet. 'Dive on it,' Thomas shouted. 'Somebody fucken dive on it.' A woman behind us hit him with her umbrella. He turned and scowled at her, ruining her with a look of hatred. These were the first words I'd heard him say above a mumble since he'd returned. I gave the woman a similar look, the kind of look that one hopes the recipient will understand well; that they are a fool unworthy of a tongue. The ball bouncing off feet as grown

men hacked. The sound of shins clattering, knees sprigged and torn, fists bursting into the faces of other men. Elbows, ribs, kidneys. Mud and water kicked up and into our eyes. They were just feet away. Marya was standing right on the dead-ball line. The hooker from Hawera took a speculator, the ball spinning off the side of his foot backwards into the in-goal area. It came at us, at Marya. The ball still in play, the game still open. Four of our players descending on it, ready to fall on it. It bounced, rolled quickly, spinning in the wet grass. Our centre leapt and threw out his arm as Marya panicked and took a swipe at it with her foot. Oh, dear Jesus if she didn't connect and send it to the sideline. The referee blew the whistle and ended the match and the hopes and deep wishes of all. The crowd went silent and the mud-soaked players lay in the grass staring at the place where the ball was moments before. The instant before my sweet sister kicked it out of reach and out of the game.

We went back to the car. I started the engine, turning the crank, and got inside. We sat in silence. 'It was going to hit me,' she said. 'It was going to hit me so I, what? I kicked it.'

'You little shitter,' Thomas said.

'Steady on,' I said.

'You stinking little – you little bitch.'

'Thomas,' I said. 'Don't.'

'I'm sorry,' Marya said. Her face was breaking. 'I just –'

'What kind of little cunt are you?' Thomas said.

'Don't,' I said. Thomas spat and his saliva splattered against the windscreen. He thrust his forearm across my neck, pinning me to the seat, his elbow at my Adam's apple. I flung my head back trying to get out, but I was pinned.

'You shut up. You shut up and listen to what I got to say. You little fucks. You listen to what I've got to say.'

Marya shouted out something crude. She leant forward and bit on Thomas's tricep. Teeth in muscle. He grunted and

his arm came off my throat. Whether he'd felt me choking or not, I don't know but I breathed great armfuls of air as he put his face into his hands. He was panting hard. Sweat was pouring out of him, dripping from his nose and chin. The sound of his breathing was hypnotic, and it took some time for me to realise he was trying to speak.

'Forget this. Please. Do that for me. Christ −' he went on in a low plead for the two of us to forget what he'd just done. My throat ached and I put my hand there to feel the bruising.

'Shut up, Thomas,' Marya said. 'Don't ask me that.'

'Please,' our older brother asked. 'Come on.'

'Don't ask me that.' She put her hand up to the back of my head and whispered that she wanted to go home. I mumbled and started driving. The three of us in some poverty of hope that this hadn't happened, wouldn't happen again in our minds. That was my thought for the three of us. Involuntary dismissal of the violence that engulfed us in the Ford. I try to see her face, but it is gone. Vanished in time's shadow. I wonder now, rethinking that afternoon, if she was too young to forget, that she didn't have anything she wanted to forget. I wonder too if that is just this older version of myself thinking back. But then that evening with my brother at the pub getting himself primed to get into a fight she took my arm and we walked in the gravel out in the front of the house.

She was crying, a wet face in the soft dew falling. She started talking: 'People like that. I don't want to hear him speak again. Don't let him speak like that again.' I held her and she was small and shaking. We stayed outside until we were both wet and I had to head to the pub to collect him for dinner before taking him to the dance.

The three of us, it all seems entirely precarious. As if any memory we have is liable to slip off time's wheel and vanish in the mud. But then I think, too, that it is not time that

holds memories in place but something quite other. Hope, love, blind anger. Such things.

Eventually I come out of the mountains and find riders harrying to the sea. I join their packs, though within sight there are no men I know.

At Villefranche de Conflent we tear through a town so ancient it seems made of pure past and the stuff the past is made of, rumours and dust. A fortress town of walls and buttresses and lookouts and great doors which we make through like knights setting out. Walls that won't be breached until the earth beneath it cracks and the mountains lurch skyward another five feet. That is when history happens, when the land is done with you and the scholars must remember without firm advice.

The road to Perpignan.

15

Perpignan. Men with eyes that no longer see. Some hardly pedalling as they come in. They lean on each other at control. Others ignore the fact they are still living and lie in a heap, discarding clothes and watching their wounds weep. Most barely know how to talk. I stand staring in the street. They totter as if hit by a hail of stones, stoned as certain parts of the bible seem to suggest is an apt judgement for men like us, full of prideful dilemmas. Shouting comes from team lackeys and whispers spill from men like me who still know how to stand but for whom words are now brackish: the taste of our own skin has entered our mouths and we are barely brave enough to speak.

In Bagnères-de-Luchon I rode in at 11th. I was 15 minutes behind Opperman, two hours ahead of Bainbridge and Harry and Percy. Here I took us home. And here I watch the return and it seems I should not be in this position. Harry glares at the road as he steps from his bicycle. He is used up and doesn't let me take his arm. He has a cold and should not be on a bike. The rest sit hunched. I feel guilt as if my small success is a violence on men I love. Somewhere back in the mountains I should have hung back and stayed with them. But I didn't. I rode forth and somewhere in the murk I went past Hubert.

Monsieur France comes to me and stands with our young interpreter René de Latour who made friends with Opperman back in Paris. He asks where I was. I tell him. He asks me my time and I tell him. I was 15 minutes over 13 hours. He walks away and I call out, asking him if he knew where the Discuter team were staying. He asks why and I shrug. I wish to see the boy, the Spanish boy. But I say nothing more and start to walk. I wish to see if he made it through.

In the minutes before our departure, I saw the youth with his body bent as if leaning on a cloud. I gave him the opportunity to inhale the cocaine given to me by one of the team managers. A return of sorts for the charm of his offer that full week before, of wine and friendship. He managed a smile and shook his head. He opened his satchel and I saw he had all he needed. Vials of dynamite. The bonuses of proper management. He seemed happy, aware that something was happening around him. Perhaps his end was coming sooner than I thought. That he would be replaced at the terminus of this stage. I could understand if that were the case. He'd seemed thin, like sticks bundled. He was also rosy cheeked and ready as if adrenaline was overriding his malady and his need to escape this race before something broke. Each time I have seen him on the road he has smiled, and that is something.

Two days ago I was held up. I was stopped as I rose on Aubisque between two bunches of riders. My neck was out, it had been for days. From my forefinger to the crown of my head, a stream of signals made the injury known as if volts harrying through wire. Occasionally it pinched at the muscles across my cranium, tightening them, and the pain was quick like a nail thrust home. My arm became weak also, like the muscle was unhitched to the bone. I fell sideways on

133

that impossible mount and onto the side of the path; the only rider in the history of the race to fall whilst climbing. I pulled my bike into the small gap in the stones that line the route so not to be a hindrance to the riders coming up behind. I closed my eyes and let the pain pierce its hole and leave. I intended to get back on the bike immediately but instead I glanced back at the trail we had made up the side of that mountain. An impossible depth below. The cut of the path seemed hopelessly haphazard, as if drawn by a child with the sharp of a compass. Madmen ride this, I thought, madmen and me. I sat for only seconds and soon found myself riding again and once more moving upwards. I laughed for the sight of it all. But any sense of amusement began to go hard, as if it had developed the material of a horn about its skin. I sensed the anger, the frightful thing that makes me go so rigid at the sight of the world and too gives rhythm to my ride. I commanded myself to make time, to undo the waste my damned neck had made of the last few minutes. And I did find rhythm, I looked back behind at the 17 switchbacks I could count below. I felt the idea that it was impossible that I had ridden those lines, that child's idea of a race. That within those lines was a pattern of knowledge I was unable to conceive of, brilliant like a fine lie. But I had and I rose. I rose and felt myself drawing a group ahead towards myself. Finally I saw it was the Discuter team. They were crawling. I went through them, barely a word was stated because at that altitude words are wind you can't afford to blow.

Only the Spanish lad had called out, and that is what I remember. He shouted out a sound that might have been my name. It was pitiful, a fragment through accent and dialect. I didn't look back until I had made the summit, the col.

But now I don't see this boy. I don't have a question for him in any case. I just want to see whether he'd made it through. So I leave. I walk and find the woman in the hotel

she'd stated would look towards the Palace of the Kings of Majorca. I expect to see the sea from her room. I stand at her window staring out looking for the shore and the opulence of loungers and bronzed bodies hazy at the Mediterranean. She asks me what I see and I say I see nothing. There is only city and houses and more land.

She laughs cautiously. Celia.

Celia. Some moments in the last few days I have caught glimpses of her in the car. She rides up ahead, or far behind, sometimes close enough to know it is her, the yellow shimmer of the Citroën. Some hours I don't know what I know and think I've seen her hair amongst the crowds who shout us onwards, calling my name. If I see her there I see her hiding for she never wishes to be seen by the crowds, so she says. She says she watches from the verges and I stare at her hidden in the folds of the throng, sometimes running to her car doors. I think to call out but realise she wouldn't respond and my mouth remains half open. She doesn't acknowledge me in the mélange after either of the last two legs when all gather and salute the day's winners and slowly remove our garb. I come to know her by the way she avoids all eye contact.

She tells me to go to bed and close my eyes and shut out the light. I eat what I can, bread and beans, chicken, bananas. Then I take her advice and lie down and breathe in the smoke that smells surprisingly sweet, and begin to dream with the sheet pulled up to my face as if it were the sheepskin I had as a child and kept close and would rub under my nose. She is, it seems, as much present at that moment as she is any other.

She says she is from Algeria, the self-same land as Louvière,

135

though she is pale, alabaster, a scarf wearer against the sun. Algeria, Africa. The continent of Arabs and animists, Boers, Egyptians and Kenyans and Congolese, tall men impossibly thin without shadows on the plains, caravans and camels, lions, simians, and the Mountains of the Moon. What do I know of the place? I have just listed it. The lot, the entirety of my knowledge in a list! She announces stories and dreams of an ancient city. Algiers. Algiers the White. She describes the city from afar on the waters of the Mediterranean Sea, the buildings crawling up the hill to the crown of the Kasbah, the citadel at the head of the city built by the deys in the years of the Ottoman. She describes the interior of her childhood home, a courtyard within the sprawl of the house, vaulted archways white and gleaming with porcelain tiles, with the intricate latticework of the balustrade beneath which her father and her father's father and his friends would sit and bet on cards and tell old stories of the old city beside the drip of a fountain drawing fresh water from a well until everything was old and the new was only an intrusion. She tells me of her father and uncles, her grandfather and brothers, how they export furniture, shipping it across the Mediterranean in large boats like the Moors had for centuries. Her father rich, moneyed beyond my comprehension. She tells me now as I lie looking at the ceiling how banks open and close on his whim.

'But don't believe me,' she says. 'It is dangerous to believe such things.'

I blink and wait for her to go on, but she doesn't. Instead we lie on our backs beneath imagined clouds. We lie within dreams, scheming outrageous in the bloom of quite conscious minds.

She later offers jars of pills for the whole of the team but I wave the tender away despite what the race is doing to us.

Here, I've made her a list:
Sprained wrist.
Broken finger.
Dislocated thumb.
Abdominal bruising.
Broken teeth.
Nipple rash.
Boils.
Back strain.
Diarrhoea.
Gravel rash.
Abrasions to the knees, elbows, forearms, forehead, torso, shoulder, ankles.
Influenza.
Cold.
Sprained ankle.

We lie in the bed where our bodies separate into feet then toes, twenty of them in the still air, mine bent and pointing off in strange directions, hers slender and small, the little one red and permanently curled. 'I have known him for nine years,' she says. 'Louvière.'

'Just after the war?' I ask.

'After the war.'

'How long have you been following this?'

'A hundred years,' she says. 'Long years. They stretch out.'

'Just the last few years —'

She nods and looks at the end of the sheet. She has a fan of oriental origin and she uses a long nail to run along its ridges so to make a collection of sounds like a tuneless xylophone.

'What will he do?' I ask and notice for the first time the way she closes one eye when she isn't going to answer a question. A slow unconscious wink and I am reminded

of ice and the way it falls. Seven years ago I drove with Thomas and Katherine on the South Island's West Coast during the month prior to my race in the Timaru Classic. We walked to the face of the Franz Josef Glacier carrying small ice-axes for show. Katherine wore a set of my brother's trousers and looked somewhat triumphant there in front of the ice standing 100 feet above her. The depth of the noise as a sheet fell away. Celia blinks and I think of this, the long wait for the ice to distend, drift down and collapse in a white rush. I look at her and wonder if she has any means of knowing where my thoughts run. 'You know him, though, don't you?' I ask.

'François? Of course,' she says. 'I know all of you, every racer.' She smiles for me, and it's a small smile, one which states she is making me into something I will struggle to escape. She shakes her head. 'Tell me about the ride. The mountains.'

'I met a girl,' I say.

'Oh yes,' she says. 'A pretty girl I hope?' She wafts the fan at my face and a petite wind beats over my head.

'What other kind is there?' I look at her for reaction but she just smiles.

'There are many kinds of girls.' Her eyes tell me this is a fact that I hadn't fully comprehended before. I watch her mouth move and don't feel any need to explain the girl's rejection of my presence as I tried for the soft parts of her. How I had to take rest on the street before finding that deep sleep. Rejection is the key to one locked and miserable room.

'You know I looked out for Louvière, today, during the race. I looked for him everywhere.'

'He's in traction. I've had my spies tell me everything.' She kisses my brow and whispers the smoke from the pipe beside my mouth.

'But before the war,' I say, 'did you meet him then?' I report words but I don't know if they truly are words or the sound one makes when confronted by extraordinary choice. Celia replies, speaks in a language I don't know and soon I am drifting. I lie quietly and eventually sleep. The morning passes into the afternoon. The light stands naked in the room and I'm summoned to get up and walk as she sleeps a deep untested slumber. And I do, I walk out into the streets through the centre of a dream.

A boy offers flowers. He speaks and I can name the vowels or consonants but little else. It is a Sunday, he walks with me towards the church and we catch up with his parents. He takes my hand and calls me Monsieur. He feels so light and small, a weightless soul to hold up and smile into. I feel his parents gather in concern. They watch my approach and call the boy to their side.

I stand looking up at the church as the family make their way up the street. A man approaches me. He turns and comes up close with wine breath.

'Bonjour,' I say.

'I met your father,' he says, his face next to mine. His eyes running over my own, over my face and the air about my face. 'In Cairo. In the war. I met him, I have been there.'

'Where?' I ask, quite intrigued.

'1915, I met your father.'

'My father. My father was never in the war. Not my father, not my pop.'

'I met a man. So,' he says and kisses my mouth. I hold him for a good 10 seconds before he pushes me off and leaves. It takes some getting used to, this being kissed by men.

I head indoors to see and watch. I immediately remember the comfort, the smell of wax and incense. The scent of tears. You forget the smell of tears until they are once again

on your cheek. I watch as two priests come into the nave from the vestry and complete a service as I sit impassive. They offer each other communion, they eat and drink as all good people do. The things we do each day to survive. Eat. Drink. I think to call out to them as they light candles and quote verse. But I am only a calm observer. They move softly from moment to moment, the wine, the bread. I watch. On evenings like these, I think to myself: Some days you eat, some nights you just drink.

I'm soon out on the street. Harry is near. Harry walks me away. He returns me to our rooms and again I sleep. I dream and wake and dream and within it I am wet with a fever. I am told by a nameless face I must ride back to Luchon. Back to the steep of the Tourmalet and the dark and there I must speak to Louvière. Dreams set out vast cruelties. What makes us follow them, I do not know.

16

We drift on the plains, Harry ahead. He rides well, clean in his rhythm. This morning we saw *Match L'Intran*'s Table of Honour for the Pyrénées. His handsome photo amongst the climbers and winners. They like to put fighters on their pages, men of heart. Harry rides ahead and I find myself at the back, then, when it is my turn to take the lead, slowing the pace. Only in the afternoon when I ride alone with Ernie do I feel the energy to talk, to respond to questions and listen to the old rider's stories. We ride at a decent pace, enough to keep our place in the field for the next few hours as we make the move to the north. Ernie rides in front of me for a half-hour, and then we swap and I lead the way before my legs struggle and the veteran is once more in the pained position of having to be my leader.

Fields run out before us, a sight I am happy to read. I can't see a hill in our path, nor to our side. Everything is flat save for mild undulations. Workers visible far to our left. They put down whatever implements they have in their arms and wave out. I lift my hands and put them over my head. Ernie does the same. We slowly begin to make our way towards the east, another shift in the continual ballet on the compass that, until this moment, had been stilted so the curve of the great bay we corner over the hours on the way

to Montpellier is noticed only by our relation to the sun. It sits hard in the sky, unmoving, tamed by the summer of its making, its face quite in agony. When even a plain day such as this seems dramatic I wonder about myself.

I think I see them, the stones in rows. I arch my neck looking over my shoulder and slow, certain at what I have seen. Cold blood flushes through me and I take in quick air. But they are never there, rather it is the light on a fence, or a barren stand of trees, dead from fire from a strike of lightning.

Two teams come at us together. For a time we ride amongst them, Ernie talking on despite the company. We match their speed until I don't last and we fall off the back. We watch them disappear, strange dancers fading into the light. The first time this happened, the second, the third, I felt guilt. Back on the other side of the continent riders went through us, ten of them as a pack, JB Louvet; they rode at the coming sunsets brilliant on the light. Their team is now decimated, broken so they too creep along the plains. The guilt was heavy then, and slowed us more, encased my legs in its weight like canvas. There was never any coming back and slowly this became the reality. But we remain and we aren't letting the air of our pride escape completely, we aren't the breath of a black-eyed fighter waning in the mud. Opperman is in the top 15, Harry and I in the top 30. Some would say we are fools, but these numbers don't say it, they say something quite other. But today, today I am the cold stone dropping to the floor of this old river.

Despite this poor showing, men, women and children cheer us onwards, shout for our efforts. I can't help but admire them, their ability to stick with us. I look in their eyes any chance I get, so they know they are a part of this. And there, a pair of black-robed priests. They stand under the gables of a stone church, smiling and talking, watching us come through their village.

'What's their interest?' Ernie asks.

One lifts a hand and shouts as we come close. I start to sneeze, tears are mingled with my sweat.

'Ah?'

'What's their interest?'

'We're racing, we're in a race,' I say. 'You never seen a priest before?'

'I've seen plenty, plenty-plenty. You go to a war, that's one thing you see plenty of.'

'What then?'

A crowd of men, women and children as we bend through the main street. The voices rise up, men with beer in long glasses. I wish to reach out and grab them, instead I listen as Ernie says, 'I'm interested in how. How is it they care?'

'You want me to call you an idiot?' I say. 'I'll call you an idiot.'

'Call me an idiot,' Ernie says.

'It's the dirt, Ernie. It's the filth.'

'I mean. But we're a couple of jokers, a couple of jokers in shorts and shoes.'

'They listen on the radio. They read about us in the papers. It's the mud on our faces.'

'Yes,' he says. 'But how? How the hell did it get to this.' He laughs a little.

'They hear our names on the radio,' I say. 'Read about us in the papers. We're inching our way forward.'

'We're hardly conquistadors, mate.'

'Yes, but who's to know that? We could be in the throes of a big move. We might be making a move, we might be coming up through the field after something has gone awry. I'm a hero. I'm taking old Ernie with me to the finish.'

'You're done. I'm dragging you.'

'I'm just playing for time,' I say.

'Playing for time,' he repeats. 'I'll tell you something.'

143

I watch him peel off and slip in behind me, shadowing me. We dip our way through a ford. The water is launched up over our legs and I feel it drip down my calves and into my shoes. It's cooling, and that makes me feel better about the day. But the bike becomes rough on the road. The clatter and weight of a ruined tyre. I look down and see my front tyre is flattened. 'Shit on a shit,' I say. We both stop beside a fence and jump off our bikes. Ernie helps me get the wheel off. I fumble with the tools. I think how I've seen priests – those same priests it always seems – blessing riders of this race. Men knelt, eyes down, the padre in prayer, words repeated and adored. The things a man might be filled with and the way he staggers in the after moments. I want that now. I fill my tyres and want a robed figure uttering phrases that'll make us greater, fitter, sturdier in our staying. Blessed and reconciled against the poverty of our bodies – so thin now if there were a soul we'd certainly see it clear between bones. But we are alone, so I say: 'You got any idea – 'bout this?' I pull the pump from the valve. The hiss of escaping air, I glance back at Ernie. 'Any idea what this is about?'

He takes his right hand and puts his fingers through his hair like a rough comb and shifts a dingy lock to the side. 'I have no answer. But I'll tell you something.'

'My sister once said that answers are for the weak. She was a joker. I don't know either.'

'Ha. Well, no. I was talking about everyone watching, just before, everyone watching us on the side of the damned road. I was watching them and I realised I think about quitting. Here's an admission, mate. I think about quitting. You do it right? You think about it? But I think about something else too. We ride and it's a constant companion, quitting, but I think somehow it isn't. Something I heard once.' I wait for him, but nothing comes, just a quiet pit of thought. We climb back on the bikes and the pedalling begins again.

The rhythm returns. I flash looks, wondering if he is talking and the sounds of our wheels are overriding him, but his mouth is still. We go on and onwards, me waiting, him riding. Thinking, and riding forward. The road dips to the right for 20 yards, then races through a stand of trees, a creek in its centre, and we burst back out into the light. Suddenly he is speaking once more. We break into the sun and it feels as if he was waiting for the trees and their shadows to pass over us before he talked, for that small marker to pass. But now I'm not sure it is his voice I hear. He sounds altered, a new person in his stead steering his cycle. He speaks, he says: '"To drop out is to die."'

'That's dramatic.'

'You ever hear that?'

'I hate the idea of it,' I say. 'Makes me filthy. Dropping out.'

'You ever hear that though? Not sure if it's a saying, but I heard it once. Twice, I heard it twice.'

'Not sure. Sounds like something I might have heard. Sounds like something someone might have said: then became something people say. In jest or to be dramatic, or for whatever reasons people say things. I don't know, Ernie.'

'I met a man in Melbourne, in St Kilda where I was on a weekend with some of my boys from the army. We'd met at the pub at ten in the morning and we weren't quitting till they kicked us out. This was back in 1920, I think. I had been home awhile. But you come home and that doesn't mean much for a while. Takes time. You know; you have a brother. But we were drinking and telling stories. Telling the same stories we'd told before. We told them again because they were the stories we have. We have others, but these were the ones we told when we were together. That's just the way things are. And I'm not going to tell you my stories, because, well, I'm just not.'

He pauses and I nod in his periphery and I doubt it matters whether he sees me or not. I just do it because it is a part of the rhythm. And I say it too because it is part of the rhythm.

'But there was this joker. He was fat, that was my first impression of him. Big fat lad who'd had his fair share. He was sitting with us. I didn't get his name, or if I did, it didn't stick with me other than he was of Irish birth and had moved out to Victoria when he was a tyke. But by lunchtime when the sandwiches were brought out he was talking. He was talking like he'd just won at the races and he couldn't be stopped. A man and luck – such a damned combination, mate. You can't shut a winner up. But this guy, he wasn't anything like that, not when you realised what he was saying. He was talking about Turkey. Of all places, Turkey. I thought Gallipoli and the peninsula and was ready to listen to all that again, 'cause that was what we did. Listened and forgot so we could listen again. But no, he wasn't a part of that. He was a mechanic. He fixed planes, but he operated in the Sinai, and then after that out in Kut.'

'Thought they were all Poms out there,' I say.

'No. Not at all. Indians, Aussies, and Poms for certain. He was an airplane mechanic. I can't imagine it. How fiddly those things must be. To make something fly? I can't imagine it. But anyway, you heard of the Berlin–Baghdad Railroad? A track through from Mesopotamia to the heart of it all. What a thing to conceive, but it was conceived and the Germans and the Turks, they were trying to get this thing done in the middle of the war. Made slaves out of 12,000 POWs and the rest. This fatso was one of them. They were marched across the desert into southern Turkey, then to Anatolia. 900 miles. Jesus. He told us this and I'm looking at the fucker thinking, boy. And he says he was a part of it, he was made to walk. For weeks and weeks they were strapped and shoved with rifle butts, hit and hit over again.

Barely a drop of water. No food. If they fell out of line they were kicked until they got up or they just lay there. It was a death march, this guy told me, that's what he called it. The walk of 12,000 barely dead souls. Men with feet rotting, feet blistered and caked in sores. They went through valleys of stone, rock twisted and hard. There were deserts, broken places he said. Moonscapes of grey stone cratered with age and the hard facts of so many things lived. One night he fell asleep with his head on this one chap's thigh. He was woken up the next day by something moving beneath him. The bloke under him was dead and there was a great gash in his arm. A dog was pulling at the man's leg and another was trying to get some flesh away from his bicep. Another day they were marching and an Indian officer tripped and fell. The Turks were on to it and went to beat him but as they got to him they realised he wasn't breathing and just stood around looking at one another. He said there was a sudden peace, a tranquil pause as they stood there waiting for something. And another time, and another time. Death and violent death was just a way. Disease and malnutrition. Starvation. He said he tried sometimes to redirect his pain towards awe, awe for the fact of the land they were walking through. The bed of civilisation, of writing and numbers, how many religions and how many wonders. All of that. But he couldn't summon it, it meant nothing he said. It meant nothing because if this was what civilisation had amounted to, he didn't want to know. It was a place aghast at its own severity. His words. I wouldn't say such a damned thing.

'Eventually they were taken to the Taurus Mountains. That's where they worked on the railway. They built viaducts, worked in tunnels for days at a time. One in four died, he said. One in four. But it was back last year when we were racing in the Dunlop, and this is why I say this, why I'm telling you. That was when I remembered this guy, so

147

damned fat it's hard to imagine he was ever starving to death. Jesus. But I was riding in the sun and half baking. I was with Percy and Harry and Opperman and a few others. So deeply, bleedingly hot. We went past a cool-looking pond and one of us called out and all just jumped off our bikes and leapt in. Jeez, now that's a kind memory. I'd do it right now if I had a choice. Anyway, we were larking about and Percy lost his God-damned shoe. We're all climbing out of the pond and ready to get back on our bikes, and he's fishing about for his shoe. We're all in hysterics, ready to leave him behind. He and Harry are bopping and diving trying to get this shoe. We're saying we're going to leave them behind and we make to ride off. Then Harry dove under and he popped up with this big grin on and he's holding this shoe. Soon we were back riding, sopping wet but happy for it. Percy and Harry had to catch us up half a mile. But pretty soon we're riding and teasing poor Percy, saying how we would have left him behind. He became indignant, sullen. He said nothing for half an hour. But then he suddenly shouted out: "To drop out is to die!"'

'He said that?'

'He said that. And I'll tell ya. I felt a strange shock. How he came to say this I wasn't sure, how those words went from one place to another. One mouth to another. It got me thinking that there's nothing we say that isn't part of something. I thought that because Percy yelled it out and I remembered suddenly this joker, this fat bloke, saying these same words in the pub. It was something he'd said. He said: "We were driven, beasts driven into the desert," he said. "To drop out was to die."'

'There was no choice.'

'Well, no. There never is choice, not if you get down to it, mate. It's always one thing, because there's only one thing you ever do. The idea that there was a choice, that's

an illusion mate. It's only in retrospect you seem to have a choice. One of time's tricks. Choice is the trick of time and money.'

'Money. Ha. And you say volition, it just —'

'Not there. Not after what we saw. And not after I heard that story. We were a part of it. And when you realise there's no choice, you just get to thinking some things, or all things are fated. I'm not getting past it. Maybe one day, but not yet. And think of that bloke's fate, the guy with his leg being eaten by some cruel animal. I think, has it vanished? If so, what came in to take its place?'

I fear I'm unable to argue with any man in flight like this. I doubt he knows I'm watching him. I try to answer his question, even if it wasn't posited for answering. 'Regret?' I say.

'The right to regret. God. Or to forget. The opportunity not to forget? I don't know. And the right to regret. Yes. But I do know something. Every moment since the end,' Ernie says, 'feels like the fade-out of the last scene at the flicks. It's as if my life and everybody else's around me – you, Jack 'n' Jill, everyone's life – was lived between the years 1915 and '17. Between my age, between 26 and 28. All the rest so far, it's like I said. A slow fade-out. For men to stand up in the metal? Christ. If you want to know, this is it if you want to know: we were all a part of some unrelenting fate, if you want to know. That's the only way to look at it, otherwise – well. You're a madman: you did it by choice, then you're a madman.'

'What did you see?' I ask.

'Me? Nothing. These eyes see nothing.'

I look over at him and he nods and that is the end of the conversation. Something concentrated about his presence as we ride, as if this new revelation has compressed Ernie into the bones and skin riding beside me. As if he has passed

through the lens of a camera and is suddenly described in light and sound. But we ride on and I realise that I have never before recognised his voice over others, it was never a voice that I could have pulled from a crowd and named. But moments ago, as his voice again found its familiar range, I realised there is far more to know of any soul than just their long fibrous tales. There are the stories one doesn't tell, doesn't give away.

The coast comes and we see it, the Mediterranean. A great wash of blue, ships on the blue, clouds skiffing on the distant blue, the sky on the blue. Scud, screecher and foul: maritime words. White sand and broken rocks. Seabirds diving and hitting the water in small detonations. A stretch of water, the great waterway; somewhere out there the key to Western Civilisation. I say out loud so Ernie can hear me: 'You see that though, eh? Old man, right? You see that?' He laughs and lets me take the front. I feel energy return as I head into the light diminishing somewhere out beside the edge of the sea. Slowly I put space between us. He says farewell as I pull away. I turn and wave and he waves and we watch each other and the sound of the sea washes and he smiles and waves, and it is as it always is when you bid goodbye to a friend: as if we'd shared a secret.

And he is gone out the back of my periphery and I take a banana from my supplies and peel it, I eat it and wash it down with whatever liquid is in my second bidon. I bite through the fat of a cutlet and chew it thoroughly. I drink. I have been sipping from the first most of the day and now I sip from the second for it isn't just water and soon I'm not riding entirely alone.

17

That night we drink. At least I drink. Quantities of wine. I hear Percy lamenting the lack of a lager to cool his chest burnt in the white sun. Exhaustion demands we celebrate something, anything that isn't the ride. We're in a café. André Leducq won the stage and is seen pissing onto the floor from his table. The celebrations of men can be the oddest thing.

Harry is sick and drinks to revive his spirits. He has influenza and it is manifesting itself through his bowels. He shits constantly and takes on salt and sugar and water. He is barely putting up with me as I recount Ernie's story from earlier in the day and we watch hurting men dance with young ladies. Out on the pavement a scuffle is ranging up. Two riders.

'You know them?' Harry asks.

I shake my head. 'Belgians? I think. Walloon boys. Maybe.'

'You want to —' and soon we are both standing and we arch our necks to look. Opperman and Percy join us and we walk outside together to watch as bad punches are thrown. The two of them are barely connecting, but there's blood on their faces. A torn lip and the red has transferred to the other. We watch them prowl on the cobblestones. Arms

out ready to grapple, I see one has a nail busted and that hand is dripping on the ground and he steps around his own puddle. They snarl, though it could be speech. One lunges and the other dodges, slipping. An ankle goes over and a grunt ricochets off the wall.

Harry drinks the brandy and winces. He wipes at his mouth. 'You know, if we were Greeks and we were back in the age.'

'They'd be starkers.'

'And we'd be doing this race starkers,' he says.

'Lord,' Percy says. 'The Lord's mercy.'

'Our bits waggling about.'

'And they'd kill us afterwards,' I say. 'Lions they haven't fed for two months.'

'That was the Romans.'

'Romans, lions. Who cares? The point is we'd be starkers.'

'And then, they'd put us in a corner and stone us,' Harry says. 'They'd stand around throwing rocks.'

I lean on Harry's shoulder. Grunts, the swipe and slap of amateur hands.

'Not much cop, huh,' says Percy, nodding at the fighters.

'Think they'll ever make contact?' I ask him.

'That's a lot of flailing you're seeing there, arms and hair,' Percy says. He's shaking his head, vaguely appalled. I put my hand on his shoulder. He looks at me and smiles, then grimaces as one fighter leaves the ground trying to land a punch, the sound of knees on cobblestones. 'Hopeless,' Percy says and looks at Opperman. 'I'm leaving. Homer?' We look at Opperman, but he stays standing beside the sweating onlookers. Yesterday *Echo de Sport* described his efforts as Homeric; Homer he has become. His eyes squint, he's quietly mesmerised. The reddened hands of the Belgians swaying in front of us as they look for an opening. Earlier in the day he'd come in with the front 25 and something

152

had them conspiring to spread out and dawdle across the line, their front wheels together. Desgrange was furious, a steaming face of moustache and gutter words. He made them sprint a lap of the velodrome so to make proper winners of the leg. He threatened the last placegetter with expulsion from the race if he did not try. So they went once around the track, like scolded children. None of them recall who placed where (except Leducq, who merrily claimed victory). Instead, those first 25 bonded in amusement for their antics. Percy turns out of the crowd and quickly vanishes.

A punch is lunged and blood comes from the fist and slaps an Italian on the cheek and there's a moment where laughter brightens the din.

'Replacements,' Opperman says. 'I think they're replacements.'

'Oh, fucking replacements,' Harry says and steps back and I find myself doing the same thing.

'Whose replacements?' I ask.

'Discuter, I think,' Oppy says.

'Discuter. What do you think, Harry?'

'Seen better on a footy field.'

'Everything's better on a footy field,' I say. I look at Harry and realise there is no hint of violence about the man, no snarl or flame in his features. I'd called him the Priest a few years back, and now the French were doing the same in the papers. René de Latour started it, saying he looked more like a priest than a cyclist and it spread. My secret name hasn't taken hold. I say 'Prince' to people, and they look back glumly.

'One time,' I say, 'we were out walking on the farm, me and my brother. We went down into a culvert between two paddocks and he suddenly kicks my legs out from under me. Wham. I'm on my back in silage. You know the stink. And then he puts himself down on top of me, jabbing at my ribs

153

and kidneys. My ears were filled up with mud and I couldn't hear if he was saying anything. Just wham, wham. Jesus, you wouldn't believe the capacity of some people for mindless rage. He sat there in the mud later crying. Not out of sadness, or regret. Just out of confusion. Damned confusion. I pulled him up and guided him home. That walk of his.'

'Your brother. I always thought there was something dangerous in his movements,' Harry says, and turns back to the fight. I forgot that he'd met him, spoken with him. So much of our lives is forgotten, left to drift in the sea of displaced memory. A knuckle catches one of the Walloon boys and the crowd seems to go silent for a moment as if something real had finally caught a hold of them, stunning their yelps and calls.

We find ourselves moving around the harbour. All the old stone. The Mediterranean lapping at the sea wall and the boats tied to posts older than New Zealand and older than her mountains' multiple names. The smell of the salt water and the way it overcomes things. Something so near about the smell, as if it were designed specifically to make us feel whole, that no matter where we were in the world we could be rectified by the smell of brine. I say this to Harry. He agrees, for once.

The sense of fist and faces. Faces twisting with the hit and skin torn on the knuckle. The compulsion to watch sits uncomfortably with the aftermath of revulsion. A sense that we are burrowing in another's pain. I walk with this, I walk with the burning drive of the ephedrine, I walk with the alcohol in my legs. We walk in the yellow haze of the old stone that lines the harbour and the buildings that fortified her in the days when battles were still fought on the sea and in harbours and in fields cleared of cattle and not the things my brother crawled through back then, the wire and the wet

sand and the trenches of dead Germans and their rot. Christ, it's a fine life this Tour and the rest.

Harry and I find the Spanish boy sitting alone in a café. I'm surprised to see him still with us. He hails me with a version of my name I don't recognise but accept. We sit with him to talk, to listen to the lad jabber in his particular English. All about us are tables and glasses of wine and their owners' arguments. I'm relieved to see him, relieved to see that he has made it through. I can't bear the idea of him not finishing when his end is so near.

'I haven't seen you on the road,' I say. 'I've missed you on the road.' I'm not sure what I mean by that quite and Harry looks at me side on.

'I have missed you,' he says. He drinks from his glass which I realise is water. I laugh and he joins me for a moment.

'But you are still riding?' I say.

'Yes. I am going to be replaced in Nice.'

'One more day.'

'Mmm. Yes,' he says. He sounds warm and full of hope. 'Fresh riders.'

'Fresh riders?'

'Yes,' he says.

'Well,' I say.

'I have banged –' he pauses and furrows his brow. I notice he is touching his elbow. It is bulbous, swollen by its own juices from a cracked membrane.

'Elbow?' I suggest and he nods.

'Yes. And I have difficult steering. So they replace me. Gracias.'

'Thank you,' I say.

'Indeed,' says Harry.

'We could do with some replacing,' I say. I elbow Watson. 'The lot of us, but especially this one.'

'My cold,' Harry says, 'what I thought was a cold, is the flu. It's uncontrollable.'

'He's miserable to be around,' I say.

'Cold?' the lad says. 'Brrrr?' And he raises his eyebrows and wraps his arms around himself.

'Um, no. Sick. I'm sick,' Harry says.

'Si, I know. I know.'

'Influenza,' Harry says.

'He throws up in the street,' I say to the little Spaniard. 'Vomits. Blurgh,' I say and the lad coughs. He pulls up his shirt and then his undershirt to reveal a thick carpet of scab up his side. I nod. A group of men come into the courtyard and I wait a moment for them to pass, then I stand in the street to peel my trousers down and show the red bleed of my thigh, the result of my dual crashes two days ago in the mountains after I'd spoken to the old farmer of this and that. It's long and feels like blunted sandpaper.

'Mmm,' the Spaniard says. 'My toe. It is broken. They say it is broken.'

'Percy,' I say. 'Our Percy, his ankle is sprained, but I suspect it's broken. One of the little bones. He can ride still, but I think it is broken.'

Harry nudges the boy and nods his head at me. 'His father is a doctor.' The boy nods slowly and flops his bottom lip out. 'He can say anything,' Harry continues, 'and who are we to contradict him?'

'Who are we to contradict?' I say. I laugh, but it goes by unnoticed.

'Señor Doctor,' the boy says.

'Señor Doctor,' I say. I feel no need to tell him it is not I who is a doctor but my father. It's a great deal more fun to be someone another has invented for you. I'll act the pig farmer

if I have found myself mixed in by an erring conversation. I'll talk for hours about trotters and swine if words will have me. Once, for an audience of aunts unrelated to me but to a girl I believed I half loved, I was a pilot. A pilot of disaster. I crashed in a field in '21, was my narration, and walked away with a bone piercing my chest, another turned inwards by the joystick and pushing on my right lung. 'It is withered now,' I told them. 'If anyone asks, it is withered. I ride on one lung, the other like a dried leaf vibrating in my chest. Each breath like a song. Here, listen,' I said and offered my chest for the aunt to lean on and hear. I am the great singing cyclist of the green Taranaki, I told her. She said she didn't hear anything and I surmised that not hearing something doesn't necessarily make it untrue, just makes it slightly more intriguing.

The boy fishes about under his seat for his bag. He puts it on his lap and takes a few things out and places them on the table. He puts the bag back on the stones. He picks up the pack of cards and removes the ribbon which held them together in a set and I think we are due to receive a magic trick. I feel a nervous twitch. Perhaps it's excitement, I'm not sure, but whatever it is, it runs its fingernail down my neck where all the hairs are made to rise. He carefully takes the cards and splits the deck and I watch his hands spread the cards out on the table amongst our glasses. Harry points to a card and says, 'That one. I choose that one.' But the lad ignores him and I realise he is looking for something. Finally he collects them all up, barring one, and puts the deck back beside the ribbon. 'My,' he says and turns over the card to reveal a picture of a young woman glued to its surface. 'My girl,' he says uncertainly.

I stare at it and look at him and he gestures that it is okay that I pick it up. 'She's pretty,' I say. 'Harry, have a look. She's so pretty.'

'She's your girl?' Harry asks as he takes the photo from me.

'I tell her I will be back, but I'm not sure.'

'What do you mean you're not sure?' I say. 'She's something spectacular.' And she is. Familiar and distant. The sit of her hair and the shape of her shoulders. I think of my brother's wife. The thoughtful weight of her visage as she considers whether something pleases her or merely amuses. Katherine and all the things you mistake for love.

'Oh,' he says. His skin is smooth, soft and kindly pale.

'How are you not sure?' Harry asks, then hooks his thumb at me. 'Ignore that one, he's drunk or something.'

'Show him your picture,' I say to Harry. 'The one of your wife.'

'I have her waiting,' the lad says.

'That's not very nice,' I say.

'She's nice but I think maybe not. Maybe not my girl.'

'That's wrong,' I say. 'Write to her and say: "I love you. Keep your lips for me, your mouth and eyes, for me and no other." I demand it. Harry?'

Harry puts his hand to the top pocket of his shirt.

I take the photo back up and look at the girl. She has a loneliness, a plaintive searching look as if asking for sympathy from some near creature. I nod and say, 'She's asking the photographer to stop staring at her.'

The boy looks at me then at Harry, then back at me.

'She's saying, "Stop staring at me!"'

'She's asking?' the boy says.

'Who took the photo?' I ask.

'A man,' he says. He looks uncomfortable and reaches for the picture, but I hold on to it for a while longer. I look again at her mouth, her lips, the way the shadow has formed on her features. She is looking downwards just a mite. She is asking something. I swear.

'A very generous man?' I ask.

'Generous.'

'He must be generous to grant a picture to your girl and let her give it to you.' The Spaniard is a poor boy, a wretched family of a factory-working father and a crippled mother. I doubt he could have the hand of a girl who has so many pennies she might spend them on a photograph.

'She didn't give me the photo.'

'No,' I say. 'No she didn't.' I look at Harry who is sorting through the pictures he carries with him. 'No,' I say to him of his wife, of his child. 'Put it away.'

'What?'

'Put it away,' I say. 'He doesn't want to see your pictures.'

'What are you doing?' Harry asks.

'Put it away,' I say.

He shows it to the boy and tells him her name. They smile together, and when he tells him she's pregnant the boy makes a hushed sound. The boy's photo sits on the table and I can't look at it. It's the only thing on the table. The only thing I am aware of is the girl on the photo, the bright of the flash powder and the startled glint on her cheeks. I have to stand up to avoid looking at her. I feel her staring at me, the young woman. I want to ask her a question the little Spaniard can't answer. I want to ask her why she is sitting in a studio having her photo taken, I want to ask her how it feels. I want to know how it feels to have this boy so half in love with her a thousand miles distant. I want to ask what it feels like not to be here.

18

Celia asks that I stay in her room, a hotel above the town. She'd found me walking in my shorts blinking at the sun. My goggles still on my head, my mind laid out somewhere between Marseille and Nice. She took me to a room in the Hotel de Rue. Now she has me lie on the bed. I lie and study what I can of the surrounds and the roof, of all her conversation.

The day was a brute. I rode us up the mountains in unshaded heat and we fell back further. There was an argument at lunchtime, we stood about waiting for the issue to resolve itself as others got back on their machines. Eventually we were involved in a crash. The five of us along with 20 others. Clothes fell off and blood and skin decorated the dirt. I ignored the team in the hours after. If Opperman and Bruce wish to talk of our incompetence they are welcome. Celia found me walking and touched my wounds then took me up the stairs on which I sat under a fan for a time, the marble cool. The sun was almost gone by the time we lay on her bed.

The room is full of brimming luggage, things dragged up from her car by porters in caps and buttoned-to-the-neck blue jackets. Matching Goyard pieces: more heraldic craft

than mere suitcases. They seem to distract her. She moves past them as if they're owned by someone else and left on the floor long ago uncollected. They're foreign but familiar, heavy and never left on their own; if she leaves the room it's for the road. She takes her meals in here, each drink ordered via the horn of the telephone, each item of food and beverage delivered on a cart. Her calm voice thanking them.

Her bags are open and have many compartments into which she dives with thin arms.

It is difficult to know what she wants with me. But having found my prone body vomiting in the roses outside Hendaye, skin black from dust and sun and tar, I seem a part of her schedule. She follows in her Citroën, yellow like the flowers and the sun they are named for. I went to her when the day was done and she took me into her room in Perpignan and now again in Nice. But my purpose, I can't say. It would be obvious if we removed our clothes, but we don't. I have the feeling she is alone, or forced to be alone by others. As we speak I get the sense her youth was once laced with unfortunate things, that she knew the contents of adulthood before it came. Watching her I imagine alliances drawn up between her anxieties battling for superiority against black days. A guess.

I lie down and she cradles me.

She lights the pipe and soon I am dreaming with her. Leaning across the bed closing my eyes and hearing the world outside like a shower of present rain drifting up from the street. Street sounds, carts and shouts. Voices like the chimes of ricocheted water, sounds fascinating and small. Up and down the alley come the movement of voices, each quite distinct, each with a point. Voices enlarge like fish passing in the aquarium, shrinking as they turn, expanding near the glass. Peaceful wise statements.

161

Celia wears blue, the tidal wash of her eyes.

Sometimes silence, as from a well dug deep in the rock before the forest.

She's whispering above the almost-hum of the town – 'Each year, each July I come here. I follow you from Paris. I watch. I watch you all come by, the peloton, the leaders, the stragglers. The sweaty grime of you all. I nip down back roads to catch you once you've passed and spy changes to the field. I watch for the weak ones to fall off the back and then I drive on and get myself ahead. I watch from hedgerows. I wear headscarves.' She stops and I imagine she points back in the direction of Luchon and the Pyrénées. 'I hide so none of you recognise me. I don't like to be seen, acknowledged.' I touch her face, it seems guarded by a sheet of gauze such is my vision under the whim of the opium. We touch the same air, we speak in the same voice, our bodies make contact but despite this togetherness I cannot claim to be feeling the same range of thoughts as her. I listen as if a foreigner inside the body of the world. 'I'm the one who wills you on,' she says. 'I'm the one who asks that every one of you wins.'

I lean over so her hair is on my cheek and it feels as if the tiniest of razors is falling across my skin, and I breathe through the holes she has made and I listen. It seems she is talking of prayer, but I imagine she would deny that.

'I hope and ask. I drive on and watch. You each flicker through the streets, the change in sound as you hit those cobblestones. And then I hide.'

'You don't seem shy.'

'Not shy, no.'

And then I am laughing, because the smoke is in my nostrils. She begins to laugh also, lightly, as if treading on petals. 'I once sat watching a young man,' she says quietly. 'The race had passed through Metz, you were all on your way out. On the outskirts is a churchyard that looks out over

162

the road and I dare to sit watching you all sing. Beside the few very old headstones is a grotto, inside a blind Mary. It rains each time I have visited. I have hidden under the eaves peeking out from the draping vines that have grown over and down the front like the fringe of a fine young lady. I was hidden in beside this Mary –'

'You said blind?' I say. I sound strange. It is as if I had spoken long ago and only now do my words make sounds.

'Blind. Yes. Someone has scratched the marble so the round of her eyes is rutted. How long ago I don't know. Such cruelty. Such cruelty. Each year I have visited her and she has always been blind. I sometimes imagine centuries of abuse. I imagine natural occurrences: water in small cracks turning to ice. Then later in the spring expanding and taking away the marble like sand, year in, year out. People had left messages on her. All over her body, people had put their names. Everywhere. Names, sentences. Little memories.'

'Well,' I say.

She looks at me. Reduced pupils: two drops of black ink. She points a finger like a quill. 'You were both here before,' she says. 'You were both in the war? Your brother and you. Did both of you come here before? Maybe you know Metz. Maybe you were there before.'

I shake my head. 'Just me.' I take a moment before I look up. I expect everything to break: the room, Celia and the way she touches my arm, the way it should turn to water. But she isn't looking at me and nothing breaks; she is preparing the bowl of the pipe. Nothing breaks a fictive world but its author, and when he goes, it all crumbles to the dust it is and always was.

'So?' She pouts and pauses – then goes on. 'So, I watched a rider from the grotto sitting next to dear poor Mary mend his puncture. But he didn't mend his tyre, instead he rested. The peloton had long left him in their wake and he took the

163

opportunity to lie down and rest. He removed his goggles and lay under a tree and closed his eyes for 40 seconds. He began to cry, so I knew he wasn't sleeping. He began weeping. He sat up and looked at his hands. And then, then he seemed to just jump to attention and got to work on his tyre. He took the tubing out and tossed it in the garden and slipped the new in. Filled it with air from the compressor. He bolted the wheel back in place. The air seemed to become very still as if he were beckoning all molecules to stall.' She kisses my forehead. 'Then he screamed. He shouted out. He looked right at where I was huddled behind the vines beside that Mary and let out the worst noise. He pointed his face to the church spire and screeched. He put his leg over the saddle and hopped on and went on his way. It was then I knew that none of you ever lose.'

I hoot, a little owl.

She's coughing and waits for it to settle. 'Nobody will ever lose this silly race. You will never lose because slaves don't place.'

I laugh and summon enthusiasm. 'Tell my father. He isn't keen on my losses.'

'Yes, I joke. But he screamed and screamed on. Then he rode off.'

'Who was it?'

'A rider.'

'Who?'

'That first year I followed Louvière.'

'Louvière? It was Louvière? You know, he was supposed to be on our team. He was supposed to ride with us.'

'Why would he want to do that?' she says. Her face is so bright. When she laughs she has a beautiful laughter, it shines across the ceiling amongst the banisters and slides to the windows.

'You met Louvière back then?'

'Louvière, yes. He's always been near. He's bitter about this. This crash and the rest.'

'It feels thin now. I feel thin when I think about him heading off that hill.'

'Airborne Louvière. He's bitter. I say it again; it's the right word. He flew off the road and survived and he's bitter the race goes on without him. Did you see?'

'I was a few hundred yards behind.'

'Behind. There are a dozen of you who could have pushed him. I look for men who might have pushed him,' she says.

'He just missed the corner. There was no pushing.'

She looks at the window and raises her eyebrows. I'm uncertain quite what this means. I hope for a change in subject. I wish she'd return to describing Algiers so I can nod with the vision of her voice as I slip into the depth of dream as when you dream lying with your eyes quite open. As far as I know it is a Monday and on the Saturday she told me old stories of her town. Old stories and the physical nature of her city, the white stone and the steps leading everywhere and the markets and the mosques, the charmers and the peddlers and fossil hunters and the smell of that North Africa untainted by the facts of empires and republics and the rest. It's all desert without her words. Such is the illusion rendered by this smoke we inhale as I imagine Chinamen in their dens take it in through the vestibules and tubes of their lungs and further into their imaginings in brutal Singapore. I feel I am somehow allied by this act to an unfurling history, and to Tao and the Buddha, to shrines and wise words I do not understand.

'My cousin wrote to me,' I say. 'She said he was something to watch. You can't help but watch. I have ridden behind him; I know what she meant. They look, people look. Stares, stares and the joy of staring.' Celia watches me as she rubs her forefinger and thumb together, thinking, as if

between them was my slim knowledge of the world. She is at least ten years my senior and fixed in place by a deft beauty that doesn't seem to shift with the hours nor break with the dawn. She snaps those fingers so I'm lifted from my abstraction.

'But the truth. You'd like the truth?' she asks. 'You want to know the truth of the man?'

'About what happened up on Tourmalet? I believe he missed the corner.'

'The truth. You want to know the truth of the man?'

'Quite probably,' I say.

'He's a vile hindrance to the progress of evolution. He coughs and farts – birds fall from trees,' she says. She makes a sound of avian distress. 'They think he won't ride for a team because he hurt someone, somewhere. That he was removed from Discuter for the love of a faint-hearted girl whose heart was broken. Perhaps, but I say he rides on his own because he hates to share the prize money. They call him the Eunuch of Paris. He won't dance, he won't kiss, and he won't fuck again.'

This is the first time I have heard a woman of means utter this great word and I feel the blunting instrument of the opium run from my body and my senses harden and I try not to let my provincialism show, but I can't help it and she smiles. Her short dark hair bounces and she looks sorrowful and intelligent like a big cat stalking something outside of the picture frame. Every creature has its rituals; hers involve the pipe and this moment when she is high and high outside the worldly and spirited familiarities of such a young man as me. She touches my face and leans in so our bodies are touching, her arm on my waist. 'Really?' I say.

'You know what Desgrange says? You know?'

'He wants all of us mad. Names us all mad. He controls the idiocy.'

166

'It's easier to sell newspapers when there's madness involved. It keeps it at a distance. We're happy to give money to it. But, no. No, I'm talking about something else. Yes, he owns the madness, but it is something else. He says, he says if there were just one survivor, it would be the perfect race.'

'He should hide men in the bushes with clubs.'

She falls away from our half-embrace. She reaches for the pipe and packs it once more and makes sure it is in there clean. 'You're here for the ritual,' she says, and then sounds almost girlish, 'and me, I'm here for something else.'

'Mm hmm,' I laugh.

'Yes,' she says. 'I wait for you to get drunk, get – erm – relations, fall on your faces. Now –' She pulls herself up and goes to the smallest of her cases from which she pulls out a camera. It is the same make as the one Katherine brandished all those years ago as I rode from Timaru, Butchers Carbine. 'Sit up,' Celia says and I do. She angles the lens and she has a look on her face of slight agony as she tries to capture something. What, I don't know. I have always wondered what men and women are trying to find when behind such devices.

Indeed, a cameraman once came to our house with his equipment and ideas. It was the March before Serbia and all the confusion. The man brought in his tripod and camera, the three of us children were told to change into our smartest attire. Marya wore a pinafore and Thomas a tie. I recall nothing of my clothes, but I do remember my shoes were shined for me by my mother. The man with the camera was affable, a tight-lipped serious man whom one would expect to work the vaults of a bank if it weren't for his particular skills. He smiled at our tired jokes and japes, until, that is, we refused to respond to his requests to pose in a reasonable way. Marya ran out of the frame just as the photographer was saying '. . . aaand'. She returned holding a

vase coloured like damp sand, one of my father's acquisitions from his year 'on the Silk Road', as he liked to refer to it. She held the vase as though it were a baby, looking into the white-painted clay as if her life were a part of it, and as beings they were linked beyond propriety, sharing blood and all the cells that move and pulse and squirm, all the soul that makes family. She was 10 and had yet to begin to walk at night. The man behind the camera refused to flash the lamps and open the lens and mark the picture. My mother, full with bright humour, asked him what the matter could be.

The image lives now in its frame on the mantelpiece not far from where the coarse vase rests. My brother and I look identical. Marya: a better version of us both. People smile and ask if we still own the piece of pottery when they stand before the picture. Marya, serious with her own delight. She looks out and tells me to breath.

'When you first came here,' Celia says as she lights the pipe once more, 'when you first came, did you fight in the north? Or were you in the Middle East? Jerusalem?'

'Me?' I ask and she nods and looks out the window to the dark and the sounds in the dark. I feel my mouth move. 'Not as such. Yes, but not as such. In the north. I went down there.'

'Where? Do you have scars. I have an interest in scars. Burns, marks. It's morbid, yes? That I have this, erm, thing.'

'I crashed in the dunes out in Belgium.'

'You talk about it, tell me about it. Talk about it. Tell me.'

'No, but – everything I have to say, it's everything you have heard before.'

'No. That isn't true.' She kisses my neck lightly. 'When people speak, it is always a secret,' she says. 'I saw nothing, I know nothing. I lived a plain life waiting for it to come to me. I waited for men to come to our house and for

everything to change. For the door to open and for men to stand in the frame surrounded in light. Their features in shadow, but you'd know what they were there to do. What they were going to say, even if they wouldn't say anything, you knew.'

'No one came?'

'No one came to the door.'

'You had a brother? A sister?'

'I had no one.'

I awake in sweat. All the water of a summer rain in my hair. Noises, sounds of foot and claw. Animals seem to be outside the room. Celia has the covers pulled up to her neck. She is shaking, the wind banging at a door. What sort of wind bangs in the summer night? What kind of shift in the atmosphere makes this occur? I think of the glass in the window and how it might shake if the clouds I'm imagining expanded to the black extreme implied by my dreaming. Oh, and how I can dream the worst. As a boy I summoned the demons as a widow does the ghost of her most hated husband, a man I imagined strapping the rear of the steely woman's cracked thighs; evil men were everywhere. Evil skies beckoned with fists in their murk. Celia puts her hand on my chest as I try to exit the bed and see who is there, what or which phantom is angling to enter our room.

I stand. My cock like a startled goose neck in the breeze.

'Back in the cover,' she says. 'You'll pimple in the cold.'

But I stand and listen at the scratching. A dog with a wet, fascinated nose. A rat. Though it isn't that kind of hotel.

'Back, back,' she whispers, and I'm beginning to fall in love with the creases at the corners of her mouth that, despite her age, must have always been there, for her smile seems timeless, a clock without hands.

'Louvière?' I whisper. I turn back to Celia. 'He wants his women back. He wants to eat them with coffee and truffles.'

'Vous êtes plein de merde, stupid Australian.'

'That's where you're wrong.'

She murmurs my name, I think it's an apology. Her voice says something more, it drifts.

'Louvière,' I say. 'What do you want from me?' I creep to the door. 'Is it Celia you want?'

'You vile man,' she says.

There is no more noise (if there ever was one) and I turn and head for the window. I pull the curtains apart to the city and the sounds of a near night, a faint glow from the street rising as if a mist from a river warming in a morning distant. People call out in another part of the city. Tentative words projecting familiar tones which bounce off the yellow-white stone and come to us mellowed and plaintive.

I am reminded of hours we spent anchored at Ismaïlia, the city at the border of the Nile Delta and the desert. The *Otranto* had sailed the Suez Canal; all assumptions were we would continue to Port Said, towards the shores of the Mediterranean, but we weighed anchor for eight hours in the lake harbour of Timsah where the canal was suddenly widened, where it seemed as if a sea was threatening to engulf the surrounds of white sands. The night came in as the ship swayed and we heard the call to prayer for the first time, voices riding across the harbour from the minarets pointing from a mosque that remained unnamed in my mind until an Egyptian trader came through the ship and I asked him to give a word. He said it several times but I couldn't recreate the precise sound of the syllables as I tried to repeat them in my mind. I had him write it down in my diary:

مسجد ابو بكر الصديق

Often I find myself looking at those marks on the page and mouthing shapes so I might know what it was that the trader said. I made a fetish out of his scrawl in my efforts to untangle the lines and loops. It is beautiful and perplexing, as too is the sound of the people meandering their way to me in this hotel room from which I have a view down rue Massenet to the sea and the promenade. I sometimes wonder if beauty is the effect of something seeming so near, so close we believe we know it truthfully and without blemish. I wonder too if the souls on the street knew on whose ears their sounds lighted, whether they would change their subject.

Celia sits up in bed and I return.

In the hours after, I am with him, with Louvière. It seems I walk to the window once more and open it so I stand above the street on the balcony, that I take myself from the balcony to the next by clinging to the ivy and swinging my legs around, over and over until I am at his room six storeys up. His curtains billowing as I enter his chambers. His room is cool as though I'm treading near ice. I put myself at his bedside. His thigh bone gleaming and puncturing the air with that pointed end like a tooth loosed from the mouth of a fighter and glinting. I say nothing and wait. The room is still until I see a dog in his corner, a mastiff breathing through his nose.

An hour seems to pass. Suddenly he speaks, but I feel no surprise: 'When we collapse they take whole parts of us. They, they take them with them,' he says. I ask who. 'The people who call out.' His voice is straining against the morphine. He speaks in rasps. 'The old ladies and their husbands. Men who tear open shirts and glisten and cry. Cry from alley once peloton passed. Hairs greyed. All wonder. Babes in swaddling and the women who leave them in the

171

cot to cry not because they must see me. No. But because
need is to let out another cry. Congregation clinging to
balcony and its balustrade waving and shouting. Shout my
name. They fall to the street. They a hungry pool. Writhing
arms and twisted legs snapped and jagged.'

He nods at the phial near the bed and I nod and take a
syringe and needle from my shirt pocket and tie off with a
belt and push the contents of the vessel into my arm, though
I have no waking knowledge of how this is done.

'You should take her,' he says. 'You should dash her head
against rock.'

I stay until morning. The room smells of hot prone body.

She lies with her head balanced on her palm. She says
my name – loudly or softly I can't tell. The way she shifts at
her voice I know she can't be far from standing and being
half naked before the light of the brilliant morning. She just
needs it suggested. Her mouth open and her eyes roaming
under their lids. I open my own mouth to speak, to offer her
the contents of my dream which sit in my body like unready
wine. I say nothing. I eat five hot rolls and quaff four goblets
of wine. I stand at the window. The remains of the original
162 are seen walking in the streets. We are skinny men like
candles without the light; half of us ghosts. Skinny men,
snuffed candles, puddles at our feet.

19

We made our bodies fit while on the *Otranto* by placing our cycles on rollers and riding stationary, drawing in the miles sitting quite still on the saddles. The boredom was exquisite. We sat and watched as the sea refused to come closer, pedalling towards the horizon off to port; all that came at us was the swell and the thought that if it ever arrived it would be with water vying for room in our lungs as the ship went down to the bottom of the sea: the site of all things we can't know or ever hope to know.

And now I think something similar as we angle our machines towards the Alps. The Alps, distant and without advent. I come from a country precipitous and layered in fern and grass and forest. I have been amongst our Southern Alps. They seem spawned by great violence, by the heaving nature of earth's propensity to gnarl and twist. Hard ruptures holding glacier and rubble from many millions of years in one colossal hand, the other fist punching at the sky. In fact the mountains seem born of something other than the lavic ructions spitting up mounds and steam and new hot earth that are apparent in my North Island. And so too does their title seem born from other forms of hostility. I was 19 when I discovered their name was borrowed, taken from another set of splendid peaks. At this discovery I'd felt quite

weak-kneed, a disappointment beyond the usual. How could you name something unique in such uninspired fashion? In this way they too never seemed to arrive, waylaid by idiocy.

I was with Thomas and Katherine when we visited them in the south. We drove the coast, the rutted roads that map the west of the South Island. We came upon the peaks looming beyond the cut valleys. The white ice in a measured fall. All land from the terminus to the sea seemed the deposit of torn valley walls, stripped mineral and heavy metals, of decades and centuries and minutes counted between your arrival and the eventual decay of awe for other things. Franz Josef; a conveyor of time and earth. A conveyor of perspective.

Katherine and my brother stood under its terminus. It was a month before my vague triumph in the Timaru–Christchurch Classic; bravado had yet to rise and long silences had taken hold. The columns of ice, the huge banyan-like structures that collapse there to become water for the oceans and sky and lakes and limitless cycles of hydration for idiots like me to perspire and drink and piss. They held each other's hands waiting for the sound to hit them, for a glimpse of the power a glacier has over time and the physicality of time. It groaned in its deep and we eventually left, slowly walking away, our backs to that patient ice. It was vital we stepped quietly and stayed silent. We said nothing, Katherine and I. We joined my brother in the deepest of quiets. We trod softly amongst high boulders and ice. A silence that seemed to bring closer the size of all things the glacier represented. We let it grow inside us as we stepped, waiting for the sound of ice hitting the floor of the valley.

I'm heading inland, but in Nice I sat in the sand, then walked out into the light surf, the water warm on my feet and legs. I tried to imagine Katherine there, a bathing suit wrapped about her form and the quiet that would envelop us if the

conditions were right. I tried to invent a conversation, a burst of speech we might have had, had we been allowed to sit in that salt-heavy sea and float together for a few hours. A perfect tide between the two of our bodies. But despite my best effort, the image didn't take. Instead I was drawn towards that other coast; damp and wet on the Tasman's eastern shores. The West Coast. A true day, though one that eventually ended in lies. Whether it was the long hours of the driving, or the effect of staring at the white blue of the ice amongst the shadows of peaks all day, or the fact we had run out of conversation, I wasn't sure, but it seemed to hit us all with a shock when we came upon that day's date. We were sitting in the dining room of the large white hotel we were booked to stay in at Fox, and remembered.

'I was not going to say anything,' Katherine said, 'but it's here. It's a fact. Look at it.' She pointed behind us where a calendar was pinned to the wall.

'Her birthday?' Thomas said, a half-hearted run of surprise on his face. Or if it wasn't surprise, something else quick and weighted by unseen change in emotion. I thought of the tree Marya used to sit under in the centre of the drive. A great deciduous thing in the autumn losing its leaves with the thought of the coming cool.

'I look at dates and look at the gaps between them,' I said. 'I start thinking: they're the only keepsakes, only reliable ones at least.' I looked at them. 'Dates. I'm talking about dates.'

'What's he saying?' my brother asked his wife. Katherine looked startled at the question. His voice a rare thing suddenly ringing.

'In the past,' I said. 'All the rest – I don't know.'

'He thinks he's being serious,' Thomas said, his fork amongst his potatoes and peas and beans and cabbage.

'It's a theory I'm working on,' I said.

'He sounds like someone who's run out of dinner jokes,' he said. Thomas's voice was rough, as if small stones lined his vocal cords.

'Sounds like an excuse, you mean,' I said. 'I sound like I'm making an excuse.'

'For what?' his wife asked.

'It says nothing's up to par,' I said and shrugged.

My brother rightly ignored me and ate his dinner. It was the anniversary of a number of things: the anniversary of the week he made his march around the house in his slow walk, the anniversary of his pauses and pants, the anniversary of his proximity to our sister. How he stood in the hall and whispered in her ear. Both quite asleep in their own ways. The date, however, was not known because of these things, but rather because it was that dear sister's birthday. And dear sister's birthday was close to her last day.

There isn't an easy way to think about that week, the hundred things that happened. The car and her wish to be taken out in the car. We each sat, glazed eyes, cigarettes resting in the ashtray and the food unwelcoming. I started thinking about his arrival home and found myself speaking out loud, the end of winter and the trains that brought in the broken. 'He was wifeless,' I said, and hooked a thumb at Thomas as I gazed at Katherine. 'My brother. No wife.'

'Quite so,' she said and arched an eyebrow. 'When?'

'Dad and I picked him up at the train station,' I told her. 'He was blue. August.'

'Be quiet,' Thomas said.

'What?' Katherine said. 'Why?'

'He was blue. People don't look blue, but he was blue. Dad said we'd down a lamb's leg for dinner and we got home and mum had the house full of roast fumes. He wasn't saying much. His face was like porcelain, but translucent. We could see right through him.'

'They didn't let me see the sun,' Thomas put in. 'They thought me too frail.'

'He wore pyjamas on the deck of the ship,' I said.

'Don't be ridiculous. I wore my uniform.'

'He wore pyjamas and he didn't touch the meat.'

'Of course I didn't touch the meat.'

He'd arrived overnight from Auckland, the sea black beyond the platform. Cold air off the Taranaki Bight and families gathered dressed as if for the opera, though I doubt there were such a thing in that town in those months. He stepped from a carriage full of stone grey uniforms in that light. I touched his arm and he looked at me, then at my father. Men around us embraced amongst tears. Katherine wasn't there, of course. Her two brothers would return in the summer once it was all over, just as her father had years earlier from South Africa. Bleak, a part in the middle of them torched by the uneasy anticipation of returning to an unchanging home. But things had changed, despite what my brother would later claim.

'I wonder sometimes,' Katherine said, 'only sometimes, and not out of love or anything close, but I wonder about the Austrians, or the Germans, or those people. Their husbands, brothers and fathers arriving off the trains, out of packs of lousy men. Even the Russians.'

'Who would, why would you care?' Thomas asked.

'The war lost and they come home; the sadness and pride?' she said. 'I wonder about it. When my father came back from South Africa, the Boer thing, he said he missed the families he met, the old Dutch. He was big enough to worry for them.'

'Why?'

'And the hopelessness. I don't know. God, I have never really thought about this. What he meant by worrying about them. What do you think? The Germans? I'm talking about

177

the losers, of course. That's who I'm talking about. We were so happy. So happy. And they, well, I don't know.'

'Depends,' Thomas said. 'It depends. I don't think they even believe they're beaten. Things you read.'

'How was it to see them come home?' Katherine says. 'Faces and how a beaten man looks. What kind of joy did they have?'

'Much the same,' Thomas said, 'just in a different language.'

'This bloke didn't speak for six months,' I said and remembered something and then we were all quiet. It was Marya, of course. Marya standing in the hall welcoming him home with her hands at her side, her night shirt all askew. He did say something. Something was said. Something whispered in her ear. He spoke, put something in her ear.

'What do the beaten carry with them?' she asked.

'The same,' Thomas repeated.

A trek of British arrived in the restaurant at that precise hour and made great noises as they began drinking. One still carried his ice axe from his day on Fox Glacier, he bore it like a pig hunted and shot, later to be hung on the wall after the taxidermist had had his way with it. Katherine bent over the table as if to whisper something, or as if to listen to what we were saying. She smelt of something warm and soft and strong. None of us were speaking and she sat there, preserved in this position, waiting.

After quite some time, after the British had gone, it was plain and obvious the last of the staff desired us to vacate the dining room. We did; we went and sat on the outside seating. There we watched the birds fly low over the field out in front of us and up into the hills before the mountains, the forest and the heavy sky above. We watched the mist in the trees, the haunt of things slowly rising and the threat of their fall. Ghosts and the fear of ghosts. Mist climbing

until it's rain; everything is in a race to the sea. Even the mountains. And even the mountains were gone, a heft of cumulus taking their place. When you can no longer see what was once there, the easiest conclusion is not that it has vanished utterly, but it has been replaced.

Thomas spoke slowly. He breathed into his fist to warm his hands. It was summer, but cooling in the late evening. He said: 'If you're still wondering about them. If you're still wondering, they go back to work. Just like us. The Krauts, Boche, Hun. They go back to making a living. Making families. Making things. Making bread, making faces at babies. It doesn't matter if you win, if you lose, everything stays the same. We eat, we drink. In the end we fight again. In the end it is all the same.' He looked at us, a bright gleam dancing on his eyes, as though he'd been drinking and had hit the point where all ideas are good ideas and all eyes seem welcoming. He sat back and leant forward. He clicked his knuckles and started on his way. He spoke until our glasses were taken away, until our glasses had been returned filled and emptied and refilled by the last staff member willing, and on and on. I learnt about the towns out around Wissant and Calais. We heard about flight and sound of flight, and learnt about all that too. How the gun fires timed shouts of glory through the propeller. I learnt about places he hadn't been, learnt about Verdun, learnt about the arrival of the Americans. And then we learnt about Persia and the Turks, how they had India in their sights, how Arabia was promised to the Arabs and how it will never be given. We learnt about the north, the brutality of the north. We learnt about being quiet as he spoke and not giving in to the need we both felt to interrupt. He became a man beside a deserted restaurant, telling stories, we his audience, polite and weak.

179

Late in the evening, when I saw Katherine in her nightgown walk through a certain light, I thought of taking it from her and seeing the inches of her skin white. Later I thought of my brother squirming and in pain. I imagined it because it was something I could imagine.

And then later again, Katherine held me. She held me close and muttered things not meant for my ears, nor, I suspect for hers. She said, once she was finished, she said: 'Do not ever think. Do not ever think if we do this it is because of love. It is not that, it will never be that. This is about distance. Distance from him. Remember: only love is about love.'

And I said: 'Love. That's something. What name do we have for love when it isn't around? I'm asking. What's the term for an act of love when there is no love?'

The two of us stood just inches apart from each other, the fine pant of our breath. Everything so close: mouths, breast, hands, skin. Distance in this instance is made of time, the way it separates the smallest things. She watched my face for over a minute before she left, looking for the thing that brought her into that room in the first place, but we both knew it was gone. She left me without the warmth of her body, without a dram to take me out of the gloom that accompanies me on memory's many divided paths.

These were my thoughts on the beach, a long-ago conversation and how we tried to acknowledge the precise nature of how things were changing. We tried with our bodies, then found they couldn't touch. And perhaps that's why things never seem to arrive, everything is always on the move, always shifting from one thing to another. And yes, the Alps come near, but they'll never turn up, so it seems. We have no ability to stand on the outside and peer into the things we make and forget we make. We name a mountain so we might behold the mountain.

180

We climb in air I hope will rapidly cool from the deep temperature of the heated southern cities, but it doesn't. We spread out early. Percy then Ernie let go and fail in the evening. In Grenoble we wait on their return. The town resting in a deep valley, alluvial and flat. A place once of river and stone.

Percy and Ernie, they take last place and the Spaniard is no longer with us.

20

'You know what it is?' Louvière asks.

'Yep.'

'Do you know?'

'What's that?' I ask.

'It's the anticipation,' he says.

'What is?'

'It's the expectation of whatever,' he says, and he nods that bald head. Bald but his voice sounds like Ernie's, Australian and puckered. 'Of anything, things, things you can't know.'

'Things you can't know? What's the point?'

'You can't know without relentless, bloody agony.'

'That's it?'

'That's terror, that's dread,' he says.

I smile for him. He makes a laugh. 'Where are we?' I ask.

'We are in Hendaye and you are speaking to me in the café and we are drunk. Men slipping on the vomit outside the stalls. They call to you. You come from their mouths. You know you are here because Harry has just left and you are alone in this conversation. I can smell you. You are "the Prince of New Plymouth".'

'How's your wife?' I ask.

'She's putting out the soup,' he says and quietly Louvière starts to look like Harry. He speaks in Arabic and then I

am awake, or I am already awake and this never happened. Celia mouths certain words and I don't make them out. I arise and from beside the bed I take what she has left for me. I walk out of the hotel in the dark at 2 before the sun.

21

We climb the four mountains, hit the peak of the race, the highest point of the damned 3,000 miles at the Col de Galibier. There is no pause to think, no admiration of the view, no thoughts of understanding and awe that mountains are so adept at producing in people, there is just a man watching at the mouth to the mountain.

※

Four days before she died, my sister spoke of Egmont, of the volcano that leaned over our view outside the curtain. She was deep in the illness and barely making words. Dying, oblivious, charming. She asked me if I would drive our father's car, if I would drive it into the foothills so she could be on the mountain one last time. I told her the road didn't ride so high and she said she knew. She said she only wanted to feel the air cool and trees close in. She said she didn't mind we weren't going to the summit, she only wanted to feel it near, sense she was a part of it. I thought of this as we waited to leave Grenoble, the tremble of her voice, the hope in her face quite ashen. We hope for great things when we are reduced, reduced as our body shuts down, closing out the peripheries. There is little left but a few verbs and organs, a

couple of eyes and their increasingly tunnelled vision. To be able to walk again, to see the land and feel a sense of size, but to know that one doesn't need legs to imagine the scope of the world. That is what let her mumble her request. And we rode a timeless straight out of Grenoble. I imagined her in the crowd, waving a wan hand. I waved back to her, happy to take her on any ride I make to the mountains. I take her everywhere, it seems. Into sleep and into these hills and the madness they make.

Finally we angled left at Eybens and began a slight incline into the green. There time seemed to switch back on and I told her to close her eyes, to shut out the sight of these men beside me. The things we become, I want no love to see. We hit Vizille. Its road the thinnest lane through the township, only enough room for two to ride abreast. We squeezed past shouters – I believed them to be the same people carted from hamlet to village to commune to city. Above us, just a few feet above us, families leant from the shutters and yelled. The flapped flags of unknown provenance, bosoms and dawn shadow on the faces of men. The shaven and the unshaven shouted. If I knew what they said I would report, for the words were repeated and repeated and they began to hum in a resonance that touched me, though I can't say why unless I make meaning of their words afresh: name a noise a noun; name another a verb. The birth of sentences teeming with life.

Soon we were alongside Les Rivoirands amongst the trees rising. Then we saw it in the moonlight, the massif. Black, white; a familiarly dangerous formula. We are a river, we are a vein, we are a disease in a vein looking for the mountain, to knock down the mountain. Close your eyes, I told her. Close out the light.

185

We hit Lautaret in slow motion, some walking, some leaning on their cycles as we went through the snow like craters in the surrounding landscape. Glaciers hung falling in the peaks high above the first col where I played a game trying to keep up with Frantz amongst such immense altitude. He stayed back when Fontan made an early move 500 feet before the summit and Maurice De Waele went with him. I stayed with Frantz waiting to see how he'd make his move, to watch and see when he'd start pedalling in pursuit of Fontan. Slowly I understood he was waiting until we were on Galibier before he attacked. I was determined to hold on to him when he went. Take his speed to the top, be meilleur grimpeur. We sat in the peloton until the road became a mule track and men started falling off. At Lautaret we stopped and were signalled by a man holding an oil lamp to take a left; all I could see was a path like a tramping track jutting off the side of the road. We halted and changed our back wheels and ran at the path, jumping up the two feet to where it began above the col. Frantz ran 20 metres before putting his feet on the pedals. I groaned and spat and caught him. We rose up the hairpins, my lungs bullied and beaten. I thought of George Mallory, I thought of men passing – it seemed obvious: surely one of us must die.

Rhythm, breath. Concentration a battle over exhaustion.
 This road barely a road.
 Closing.
 Head and thought fade. Muscle clenching the hemispheres.
 Utter splendour, peaks and distance; sand in my eyes.
Snow.
 Closing in, closing.
 My bike, I named him George.
 A dowser over the light.

Men, hundreds it seemed, lined the path and shouted, one came at me slapping my back as I stayed with Frantz. I began telling him I was crying, but then realised I wasn't. I then realised I wasn't speaking because I couldn't speak. We named our mountains the Southern Alps, but those are not these.

And he pulled away and I felt the creak of my bones as I forced the cranks. The terror of burning muscle. I sat behind him and we could see Fontan ahead with the Belgian, they were the first to the tunnel the French army put through last century, and we approached riding hard. I could see its mouth and the way it opened into black. Frantz was three, four bike lengths ahead and his speed was increasing. I felt myself slow. My legs were like wood, men were shouting at us, men standing amongst mountains yelling, cars pulled to the side of the road and barely room for us to ride. I was standing on my pedals, my head so full I felt my temples crack and I let him go. I stopped. I put out a leg and felt the earth rush through it. It was as if my limbs had become dust and all atoms had collapsed into fear. I went sideways.

'Get up,' someone said in English.

I had nothing to reply with.

'Get up. Lazy.' A woman's voice and I expected it was Celia. I lay prone with my bike on top of me waiting for something to tell me it was her. A wash of scent, a peel of sound from her fan as her nail went through its vanes. Nothing came, no hand to lift me. I drifted into the fade of glancing light. Voices, sound. Clouds in the near surround.

Though soon, without memory of how, I was back up and walking. I looked around, the edges of my vision hazed. The ground evened out and I put my leg over the saddle and I looked around. I saw a woman with short black hair amongst leather-clad Frenchmen who had made it this high on motorcycles and looked oiled and ready for the end. The

woman wasn't watching me and I pushed off towards the doors of the tunnel. Beside the entrance was the figure of time.

I recognised him from photos, from brief glimpses in the tent housing control, from rumour and film. Henri Desgrange, the Tour's cruel inventor, stood moustached. My face covered in saliva, blood on my knees and my ribs breaking through my shirt. I was the man he wanted to see: alone and willing, passing into the belly of the mountain.

I went close. I wanted the old man to smell me. I started speaking, saying one word over and over. 'Prince,' I said. 'Prince.'

<p style="text-align:center">❂</p>

At the end, I fell from my machine in the square. I was helped to the tent where a man stood over me shaking a bottle of water onto my torso where my bones stuck out. Thirteen-and-a-half-hours. I was surprised to notice that I was breathing, as if it were the first time I'd realised the body does such a thing. I asked and discovered each of my teammates was still on the course. I waited in the square drinking sugared water and watched the riders arrive. A fitful attempt at a sprint among three from separate teams saw a crash in front of the crowd who only wanted to shout and cheer. Knees and elbows cracked. Skin left behind on the cobblestones. Opperman arrived five minutes later. He signed in and found a bed then went to it. I sat with him for over an hour. We said nothing.

Eventually I returned to the streets and took up my position beside the lake and watched riders return. An impossible fatigue hung in my body like damp sand. A man sat nearby and I saw him list then slip into a slumber. I called to him. He opened an eye and soon closed it once more. My

legs became stiff. My back and arms became hard. All of me turning to stone. I waited.

Waited.

❖

Now here he comes. Percy at the finish: a bandage about his head. He hands his bike over to a waiting helper from Ravat Wonder then stands still in the square. I go to him and walk his body to the seat where I sat myself sometime earlier. At our backs Lake Geneva and the stillness of old water. We sit and wait for his breathing to return, his sweat drying in the last of the sun as he drinks continually from his bottle. The rest of the field enters the town as if scattered gravel.

He speaks slowly. 'Who's –' he tries to say.

'Who's out?'

'Who's out?' he asks.

'Who's still on the road?'

He tries to nod and his head bobs and his chin stays on his chest. He waves his hand as if drunk and arguing with his own stupor.

'Harry,' I say, 'and Ernie.'

'Old Private Ernie Bainbridge. Digger.'

I look at him, his eyes mostly shut. He nods to himself. His bandage showing at the sides of his cap, which sits lopsided on his head, the gauze the keen blur of a spinning top ready to fail. The last two rides he's staggered to the line in last place. I think of Bainbridge and Harry and I say: 'Percy – did you see them, Harry and Ernie?'

'I watched the lights,' he mumbles, 'the lot of you blokes looked like fireflies.'

'What?'

'This morning, up on the mountain.'

'The headlights?'

'The way upwards and around those bends, the sight of the hills. You remember?' He sounds out as if in fever and puts his fingernails into his beard to scratch and watches my face with eyes whose colours seem cooled by the air off the lake where the last of the sun's rays play on the tips of the waves.

'I remember. Did you see them?'

'Not since this morning. The night had a hardness, do you know?'

'I know old boy,' I say.

'Everything felt close. I was watching and everything, everything felt close. Like, what?'

'Dunno, Percy.'

'Old walls. Cave walls. Like the walls of a cave,' he says. 'Taking us to what? This place. Wherever we were being led. Smooth walls.' His head nods again so his chin hits his chest, but this time it bounces back up as if sprung with the memory of metal.

'When? Which hills?' I ask and stare back at those eyes. Several times we set out in the night. Twice I saw the spectacle of lights as they rose up mountain tracks. Twice I thought of my sister and the drive we took near the end. But during this morning's climb, I saw no lights. I saw nothing but the black shape of the hill and the ride we must make.

'That was this morning,' he says, 'wasn't it? We were headed to some place.'

'That's right,' I say.

'Where?' I look at him and realise he has quite forgotten our location. He has his shoes off, his feet are streaked with the usual lines from cramped leather and blood from blisters. He stretches his toes and I can see it makes him feel better in some way, that a mote of the pain – which I know, which I understand so well, just as I know that the passing of this time we are stuck within is only temporary – is teased away.

190

'Here,' I say, 'this is the place.' I laugh, hoping to ease his pain a little more. I fear I sound like a doctor, nervous beside the patient under the stare of the nurse who knows.

'Where?'

'Évian.' I'm smiling for him. I nod at the lake in front of us, out past the arrays of flowers bending in the breeze off the water banded by lapping shores. Percy nods also, then points at the lake as if it contains the opinion he's seeking. There are isolated white caps where the water is broken and its wave is torn in two. Somewhere out there France ends and Switzerland begins. Such a tempting idea. And I mean to say to my companion, 'Out there, out there in the middle, there's the border. That's where we are, at the border.' And I want to make a joke about stealing a boat and heading out into the centre of the lake so we can say, 'Fuck those who think we'll ride again!' But I say none of these things.

'We looked like something,' Percy says. 'Everyone riding up. Like something else, I'm not sure.'

'Like something else?' I ask.

He nods his head. 'We looked like something else. Those Chinese lanterns they let loose on the river.'

'Which river?

'Not sure, just that they're set free to float loose. Candles in paper boats, prayer lanterns.'

'Like in Siam, I think?' I ask. I believe I have seen photographs of such things.

'Perhaps,' Percy says. 'Perhaps Siam.'

'Prayers floating on the water,' I say. He nods and I look away. I have seen photos of these somewhere, in a book at my uncle's shop in Wellington. Maybe in an encyclopedia, it doesn't matter. Not so much as his revelation. I touch his arm. 'I've seen pictures of such things,' I say.

'I don't want to think about it.'

'My uncle has a bookshop,' I say. 'It's like living with a library in the family.'

'I never believed in prayer,' he says. 'Not a dot of it.'

'How so?'

He shrugs and spits into his hand then rubs the stuff like an ointment into his forearms, which are dry as paper. 'Look at them,' he says and points. He half-stands and indicates west along quai Baron de Blonay and the small rise down which beleaguered riders come. We turn and I stand upright. The rattle of lose bolts and cracked joints. They are barely cycling, legs flopping, knees askew, all form damaged by 327 kilometres of crippled roads, dust and shingle, mountain and knowing insects huddled at grey water ready to swarm and follow you and your sweat. Some men are crying as they come off their machines. Heads in hands crying. More of them arrive, legs shaking and bodies in a debt to their muscles eaten away and shrinking like old fruit in a wooden bowl. If I had a toffee hammer and I tapped on any given limb I fear it would shatter, leaving only the remains of a once vital man bent on winning this race of all races. The teams are broken and scattered. Officials gather around riders asking where their companions might be and they squint up at their faces as if caught in the cramp of hunger. One man is helped to a stretcher, unable to walk.

The large crowds of earlier in the afternoon have dissipated, but still some linger over these last rites as if a congregation filling itself with the prayers of desperate men, the vestiges of which drip from their mouths in oaths and tender mercies. They watch and know they can't imagine the torture of this day. They mill, they come close. I stand. I turn around to shake the feeling that I'm being watched, and of course I am. I'm conspicuous. Once our bodies are off our bikes we are used meat, distasteful, reeking.

I imagine Percy watching us from below, the four of us ahead up the mountain within the remains of the peloton. The power gathering in our legs as the pack surges and we

feel the control of a will we can't see, we can't breathe, only act in response. The hurt that resides deep in our muscles is condensed to a keen part of the mind and ignored, the deep massage of this communion, the spiritual ructions smoothed to a collective beating of hearts. I close my eyes when I ride, I close them to feel the presence of my fellow riders directing me with their proximity. I bump into hips and shoulders and open them again. I am riding in my head once more and the idea begins to make me feel off-colour.

He taps my shoulder, I turn and watch more riders. We are eager for a sight of Bainbridge or Harry, but neither is in the bunch. So many have dropped from competition, taken the refuge of a support vehicle in the rear, headed home to Paris or Bruges or Florence or the bottle. Such disappointment. From the 162, only 70 are left. I find it barely credible that such drop-outs have tallied. I am mildly disgusted, the thought of them abandoning the race we have travelled 12,000 miles to battle. I am certain it is their proximity to home, their wives and lovers, the fact that they've been paid, the facts, the lies. Perhaps too it is the knowledge that only a few can win and the rest will be forever losers. Is there more pride in returning to your village offering injury and hurt as your legend than waiting until the end to admit defeat? I ask Percy and he shrugs.

'You know, there was something beautiful in watching you all floating away,' he says.

'What?'

'You were floating up the hills. Little globes in the sky.'

'You know,' I say, 'they have lanterns too. I recall lanterns they let out to the night. Wishes written on their sides. Is that right?'

'Prayers,' he says. 'Prayer lanterns.'

'Yes.'

'Prayers, they write prayers on their sides.'

193

'That'd be a sight,' I say. 'A hundred. A thousand. They last till they fall, I guess.'

'Yeah. And I'm thinking now. What's a prayer if not a hope. You all looked quite unreal.'

I look at him and realise how pain is sapped by odd rituals. How we nurse ourselves with the familiar no matter how odd or displaced the action might be. Talk. Talk and how talk shifts the unknown into the real. How real we seem when conversation repurposes the mundane for tasks of rehabilitation.

'It's properly all right if you want to give in,' I say.

Bainbridge arrives during the evening, hobbled. The second to last in. He is covered in lumps, his body weeping. He strides past us as we go to his aid. His mouth open, his cheeks skeletal and a face full of tears. He's barely walking, indeed those strides I mention are more staggers. It's important to remember him well. He doesn't head to control. He refuses our comfort or conversation. I love these men. We bleed for one another. This one won't let us see the hole his body has finally become. Bruce Small leads him away and there is great melancholy in the action, as if all were at an end.

And Harry's still on the road. I fear he has been hit. I fear his legs have been taken out from under him and he has gone off the side of the mountain into a ravine where he will rot and be the carrion of every eagle, falcon, hawk eager for food. I say nothing of this fear. He hasn't been this far back in the field at any stage, indeed he has never been behind Bainbridge – but we look to the road and we see nothing.

'I'll show you something. I'll tell you something,' Percy says, and stands. He removes his hat and the bandages

wrapped around his head. He reveals a fresh graze above his ear, hair and blood. It isn't deep but I can tell some force has thrust itself upon him: there's deep blue bruising around the wound. 'I was arriving out from the bend at Saint-Michel,' he says. 'I was only 50 yards behind Ernie and I had speed. I had hardly pedalled since the col. My legs were going in circles; they were just rags being pulled by the cranks. I looked back over my shoulder, I was hoping for Bruce and the car. I needed to stop, I needed to have my legs stopped for just a moment. Ernie was ahead of me. I tried to put some sense into myself and drunk down one of my bidons and God knows what was in there. Whatever, my legs came alive once more and I felt the urge to chase him down, I stood on my pedals and rode, I cut corner after corner, the road widened and narrowed, you know.'

I nod.

'I had speed.'

'Open grave?'

'Right gaping open. I had the sense of walls closing in and riding straight through the gap. I could have been sleeping. I leant low to the road in corners. I felt the nearness of the gravel. How close we are to dying in those moments, mate, no one knows. I felt the speed like it's no longer a number. I drove hard, right at the apex, on the perfect line. Then the full grille of a car was all I saw, my eyes full of the blue bonnet and then I was braking but too late and that was me strewn on the ground. That was me gasping at the air. Lungs crushed flat like paper bags and there was no air. I saw my bike 20 yards away. The front wheel looked cracked, the tyre hanging off, but it still had movement; some of my momentum was still making it rock on the axle. I looked at it and made a small sound. At first I didn't know what I was saying. But I was talking – gibberish. Then I realised. You know what it was?'

195

I nod. 'It wasn't gibberish.'

'That's right. It was an entreaty,' he says. 'That was the sound I made, a prayer. And what was I asking?'

I put my hand through my hair. 'I know what you asked.'

'I asked that my legs be broken, that they stand me no more and I go home. I return to my wife who is so sweet, and like as you say for those French quitters. It is so easy when I think of her. I just push off from the shore in some boat.'

'I know,' I say. And I do. Every day I crash and I hope it's the end.

<center>❖</center>

And each day I go on.

It is 17 hours since we started the day, it is dark and it is last place that Harry secures when finally he arrives. There is little about him that seems real. I take his arm. I expect it to fall to dust, to float dutifully away on the cooling breeze towards Geneva, or Monteux, or to the place he desires most. But he has no desire as I hold him, only what remains of a rider when asked to pedal out of hell.

'How long?' he asks.

'Enough.'

'How many hours?'

'17.'

'17,' he says then swears. There are tears making their way through the dust. I am crying.

'They will mean nothing tomorrow,' I say.

'Last place is —'

'It's an utterly necessary place,' I say.

'—'

'It has to be taken,' I say.

He smiles, he nods, he snorts. He's crying and so thin now.

<center>196</center>

And time is temporary. I made this claim earlier. I claim it again because we remember seconds so poorly, recall hours so mundanely, like the fall of drizzle or misted rain: by morning it has gone. Only the pain remains. Somehow, it's the proof of passing, the measure by which we count. We leave that town two days on with little but the cracks in our bones and the last great hill reduced to memory and forgotten prayers, the mumbles of broken men. We are a flood and we fill the valleys.

22

Last night in Évian I felt my voice change as I told Celia what it was she wanted to know.

'It wasn't that I was infected,' I said. 'I wasn't infected by any disease they knew about. They thought I had a cold, or influenza – but I got sick with something else. It wasn't ever named. I had been in Cairo six weeks at that stage. Doctors kept taking my temperature and being dumbfounded. If I tried to get up, I fell down, there was nothing in my legs. A nurse mopped my brow, but I wasn't hot. My neck was swollen where the nodes had swelled up so it was impossible to swallow. Under my arms, all over my body. The doctor just started to ignore me in the face of worse conditions, real fevers. Word got out around the mess that I wasn't sick, that no one could figure out what was wrong with me. Word was I was faking it.'

'You're going to tell me how you broke your . . .' she said and pointed at my leg.

'They got me out of bed and told me they were taking me to the pub. Just the mess bar, but they had me up and got me to the stairs and one of them, he slapped me on the back –'

'They thought you were a coward –'

'– and I tried to compensate and stumble down the stairs

away from their hands. And I fell and –'

'– you fell and you broke –'

'– and I broke my leg.' I looked at her watching my lips, and watched her mouth my words back to me. She didn't flinch, didn't query. She appeared to be following me faithfully as if along a track dividing and splintering and coming back together. All the while my voice was telling her which way to tread; all the while I was expecting her to stop and protest she couldn't step any further; all the while I was quietly surprised at how easy it was, this lying game.

'So, what was wrong?' she asked. 'In damned Cairo. So sick, unnameably sick? You slept with a prostitute. Fans going, flap, flap, flap. You got sick, little man got sick.'

'Not so much,' I said.

'You all slept with them, even those who didn't wish to, they slept with them.'

'Up to our eyelids. We all did.'

'Galoshes to keep diseases at bay,' she said.

I nodded and laughed, slowly and right through my body. She put her hand on my chest.

'Young men. There ought to be a law. Men standing around throwing whatever at belly-dancers, watching the coins glint off the light as they flick 'em from their thumbs.'

We sat silently, waiting on the sun, on something strong to begin the conversation once more. The grass shimmered and I realised the wind had changed direction, that it was now coming down off the mountain instead of the lake. She put her hand on my arm. It was warm, how a relative's should be, but never expected.

'And when you were out of plaster,' she said. 'Once they cut it open. And you were told to stand up and your legs were all weak and you smelt so bad and the nurses, and you stood and it felt like it meant something. That's when –'

'I knew they were all gone. At Gallipoli. Not all, but –

199

they were all gone. So, what?'

'What were you going to do?'

'What was I gunna do?'

'Sail after them on some chartered ship?' she suggested. 'Charter a boat and run after them all.'

'Jump overboard at the sight of land and swim to the shore, waving.'

'That's right.'

'I was awaiting court martial.'

'But it never came?'

'No. I fell in with the British,' I said. 'Luck and the British.' She didn't interrupt so I went on. She heard how Thomas met five British servicemen ranking from lieutenant to major as they visited the officers' mess at Zeitoun. She heard it through me and there seemed no question, no query asking if I was lying. I went on and onward. They'd come in to cool themselves, they told my brother, some of them stifling their sweating bodies by hiding them inside layers of cotton. Each time he told me about these officers there were more of them, but I kept the number at five. For hours they talked and drank beer. He met them again one weekday afternoon in the souk at Khan el-Khalili. Thomas was dehydrated and sitting alone in a corner, dazed from walking in heat without water. They picked him up and revived him with tea under shade of a vendor's roof. Once standing they had him join them in their walk in the city as they looked for inscriptions in stone. 'I would walk about Cairo with a core of the officers,' I told her. 'Men who each seemed to know where they were going. They had notebooks and hand-drawn maps and spoke short sentences. There were five of them, sometimes six or seven. They seemed to have agendas. I can't name them, but they were always looking for a building of one name or another. Small, obscure mosques, of whose past they knew a great deal as if they were born

200

with a map of antiquity in their heads, a homing instinct for extraordinary places and people. On one occasion I found myself in the small courtyard of a house drinking apple tea and smoking cigarette after cigarette as two of the English officers spoke with an old man who must have been in his eighties, or older. He was gentle and was looked after by his daughters – in fact, no: his granddaughters or great granddaughters. They were young and beautiful, or such is my memory. Pretty brown eyes batting long lashes at where we sat under a sycamore whose roots were cracking the tiles so the floor seemed restless.'

'Who was the man?'

'I didn't have any idea, I didn't know until much later when I was in France. But he talked so quietly I could barely tell what he was saying, whether he was imparting his knowledge in English or Arabic. I would nod, as if falling into a light sleep. I imagined I was dreaming. I remember it clearly: he was talking in this voice and the wind was shuffling the leaves of the sycamore tree and it all seemed so improbable. I drifted and felt a lightness; like love, but it was just air. It was the next day that one of the officers took me flying for the first time. I was a lieutenant and I was asked –'

'The Air Force?'

'The Royal Flying Corps.' I gazed past the hedge to the hills from where we sat on the balcony of the hotel room. The sun was on the horizon, or at least evidence of the sun: a purple blue lifting from the foothills. Thomas travelled to England after Cairo. He joined the RFC, indeed became one of their pilots. That was how he came to be shot down. How he ended up in the dunes on the wrong side of the mud. How he lived with the decay of the dead for seven days before he was frightened from his hole and found his way home. 'That is the story of how I went to France,' I said to her. 'That's my story.'

'And then the Fokker curse,' she said. 'That's what they called it, was it not?'

'Fokker plague.'

'Fokker –'

'Plague.'

'Fokker curse,' she said.

'God.'

'Which one?'

'Fokker scourge,' I said.

'Really?'

I nodded and shook my head. 'Then I went down. An exhaustion, so deep, like a dream out of control. That was the weight of it. Time was another thing, a broken thing. I am yet to rectify it.'

'How long?'

'Days in the sand. Two days in an old mine.' I say the word two because I have to lie. I should expect no sympathy for my brother's misfortune, that is not the aim of this. 'When the French came I pulled two bodies over me. I didn't know if they knew English and I was beyond reason to reason with myself. On the second day it rained and I collected water on my tongue and in a German helmet. It tasted of metal.'

'Blood?'

'Metal.'

She nodded.

'And the officer was killed. The one who took me to meet that old man. It was only a few days before I went down that he told me who the man was. The one in the courtyard with the sycamore tree and the beautiful daughters. He was on an archaeological dig. That's why they went searching for him. That's why they sat with him and spoke. The archaeological dig, the one at Hisarlık. That old man. He was there in 1894 with Wilhelm Dörpfeld. Was that his name?'

'Whose?'

'I'm talking about Troy.'

'I know what you're talking about,' she said.

'I met a man who'd been there. Who'd stumbled upon the walls. That's who they were looking for,' I told her. 'That's who we met in Cairo. He'd walked and mapped and dug at the site. I only found this out a few days before I went down. A real place. I find it extraordinary that I met the man, that he was there and I was in his courtyard with his granddaughters.'

'Do you ever think you ended up on the other side of the Dardanelles? That you ended up in some other time and this isn't the place you left?' she said and looked out at Lake Geneva, in much the same way as Percy the day before when he spoke about his lanterns and tried to recall where he was.

'Perhaps,' I said.

'And these men you were with, they went looking for that old man. You followed them and you walked the old city looking for him in the streets?'

'I didn't know where we were going. It was some task, it seemed. Something that went on alongside the war. Two of these men were from Cambridge; I assume they returned there after the war. This was an exercise, not to replace the war, or forget about it, they wanted to legitimise it. That was the thing, they wanted to have the conversations, long conversations that were somehow a reasoning of their time spent away from their offices and desks and the libraries. I imagine dark libraries.'

'Dark libraries,' she repeated. I think she laughed. 'What about now? Is this racing, is this about legitimising? Coming back here?'

'I came back here to remember. That's why I'm here. For them it was about the conversations.'

'That's what it's always about.'

'I guess. I guess we used to talk about things,' I said,

203

'to distract us from the real thing which was about killing people. Everything we did was about killing people. All the photos I took from my cockpit were funnelled into a system that was designed for the killing of people. We'd clean the latrines, all with the purpose of killing someone. And it's not like you finish your day and you say to your pal, "So, who did you kill today?" And it's not like they say back, "Leonard Braun. Captain Leopold Braun."'

'Leonard.'

'You never ask if you killed someone. Which seems somehow ridiculous. You hear about girlfriends and wives and sisters and mothers.'

'What about your sister?' she asked. 'Did you ever describe your sister to your British officers?'

I shook my head. 'I never let on that I had a sister. Never. She's the only one, Celia.'

'She's the only what?'

'The only one.'

She asks again, her voice alone and distant, cheerless and lingering. She's knows I can't say. As Percy had said, it's so easy when I think of her. But it is so hard to speak, so hard to see what you need to see when all about you are the words of others.

It seemed extraordinary, as I spoke out the contents of his story, that they were real events, a set of events that were somehow true and somehow related to my time here. I'd heard this narrative at Lake Wanaka at the back end of 1921 a few weeks before the race out of Timaru. From there we drove to Queenstown and deeper into the south. We doubled back to Mount Cook, and from there, Timaru. The entire time he spoke on and on. I rode up the east coast

and found myself in that strange trance which may not ever have been broken, not even by the fist that caught my chin and sent blood and tooth into the dirt. And despite that we went on and carried it all with us, every word spoken, every attempt to forget. Six years later I left for Sydney, then Melbourne, then Perth, then Colombo, then Ismaïlia, then Toulon, then here. This hotel beyond the Alps, I can't name the region because I seem to have forgotten to remember. The town is Pontarlier and I have no desire to explore and here I tell it all again. Celia is beside me. I can't tell if she is sleeping or in one of those dream states one reaches for but only finds on the end of that pipe. I haven't the energy, and I fight any thought. I notice in the quietness something deep and unrelenting creeping at me. Melancholy doesn't so much have claws, rather it has tides.

We sleep – or at least I believe I sleep – for I speak to him across the room: Louvière and his face hidden by the fall of shadow.

Such lies are dreams, I'm terrified I report them at all. I turn him off and wake. I lie with a sheet covering my nakedness though I feel no cool air. Celia breathes as if instructed, as if she has trained for days and months to learn the correct pattern just for this moment. Her rump glows in the slight moonlight in from the window. I kiss her hip and expect a change in position but her belly undulates in the same precise manner. I kiss the hollow of her waist and hope she will turn and face me. But the breathing continues and I lie back in the throes of calculation, trying to surmise how curves and angles happen to be perfect.

'He's writing to me,' she says. She stays in the same position, supine. 'He wrote from Luchon.'

'Louvière?'

'The post is quicker than you lazy men.'

I watch her in the dark, wondering where her mouth is precisely.

205

'He's in a state. Great sadness. He's greedy about being sad. He desires to rejoin the race – he wrote this – any way he can, he wants to rejoin. He asks that his leg be amputated and that he be allowed back in. He says he knew comrades in the war who'd lost a leg but who manage to ride, a sight difficult to conjure without having seen in action. People rush to watch them pass.'

'Where?' I ask. 'I want to see this. Where do I have to go –'

'Belgium. He has friends there. We both do. You know, I lied,' she says. 'I wasn't in Algiers. I was in Belgium. I lie about that fact. I don't know why I said what I said. I was stranded in Belgium at the start.'

'Stranded in Belgium, what? When they came over the border?'

'I was stranded in Belgium, yes.'

'How so?'

'I was teaching in a small town; a few girls were teaching all over Belgium. Something that had been arranged for us by our college. Time abroad to widen horizons. Such was our life then, such was the way things seemed driven by something principled. It was summer, of course, and most of the girls had returned home at the end of term. I hadn't, bless me. I stayed on. I'm a girl lacking foresight.'

'Then Sarajevo?'

She says nothing for a few moments and I assume she is nodding or thinking about nodding. 'And we thought: Russia. After reading all the news, hearing word of mouth, we thought Russia. They'll fight it out for a few weeks and then things would calm down. No one said to us: "Get out. This is a situation. Get out." No one said to us, no one explained that they would come through Belgium. Serbia. Russia. Hungary, Germany and Austria. France and Britain, absolutely, but the way I was told, the way it was supposed

to happen – it would work out differently. But they bullied their way in quick smart.'

'I try to commit it to memory, what happened. The origins, dates, the –'

'But you can't, can you? You can't repeat it because so much happened in days and hours. So much happened beforehand. So much happened in countries and cities you had never heard of but it happened and you didn't know, then you knew all of a sudden.'

'People saying the names of Dukes, they said Belgrade and Sarajevo and the rest. My brother was so excited. His whole team, his whole football team.'

'And then they came. We were in the north living in a border town near Liège. They walked into Luxembourg. Then there was Visé. We were nearby and quickly we made our way out of the village and south. That was the 4th of August. We didn't think we needed to go far. A woman I was travelling with had family at Gembloux, so we headed there with hundreds of others. August. The whole of August there. And then September came and we got out. It took a long time to get across but we did and we got to England from Dunkerque. Small boat.'

'How did you get across? Belgium, I mean across Belgium.'

'Slowly. Farmhouses and hedges as cover in the night. There were four of us trying to get to England.'

'Why England?'

'We thought Paris would fall. We thought France would go, and then. And the. And the things. What we saw, we had to get away. Sometimes you need to cross whole borders and seas.'

'What things?'

'What things? They were butchering people: women, children. Who knows what they were doing to the men.

But I heard what they were doing to the women. And I saw. So that was why England.'

'What did you see?'

She said nothing. She rustled the bedclothes as she moved position.

'Where were you?'

'Certain moments stay. Remain inside. I was at Gembloux,' she says quickly. 'In marketplace. A woman. Any woman, I don't know who she was. Any woman, I wasn't from that town.' She sits up and leans forward so I can see her. She takes my hand and her voice is barely audible and I think of the first time we met, how any harshness in her voice seemed somehow eradicated, as if any volume it once had had been suppressed or disconnected. Things, events, something, maybe this, maybe another day, had done something. I touch her face and expect something other than the warm skin. 'They strung up her body in the market. Her breasts. Her hair. Cut. They cut her breasts off. Mutilated. Her organs, we could see her insides. And that, we saw that and didn't pause to think about getting out. Babies. We went across the front, that was the easiest part.'

'Babies.'

'We stood in the grass with our backs pinned against the stone of a coal house in bramble of an untended bush, listened. They were nearby. Germans, of course. I'm not talking about Germans for the sake of saying Germans. I'm talking about insane people. How they went from normal peoples to those things. I don't understand well.'

'Where?' I ask, but she just shakes her head and I know only because my hand is on her neck and I feel it twist.

'Between us and them was small stream running between the house and this little structure by which we hid. I saw a woman come out of the house and run. Her dress was half removed, torn I guess. She went towards the soldiers, as if

she hadn't seen them, and then back the other way. She was carrying a baby and dragging a toddler. The tot's feet in the mud as he was pulled. She was crying, the mother. Everyone was: the children and the mother. Then she zigzagged directly away from us. Men came out of the house after her. They stood laughing, one in his breeches. One of the soldiers pulled out his side arm and shot her in the thigh so she went over. Then they were laughing because of the way she fell and how the baby went forward and landed on its head and then slowly went over and its little feet bounced up. And there are things I'm forgetting to say, I'm forgetting to say how much noise there was coming from the woman and the toddler. The baby too. But I remember the smell mostly, somehow that's in my memory. The smell of mud and stream, smell of the stream. But it's meaningless to relate any of that.

'And then, I'm not certain what they did to the woman, but I imagine. They carried her inside and the other soldiers who hadn't gone into the house stood around looking at each other. Then one was walking straight at us and I don't know why but we just stood there. I don't know how he didn't see us. But he came within three feet of our position and didn't see. He had things he was looking for in the coal house, and he found them. A box with nails and a hammer. Whether he was intentionally looking for them, for those specific things, it is hard to know. But sometimes I think about it. Where his intent lay. Did he know what he was going to do before he did it, or was this toolbox some kind of, I don't know, was it some kind of impetuous –' She pauses, not able to name the thing she wishes to identify. Then: 'I don't know, but I search around in the options, trying to find the nature of this event. I search for motivation.' I hold her arm as she speaks, my other hand on her foot under the sheet. 'A war is a thing of animals, of grunting, fucking animals. What is it, how is

it that they can finish the war and continue? To go home to families, to their own children and know that on a Saturday in 1914 they were at a farmhouse and they took a small child and put him against the wall of the house and began nailing. Hammering as his mother was inside being tortured by men's cocks and fists. They put them through his legs and arms.' She stopped. She breathed slowly, deliberately as if looking for a reason to keep telling me what she was going to say. Her voice a tremor, the susurrant conversation of near grasses. 'The baby,' she says and stops. She cradles her chin in the palm of her hand and looks for a place in the room to rest her eyes which holds no distraction. 'The baby they kicked until it stopped making sound, and then for some time after that. I remember one of the men bending down to pick up the thing by the foot and how the leg and the body separated and how he dropped it. The look on his face, the look of sudden disgust. He shivered and then turned to his comrades and shook again for them – exaggerating his initial revolt like some pantomime. He looked at his hands, as if they meant something or said something, he looked at them and cocked his head as if they were something curious and new.'

'That's the main thing, isn't it?' I say, barely moving my lips. 'The main thing that stays with you.'

'The way he turned and looked at his friends. If they were friends. Do friends do that kind of thing? I have no idea. The way he turned. He looked, his face caught by the revulsion deep in that moment, his eyes retreating and his body shivering and how quickly that deserted him when he deliberately shook himself and then smiled. I think back and I think of his quick shift to a smile. I think how hard it is to fake that kind of thing. So I believe he wasn't faking. There's no undoing who you become. It's the attempts to hide who you were, that's what defines people. I was a teacher and –'

'And the war was only a few weeks old,' I say. I'm no longer looking at her, rather at the sheet hem so delicately sewn, so finely made by deft, intelligent fingers.

'Count the weeks on your hand,' she says.

23

Frantz drags us behind him across the land. He nods to me when he sees me. We can't catch him. We ride for other reasons now. It is clear, has been for some thousands of kilometres.

I feel the move towards it. The road bends, we tend north. We move in an arc through time and history. Soon I will have to remember, I will have to recall. It seems inevitable: memory must arrive out of the land and be part of this ride. Wars have dragged horse and men, carts and guns, artillery and tank and stock and sword and lance and mace and men and the nightmares they die with across fields like these a hundred times. We ride in their wake. I think of the death sentence of the war and how despite the shells, despite the wire, the smoke and gas and the lungs full of fluids and the faces burnt and legs cut in two by thick bullets and the meat men become, how people live on. They take physical form again and again. I fear this, that I have to recall any of this.

France. I am in awe of her. In her cafés and bars I look for men half-broken. I look for men who will speak mad sentences and whisper. I never expected the words I heard when Celia spoke. They sit with me, in my bones as if marrow diseased yellow, a rare sick feeling that can be countered only by higher rituals.

We don't sleep now.

We ride as a pack, the four of us in unison. We feel slow, despite the slowest of our party no longer riding with us. Our bodies do little in the way of making up on lost time. The Alps have taken much from our determination and replaced it with a kind of grey silence. We were rested for a day, but it wasn't enough. A week and we might have begun slowly healing, but only hours were offered. I feel a lag in the connection between my arms and the handlebars, between my fingers and the brakes I wish to tug tight to draw the day to a close, a lag between my capacity for thought and the thought. I am, strangely, enjoying myself.

We come upon a church which we saw from quite some miles out, its steeple pointing to the moon that's distinct in the blue sky since overtaking us through the morning. I hear Percy begin to sing. It's a long melody, and his voice is neither sweet nor good but it is kind and we join in. Humming. There's a game that develops as we head down the country lanes through this lazy wine country. We take turns recalling hymns when we see a new spire ahead. I have a poor memory for song, so I make them up. Appalling words, borrowed melodies. Oppy can harmonise, as can Percy. But together we're blunt with tonsils like wire. Song is self-sustaining, it's everywhere, in all lives, on all roads.

And we'd done something similar, Thomas, Katherine and I, when we finally left the West Coast and drove over Arthur's, then south again into lake country amongst the Southern Alps, though our song was not based on the sudden

arrival of a church steeple, rather the sight of any building we saw rise out of the land. We sang long and in harmony, at least Katherine and I did. Thomas mouthed the words. He mouthed and conducted Katherine and me.

※

Harry is barely with us: diarrhoea, dehydration and sores, these have made him a ghost turning the wheels. I think of what Louvière said last night in my dream, or perhaps not a dream. I suspect I now talk to him quite consciously before I sleep. I open my eyes and he's somewhere near. He said that by the end of the race your brain aches, it hurts as though it has computed the stars', and all the planets', trajectories, their light and their future, then explained it all concisely. It is as if he knows this because he has studied the night sky through a telescope and felt the significance of our narrow horizons. In truth he knows it because he has completed this race and felt the numbness of a mind depleted of its own brain matter; the body begins to eat its own by the time this is done. And Harry's time in the mountains was a particular nightmare, worse than I can conjure in my conversations with Louvière. It has made him quiet like the lie of a ball forgotten in the rough. I ask why he goes on. He shakes his head.

'We stop,' I say.

'I don't stop,' he replies.

'You take the car to the nearest town. Bruce'll drive you,' I say. 'And then. And then from there you take a train to another station. You carry on, eventually you arrive in Paris at the Metro. From there you go anywhere. You mingle amongst the people, the damp platforms.' I stop for a moment and put my hand up to my eyes. The wind wraps around us and sends up dust but we seem to ride through it

as if it were a real tunnel and a shelter from all the elements including the sun. He remains quiet. 'You could be with your wife,' I say. I slip behind him and take his slipstream. I watch his back, his head still. I think of his wife back home, so pregnant that surely his only thought has to be for her, for her and the child's arrival. I ponder that likelihood, her swollen belly, her feet in his leather boots surrounded in snow as she stands at the gate looking off toward the Port Hills from which he will eventually ride. I think of her hearing the milkman's cart making a noise up the street and imagine her stretching her neck to see, but it is only that man slowly coming with his canisters of milk fresh for the homes of the few that live on this last street before the gardens beyond where Harry's parents dig the soil and plant the seeds for the vegetation to grow. And she feels the sigh of her child as it turns in her womb, and Harry feels it too, such is my imagination. Bludgeon me for being a romantic, but I imagine that is what he feels when he looks with his eyes across the plains and our front wheels are pointed south for the brief moments the road is turned from its purpose to take us north. There is a boat in the harbour, ready, waiting. I imagine he is capable of seeing things that the rest of us can only speculate upon.

We ride through the afternoon, the threat of the hills nearby. They remain on our right-hand side, looming as we head down valleys and across chequered plains. At times the clouds shroud the peaks but mostly the skies are clear and we head towards the German border and Strasbourg. We head north. We are the rain in the valleys and we head north.

I'm watching him in thought as he rides. I have an urge to break into his thoughts and stop him from thinking. Tell him something small. Tell him how hungry I am. I whistle, but it sounds out so thin I wonder for a moment what a real whistle sounds like. He only coughs and keeps going.

There is a pain in my chest. A raw twitch. I concentrate on my breathing, as I was told to do not so long ago, a man in robes with a surprising array of English words for a monk. Anapanasati. Anapanasati. We were at Gangaramaya, a temple beside a lake. With our ship paused in Colombo we took to the streets and walked for hours in the heat that had our bodies pouring out all sorts of odours we'd picked up during our horribly idle hours on the *Otranto*. The three of us stood before an array of young Buddhas seated in a gallery overlooking the courtyard. Each made of stone, sitting, staring at us. And we stared back. We watched as if they were seated in a stand, perhaps watching the ongoing pilgrimage of those who came to look and pray. I was reminded of the cricket ground just to the north where we could hear the occasional yell and gasp. A monk came by and spoke to us in a pleasant English. When we told him what we were doing he said to be mindful of our breathing. Anapanasati, he said. The physical mantras that take you outside of the skin that hide muscles and blood and organs. Breath, be mindful of breathing. Anapanasati.

'You ever wonder why we are racing?' I ask. 'You ever wonder?'

'Because we were God–damned invited to. We race because it is the right bloody thing to do.'

'But you wonder, right? We could be anyone. Anyone could replace us. We're just here to remind people there's a race and they're a part of it. We don't matter, interchangeable. Swap us out with any gullible sook. It's the line we draw around France that matters. This is France. We're just reminders.'

'Or, we were just asked and that's why we're here. It's practical to continue. You feel your legs?' he says. 'They're disappearing. Your muscles are fading, you've never been so skinny. Never. That's the wonder. If you think there is a

216

wonder to be had,' Harry says and says nothing more. He seems content to ride in silence. He gazes straight ahead, the road and more road, the ever-unfurling road. Silence is the right of all men, silence and the right to hold it. We pass through hamlets and brief flurries of excitement. We round steeples, we ride into stretches of cloud cover then light. All silent. But suddenly he speaks, he says: 'You've never been so skinny. That's true. Truth is always a lot harder, a lot colder than you want it to be. Truth is always cold. Muscle is running thin. My body is eating its muscle to stay alive.'

'Nasty.'

'You haven't noticed it. You haven't noticed the same?' he asks.

'We're only ever half here anyway,' I say.

'Who said that?' he asks and coughs. I waggle my head as we are overtaken by the Belgians we had seen back in Nice. They have speed and take us on the outskirts of a village before the road turns to cobblestones and threatens to topple us in the turns. They say something but I have no idea what. I hear the word Australia and that is it. They look back at us expecting a response. Oppy is up in front and they exchange words in French. 'Who said that?' he asks again.

'Someone, not me,' I say.

'Well, don't believe everything you think,' he says. 'Not everything. Sounds desperate.'

'I don't even know what it means. Something Marya said,' I tell him.

'Marya? Little sister. How old was she?'

'She was sick. She was dying, I guess. People shouldn't have to go through that. They should just die. How can you trust someone who's dying?' I ask and feel the embarrassment of my comment and my face heats. I spit a dry tangy glob from my mouth. 'Forget about me,' I say. 'I'm in mourning. My body and the rest.'

'You miss your sister?'

'I always miss my sister, I always want her around,' I say. 'But I get you instead. I get Harry bloody Watson. Harry Watson, Mile Eater.'

I watch him nod. Solemn and in time with his pedalling. We ride with such precise rhythm. Our strokes each equal as we are sharing the same gearing. Ratios Louvière gave us back before the mountains. Unused by him, of course, but trusted by us. When I think of things such as this I get the sense we've become part of some greater ritual. Blood, wine. Et cetera. Pain and repeated words. Harry stops pedalling for a moment to laugh and it's a relief. Then says: 'It feels like someone's revenge, this whole thing. What do you think?'

'That you're a bit stupid.'

'Don't say that.' I expect him to laugh again, but he doesn't, instead he puts on a burst of power and we speed, coming out of a bend and into the hill. 'Where's that woman?'

'We don't see each other every day,' I say. In fact I haven't seen her at all today except for a moment, a brief moment as she leant into the interior of the car I've seen trailing behind Discuter, who collected her all the way back in Caen from outside her hotel. I have seen her amongst the men who step from that vehicle, I have seen them talk in slow whispers. But today I only saw her thin back as she leant inwards. I look for her in the crowds but most times there is no one of her description. I told her what I told her, she has been absent since then. Since she told me what she told me. 'I fear she has taken that car from the road, plummeted.'

'That's what this is like. Makes one fearful. You fell in love?' he asks.

'Easily. Look at me, it's what I do. I am a bunch of holes, I'm waiting to be filled up.'

'You want to fill them in with bad loves.'

'She thinks I'm older than I am. She thinks I was here

218

before. She thinks, you know —'

'You were in the war?' He laughs. 'You look older. Since I met you, you've gotten hard in the face. Not kind words but —'

'It's the wind. You got any idea how old the Spanish lad is?'

'You say "lad", so —'

'20.'

'How old does she need you to be?' he asked. 'For you to have fought?'

I shake my head. I don't want to talk any more of her, to hear her voice in my head, for I fear if I do I will repeat all the words she has said. I say it again: they sit within me. Metal and flesh and horror I doubt can be honoured by any kind of remembrance. 'I'm desperate to destroy my body,' I say.

'How is it holding together?'

'It's dandy. I'm not trying hard enough, obviously. Gotta find other means.'

Harry laughs and breathes. He coughs twice, then laughs, and then once more he coughs. As if he has something caught in his throat he keeps coughing. We sail on for a hundred metres and he's still coughing. The road smooth and clean. His eyes pinched. He takes his hands from the handlebars, the bike veers, it heads off the road towards the fence barring the farmland from our wheels. Coughing and more coughing. I shout. He comes back the other way into the centre of the road where the gravel lies in mounds. He jumps off his cycle and stumbles forward whilst his bike continues on its way, its cranks still stirring. He dips into the ditch on the other side of the road. I hear him retching, but I see nothing come from his mouth as I too jump from my machine. Riders behind us skirt our bikes and merge once more. I run to his body bent like a card marked by a

cheat, a trickster. He coughs on and on. I thump his back as I arrive. He punches the air behind him, warning me off. But it is not stopping and I notice the race is slowing for the sake of men staring, watching my friend choking on the air, for it seems there's nothing but oxygen in his throat. His noise is the harshest scratch, like wood dragged through rough stone. Each time I approach he waves me off with a hand. His convulsing body, his lungs rushing to fill with air in the brief moments he is able to halt his rasp, and then, like a carpenter's hammer the harsh wrack continues unabridged as if searching for a perfect melody as it bangs out its rhythm. He kneels in the ditch, beside him the bones and fur of a fox massacred by the wheels of a car angling in the night to the small eyes its driver spies from the wheel and feels the desire for death and blood and ridicule, but Harry doesn't even notice for his life seems to be breaking itself in two, or four, or a thousand as he coughs and coughs, this unending noise attempting to escape his body and show itself to the world.

'Hey!' I shout at those who have stopped to watch. 'Hey!' I hold him and I ignore the decay beside us, I ignore the dank water. He's coughing and making a sound as if trying to speak, as if this is how new words are forged.

In the later hours he tells me it isn't. I argue with him. We fight in a strange language.

24

Airships come near. The width of their shadow leaning over the land, a cigar in the hand of a monster and the clouds seem somehow bigger in its presence. One of many ghosts. I'd never expected to see anything such as this. It is colossal. It will fall quickly if punctured, that's my first thought. We ride beneath, the four of us together barely able to watch the road. I look up hoping to see the controller, but there is only glass darkened by afternoon sky.

A machine built for speed is forever more beautiful than one built for the sake of its own splendour. I'd once heard this claim and Zeppelins prove the argument. Though they seem to lumber, it is the line they take across the land that makes them pure: machines ploughing through the sea of unknown things. They rise past us like the laden thought that the sky may one day be full of these things, lighter than air.

For an hour we don't speak, we don't listen.

※

Beauty: it seems the great placeholder of memory. And sometimes, memories, they take days, weeks, years to come back. Last night as we sat in the warm evening and

a night crippled under a blanket of cloud I was surrounded by some of the remaining touristes-routiers as they sneered at their meals and made jokes of the team members, like us, who struggled to survive. They are poor men, as most are. Working class, peasants who have found a way out of their hard lives by living another hard life on the road. Professionals for whom each race is a way to eat, a way to sleep. They scramble for position at the end of each stage, trying to earn another franc more than their competitors. They despise Nicolas Frantz, hate the fact of his upbringing, his wealth and ability. They would hate me also, if they knew how to ask where I come from. I am no peasant and the only poverty I know is of restraint. These are devout men I describe; they have faces almost scarred by the deep lines that come from furrowing their brows as they race.

I sat with them and listened to them speak. I could pick out words, small phrases, names. I heard them say 'Zeeland'. I let them murmur it and laugh. I heard them say my name and I took wine from their bottles. I ate a loaf of bread and a large round of cheese, which makes me sick, but I could not stop eating it until it was done. It smelt of urine but tasted like a kind of heaven, as if the cows of this area are force-fed salt each half-hour of the day. I washed it back with the red wine that they drank each night. I fell drunk quickly. The room swimming with names; they were telling stories. Old stories. Octave Lapize. He was the first over the Tourmalet, 18 years ago. They spoke of that. One of these riders was there, an aging wreck of a man with little hair and a face like the loose skin of an elbow. He repeated Octave's name over and over, he pointed and gesticulated his way through story after story. I couldn't separate the name and the thought of two strings struck and ringing out simultaneous harmony, it's impossible and I wondered how his name came to be on the lips of his parents when they named him. The first man

over that hump. Lord, and it struck me that I had done the same. That I had ridden over the top of the same cruel col and flown down the far side.

I had, indeed, forgotten the torment of that day. And, I ask you again, is that history? That resonance of the past with the now, is that what we call history? If so, then there is no circularity, just a plainsong sung in the ages.

The night finished with eight of the drunk riders – half of whom revealed they were no longer a part of the race, that they had quit with under a thousand kilometres to run – out in the street shouting curses. Two men yelled and threw rough punches at each other's heads. Their blows glanced and faded. I recognised them and they were the Belgians we had seen in action in Nice. They were weak and neither could make definitive contact with the other. I understood they had replaced members of Discuter, the Spaniard and another. I realised I wanted them to hurt. I wanted them to bleed. They flopped and swung their arms in loose haymakers but rarely touched each other. They flopped, yet, somehow, each managed to break the other's nose, blood dripped onto their shirts as they held each other, a warm embrace but still fighting. I felt a welling of pity, of pain. I had an anger, a cold white anger inside. It seemed aimed at the Spaniard, that little lad out of Catalonia: how he could leave and be replaced by these men when Harry is forced to carry on in agony and Louvière lists in his bed? Punches, drunks. A man cried. Then it spread, five of the group began to weep. Clothes and faces quite drenched. I recalled my moment in Vannes under the odd stare of that peculiar saint and how it came over me, a rush of love and deep sorrow. I wondered: when the moment comes, when love overcomes hurt, what sure thing separates them.

But I was talking about memory and how beauty holds it in place. In Belfort we finished as a group, the four of

us remaining: 23rd place for Oppy, 24th for Harry, 25th and 26th for me and Percy. A kind of soulful jaunt we made across the finish, we linked arms and rode in with our wheels aligned. It was a good showing and my heart was drugged with love at that moment. The crowd that had gathered shouted out our names and I saw Ernie, not for the first time, weeping as he embraced each of us. I wish to share my better self tonight and I do not seek out Celia though I know her hotel's name, I know the room to which I would strut if I so desired. But I have none. Instead I sit with the boys and we yarn of the girls, friends, lovers or family we love so hard and so gently, and quickly it is me who cries once more. I cry at stories the men tell of loves so far distant, so near in their breath I think of Marya, the two of us in the clouds. The two of us on the mountain, the volcano in the middle of the Taranaki.

We once climbed its cone in a summer when the peak was near without snow and the land out beyond utterly clear. We swore we could see the edge of the South Island, so light was the atmosphere. To the east the gigantic hulks of Ruapehu, Ngauruhoe and Tongariro. They waved in the thermal energies that rose across the land. Marya removed her boots and socks and put her hands in the air. She reached out, her feet and toes stretched like her fingers. Her hands above her head as if she were carrying the sky, or something large of the sky. She hummed and I saw her eyes close. The immensity of distance seemed broken, even if just for a short time, an instant, a moment. And a moment long enough to know something with complete precision, that was what her face seemed to show. She held something inside the instant and let it fill her. I recall our times on the mountain effortlessly with this at its centre; warm, blue and undying. It was 1916, November. Thomas had been gone for close to two years. Two more and she'd be no longer. I cry and

the men watch how my hands quiver, shake with the presence of loss.

<center>※</center>

We are in the land of old irredentist hope, Alsace-Lorraine. Today we crossed the front for the first time, but I'm not aware until Bainbridge mentions it at the bar. There's an old sadness in Ernie now, as if his departure from the race delivered to him a knowledge containing the absolute nature of defeat. I can see it in the way he seeks solitude by making others question the point of our continuation by his mere presence, then offering no answer for even himself. He informs us of our place on the map and I realise something unsettling.

It's the gentle rolling hills that get me, the undulations that seem quite unlikely to hide armies and artillery and guns. I grew up with the names of ridges and towns inked into memory: Messines, Vimy, Verdun, Flanders. I had imagined great rising lands, precipices to conquer and fortify, but I am reminded that their part of the war was a front of gentle mounds on the apron of some poor farmer. It was desperation that made these hillocks into mountains, these gentle rises into great ridgebacks on which life was fought and held. I saw nothing as we rode through. No sign of life or death. Instead I daydreamed, I daydreamed and missed it all.

We arrived to another medieval sight. Strasbourg in the afternoon. Now, we walk over ponts couverts from tower to tower. We walk in streets surrounded by white homes with such distinctive black trim, buildings so old now I fear who might believe they have ownership. Surely nobody could claim such a thing of something so old. Percy keeps looking

<center>225</center>

at the river; he keeps saying it's the Rhine. Opperman argues with him and they come to the conclusion they don't know. There are rivers everywhere and, when they ask, they hear only German in reply.

I speak to Harry and Harry knows what it is we are looking for: a cracked stream, a burst wall, anything to break the beauty of this place.

The road seems broken in places, as if chalk marks scrubbed out by an invisible hand, then reappearing once more, furrows where the horses have dragged their carts and men have stood alongside shouting in a language only horses nod at and make noises back to. We are a song and we ride humming.

But I am lagging. It is a short leg but I am behind. 115 miles. I believe Percy and Oppy are in front, somewhere, some distance of probably miles. But here is Harry, he fell off the back of the rest of the team early on. He's coughing violently, I ride beside him, his head on my shoulder at times as I put my arm around him. An hour folds in on itself as if in the blackened hands of a typesetter compiling the words as we speak, making the octavo fold before the cut to make the page. I puncture on the outskirts of Saverne and I ride on like that for two miles until the sound of it in the forests before the Vosges becomes too apparent. I only stop when he calls out my name. I toss my machine into the dirt at the side of the road. He circles around and I know he cannot stop, that if he stopped it would be for good. I tell him I will catch him up. But I never catch him. I dawdle through the hills and find no one back in the reaches of my periphery to harry me forward.

Geldhof of Louvet dropped out after yesterday's ride from

Belfort to Strasbourg so the official count now is 60, 60 of us left, possibly less, certainly no more. Today it is my turn to carry that number on my back. Number 60.

I see a house shape amongst rubble. I see limbless trees. I stare and try to recall the lines on maps I used to read and think where the artillery stood that rendered these things so. I look to ridges and stands of trees for an inkling. You see how nature starts to remember and force its way out of the cracks and chunks of masonry, limbs of trees wriggling out of stems from seeds and pointing their leaves at the sun, you watch and then you ride on into the hills where they once made trenches across gully and spur.

On the outskirts of the coming town I keep vigil, my eyes on the churches for a grotto, for a blind Mary. I hope I won't leap off my bike and run in and look, but I can't promise myself anything. I know I would want to see her face, just to see if there is any connection between the two: Mary Mother of God and Marya my little sister standing atop a mountain, a volcano, a southern Vesuvius. They look quite the same, I'm sure.

25

Metz and I hit the bridge and the signs of a city become apparent. The railway lines bunch and rattle the bike so my arms are made numb. A man signals for me to turn and I pass by lines of housing on my left, a high brick wall of what I imagine is a prison on my right. I think decisively that I will not be able to finish the stage. That I should crawl against the stone and sit resting my head and let Bruce and Ernie pick me up out of the grass. I coast. I remember the stories of men in the early years being dragged by wire, a length of it tied securely to the rear of their support vehicle, a cork at the other end on which they bit with their teeth. I imagine the same and let myself be pulled by the idea of it, the rubber-like wood. I bite the cork and head on to a new river's edge. In the end I am the final shadow to see the sight of it, the glow of Saint-Étienne de Metz high above the river. The afternoon is full of dark clouds, but the windows are bright with the gigantic glow coming from inside the cathedral. A grand throb of light held in the globe of an ancient chapel. Behold this thing. Do not step back. I spit the cork; all symbol tastes sour at such a sight. I wonder if Louvière has seen this. I'll ask him in my dreams what he said to himself at the sight of it.

Harry and Oppy take me from my bike whilst I am still pedalling. I know I am crying. I know that all about me men cry. I take on water but throw it up. They hold me up at control and I sign at my name. I write, 'This Man Died Three Hours Ago.' The officials don't blink at the extra syllables.

I sit with the boys at the side of the courtyard where we have gathered. There I open my musette and pull out what food I haven't consumed on the road. I find a raw egg still in one piece, I crack it and swallow the contents. One gulp. I slowly come back as water is put into my system. I hear how Opperman punctured once, Osborne twice, each waited for the other in the verges as the sun grew larger. How they lost two minutes at the gates of a railway crossing closed against them. They rode together over the finishing line with their arms locked: 19th, 20th. Hubert is now in 17th in General Classification, a slip by one place. What could have been if he'd some real riders, not us sick men in need of sleep, water, food, bed and home, in need of him to drag us to the end. To think of this is to think of other worlds.

I hear Frantz was penalised for interference, but still he held on to win the stage. He and Leducq scrapping it out. It's another race they ride. I've seen a photo of the two of them from last year. Their arms around each other as they ride, great smiles, great friends by the look. But I know this is not true, can't be true.

I drink wine in the evening. I lie on a bench and listen to Oppy. He is one full of facts and he gives a new one each day for my book of wonders. This is the town from which Gregorian chants arose, where voices found their invention in the back of monks' throats. He has a slight look of joy when he offers these morsels up, as if in each word he gains karma and deeper worth, and I don't doubt it. At each new

town his fight to keep alive in this race is celebrated, the number of lips that have grazed his cheeks are uncountable. I ask him what they sound like, these chants. He shrugs for me. Gives a full French shrug with his bottom lip protruding and Percy puts his arm around his shoulders. It is a quiet evening, one of candles and half-light.

Tomorrow is a short run to Charleville, a distance of 86 miles. We will be riding out at 10am. An easier day by some kind of measurement and I'm not concerned for my late night wandering. I walk back to where the racing was completed and soon find the street lit up enough that I know the direction I must follow. I find myself walking towards the great lantern above the waters' run. I come closer and the building seems to grow, to loom as if the walls of a sheer valley carved by glacier and time. From this angle it seems the church is built on top of the five-storeyed buildings I can see beneath. I walk slowly then feel myself rushing uphill; I fear the cathedral is about to shut out its lights and close its doors. I can hear singing, the shuddering harmony of a massed choir. It diminishes and rises up. It seems to float, so much glass lifting it, and it seems floating in the air out over the river. Each wall constructed by the spectral array of stained-glass windows spilling out the light of how many thousand candles. I try to hurry as I come to the lane that puts you at its doors.

I run my hand along the surface of the exterior of stone, almost a millennium since it was put down here, a thousand years after the man it honours walked about the desert land of Palestine and Judea. I have no concept of history, I have no means to consider its depth. Nothing this old touches the earth in our land, nothing we have made. Only mountains and trees reach this far back, and even those we have turned into other things, ships to take us away from the island, buildings to lift us up. No man had set foot on our shores

when this was put in place. This stone upon stone. I touch the doors, I enter the cathedral.

Hundreds standing in the mass. Somehow I have no problem hearing the words coming from the far end at the apse. I look up in the nave and feel a giddy rush. The roof is impossibly high. I walk softly to the aisle on the gospel side where the congregation is sparse, I have my hands out, feeling for the pews. I sit as the congregation sits in a rumble of shifting wood and shoes.

I watch proceedings, the priests at the front distributing incense and the smell of it is quickly everywhere and I wonder where it originally came from, what part of the world gifted that particular technology to this ritual. The liturgy begins, the tone of rich words so many times spoken. No one looks around, all eyes to the front, though some seem not to focus, faces limp, others smiling and others still frowning, the deep lines of concentration, the moods of many as we heed the word.

There, off to the side, are the robed figures; I'm guessing the descendants of Oppy's chanting monks. They blend in here, seem quite a fixture as if statues or carvings in wood. Each face hidden behind the shadow of their hoods. Gradually I realise you don't look for faces, for eyes and features; you take them as a whole, as another mass within the mass. Sacraments themselves. They are the low hum in response to the presiding priest's recitation.

I listen and understand nothing. But my ignorance is trivial and extraneous, as if the invisible thing of a child's complaint. It's the fact the words are said. It's not the words so much; it's the extraordinary fact they are spoken at this moment, at this time, in this place alongside this carving under these windows in this light. This physical instant. Latin, Greek, French, rhythm and the stage. Here's the blood, here's the bread. I sit through the moments when the

congregation are seated, I arise when they get to their feet. The choir stands and they open their mouths in harmony. Colossal, massed. There are boys singing in robes. The whole building rumbles with the sound. Nothing separates me from the voices, certainly not comprehension, that is the last thing I need to be concerned about. It is in this moment, this physical moment, that these words come the nearest they will ever be to having a relationship with the hard edge of physics. That is the effect. Germ-like, hopping from breath to mouth, breath to mouth. All a remedy for miles, for the invisible miles and the distances we make.

Don't believe everything you think.

The singing gathers once more, a swelling that reaches around you, holds the small elements of yourself in the whole of the cathedral. This is the sound of hope on a scale that lurks over mountains and divides seas. The things of religion: they are the relics of the great lost love story. Hope and song and the nearness of dreams. Everyone here is hope, hope surrounded by hope. The song of a thousand-strong voices willed by the promise of victuals and drink, by the collapse of the chasm over which faith makes its bounds. Somewhere within it I hear a voice. A note whose timbre sits alone above or below, or beside the rest. I look around for a mouth, the face emptying out this familiar tone. It is so close, I look down rows, I peer over heads, over families, over young men separated from the young women and children dressed so fine. I see two riders from the Tour, I see five more and I put up my hand to wave, though I don't wave. Faces flicker in the candlelight, men holding on to notes they can't hear but for the mass they are within. Then something, something else. An ear, a neck, a shoulder. I hear a voice apart from the others, a breach in the side of all this sound. Slowly she turns, a book of hymns in her hands, her mouth open so I can see it is her breaking the song.

Through the last three days I have ridden without white pills, the cocaine, without the help of the ephedrine, and my body has felt the weight of itself, the weight of its damage. My knees are weakened, the muscle weary and (as we keep saying) eaten at by our inability to make them anew. Tendons seem to sag and ache. I drink constantly to rehydrate but it seems to have no effect; the weakness expands. Celia has me lie on the bed. I do not remember how we made our way here, though I recall voices. She certainly would've needed help: if I did not walk, she did not carry me. I have not mentioned her size. But she is small. For her to have carried me she'd have to be part monster.

We eat slowly a meal of fruit and nuts and berries. She orders a salmon and it arrives under a silver dome.

I can't decide to ask her whether she has ever been to Algiers, or whether it was a kind of lie to make me love harder.

We speak, I'm talking. I say to her: 'At a dance. 1919, I think.'

'You think?'

'I believe so. No. '18. It was 1918.'

'She's your wife.'

'She's my wife.'

'A dance, where?'

'Out of the town, on the coast in a little town hall. My younger brother took me there.'

'Little brother. How old?'

'He sat me in the shadows and I was bleeding. Had been bleeding.'

'Show me where –' She puts her hand on my face.

'An hour before he collected me from the pub where I

was fighting. Outside, I was fighting. He collected me and took me home and had me bathe and change into a suit and he took me there. He must have been 16. I didn't speak, I didn't know how to speak, not yet. Speech was cold and not moving my mouth. Katherine was there. I saw her in the light of the dance hall and the band played and she walked around in her dress, the pleats made it seem she was walking on air, which I guess is the desired effect. I can't say.

'It was winter so the only thing keeping us warm in that hall was bodies, a hundred or so bodies in this little wooden hall with a band with a violin, a piano, a banjo, and boy with a drum and some brushes. My brother went to her first. He asked if she would dance with me. What a thing for a little brother to do. He was covered in spots, the kind that later make your face hard when the sores empty out and scar. She was sitting, I remember that. Perhaps it was out of sympathy but she agreed, I can't say why, but he took her hand and she stood up and put her arm under his elbow and he walked her over to me. She took my hands and asked me if I would like to dance. Which I know is forward, which I know should not have happened, but she did it and we danced slow in the hall. That was the first time I met her. She let me cry in her hair. Or maybe that was the next time. Maybe that was in 1919, when I saw her next.

'My brother took me home and that night I saw Marya walking in the hall, she went into the kitchen and came out again. She seemed quite awake and I tried to talk to her, but she gave nothing in reply. She was quite oblivious to my presence. Some days I want to go to her and stand with her, but that can't happen anymore.'

'Come back to England with me, when this is done,' she says and lies back again. 'Come back and stay for a while.'

'You're from England then,' I say.

'Thereabouts. When did you get married?' Celia asks,

and rolls so she is facing me. She's been on her back and and I liked talking with her in that position; lying supine together seems to be the place from which stories come.

'It was later. First the war ended. I heard it on the wireless. Dad and Mother and the rest of the family were in Wellington at my uncle's house. They were there for two weeks and I walked the house alone for hours at a time. I would walk from the lounge to the dining room. From the kitchen to the lounge to the parlour, from the dining room to Marya's room. From my room to my parents'. From the kitchen to the parlour. From the parlour to Marya's room. From Marya's room to my room. I made sure I covered every variation I could. It was how I passed the days. I listened to the wireless at noon until dusk as I walked, the volume dialled full in the dining room where the radio sat. Each day I made the journey about the house, making the exploration complete. I'd listen to the reports from Europe, the day-old news. I'd listen to the predicted dates of return for the infantry. I waited on those days. On the particular invasion of the town by the town's very inhabitants who had been gone for all those months and years. I waited for men like me to return.'

'Where was Katherine?'

'I have no idea. Somewhere at her parents' house I believe. We didn't see her again until March, she wasn't in my mind, maybe my brother's, not mine, not yet. I was waiting on the end of the town's empty years, that's how it felt during those months since I had come home from Scotland. Empty and waiting. Waiting for empty men like me. My family returned and they were cautious around me. I felt it. The end had come and they were cautious around me. Finally the first men returned and I went to the train station to watch them come off the rail. Men like me. I drank with them when they arrived. Men like me. I fought with them.

I hugged them, we drank all the beer in the White Hart there was to drink. I stood on the upstairs balcony and swayed with men still with their sea legs making them unsteady. Men full of illness from the front. From the ships. A lot of the men were sick, but what was I to care? I embraced them. We poured beer on one another, we danced to invisible music running through the crowd. If we sang, I recall no tune. It was summer then, and everything spread like a fire in scrub.'

'And that, that was how Marya, that was how she died? The flu?'

'Aha. That's how she died. Or, close enough. Irresponsibility and idiocy. Two things, they always play their part. My family had returned. I came home from the White Hart and I must have stunk but I came home and I walked about the house. I started walking like I did. I was tracing my steps from the kitchen to the parlour and that's when I saw her. She was standing in the middle of the hall looking I don't quite know where. I went to her and stood in front of her. I watched her and put out my hand and she took it. I moved close to her and I put my arms around her and held her. It must have been for a full two minutes. I held her. I whispered in her ear and she whispered back. She opened her eyes. She was the only one. The only one I came close to killing in that whole war. They call it the Spanish flu, but really, it must have been born out here, somewhere out here.'

'And she screamed?'

'She screamed,' I say. 'She screamed and God, if the house didn't wake up.'

26

She screamed. That's what I told Celia. But that isn't quite true. I stated it for effect, for the sound of the word, to match her story of Louvière screaming at her Mary. That's how we make narratives: we put like with like and damn the rest. I told Celia the hours of Marya's sickness were uncounted, as if halted, or slowed, the speed it reached deep into her body and hard chill that made tremors on her skin. She shivered like a solemn music, a minor cadence closing in on its coda, the song at the end of songs. She died so quickly I couldn't count. But Thomas could. And whether she screamed or not, to me it sounded like a line from a music not yet written.

I told her this and then I slept. I slept until 8:30 at which point she woke me with a hand on my back. The cool of her fingers down my spine. We spoke no more of Belgium, no more of the things that follow her. Once is enough, the topic's absence seemed to imply, once and that is all. I walk now to my room and collect myself, feed myself. Soon I am back with my team. We are at the start, the four of us and Ernie looking tense, despite the ease of us now. There are only four stages left, no mountains they have told us of, just cobblestoned roads and the end and the remains of the end.

Today we are last off the line and we watch the other teams prepare for their ride out under the stare of dim stained glass

looking down from Saint-Étienne de Metz. I'd tried to find out the name of the mass I had entered last night, but had no luck. In this morning it seems empty, a firepit after the feast. Whatever I underwent in the nave under the voices, the ice-like robbery of my heart and thoughts, it was gone, snuffed, vanished. La Lanterne du Bon Dieu, that was all I found out about the cathedral, its nickname for the locals who must see it every day and walk past its doors and empty wings.

A woman circulates. She has an urn of coffee and a couple of small cups from which men take in a gulp, putting their hands to their mouths as the liquid scalds their tongues. I take a hit and make a meal of it and end up spitting it out on the cobblestones. The woman bursts out laughing and says something and I nod and laugh with her and I am briefly taken back to the start of all this, the beginning at Paris, the young woman who leaned forward from the crowd and caught my and our attentions. I wonder where she is at this precise moment, I wonder if she has followed our movements around the map they publish in *L'Auto*, whether she looks for our names beneath the pictures they publish, whether she ever swooned at the recklessness of all this. I wonder because it is something I find myself doing. I think back at the Alps, the Pyrénées and that is all I am able to do, think. My imagination does not allow me to recreate it any more than it does my brother's days in the pit. The woman pours me another cup and I sip it gently and smile for her and watch her become demure, an act I'm sure. One built to make a man's knees quiver. Everything, eventually, turns to myth.

She moves off and continues her mission with the coffee, laughing and joking with all the men. I see Discuter. I have come to understand something about the Belgians. The man Celia goes to see, who rides the blue car, a Mercedes I am now told, he manages riders and races. The Belgians come

under his wing when not in this race. I haven't been given a name, but Celia has explained he used to ride, has ridden the Tour, used to battle with Louvière as often as anyone. The Belgians stand with the rest of Discuter. I haven't seen them on the road for a few days as we have been at the opposite end of the schedule. I have the urge to relieve myself and ask Percy to hold my bike. I run into the café from whence the woman had arrived minutes before. I find myself in the toilet and emptying everything in a horrid rush of black devilish tang. I feel light-headed and step out into the café where several men have gathered. One lifts a glass of red wine as a kind of salute as I come past. I nod and grin and he signals to the man behind the bar and soon I have a glass in my hand. The smell of a deep rich red and I gulp it down and everyone laughs and I shake the man's hand and head back.

I thank Percy and he looks at me and asks if I am all right. I eventually nod. My stomach is raging up but I don't believe there is anything more to give. I dare not look around for the fear of catching someone's eye, but that is precisely what I do. It's the Spanish lad standing with his bike, red cheeks glowing in the fresh morning. The quick shutter of eyelids as he sees someone else in the crowd. He calls out to this person he seems to know, making a hand into a fan that waves. The boy's back in the race and the air is cold. I say something but it is just distorted air.

Percy is talking and I'm not listening, and then I am and he's saying, 'Bring us back a bottle next time, mate. I know it's early, but for the love of Christ.' He's facing in the direction of the mademoiselle from the café. She is laughing, letting André Leducq tell one of his jokes, letting him stand near with his arm about her waist so her bosom is against his chest. I like Leducq. He once said through Hubert that I reminded him of a duck, a plucked duck still swimming.

I had just finished my lap at Marseille and was high as an eagle stretched out on the tips of its wings glaring down at the two of us. I laughed and he laughed, a ripe rip of sound that stirred those around us. Now I look back at the Spaniard and he too is watching the Frenchman, but he isn't smiling. He has seen me, I realise, and he knows I am not laughing.

I stand staring from under the view of the cathedral's great panels of dark glass. All eyes on us, all cheers for our pluck as we get on our bikes to ride. I give glances to Percy, just to see if he notices how empty a lantern can be when you put out its light.

❖

It's near Charleville that I first notice the oddity. The startled colours of Alcyon-Dunlop: four riders, three domestiques and the yellow jersey, Frantz. I can see it is him, even from 200 metres back, the shape of shoulders, the aspect of his form, the shine of yellow. Over 19 stages, plus the other races run, we come to recognise the way men ride. I am used to seeing this pack, this jersey in the middle of four or five men moving away from me, but now they are slowly coming closer. I am a magnet, I am riding well, but still, this is as unlikely as a creek rising in the heat of a drought. And there, out beyond them, is Opperman. I know his lonely shape better than any rider's now.

Four hours ago we'd departed Metz and entered the Ardennes behind Discuter who themselves were following on from Alcyon. I am yet to see the Spaniard or any of his team members – they too must have passed by this strange sight. At the exit of every corner I seem to be gaining ground. I suspect Frantz to be ill or injured, his teammates helping him along by making a gap in the air, a pocket within which he can ride without interference. The flu has wrecked many

240

in the peloton, made good men and great riders grotesque with vomiting and fits of coughing; you see them hunched, faces screwed up, each weeping like a baby shoehorned into a stiff boot. I make an assumption that this has taken hold in Frantz. I desire to pounce.

I force my pace running beside a wide river I have not yet named. I straighten my angles and pierce the air. Then cobblestones. There is no comfort in the ride, pain that vibrates until you're numb. Despite this, against this, I find rhythm. I'm a song, ragtime running through me.

We hit the medieval haze of Mézières, its fortifications leaning towards us across the bridge, in its centre another looming cathedral, but with thanks we do not approach but angle to the right down towards what appear to be government buildings. We are deep within occupied territory now, this is the crossroads where the Americans came and fought, this is where the last battles were hammered. I know this: I was told last night how Mézières and Charleville combine at this river. Water and steel merge here and so too did the Germans and Yankees.

Now I too am merging with them as they come closer. We clatter over the cobblestones towards the end and I feel them near my wheel.

The river seems to be everywhere in the town, cutting back and forth, circling mounds of land and then under bridges old and older than I can say, a canal from what I can make out on my right. And here, here we slow. The rubble of some crushed building still apparent these ten years later means we slow more than we would normally for the next corner and the next corner after that. Bombardment marks out the shape of a town and leaves little else. But they stay, the towns. So too do the streets, their borders having been wiped clear, but they remain intact on maps kept in sacred rooms locked until a city must be redrawn on burnt land.

All scrolls are sacred when all else is forgotten. We are riding slowly because it is hard to race at the site of broken things.

A bridge once more and a marshal points right a few blocks along. I am racing again, hard into a breeze. Alcyon, pushing. The invisible mile, the shift as the distance becomes nerves, tendons and blood. Pain becomes a mantra, an index running through your body. Frantz pedalling at a curiously faster rate. There the small stadium; there voices call out and shimmer about us. We break into the structure and onto the track. I'm riding on the tail of Nicolas Frantz and I hear the sound they save for him. His gravity pulls the crowd around so all eyes and voices are concentrated on us, each breath is gauged to shout outwards, each iris glints and stares. Each eye looks and we are dragged forward in a sprint, our breathing focused on pumping oxygen into our blood and rushing it into our muscles. Louis de Lannoy sways outwards, blocking the inside running on the top circle and my hand comes off the handlebars and I shove at his hip and pull on his shirt and feel myself go round him, I don't look at him but I am aware I sound like a bull as I shunt every bit of juice down into my limbs and feel the spin of my wheels. Louesse comes at me, weaving, so I am forced into the outside of the track, but I don't take the outside of the track, I dip into the coming turn and into their pack, five of them, hungry and near the end. We make grunts, curious noises, sharp groans only we know the meaning of.

'You filth, you fucking come on,' I say to no one. I feel pornography in my voice, a shout of base terms. 'Fucken, fucken, fucken,' like a bad train. Elbows slam at my kidneys and the roar is everywhere, it does not stop. Flags.

Frantz shouts. 'Look at me. Look at my bike.' I thrust a hand backwards, once, twice into de Lannoy's mouth and I momentarily feel the hard white of his teeth and the flesh of his gums. 'Fuckers,' I shout. I feel a fingernail against my

242

eyeball and someone grabs at me. I close my eyes. I close my eyes and I don't care how hard I have to ride. I turn and spit and see the glob land in Louesse's ear and I note how he winces and I am standing on my pedals and Frantz is at my side. 'Ride, you fucker,' I say. The crowd standing, the entire expanse of people standing, the ebbing rumble of their voice that stands too, as if summoned by some drunk priest to their feet. Flags. Australian flags. The sound of how many thousand, the way they hear the man next to them, the way breath is voice and the way it cracks the air when you hit the line and my wheel is in front of a man who can't be beaten.

We coast together, Frantz and I, we let the momentum of the sprint flow us back around the track. To brake would be to dismiss the effort that took us here. We let gravity and the air in our faces slow us. Our speed slowly unwinding, the din sustained on a plateau, its pitch somehow deeper. Australian flags, hundreds of them. I wave as Hubert must have a few minutes earlier. My name, my city: these are shouted at me and I laugh and wave and nod. Frantz claps my back and I feel at ease to smile for him. I turn and I look. I finally see, I see what he wants me to see and I suddenly know what he was pointing at and I hear the crowd burst and rain clapping hands upon us and the way it slowly falls away and the way time slows as they say it slows and the way the stomach goes empty, the way the mind seems empty and I believe I know the hollow, the pit men go to when they are utterly alone.

Finally he dismounts and I too step from my machine and I go to him and stand beside him. We both look at his bike, it is not an Alcyon bike. It is not a man's bike. It seems half-sized, though it's not. It is a woman's bike with small cogs made for the village, its handlebars a simple set for riding upright, its seat sprung for comfort and its frame angled so a

lady might not undo her honour as she dismounts. A hollow there, and a hollow in my body and I know not how to fill it until I remember to breathe and what the man in Colombo had said. Breathe, be mindful of breathing.

I stammer my name at control and sign after a long pause thinking what else I could do with my time. All this time I have wasted turning muscle into air, turning time itself into speed, turning it into long dreams and prayers to no one but myself and the dead. The gap I closed merely an illusion of distance passed. Perhaps I could holiday now, perhaps in the places I have passed but not been able to describe. Provence and Nice la Belle and Mouton, Bordeaux I have barely mentioned. Places I promised Marya in the hours before she went. Perhaps England, perhaps home on a trip through to North Africa. I sign and turn and the Spanish boy leans behind me. He reaches for my hand at my side and I wince, I squeeze one eye shut and realise I have no words for him. I breathe hard through the back of my sinuses and my mouth fills with mucus. The people around me keep smiling though they should really turn away.

That night I walk in the town. The bridges across the river double back and back again before heading off into the Ardennes. I walk in what I believe to be circles as I keep crossing a bridge. I convince myself I am lost, but I'm not. I convince myself that I will soon walk into a café and look someone in the eye and they will stab me and I will turn and fall out the door and I'll cry out, arms flailing, and someone will come to me and I will not have to race anymore. But I am not lost and there is no man waiting with a knife, no man waiting anywhere. I walk the site of the old town hall

which is a field of rocks and masonry. I'm not sure what I am looking for, perhaps the idea of the building. I was told what used to be here, how impressive it was, but now is wasteland. I pick up a piece of rock and look close and see part of the edge of a letter. I rub it clean and put it in my pocket.

He hit the level crossing at pace did Frantz, snapped his frame. East of Longuyon is where he went down. Things happened quickly. Arguments with his support, with management, with marshals. In the end he saw a woman with a bicycle and persuaded her to give him the machine with the promise of money. The bastard rode the last hundred kilometres, two-thirds of the stage, on this undersized bicycle. His lead dropped by 30 minutes, but he is still leading the race. I barely beat him in the sprint.

I find myself welcomed back into old thoughts, old events: the day my brother knocked my tooth out on the banks of a river flowing out to the sea. The day of the Classic out of Timaru. I recall how I was caught by the wind as I struggled north towards Christchurch and the aerodrome. Somehow I found it easier riding into the face of the gale. I was able to find an even pace that I suspected others would struggle to match. But then the bridge and the sight of metal raging towards us.

The bridge was a dual apparatus for both rail and road. Cars, horses and trains shared the one lane. And so it was that it served us on our two wheels racing north in the heated wind. The truck that came at us was headed for a local farm, coming from another such station just a little further north. The race officials hadn't a chance to see it or halt it, nor warn it of our presence, nor had they the chance to tell us of its approach. It came down upon us. Riders in front leapt from their machines as they hit the bridge. They dived into

the shallow river and their bikes were crushed. The noise, the rupture of metal. I veered off into the gravel at the river's side barely in time before the truck took me into its radiator and swallowed me and spat me like a pip. Goats who had fallen from the truck and landed only moments before I'd come off the bank writhed in the grass. I heard no noise. I saw blood, I saw bone and the way it went through their hides. They were newly shorn. They moved in a slow, slow animation, as if something had grabbed time by the scruff of its neck and yanked it backwards. Everything slowed, time winding down. I felt the air become thick and my body become light. I could make out extraordinary detail in the air beside me, the mites of dust, the insects which fought their way through such air. Everything about me seemed simultaneous. Everything seemed linked to a time in the future. I veered and shut my eyes so the goats stopped bleeding for a moment and leant my bike so I passed into the river's bed beside the rush of its real waters and rode until I came to a narrow patch. I jumped from my seat and ran into the stream with my bike over my head. I hardly noticed the torrent, I found a path made by stock and went across the breadth of the waterway until I was back on the other side and I rode on at a deadly pace, my body weightless, my head clear like the chime of a bell undiminishing.

My pace remained solid and consistent. As riders went behind me, I realised I had been counting. That all the riders who had overtaken me in the early parts of the race – O'Shea, McNamara, Gerry Aintree, the dozen or so scratch riders – fewer than eight remained. I had overtaken them once more, swallowed them up. I found myself in a zone of strange gratitude for something. It wasn't possible that I was this fast, but I suddenly, unexpectedly, was.

The whole way I spoke, the whole way I mumbled out loud to my sister. I mumbled her name over and over.

Inch by inch, syllable by syllable I said her name. It raced with me out of that strange blue air as if she was going to come and walk alongside me. When everything went still, as it all slowed down, as those poor animals broke themselves on the rocks, all memory seemed present and ever ready.

And I try to remember that now: the detail, the way all slowed and all became light and power. I try to recall and feel I need another voice to explain it to me, another voice to remember for me. I think this because the only way I can imagine ever winning this race, ever placing higher than a loser battling against a champion on a borrowed machine is through the memory of another. Another in another time recalling this time; this time ever present in my time.

At the hotel Harry is on his bed and I tell him Ernie might return to the race. He doesn't say anything. He shakes his head.

'What do you think about that?' I ask.

'I'm thinking we should sleep.'

'I'm going to find Louvière and tell him to join our team. We'll be a force.'

'Invalids and old men,' he says, barely audible.

'After Paris they're going to be handing out a pension,' I say. 'You won't have to worry about your wife and kids. Everything is in hand.'

He laughs, but it is a laugh without purpose unless its purpose is to shut me up. There are souls I can't resent, can't despise, no matter how much I love them. An hour later it is dark and I lift him off the bed. I tell him he needs to come with me. That he needs to see what we are going to see.

Part 3

27

Hours before dawn. We drive. On the cobblestones the tyres struggle for grip. We skid and the vehicle goes looking for traction and resists our slide. Celia handles the wheel. Farmland, villages and the smell of animals. The threat of being lost under the dark sky and the faith I put in her memory to get us there and return us before we ride out. This is the way we move westward, slipping, gripping, speeding.

I lie back staring at the stars between the clouds wrestling with one another for space in the strata. She speaks and I listen and sometimes I respond. Her usual soft voice replaced with a shout against the wind. A nervousness: despite never having exhibited nerves in my company, she is now nervous. She admits it: 'Some things are certain to make you edgy,' she says. She has to shout over the ruinous sound of the Citroën's engine. Her accent becomes stronger, forced out. 'I watch kids get on the tram and I get nervous for something. They shout and sing and the way they seem so certain. Which is probably it, certainty. I am fearful around certainty. Isn't that the thing about childhood, certainty? Adulthood is one long comedown from utter faith. We're always trying to get it back, somehow get it back. Search out for fates in odd places, but no. Poof, it is gone.'

'This makes you angry?'

'Nothing makes me angry. I just am. It's the French way.'

'You're not French, Celia.'

'No matter,' she says and she doesn't pause to laugh. 'You say the Spanish boy, that he has rejoined the race.'

'Did you see him? He's quite refreshed.'

'And that is upsetting. I find it upsetting. I don't race. I have no idea what this is like. But I find it upsetting.'

'If you're out. Plain and simple, you are out.'

'So that makes me angry,' she says. She thumps the steering wheel with the heel of her hand. It seems to shudder on longer than expected and she grasps it as if the car were out of control. 'There should be a rule. One rule. Just one. Either you're in or you're out. Fair? Yes?' She looks at me for agreement; she finishes her smile with a scowl. I have nothing in the way of argument, so I nod. 'He deserves a spanking. If men like Louvière. If he can't ride – well, your Spaniard deserves a spanking.'

We have been driving for an hour, and now she drives hard with this thought tapping away in her mind. She has barely stopped talking. Unusual for her to go on like this, but it doesn't seem out of place. Which is precisely the oddity I accused my brother of beside the Waimakariri those years ago. I accused him of talking. What a thing. He had always been sullen before Marya went, always unwilling to share before the war. But after it all, after we buried her he became something else. He slowly began to talk and gesticulate, he became easy with those around him. Perhaps after his marriage, perhaps then he had started to talk, perhaps he eased into it. None of it is easy to grasp: the dates, times, the moments when he moved from one person into another. But it happened and it was only after our night in Fox that I began to notice. He learnt to speak comfortably and without end. At the river I used the word

'normal'. I said: 'You talk. You talk and you sound, you sound out. I don't know. People talk. People say things and I think they're trying to make things, they're normalising. That's what I'm saying. People repeat things, over and over and, and you make incredible things orderly, ordinary. Say nothing. When you say nothing and it doesn't feel so simple. None of it is simple. None of it.' And such was his response. Such was his response I bled and staggered forth and swung my own fists like a rag doll held in the fist of a fool. Now Celia speaks and I wonder why I don't feel the same urge to sacrifice my adoration by asking her to be quiet. Especially with the thought of her and Louvière walking together through Belgium. That he makes the 'we' in her narrative. There is a truth hidden in there somewhere. I tune back into her, looking at her face then back at the approaching land. Her voice fading in and out with the hit of engine and wind.

'There was a time when I was a teacher,' she is saying. 'You know this? I taught in a public school, young women. I taught mathematics and history. My résumé is impressive if you want me to list it. The years were part horror and part joy. You know that too by now, what I have told you. It is possible, and I think I proved it, to earn the love of girls of that age, believe it or not. When I was 15, 16, 17, I believed love was some cruel pledge, that it was something to prod us into adulthood, that threatened thing at the end of those years. That thing at the end of certainty. I went looking for men to prove me wrong, I suppose, do you know that, that I did that? To wrong me, just so I could point at them and laugh. I wanted to stand over them, but it didn't end well for me. I was at university when I met Louvière. A group of us were travelling through the south by train and boat.'

Harry murmurs from the back seat, a blanket pulled up to his neck, and what rank sleep he must be having. I lean back and pat his leg. I turn back to Celia, I watch her, her

mouth, her eyes. I think of her standing at the window in Nice, her body and gestures, the way they combined so completely to create an impression of an adult so distant from her childhood that there had to have been something which tore those worlds apart. I think of the desperate need we have to be other people, to become them so to become ourselves.

'And these girls I taught,' she says. 'I was so afraid for them, that the things I taught them, that they would leave and they'd have hearts and bodies and minds full of facts for the mechanics of the world, for the map of its construction, a manual of some kind, a book, I guess, for its operations. And I would cry for the only real fact that I could tell them: none of it matched up. The futility of all that precision I had taught hundreds of girls to keep keen, all it equated to was a broken heart for the true reality of things. That was all they'd find and I'd cry about it.'

'He was the source of your broken heart?'

'Louvière?'

'Yes.'

'Yes,' she says and taps the steering wheel as if summoning a thought. 'But I am lying. What I am saying is an old lie. I now think of all the things I taught, all of it, how they match the world perfectly. Everything about it is as beautiful as the world. Now I resent the lost tears.' She made a noise, a half-laugh. 'Huh. Maybe I do, I'm not sure. But knowledge, it is as beautiful as the world.' I touch her arm leading to the steering wheel, she glances at me, a smile full of a laughter she hadn't quite let out and I smile back at her. I manage to get myself into a position to glance back at Harry and wonder if in his half-hearing state he is able to process any of her words into sense, into memory and comprehension. In each moment she contradicts the last – in each moment she seems to come closer to the whole every person promises

when they start to speak. He looks almost dead as his form bounces with the road.

'And what a thing, beauty,' she says. 'What a thing it is. You know what it is? You want to know? This is what it is, it's the rearrangement of the world, of the energies of the world, of loves and hopes, all these things, into another new and unthought-of—' she stops, paused in effort to recall what she believes she has previously defined. 'Energy. An energy one hasn't before comprehended or allowed for. That's what I thought, and now I think it again. That's beauty, if you want to know. A new bloom for old roses.'

I slump into my seat and I struggle to move for the next few minutes. She talks on. Part of it I hear, the rest drifts past. Everything wet as dew touches down. I dream on and off. Celia accelerates down a long, narrow straight. The darkness curves away from the headlamps' beam. Fences blur and night animals scurry and time has its face torn from all clocks. She is taking us west, deep into the downlands of Picardy.

'We became friends 14 years ago in Aix-en-Provence,' she says. 'Louvière. François and I. It took a month and then we were in love. Simple. We went north together to Belgium where I was due to begin teaching.'

'Love.'

'But he is married. He has been married since 1910. He was 19, that was when he moved to Luchon. To be with her. He came back from the war quite surprised to find he was still married. She is five years younger, 15 when they married, can you imagine? And he comes back from the war and she is used to being alone. She is used to being with her family, who she left only for a few months anyway. Going back to them, it seemed to her, was going back home and there was never going to be any other home. But he came

home and that was their life. He started cycling, serious cycling in the mountains. You've seen the mountains, you know what they are. I met him during the Spring of '14. I met him again six years later and on and on. It goes on.'

'Has he written again?'

'Louvière. No. But I have made enquiries.'

'What news?'

'They want to take it off. His leg. The doctors want to take it off. They are making noises that it has to come off. But he makes noises back at them. He's lying in hospital with a rotting leg while riders come and go. Friends, old friends. Riders who don't ride this race. Family. His wife's family. Children lurking, staring. This is what I imagine. Then: crimpled tissue, snipped nerves. God – you know? There's always something. Some part of you, it is always turning to a ghost.'

We drive through a village and the morning is starting to grow out of the farmland, the buildings silhouetting. I believe we are lost. She won't stop to talk to the men who stand at their horses, smoking cigarettes in the blue morning. She turns left then right so we come out at an angle to the road in. The sky seems to shrink into the eastern corner of the stratus, the hemisphere merging with solar streams off the sun. Everything starts small, everything starts in the verges.

She starts saying names: Roisel. Moislains. Marquaix. Every few miles a new name. Tincourt-Boucly. A set of houses sparse, separated by haystacks and furrowed ground. Red brick house. The wood store, the thatch and faggot lying in the grass. A patch of burnt earth where cut scrub was set alight. Buire-Courcelles. Doingt. The steeple, always the steeple. The rise in each hamlet. Shops and stores. Fence and hedge. Dogs sniffing. Trees, their tops blunted. People slowly rising from their beds and the morning smoke in the

chimneys for coffee and bread. Shutters pushed back to let in the sun. 'Péronne,' she says.

The main road is a collection of smashed things, beaten and bombed and set alight. Here a brick oven, here a brass knob, here a pile of ash where people have since come and burned what they can't bear to retain. Beams and stone, the shape of houses and businesses. Things remain but only need a push to send them on their way. It's as if this is their true state, rendered so we might see the materials of each old structure, how simple they really are. There are houses still standing, occupied and fulfilling traditions of life and custom and the rest, but mostly it is piles of rubble and the skeletons that seem so simple to reduce to wood and brick. To stand at their side and whistle the right frequency and it would all go down. And how simple it would be to see them all collapse. But none of it is simple. Simplicity is just our desire for composition, for things to be true.

Store signs still readable, one clinging to the shell of a bakery, another to what was an apothecary. I see dogs and cats and horses and birds, the sounds of birds.

We find ourselves beside a woman in her middle age. She has her hands coated in dust. Celia speaks. The woman ignores us, shuffling in her business until I hear the familiar 'Nouvelle Zélande' and she stops. She stammers. She shows us her hands, fingers well used to digging. She says to Celia, and Celia translates for us. 'She says, "I come here most mornings. I was there, across the road when the shells hit. My daughter was in here. I ran at the blaze, a foolish woman." She says, "Isn't that me, a foolish woman running at the blaze?" That's what she says.'

Harry asks if she comes here every day and Celia turns to the woman and speaks once more. I listen to them speak, the way Celia becomes the other in the shift of her tongue.

I realise both women are perhaps the same age, separated by the effects of circumstance. 'She says, "No. Maybe sometimes in a month. Once a month, two, three. Depends on the time of the year." She lives with her brother in Driencourt, which is near.' Celia kisses the woman. We each kiss her cheek four times. We hold her in our arms, a quiet warm through her bosom and the sense we are here and will remain here for some time. Harry stands beside her unmoving. They look at each other, slowly disentangling from the complication of what it means to gaze and gaze back. We make our way along the street and what is left of the town. Things broken and piled in remote mounds. I smell buttery bread and I turn back to the car and the others follow. It's only a ghost, but I look back for the sign for the former bakery. The woman is looking at the ground, kneeling in interest.

It takes time to find it, though it was always close. The river, the real river for which all of this was named. It's beautiful though I suspect full of more broken things. Desolation in the hush and willow. I've heard how the land gives up hidden items once lost in the mud: guns, grenades, artillery, a truck sunk in the depletion hole. Men with blowtorches come and make off with metal. Nothing is going to be moved in one piece. The river is a deep winding thing. Trees hang their branches low to touch its ambulatory waters. No one is around to say what might lie beneath. We stare for a long time. The source of a name, and such a name as quiet and beauteous as the Somme.

And that is what we find ourselves doing in the hour we have before we need to turn back: we stare, stare at fields and hillocks, stare at rutted ground where cattle walk and chew. We search for trenches amongst the grasslands and seek evidence but each of us is uncertain and unwilling to

make a claim either way. I make my own battlefield. The longer I stare, the longer I look at fields whose names I don't know, whose particular battles I can't name, whose dates aren't written in the pasture, the more it becomes apparent: I know nothing, and the land will not tell me as I'd hoped it might. I am as ignorant as Kitchener's army in those first weeks of the war when they gathered, marched together to the town halls. Walked to where other teachers and apprentices, baker's boys and dustmen, butchers and grocers, shepherds and shearers, boot-shiners and plumbers, students and commonplace yearners knew only one thing: to come here, to fight. Barely a soul knew what that would mean. Such scant knowledge and the only knowledge I bring with myself is the thought, 'How could they have known?'

It takes minutes before I see anything but the words and the words of histories and newspaper columns and thugs. The whole scene described for me, details of hillock and smoke, weapon and disturbed ground, and it feels as if I know nothing.

Though I do know things. A kind of knowing. I know that after weeks of endless, unceasing shelling of the German lines the British paused for 10 minutes, waited for 600 seconds, gave respite enough for their opposition to recover before Allied captains blew their whistles and sent their men over the top. One of the phrases that lived past the war: over-the-top. Over-the-top. Repeat it again and again and listen for the machine guns the Hun had quickly remanned and watch as men fall in queer ways, lopsided, heads twisted, arms severed, knees shattered so the leg bends backwards. Imagine the sound, in a pause between the bullets and shells, the choir of the dead in no-man's-land. A constant repetition, men walking forward and falling. Walking and falling. Walking and falling. Walking and falling. Say it 100,000 times. Walking and falling. Walking and falling.

Repeat it until it becomes a mantra. Repeat it and eventually its utterance manufactures staggering men and you see them without your eyes. We stand staring to the north, the sun to our right, our hands up to our eyes like a salute of which neither of us is aware, stone cold in the morning, breathing grey.

And all this, all: it seems so long ago it can't have been a mere decade. But it is and there, as if proof, are the trees, the dead trees stubbling the land like stalks of corn after the harvest. Rows of dead wood not yet rotted. And somewhere there is Thiepval Ridge and a chateau that once looked across a much more peaceful land. But I am looking for things that no longer have the physical traits that gave them their names and I fear I will be quite mad if we stay any longer. Walking in the ghost memory of language's open dreams.

Eventually we find others are doing the same as us: parking their cars and stepping outside of the vehicles and walking a few steps into the field and staring, each waiting for the day, for the light to tear open the dark and show us the weight of what happened here. We are nothing more than pilgrims, made silent by an unwilling land as we ambulate the Somme. There is no church, just 300,000 dead. 300,000 and the sense that if we stay here we will become stone. Hard pillars wedged into the land, waiting on the real. Waiting on time to start once more.

We drive back through the meagre hours we have before the start of the stage, and I know I need his memory. I need Thomas and the memory he once had of this place, this continent. For those long months that he stared at the window, that he stared at the fireplace, that he stared at the wind making trouble with the trees that line the driveway of our parents' house, that he stared at the pane of glass where his focus seemed at the time to rest – I watched and

tried wordlessly to recall with him what he saw. All the damage, all the harm. Then at that moment in Fox under the mountain haunt of damp sky, rain and haze, he put it all in the air. At that moment, the moment he began to talk, the stuff of his silence was made ruin. Walls seemed to merge then collaspe. Something emptied out, something filled. I realise I have lamented the passing of silence and I find myself talking. I feel Celia's eyes on me and hear the sound of myself making words out of what could have only ever been dreams.

'It was spring, not long after winter had started to ease. April. Our airfield was way out west of Ypres, Wipers, whichever vulgarity we make. I say Ypres because I feel like I'm doing the right thing, but at other times I feel the opposite. I have the wrong sounds, and I know I do, but I keep using it. We were at Saint-Inglevert. 21 Squadron. This was out by the coast. These aircraft, the RE8s we flew, they were poor in the air, handled like bad air itself, like a wind tossing paper: dreadful to land and clumsy to turn. But they were our machines. Nobody could take away the fact we could fly. The thing we could do, the thing that so few others had the same right to do, was fly.

'We'd fly over the front 10,000 feet up and see the battle, see it silent. I had a gun pointed between my propellers and the photographer had a machine gun at the back. We'd fire at whatever we fancied. I never hit a thing that I know of.'

'You never flew here?' Celia asks.

I shake my head. 'We had been at Saint-Inglevert for a month when I went down in the dunes. Occasionally the war seem to be winding down. We were wrong whenever we thought that. It was early March, before Ludendorff's push. We'd be stealthy, flying low over the coastal region staring amongst the dunes for movements. People look like midges.

You go to the beach and midges crawl out of the sand and fly. Frustrating and making you slap. But you could always tell a person, a person always stops and looks up. I don't know what they want us to see. You know at the start of the war, nobody save the French and Germans thought much of the idea of flying, what use it might be in war. And even the Continentals weren't entirely sure what to do. The first exchanges were men waving at each other, flying alongside and signalling hello. The escalation came about with hand signals, men with hangovers gesturing two fingers. Next came rocks and stone. Men throwing things at each other. Imagine that, throwing rocks as they went past each other at 150 miles per hour. Then pistols, the spotter at the back with a pistol. Then rifles and then machine guns. Then machine guns timed to fire through the props. The history of aerial warfare right there. I know men who've survived that whole gamut: they fly machines with one intent to their design, to kill and avoid being killed. And you know, I find it sad, in a distracted way, that the first time most people ever get to see an aeroplane it's a machine out to cause them harm, to end their lives. They should be things of wonder.'

'How were you hit?'

'Ground fire. The same that brought down the Baron, but I was not him. In fact I'm not even sure I'm a particularly good flyer, but if you stay up, they keep sending you up. I lasted two years, which was pretty good. Luck, I guess. Luck and a good tail gunner. I had four of them, lost two to fighting in the air, dogfighting. One to illness and the other died when I hit the dunes. Broken neck, internal injuries. Trauma. That's my guess because I never saw him again. I never saw my aircraft again except as some wreckage.

'We were turning back from Middelkerke and saw a friend's aircraft out off the coast above the Channel, the English Channel. I banked and flew at a mark I made in

the sky where we might rendezvous. We fell into formation and offered one another hand signals. Thumbs up. It was towards the evening and we flew towards the sunset, which was a stupid thing to do. Right out of it came three Germans, Fokker DrI Dreideckers, triplanes. Turn on a pin and they split the two of us. I flung my craft port and towards the beachhead and the dunes which were covered in barbed wire and riddled with mineshafts. The far reach of the Western Front, the end of the line. God, you know, but that's not quite true. The front went on in the Channel, mines, the other kind of mines, prowling ships and men like us airborne and ready to shoot at whoever tried to round the far point of the line. In theory it continued up through England, Scotland, to the pole. I was pursued by two Germans. They played with me. Twice coming alongside and staring as my gunner tried to take aim, then they'd climb, flip and be on my tail putting machine gun spray through the struts. I put her into a dive from 7,000 feet. The machine shuddered as we hit cold air. Screamed, as though I were ripping its skin from its muscle inch by –'

This is the sound of my voice. My voice rolling forth over the top of my brother's life at what could have been the end. Fading through the spectacle of aircraft taken from the air, ripped from the air. The memory of another garbled forth. The attempt to make memory in the shape of the other to become this narrator. I censor myself here, for there is no reason not to. No need to make entertainment out of his hurt. Though Celia heard it all. Harry too. I went on into the sand and into the dank water and mud and wire and sheets of fire and six days of crawling and waiting.

'– I realised I was still wearing my leather helmet and pulled it off and set it on the high point of the crater and watched as bullets sang through it. I left it there and began to crawl and

as I crawled a mist came in, peeling off the sea and rolling into the dunes. The sand was damp and I made my way blind until I was rolling without volition.'

'How long was he there?' It is Harry. He has woken, or has been awake for some time. We are in a town, Celia has the car idling through the streets, barely touching the accelerator. He sounds half-broken by the sleep he has been in since we left the river and the surrounding fields.

'What?' I say.

'How long was he there? You're talking about the ditch. Thomas's ditch.'

'Six days, I dare to think,' Celia says. Her voice quite sudden, quite changed. Rounded vowels, the stuttered sound of Kentish England. 'Six days far as I know. That was what I was told. Your parents sent letters. They mentioned six days.'

'Six days,' I say. I look at Harry who is looking at Celia, at Celia's mouth. At Alice's mouth.

'His parents. They wrote saying that Thomas was found six days after his plane was shot down,' she says and looks at me. She puts her hand over her mouth.

'I hit something,' I say. 'My hand in something wet and stringy. I got my right leg up and looked around. I was in a ditch, quite deep. The walls about eight feet high. There were two bodies in there with me. One buried up to his waist, the other lying on his side, half-covered in dirt and sand. There were splinters of wood, nails and a lantern with cracked glass. It was a collapsed mine. I tried not to look at the men. I was aware of them, their proximity and location in regard to me and one another. Both quite dead.'

'Both quite dead,' Harry says back at me.

'I was just aware of them.'

'Something wet and stringy,' Celia says.

'It was the man lying. I touched a part of him. A part

264

that was once him. Skin. Skin pulled back from his leg, his thigh. Peeled up from his knee.'

'My cousin once wrote to me, Harry,' Celia says. Her voice cold, colourless. She sits up and squints in the low sun. She glances at me once. 'He wrote to me. This man here,' she says, turning to my friend in the back and pointing to me. I stare at her mouth, her voice. 'He wrote to me a few times. I live in London most of the year, I'm from Margate, but that is where I live. He wrote to me there.' She stops and looks at me.

I feel the panic, the tension between silence and speech. I go on: a Judas against my inclination to stop.

'I slept then,' I say. 'I started to sleep and dream. I lay there on my side after the concussion of an artillery hit. I phased in and out. Smoke rolled in over me. Black smoke and then it was black because it was night. The days kept switching to the night, it went on. Hunger penetrated everything; I looked in my pockets for anything I might put in my mouth, anything to chew. There was never anything. I bit my nails back to the raw, I chewed the inside of my cheek. I would stare at the dead men, waiting for them to stop being dead men and just men so I could search their clothes for anything. The sky was a dense blue that morning, without cloud and heavy like it could fall. I remember skies to remember moments of change in my life. And then I thought to dig around, to scratch about in the soil, for this was once a mine and inside mines you can find anything. I used a piece of wood to scrape away sand and dirt and look. It was futile, of course. Until I found something, it was futile. I came upon a can of beef, bully beef. How do you open a can of beef in a ditch? I searched for anything metal and saw nothing until I noticed the wooden grip of one of the men's service pistols on his belt. It was then I touched the corpse, my first corpse. I touched his hand beside it and felt the dead cold. I took the

pistol. You know, there is no point to a gun other than to cause damage. You know this more than ever when you feel the weight of it in your hand. They are revolting things no man should ever feel pride in owning. So I used it, I used it as a can opener. I held the can in front and aimed the barrel upwards and away at the rim of the lid and fired and the whole thing jumped out of my hand and I went looking for it in the mud. I found it and saw the bullet had lifted the lid so I could get my finger in there and pull out the meat. It tasted. It tasted – I don't know how it tasted.'

'How old were you when you learnt this?' Celia asks.

'16. No age. 21. I watch it as it comes to life. I'm not repeating anything. There is no repetition.'

Celia looks back at Harry and Harry says nothing. I can't look at his eyes, not the full force of them. I wait. Wait until I am forced to look. By his voice or hand, he will have me glance and I will see something. I will see a face, a look not prepared to give in to my voice. He is so close and I can't look – I fear how far those eyes have travelled in the last minutes. How many miles they have traversed, how many mountains and plains and heat-locked bands of air that take the breath from our mouths and bake everything till it is hard. I fear how little he knows of me, how little he will believe in the future.

'And I spoke to them, you know. I spoke at them for days until –'

'They started to talk back,' Harry says.

'They started to talk back,' I say. 'No syllables. Syllable-free sentences. Perhaps they were singing, perhaps they were just saying things I didn't, couldn't understand. After all, they'd been to war and I've never been to war.'

266

28

We are without time, we are beyond such a thing. At Malo-Les-Bain, Opperman, Watson and Osborne finish an hour-and-a-half off the front. I come in near the rear. We are below the line now, we crossed back over no-man's-land and into the Republic somewhere west of Lille. I said nothing, though in the morning Hubert made the comment that someone might say something. Of course, I have said enough already. I have stopped describing the lot of my speech, the rest remains back in the Citroën outside of Charleville. I went on, I went on and on. And though they knew, they didn't stop me.

My brother lay in that mine for days, a whole week, though whether that is six or seven or five or eight days, it does not matter. He lay there with his two companions until he went quite mad, I believe. Until a reconnaissance party found him half-starved, mumbling in complete disconnect. But I don't know that, nobody has told me that. It is merely the imaginings of a teenager who watched from the doorframe as Flight Lieutenant Thomas walked in the hall and held my sister as she dreamed. Of the hundreds of hours he has spoken, not one of them has measured those days in the mine. All its illumination: it's my making.

And I hear Celia's voice. Her voice undressing, unveiling

the county, the city, the village and street of her rearing, and my body in panic, reconciling the effort it took to become another, the bickering it takes to undo the mimicry. The bareness of her voice. The skin of it unkissed awaiting the mouth of another. The mouth of another to say it all back to her. I become slow trying to understand this. Rickety, a relic. Everywhere men pass by me.

I walk alone, meandering here, looking for a building, a clutch of buildings in fact. A jumble of houses my cousin wrote of back before she was the woman I now know. I haven't seen her since we quit talking. I stepped from the car and went quietly into the hotel where for an hour I slept and dreamt of her, the her before she came to be my cousin. My cousin who taught in schools, who travelled here and there. I've known for some days. That Celia and Alice, that these names matched the same person. Not everything I say, not everything I know I know. But I know one thing. In the moments after I quit talking, there was no hint of judgement. No distance other than the need I felt to escape her presence.

I changed into civilian clothes some hours ago and trekked out here at the water's edge. Nervous, the calm culled by the seeping memory of who I had become. The violent nature of becoming another for an hour, for two. I struggle to recall the sound of my voice in those moments I spoke as the Citroën rumbled.

The beach is full, the wonder of shouting families and naked bodies, amorous boys with arms about each other and eyes on the shape of women, the curved tanned breasts and slight mounded bellies. I walk but feel, as I have before, as if I am being followed. Eyes on my back; the tremor rush of cocaine also makes one weary of any looks which lurk near. Sparrows on the wire suspended between lamp posts; they wait for crowds to leave before descending on the sand to nip all the remains from the grains.

I have walked so many cities, so many miles and looked at broken buildings and the brimming wonder of architectures and structures made by men of genius and close understanding of the way we feel awe and I start again, looking. Though nothing will have the grandiosity of the standing stones, the menhirs of Carnac, nothing will give effect like their formation, standing, staring back at 5,000 years of unbroached past. A collection of buildings facing the sea; Alice described these during a time before this race, before I began to know the hurt, the shape agony makes on all men who chase it, before she came out of the echoes outside the abbey to make contact. A clutch of houses and the way their angles complicate their presence before the sea. She'd written many of the things I have seen so far and I still feel the urge to see more, despite the uncertainty I feel about her and the fictions we have made in each other's presence.

I find myself pecked by my own falderal, all this nonsense out of hand. It's a colour: blue for the sad notes I hear in the boys' talk 20 metres away, and red for the teeth of bickering men behind me. I walk and squint at the failing sun. I am on the coast of France and I walk her beaches.

And these western beaches, I half-expect my brother to be standing at a lamp post, leaning, smoking, expecting an answer to why I decided to be him. But there is no one but me and my imaginings, the buildings and the idea that if you look long enough you will see the architect and all he asked for.

Last night I spoke to Louvière. I told him about that night by the river in 1921. How we argued and threw rough punches. I told him about Thomas, things of Thomas. I explained how after that bleak anniversary in Fox, how he started talking of war. How he began to work hard. How he drank,

how on weekends he went around the rugby grounds, how he had a few friends and they would watch games together, that he rarely got too drunk, and no longer fought. How he had people to the house where Katherine would cook. How he laughed in a broad tone, his short body shaking. That's what I told Louvière. How he talked of his time in Cairo, in France, of Paris. He would decant the hours flying over the battlefields with his camera and his barely stable aircraft. The struggles they had to keep flying, the whistle of bullets as they sought to make contact with the fuselage, wings, engine, or the flyers themselves. The panic of gliding above treetops when the engine cut out and coughed and returned to life, the curious effect of air pressure on his ears and how he found himself easily short of breath once certain heights were attained. How he spoke about his transfer to the coastal region of Belgium, the day when his engine was lit up by tracer and he flew through the evening like a tarred and bright arrow.

That was where it stopped. That is where he is alone. I explained this to Louvière. My brother, I told him, he never spoke about killing. No one did, not to me. No one spoke about the fact of shooting a man in the head, the lungs, of blood and air finding portals where there should have been muscle and artery. That was the place of imagination for me, the horror of bedtime wonder. I explained his brute instinct to hurt, to fight and bully. But, I said out loud, I swear I said out loud, all I needed have done was recall him standing in the hall with Marya, because that was the closest he came to killing anyone. She was the only one. He'd never had to tell his friends about killing with a gun; he'd never fired such a thing with real intent. All he shot were images of France and Belgium, of troop formation and trench, of artillery and camouflage, of the hidden things men in huts with focused lights and magnifying glasses glared into, collecting the dots

into images that indicated the focus of the enemy's desire.

Stony silences, I told Louvière, weeks like weeds growing across months and then years. These were what I wanted, what I expected. I coarsely needed this: a sign of remedial breakdown, of damage to his self, an involuntary admission of the fact he'd been at war and brought this silence home with him. The shame and guilt of watching somebody die, I needed someone else to take the blame. That was my admission. I believed all Thomas had a right to was silence and the ache of silence filled with Marya and things of Marya.

Louvière looked at me, he looked at me and glared until his eyes started to speak. 'The walker? Sleepwalker?'

'My sister.'

'She die in her sleep?'

I shrugged. 'She was beside me, beside me in the car breathing till she wasn't. Till she wasn't breathing. It had lost control on the road back across the country down from the mountain. I hit a fence. It wasn't much. Just a fence. Palings went in the air. I'd taken her into the hills. She was half well and wanted to get out of bed and see the hills.'

He was quiet for a long time and I began to wonder if I was truly awake and just staring at the hollow in space where I believed him to be. But then he started again.

'There's always life, and there's always people. So we think of people. People who have gone. And when they go,' he said, 'when people go, if they are taken or something intervenes, things. Erm, important things, they set off, no? They vanish. Someone, a lover, a mistress, your teenage love against whom comparisons of any other love are what? Not valid? Yes. A wife, a friend who shares things. Things no lover could. When they gone, when this happen the invisible things of love, they are lost. No? We know this. This obvious. But what is it? What is it? The sound of their

voice? The, erm, up and down. Le cadence. Cadence of voice, their breathing, the way sentence begins and end. The lightness of skin. The laugh. All. The way they kiss the back of your hand because that is what they do. The balance of idea. It becomes the vanishing. We know this, yes? But it is memory. Memory is the thing lost. Shared memory, the memory that is only there between two people, only exist between two people, the memory that is unable to operate without both people. Merely the vapour of a spent morning, that is what is lost and that is the deepest hurt. Memory made by two minds, by the sound of their speech, by the way they react to words, light, music, how they dance together, how they are drunk together, how their bodies move when it's hot and they need each other. Memory that goes; this is the longest, deepest pain.'

I thought I could see him at the end of the bed, his mouth twitching. The angle of his nose, his bald head, the shape of his chin: a silhouette of my making. No light interferes, no noise back from the street. The real of a dream; bluer than blue, blacker than black, stiller than slate at the bottom of the ocean under all the silt. He made a noise as if waking in his sleep, his throat caught on his breathing.

'And, you know,' he went on, 'when they gone, these memories, they no longer. I believe this to be fact. There is no recourse, mmm? No recourse, but to a silent mind.'

I waited until it became apparent he had finished, till it seemed he was done. But I wasn't sure, so I didn't talk back. What would've been the point of talking back to a ghost, especially to the ghost of someone quite alive several thousand miles away in his own bed? I waited, the two of us poised. The night stalled as if waiting for something to shake it. Then he leaned forward, he smiled. I waited for my apparitish friend to say one more thing. But he didn't because it was morning. Light was in the room. It intruded, a

stranger pushing its way through a dark street. I kept staring at the space where the Algerian had sat and thought of the things I should have said. How I should have made a protest that my desires were all askew, misinterpreted, wronged. That someone needed to do something. But by then I was awake and he was gone.

❖

Now the sun is edging towards the end of the day, it must be after nine in the evening. The white sand is beginning to glow, a long shadow from a deckchair looks like the art they peddle in Paris. The people a ruin in heat and sun. I keep moving, never sure where I am apart from the coast nearby. And here a river, a band of soak heading into the channel the road bends around, and I follow it so briefly I am heading inland once more before a bridge allows me to cross. I stop halfway, I linger looking down into the water, the run of it, the way it has no choice in its direction; it must head downwards – always and forever. I walk on.

On the far side of the bridge the town seems to continue but a sign tells me otherwise. Dunkerque it says and I know her hotel is near. I walk until the buildings become less sparse and I am on a boulevard of sorts. Clear in front of me is a memorial, a plinth and column and a statue with an angel on top. When I am near I see written 'Monument de la Victoire de 1793'. I stand and admire its size for some minutes before moving on. 1793. These monuments mark the country all over. A year of horror and the slaying of kings and court. How long does it take for a city, a town, a hamlet, or even a family to transform ungodly acts into the righteous?

I stand in the circle outside the hotel. The sun leans on me and I have to sit before heading to her room. The weight of dreams and the way they rest with you throughout the day. I read the sign. Hôtel Aigle Bleu. She's here for the final days, the second to last night before we head for the end. God, the day is heavy. The sun, the weight of the sun and the light and this evening and all memories that I have let come and weigh upon me. The crest above the blue awning, an innocent-looking bird set in chrome tips its shadow on the ground and I feel it fall on me. I do sit. I sit briefly before a porter comes and lifts me by my elbow.

The man speaks and I just shrug as I have learnt to do. I look at the brass buttons on his jacket, the way they glint and lend clout to his presence, as if he is the one in control here, the only one. He starts to speak once more and tugs at me and I am once again standing in the full glare of the sun.

'Sit in your piss,' I say and smile and shake his hand.

'Give up,' he says and I look past his shoulder. Two men exiting the hotel in a saunter.

'No, no,' I say. 'Quite happy.' I watch one of the men and slowly feel I recognise him. He does a little jog towards the car waiting for them. It is the nameless man seen time and again. For a month these men have been following on. Driving in Discuter's wake. A half-dozen of them dulled by the enterprise of their slow drive in pursuit of ragged men.

The porter starts to speak but I hear another voice, a woman's voice, the voice of my cousin and I am being hailed in French and I turn. I wink at the porter and walk towards her. She is standing in the entrance with her hair sprung at the side and I suspect immediately she has been sleeping through the evening. Her clothes don't sit straight. And I realise as I open my mouth that I don't have her name. My mouth is empty, a small cavern at the edge of thought. All the little things I recall about her, all the dust and bites of old

story and mystery do not explain to me her name. She is so small now and I reach for her.

'Today is Friday,' I say from the bed where I sit.

'Wednesday,' she says, standing at the window. 'It was Wednesday. His wife was with him. His wife had his hands against her chest, watching him breathe, watching him breathe and the panting and the way it becomes rapid towards the end. And then she felt it stop. Jesus. So fast then his wife felt it stop.' She points at me, at where my legs rest at the end of the bed. 'Have you ever been in a room when someone dies?'

I nod.

'Every day something dies,' she says. 'At the end of every sentence something dies. Say something; something dies. But the way their bodies start to speed up. Faster, racing, every pant shallower and shallower. You blink. Shut your eyes. Each time you open them they are closer to matter, to hard matter. To calcium and carbon. Closer than they have been before. All day,' she says, 'all today's hours I have been on that mattress. I've been watching him over and over. Staring out the window, staring anywhere, watching him. Over and again. The two of them, him and his wife. Find a way to ask them to stop. That's what I kept saying to myself. Find a way to ask, ask it.'

For a while she remains at the window which is open to let in the wind from the sea. The salty airs and the thought of coastlines and ocean and escape and distance they bring with them. None of it is enough to rid the room of the heavy smell of a man's cologne that was apparent the moment I entered the room. I suspect he was the one who delivered the news, the man from the car who broke it over Celia's heart like a vase and messed her hair just so.

'In bed. In his bed,' she says. 'Died in his bed. Christ,

those weeks, those days, all that hiding. I imagine you know: Belgium is a small place. A little country, more border than beach. But it's nothing if not huge when you are trying to escape it. You're blinded by no sleep and shaking and you're trying to escape. Do you know the tremor, the body tremor that runs through everything? The way we hid ourselves in mud and hid between bodies. Listen. We found a pile of dead in a culvert and pulled them over us as the Germans came through hunting for anyone they thought was out of place and could put to the end of their bayonets. Rotted clothes and flesh on the turn. The empty eyes staring right at us. How many smells remain with us? How many hours did we stay awake? He took me with him across those fields, from farmhouse to farmhouse, shadow to shadow. We saw limbs hanging from trees where artillery had hit. The rest of their bodies, God knows. A horse with its guts blown out still making saliva as it waited for death. Death. Everywhere. François took my hand and ran me through fields. There were days when there was nothing. Clear summer days, the gentle rise of smoke from a chimney as bread was baked. Lord, we became bad thieves. We were shot at by anyone and everyone. Nothing hit. And now, now he's dead from a stupid cycle. Lying in bed with his wife who never saw the faces I saw: all other expressions gone, all gone except terror. The gape of terror. Jesus, what an expression.'

'How did it happen?'

'I've lived here how long now? I returned in 1918. At the end, I came back and went looking for him. After we got to France he joined the army and did the best he could to get killed. He wrote me letters. They arrived within hours, from the bloody front to Margate. He talked about love. He talked about death and how when it was over he would become a promise, fold himself into a envelope and whisper over the Channel and we'd be together. But what?

That never happened. Never. He went back to his wife because he actually lived. I don't think he expected to live. He expected to die and just be those promises in limbo out in the sun waiting for the wind to blow them to dust. Christ. Now he's dead. These years I've been following this so we could be near. Turned my life into another's so we could be close. I haven't been that girl from Margate for 14 years. Now what? The rest of you all free to –'

'How?'

'Sepsis, if you know what that is.'

'I know.'

'You know,' she says with cold confirmation. Her face narrows. 'How do you know?'

'How do you think?' I ask. 'How do you think, in the end, I know these sorts of things?'

'Your brother. What an ass you are,' she says and blinks that long slow blink. I barely hear her. My cousin Alice. Celia. Louvière is dead and she says this. God, what a trick to unravel and find at its centre: the dead. What an ass I am. How many years has she been following this race, how many years has she watched as Louvière has ridden alone. How many years has she waited for the moment he will come back to her, walk her back across those fields, back to the unsullied city before the war began where she taught and let herself try to understand the world and the things of the world: beauty, love and the precision machinery of love itself, how many years?

'I'm sorry,' I say.

'Come on. Thomas. Thomas, Thomas, Thomas.'

'You know my name.'

'Who cares who you are,' she says and stares at me, challenging. That I say the same thing back at her. The cruel thing, the emptying thing, the thing that will make her lose the contents of her hurt self on the floor. 'Don't. Only he –' she starts.

'Alice,' I say.

'– only he calls me that. You don't call me that.'

The way she cries, it is different to others. It is louder than her voice. Louder than speaking, louder than anything we ever wished to say to each other.

29

Teams are fragments now. Five left from Alcyon. Louvet no longer a part of the race. The four of us remain despite the lack of obvious stakes. We run south in a definitive line to Dieppe. Hubert has been dragging us for how many thousand miles we don't count any more. But we remain. Discuter, five of them still on the course. The long torture has been escaped by how many? 120. 120 deserters. We ride without their wake dragging us. And we know why we are here: if we left we would leave a legend behind stating false myths of gutless, senseless waste. We want nothing in place of our story but the one we have made.

Outside Dunkerque, 45 miles out, Opperman's forks go. They give in on the cobblestone roads. The jarring hell of those things. We sit for 40 minutes on the side of the road as he refits a new frame to his wheels and chain. We sit with him, yet he seems so alone. So far out in front of us, so far behind the leaders. He seems caught in an ownerless space, out beyond our horizon but impossibly beside us. I look at him and can't imagine him ever not riding in this race.

I piss in the trees and slip two pills into my mouth. I await the tremor thrill of their effect. The handkerchief Celia offered me way back in Caen, more a rag now. I drop ether into its dirty cotton and draw hard and hope for all the

things we hope for when near the end. I keep my eyes out for her car, for her short hair and that wave of her scarf. I watch closely, too, for what she might bring with her. Those things sleeping deep within me, between my head and my chest, squeezed between my oesophagus and skin: fear and the mould of fear trying hard to be swallowed.

Hubert finally has his bike back together and he calls us. We stand around staring. The alignment is all wrong, the bike bent. If this is the end, the end is shallow for I feel little but the smell of brine on the air drawing me back over the depth of oceans to my own seaside city beneath the weight of the mountain. My body entwined with the shadow of the thought that this is it. A morning close to noon. A field close to unsowable for the salty breeze. I expect Celia to appear driving slow, her eyes on us as if to prove a point. She would say nothing as we gave in and sat in her Citroen and felt the car pull away from the race. But there is no one, no one but two citizen riders watching without emotion. Tourists leaning on their own machines. They seem in no urgent need for us to ride on. Standing watching.

'What do you say?' Harry says.

'What?'

He nods at the riders. One has a Union Jack on his pannier bags. He calls out. 'Let's borrow your bike then? How do you feel about that? We'll borrow it and you can meet us up in Paris.' He turns to me. 'You think they speak English?'

'Leave them alone,' I say.

'What you say?' he calls out.

'We don't want their bike,' I say. 'Look at it.'

I look at Opperman and tilt my head in question. He doesn't move or speak. The men step forward, moving slowly. One speaks but I'm still looking at Oppy, waiting for what he's going to say. The machine is painted grey, stone dented and I can see where two spokes have snapped and they hang from the rim.

'You're going on to Dieppe?' the man asks.

I'm watching Hubert. He doesn't move, his eyes on the bike. It's a heavy machine with low gearing, unfit for road racing. He stands waiting, his mouth closed. 'Don't ride it,' I say. But Harry is already moving the bicycle from the men.

'How will we know to get it back?'

Opperman barely nods, but he does and then it lifts, this weight that seems wrapped about him.

'How will we —' the man starts but doesn't finish his sentence. They watch us stand on our pedals and head out into the kilometres that wait.

Hubert pushes as hard as he can but barely keeps up with us. We pace him. Riders come through us. Little is said. There's rain and the road mud becomes grey. Conversations are not taken up and there is no fight. Something in the peloton is dragging, a protest perhaps, a long slow salute to Louvière. It is difficult to say. His name is not mentioned. We ride on. The coarse rattle of Opperman's borrowed machine, an ugly grind of an unoiled chain.

People still line the roads. But there's an awe now that builds in a way as to concern me. It seems as if they merge for the fact of their own gathering, and I watch, fearing what would happen if we were simply to stop and step aside our machines. Of course, I do nothing but ride on inside my blank stare.

Of those of us who are left, most have only one chance at victory: the conquest of fear and pain. That is all we are fighting. The deep plough of agony digging at our bodies. I watch Opperman on the borrowed cycle, riding like Frantz two days ago. But no one seeks him out for a duel, no fool is looking for a scrap in the hope of false fame. He is utterly alone beside us nobodies, breathing heavy, scrapping himself along in the wet. Such a disappointment to finish

this way. Such a way to farewell a legend. The man is dead and somehow this is all we manage: a ride on borrowed equipment, faces shedding the last of our skin in the sun, and Hubert on a machine made for tourists.

Nothing is ever the real thing.

We hit the final town. An ache clamps itself to my head. Our names shouted in the echoing streets, nouns like nails. Every shouted name a little death for the things we are. We hit the boulevard facing the channel, faces leaning, eyes wide, the shimmer of flags. The awe builds. It is for their own gathering – a hymn to themselves. A woman shouts: 'Aller à cheval! Aller à cheval!'

❖

I smell the incense of a bonfire at the entrance to a park not a hundred yards from the beach at Dieppe. The waft of smoke. The smell of riverside summer evenings of damper and story. The beer and the reek of mutton come rushing. The smoke smell in my clothes somehow pleasant the next day and the days after that.

I see several racing cycles up against a fence. The man from the car that follows Discuter through the dark, the same car Celia goes to when her supply is lean, stands by watching. I nod his way then head towards trees drooping their long arms across grass green and rich where smoke wrestles. I walk into the trees and find a breeze pleasant against my warm face. A group up ahead beside the bonfire I smelt from some way out, a circle of men and children and women and racers and whoever else has decided to group together at this point. I hear the familiar grunt and stunned slap of hands against flesh, the sound of effort and force, of breaking things. I jog up to the rim of the people there and peer through. I catch a glance of the Belgians, those forever

bloodied men. One is thrusting his hand towards an unseen body or head. The crowd murmur, bottled excitement as they watch. A man turns to me and we laugh, both together at the same time. I smile and peer around him. I twist my head hoping for a view of these men once more. It has become quite a ritual, these Walloon bastards and their fists.

Earlier I stood amongst the pebbles that fill the expanse of the beach. It was wide, 50 yards from the umbrellas beside the road to the sea. The rocks undulated under my shoes and I thought of stones in the mouths of children playing a game without a name. And now I imagine these Belgians, I think of these men mumbling when asked what it is they do to one another.

I push into the circle and two men shimmy their shoulders to let me in. A bloodied figure. The two men have found a partner for their match. He staggers about, the chap not in good shape. Neither of the Belgians is looking at the other, rather at the figure swaying and dripping blood on the ground. One of the Belgians throws a fist into the man's midriff. He coughs and starts to fall and arrests himself before vomiting. Blood and mucus. The other comes at him and feints a kick at the man who seems quite unpractised at this ugly show. The kick isn't followed through and things pause for a moment. The man's hands go to his knees and I see something familiar, something in the profile and the clean bit of his skin which isn't bloodied. I see it and I see the boy's shape. The Spaniard in the middle, the lad who had rejoined the race in Metz. I step back. His head is bleeding, a stream coming down his shirt which is half torn from his body. I see him stagger and one of the Belgians runs at him and hits and hits again in the boy's kidneys and liver. The other sidles at him and thuds the sharp of his elbow into the back of his neck. Then they walk away. The lad falls and rolls over so dust and leaves stick to his face and skin. He begins

to crawl. Slowly moving himself to the edge of the circle. I see a foot come out of the crowd push him back down as he tries to stand. I shout and look out for a face, a broom of familiar hair because I know she is here somewhere. Then the Belgians are at him once more and I realise this is not a fight, it never was a fight.

The crowd disperses. The Belgians walk to the fence where their bicycles rest and cautiously set off when they realise there is nothing left of the kid, their teammate, to hit. Any pain in their bodies I doubt could have been caused during the assault. I search for faces to look into, to see what kind of words they might say but I see only blank eyes, no smiles, no tears and for the first time in this country so full of love and hate and joy and cried-out eyes and lungs, I feel a strange vacancy, a hollowed grimace that has its back to me as it walks away. Then I see her. I look for bodies to hide behind as Celia moves through the crowd. And then I can't see her. I stretch my neck. She is small amongst the crowd and is gone.

What name would I shout anyway? All names are borrowed, especially when you're a thief and take another's just to see how it rhymes in your body.

Finally I find her again, she is beside the car, the blue car I have seen throughout. It idles on the grass. Celia leans into the window. The man from the hotel, the same jaw and dark eyes.

Two men and a woman head towards the Spaniard. I watch him for a few seconds, and then look back at my cousin leaning into the car. I feel a wave of nausea ride in my body. I shout her name, but there is no response, she is still in the car window. I turn, I jog to the lad, to where he lies. His face swollen and broken, his nose spread and his cheeks cracked where they have kicked and kicked again.

Blood caked in his long moustache. I come close. One of the men lifts him up so he is on his haunches like a dog. He looks up, eyes so red I don't believe he can see; I crouch down and stare at him. Seconds, minutes, his face a mangle and I wouldn't know he was the Spanish boy who showed me his photos, who offered me his wine, who rejoined the race, who I desired to hit or to see being hit. And now my desire has been met, I have nothing to say. One of the men has a wine bottle and he tips it on the boy's head and I see it is water. I watch it run off and think that the son of a doctor should know something of this. But nothing, just the lie, the lie that I had my father's hands and how useful they might be right now.

In some final act, men from the car come out of the doors and walk to the boy and take him away. I look about for her, for Celia, but there is no sign, no indication she is near. Just the sense that she has something to do with the lad's beating. I want to look at her, I want to look her up and down, for her to know I am looking her up and down, that it has nothing to do with the shape of her, nothing to do with her hips and legs. I'd look up into her eyes and show her what stones we have become. But nothing, she has gone. I go to my knees. My arm numb. I breathe between my teeth. The coarse grab of tendons in my neck.

The Spaniard's bike is left there on the fence. Nobody touches it. Not until a few hours have past and someone might come by, a child perhaps, a boy who needs such a thing to ride about the neighbourhood, to wave to the girls and the rest, not until then will it be taken away.

30

I turn back towards the town. I start running. I stumble on legs so unused to this movement, but I run, my arm limp. I jog and pause and feel the glimmer of unusual tiredness. I run again. My lungs hack and I think to rest on the side of the road, to breathe and let sleep take me. I want to be a ball curled and warm, the centre of a skein, the light blotted out by dye and wool, the flavour of an unnamed animal in my mouth. Instead I walk in the tunnel in the middle of vision blurred and twisting. I return to my hotel. I walk into Percy in the hall. He looks at me, a hand through his thick hair, flaking lips pursed and whistling briefly. He takes my arm, feels the shaking and we are soon walking down the stairs out onto the street. I say to him, I tell him my neck is out. My arm is limp and my neck is out. He says nothing. It had clicked in that audible crunch as I'd searched out Celia. A nerve clasped between bone. Volted hits of pain. I stand momentarily looking into the eye of a donkey hitched to a cart piled high with flowers and their long stalks. I'm confused for a moment, worried who will buy all this. He directs me through a shimmer of pigeons picking seed out of the cobblestones into the café under the hotel. They take to the air and drop liquid on the stone behind us. Noise and pealing laughter. My team, men in the new moments of the last night. I stand with a white wind-cracked face.

They eat, fish and eggs and bread. They talk on and smile. Jokes. Men who want to be amused, buoyed by the thought of the final hours which will shrink to a dot at the end of the track rimed by so many thousands. Harry's eyes jump to mine and I suspect fear and a fear for the lack of lightness in my face. I attempt to put food into my mouth but can barely lift my fork. A pain deep behind my left eye like a heated nail. The room is all tablecloths and candles and shakers for salt and men in the corners murmuring into soup. There is a crust of bread in my hand. Nothing seems like food.

'Eat,' Percy says. His eyes catch mine almost by accident, they're monosyllabic and utterly sufficient. Eat, they say.

'Thanks.'

'Eat it,' Ernie says. 'If you leave your seat for even a moment, that'll be gone. That there on your plate'll be gone. Licked.'

'You hear about Louvière?' Percy asks. 'You must have heard.'

I look up at him. A certain defensive jerk.

'You must have heard.'

'What?'

'You hear?'

I nod but have the sensation that I impart no information in the act.

'He's dead. You must have got that in your ear.'

'Of course he's dead. He's been dead for days.' I squint at him trying to gauge how displaced this conversation really is, how far it is from the reality of what he thinks he's saying. 'Hasn't he?' I say. I stare at him, his fork at his mouth, his food.

'I'm just saying,' he says. He wipes a piece of bread about his bowl. A lone piece of chicken thigh remains. He forks it, lifts the meat to his mouth. Protein, flavour. He is saying that is all he cares for. 'Eat.'

Men filling themselves. The shelter of a room made purely for eating, it makes the perfect den for repeating the hours and assembling memories, looping them together into what in the future will become the day. Right now everything is translucent. I watch each of them, each in their own secret battle to make this so.

'Back in Luchon. You remember Luchon?' Percy is saying. 'I haven't got a clue where that was. In the mountains. I know you're gunna say that but – I've no idea. I really don't. But that's where.'

For the whole day we'd ridden and for the whole day I believed we rode in the trance of a funeral march. Our poor pace an elegy, an ode to the final pains of Louvière. Nothing is the same as what you want it to be and Percy proves how far I have shifted from the plain objectives of the race, how far I am from winning. I'm dead last by this reckoning, heading backwards. 'I have to leave,' I say.

'Your plate'll be licked clean. That's a fact.'

'I have to. I have to get out.'

'Where?' Percy asks.

'I have to get out of the race.'

'That's not an option,' Percy says. 'Look at Ernie here. He's desperate to get back in but he's too old. We won't let him in if he begs.'

I look at Harry and put my hand on the table towards him. I fall silent. I feel the table shape and move, my eyes unable to make contact with its surface and focus.

'How?' I hear Percy ask. 'Or if not how, why?'

'I'm not well. I have become unwell. Everything. I have become unwell.'

'How's that?' Percy asks. 'You ride fitter than me. I'm still here. You're what – some nancy now?'

'Let him be,' Harry put in on my side. He doesn't look at me, only at Hubert.

'Something is going to happen,' I say. 'Something –'

'Tell us,' Percy says. 'It's just 200 miles for God's sake. Tell us.'

'Something is going to happen and I have to leave.'

'We ride 10,000 miles and then there's just 200 left and you make a decision that it's no longer your cup of tea. Is that it? No longer your cuppa? Jesus weeping shit.'

I have nothing to say. For once in my life there is nothing. Harry looks at me. I feel my mouth open. The thing I have to say sits in my chest, reedy, waiting for a thin breath to ride to the surface. The Spaniard and the rough certainty that it is Celia's doing, that she planned for those maddened Walloon riders to take their fists and make his body soft and bled. Her will. That it is her will for my eyes to shrink and blister before the sun as if their lids have been removed with a butcher's fine blade. My fear is that the cost of saying your fears out loud is that speech makes them true. God, keep me quiet. And I keep calm. I remain quiet until I say: 'I have to be nobody. For a day. A week. I have to be nobody. Ordinary. Some bloke. A few days. I'll get drunk and convince myself I was never here. For a few days.'

'Why?' Percy asks.

'If he has to leave,' Harry says.

'Where's he gunna go? This is madness. A kinda dog lunacy.'

'He's going,' Harry says. 'Everyone has the right to be mad. To go mad. To tend to madness.' He laughs, cocks his arm and drinks.

'I can't feel my arm,' I say. 'I'm not mad. There is nothing in my arm.' I find myself once more looking at Oppy, trying to see what he might understand about this. But he is silent and I am harangued by Percy once more. I look through the noise of his voice and see Hubert's mouth move and slowly his voice comes out. He speaks and I notice the way

he can't make eye contact. He's facing towards me but his pupils are pointing like pins at the far wall of the tavern where paintings of dells and cottages look old, older than they likely are. 'There's no such thing as ordinary,' he says. 'That's the fact you learn. What we learn. There's no such thing.' He doesn't seem to take any pleasure from informing me of this. I suddenly admire him deeply. And not for the fact he has pointed out my lack of awareness, nor for the lack of pleasure he seems to get from the moment, rather I'm fond of the fact he knows it is important not to let me leave the café thinking ordinary men even exist. I watch him and wait until his eyes slowly give in and look, because they must look, eventually.

And then Percy says, once all has been eaten, all has been said: 'Ah, yer a fucker and a fool. Put him out on the street. Put him out with the beggars.'

31

I collect my clothes together into the rucksack I rescued from Bruce Small's vehicle. I cram in what I can and pause in front of the window as Harry moves about the room. The curtains flutter, a breeze in the morning sun coming from the North Sea to help all on the road to Paris. The crowds are gathering, the slow meander to farewell the remains of the race. 42 riders where once there were 162. Such is the toll.

Thousands will cram into the streets to watch my adversaries pass, they will cry, as they have in each town we have gatecrashed with our oily music, then abandoned with the smell of us deep in the clothes of those we kissed, or held, or fucked. Men with pot bellies who run after Oppy and shout his name. Women who want Frantz. Men who want Frantz, who want proximity and something they can't name. The three of our team who remain will ride to the end. Flowers will be thrown in front of tyres. Then, in the last hours before Paris, the sky will crack and the rains will come. Such things. I won't be among them.

Opperman remains in 17th place, Harry 28th. Me, I don't know, and nor does it matter. I will not be counted, just as Ernie will not be counted. I watch Harry organise himself. In the end he is standing by the door.

'You ready to leave?' I ask.

'This is the end,' he says.

'The end. Things of the end.'

'The things we say at the end,' he says. 'You heading back north? Is that your plan? Is that the idea?'

'Do you want me to say something?' I ask. We remain still, the beat of the room counting off until the next man speaks. Sounds from the exterior intrude, a cart running over the cobblestones, his horse's shoes making such a clutter but then is gone. Then a man laughing on the street. A dull dumb laughter that reaches up, that extends our silence so we find ourselves thinking things we don't wish to think. The dullard stops and I say about the pain in my neck, 'My arm is gone. My grip. I can hardly hold the handlebars. Not to race.'

'This is the end,' he says. 'Say what you want to say.'

'What do you want?'

'You have no troubles with speaking. It's not one of your problems; it's not a struggle for you to speak your mind, no matter the lunacy. Anything.' The man in the street coughs and laughs. A poor laugh, the laugh of a man without capacity, such is the dull, repetitive nature of his work. 'Listen. I don't care who you need to be to finish this. Just finish it.'

'Lunacy? That's a word.'

'I'm having a go at you. I just need you to finish. Next I'm going to ask whose idea it was to quit. That woman? Her idea? Then I'm gunna ask if you've thought this through. I'm not going to expect answers. I just want you to contemplate what if any answers you have, what they might mean. That's it. And I'm gunna watch you do it, watch you try to say one thing without falling into a pit of some mindless – down some path, on and on. I'm gunna watch you try to close the gap.'

I watch him, a long waiting stare. His eyes switch from my mouth to the window to the basin where my razor sits in foam, looking for time, for an excuse to leave because time has run out. Then the laughter again, a kind of crude interruption, the kind you'd expect from a dog eager for your attention, even if that attention amounted to the back of your fist against its rump. I spit into my hand. 'One thing?'

'One thing,' he says and he looks tired, too tired for the day's ride to Paris. But I know he will do it, I know how far he can ride if he has to. How many more miles he could ride. How many more countries he could cross. 'I am so – God. What? I am so near nothing. I'm skin and bone and tiredness. I want you to tell me one thing. I want you to say how deep it goes, how deep tiredness goes. All this. How far it reaches in. That would be useful. To me it would be useful. Let's end on that. If you can tell me that, if you can explain that, you might be of some use to me. But right now, right now, you're an empty rag.' He sniffs, drags mucus off the back of his throat, the early morning mix of phlegm and dust, the stuff he has lugged with him since Paris and before. He squints at the window. The man is still laughing, a cackle full of tripe and spit. Harry flinches, the sum of energy he is willing to offer against the annoyance. 'Shut up,' he whispers.

I shake my head. I shake it and turn at the window. I feel Harry's stare against my neck, the edge of it: a rod heated and lying down across my skin. I push the window so a brace of air hits and I see the man laughing. I see him and I shout. My voice breaks, it cracks and echoes off the walls and buildings up and down the street. A hard crack of noise like a skidded horse hoof, not human, not speech. Ten, twenty people look up: all bend their necks trying to spot from where the noise could have come, searching the sky for something other than me.

There is cloud rotating slowly above our heads, white bulbs that will burn off as the day becomes hot, slowly reducing down as separate air pressures shift skyloads of air to other parts of the continent. I ride east. I ride into the wake of those who've come before, namely myself and others. Despite my neck the bike moves freely without the weight of the race, though I can't tell you what speed I manage as I break from the coast and stream beside a river in a shallow valley. The stiller the body the better one's momentum. I am not in a sprint. I am gliding north-east, uncertain of the true direction I should be taking, I am not racing. And I am not following yesterday's roads. I am riding inland for a new sense of this country. I am in no peloton, nor is time kept for me. I ride through the long shadows of tall leaning trees who watch the river flow in the opposite direction. It's a gradual rise, an eventual gain of altitude, no more than a few feet every 50 metres. Kilometres seem to disappear.

I glide, though my legs rush beneath me. I find there are bananas in my backpack and I eat them and they feel like gathered silk melting in my mouth. I count the gaps between the trees. Each one, I believe, is 10 metres from the next. 10 is 100 metres. 100 is 1,000. A kilometre. One more kilometre further away from Celia. One more kilometre she would have to travel to find me.

I find myself running over what I told Harry as he stood at the door and the man below finally drifted away, taking his laughter and making it smaller and smaller till it was only the two of us watching the space outside the window. Harry and everything I owe him. I told him I would go north to where my brother went down, where he lay. I told him I had no choice, that I had to see. I did not speak about

Celia, he did not read fear in me. He wanted to know about tiredness. As if on our return from the Somme I had learned something I hadn't known previously.

'The night before she died, my sister, she sat up in bed,' I told him. 'Perhaps for the first time. I'm not certain, it was two in the morning and she sat up and I watched her yawn and stretch muscles that had been dormant for the week of her fever. She sat up and her face, it was sagged with slowness. With tiredness. If you want to know about tiredness, her face was dragged down by its full weight. She had no expression. A face without expression hangs off your bones until something comes to wake it. I asked her if she had anything she wanted to eat. It was the first thing that popped into my head, food. I asked if she'd like a cuppa. A sweet cup of tea with creamy milk straight out of the cow. She took a long time to say anything, to wake up out of it all. She stretched her arms over her head. She did this several times. Her voice was weak, but she asked for a cuppa. I brought it to her. She asked for food, for a sandwich of honey and butter. I went to the kitchen and brought it back for her. Thick white bread I cut with a big knife and I watched her eat, watched her face become Marya's face. We were there for an hour. Watching her chew, watching the tiredness leave. I asked her where she went. She chewed and eventually she started nodding. "I went somewhere white," she said. "Somewhere where I wasn't expecting to leave. But what choices do we have, dear brother? What are they?" She told me she went deep, right into the pit of tiredness, she said she went so close to exhaustion she couldn't see how to wake. It was no place but everywhere. "It's still here," she told me. "It is still inside me, but look, my arms move. Just, but they move. My toes move. How perfect my toes. I can't tell you," she said. "I can't tell you where it lives, what it's made out of. I can't say much except that it is here.

Tiredness: it's still here."

'So I asked her how I could help it go. She just looked at me and said, "What makes you think I want it to go?" I laughed until I realised I was shaking the bed and she put her hand out and I took her hand and held it. I then asked what she wanted to do. She raised her eyebrows at me and nodded. "The mountain," she said slowly. "Show me the mountain."'

Harry interrupted. He leaned against the doorframe. 'What did you do?'

'I put blankets around her and picked her up as if she were a rug and carried her out to the porch. I put her on the love seat and asked if she could see it. It was four by then, so dawn was coming. She said she couldn't. She told me to drive her, so I drove her. We drove into hills, how the undulations before the road went up in a steady climb so we were on the rise on the volcano. We wound through native forest, heavy forest. We went as high as the road could take us. She asked what we'd look like from below. I told her we looked like a car. A car and some idiots in the morning. And then, Harry, she asked that I have better answers; she asked that I give better answers to her questions. So I go looking for better answers.'

'That's fair,' Harry said. 'It's a fair request.'

I nodded. The thing was I wish I'd had Percy's imagination, then; I wish I'd known to say how we looked like lanterns in the hanging night. Instead I was silent as if watching her in the dawn, the dawn and the sounds we make when shown the dawn.

'We were coming off the hill,' I said. 'Marya and I. I was being careful. The lights of the car were weak, barely up to pushing back the darkness, let alone showing us the way. So I was being careful. But have you ever driven one of those cars? Model T? They have two speeds: slow and fast.

Little in between. A jerk of acceleration, which is terrifying, or those brakes that slammed you into the windscreen. We were coming off the hill. We weren't high up. The road didn't go very far, but I'd taken it to the end where it was really just a track. But I went up and now I was coming down again. Marya hadn't said a lot. She was pretty quiet the whole journey. Just made the appropriate sounds at the sight of the sun rising. The colours and everything. And I was coming off the mountain and she was very quiet. Quieter than before. I couldn't hear her breathing, not with the sound of the engine. But I couldn't sense her breathing. It was cold, colder than it was when we set out. I don't know how, but it was colder. I started to panic. Firstly I said her name. I said her name over a few times and I heard nothing. So I started to drive faster. I started putting that machine into corners at speed. And that wasn't pleasant. It was okay doing that when it was just me: I loved the exhilaration of driving like that on my own. You know that, right? You love speed as much I do. But with a passenger I became uncertain. And a passenger. Was she still a passenger? That was what I didn't know. I was saying her name over and over. I should have stopped. I should have stopped and felt her, put a hand on her, but I was terrified that I would feel cold skin. Terrified I would only touch wintry skin. So I went quicker, trying to get her back, back to the house where someone else would be able to tell me if she were cold or not. Whether she was still breathing. I hit the corners hard and accelerated out of them, wheels spinning in the mud and dragging us through at speed. Speed is a thing, Harry. It's malleable, you know? Hard, like rubber or cork. I thought speed would wake her up. I thought speed made things real and quick. Jesus.

'And then a fence, Harry. I hit a fence. I hit it. Everything slowed and I hit it at such speed. Everything slowed. Everything became easy, my movements on the wheel,

my feet, my hands on the controls, my vision. I could see everything. I could feel the light on the horizon rising, I could see a cow in the paddock look up from the grass, I could see the flies rise off the palings where a lamb's hide was hung, I could see my sister lurch this way and that as I sought control. The car hit. I was in control of everything, every mite that was in the air, everything, every muscle in my body and the movement of the car and the way my sister lurched. I was in control of everything until we hit. The fence exploded over us and the car went on its side. A blur of white and the palings flew over us and we rolled and my sister was thrown up and over the seats so, as the car righted itself, she was sitting in the rear seat, slowly rocking as the momentum of the ride ran through her until it stopped and she stopped and everything stopped.'

And I told Harry, I told him that I didn't know how many minutes she lasted after the car hit the fence. I explained how I'd flipped it, torn the roof off and how we sat in the machine rocking on its suspension. Her neck was bent all out of shape, eyes looking at me in a strange way. I told him that I sat there for an hour, half an hour, and I touched her cheek finally before trying the engine and felt it kick back in, how we rode back to the house. She was certainly cold by the time I got her there. Despite the warming morning she was cold and no longer capable of shivering. We were like that for how many hours. The two of our bodies getting colder. And then sun heating the farmland and the air and the bonnet of the car and then me getting warmer and her getting colder. There was no coming back from that.

And I told Harry I didn't know what was said in the afterwards, what words came from what mouths. At least not until I was with Thomas at the river. 'But I know one thing,' I said. 'I know that as my father took her from the car, carried her to the house in all those blankets, that it was

298

about then that I started to hate, that it was about then my anger found a measure by which to guide itself.'

Harry nodded then, and he took up his bag and held it against his chest and stood paused.

'So I blamed Thomas for that. I blamed him for her. Of all things, I blamed him for her, for trying to disguise the fact of her. That she died and it was his fault. I sat in that car and I looked at her and knew she was gone and I blamed him. I said that, years later. I said it and he hit me. He took out my tooth. And I went at him. I went at him with fast hands. Jesus. He clobbered me and stood over me and he said I was the one who drove her into a fence and I yelled at him. I blamed him for whispering to her in the hall. Talking to her in the hall. He stood beside her and whispered whatever he whispered into her ear and whatever else. Whatever else was in his breath. Passing that thing on. Then we went at it again. It never stops.'

'Never does.'

'But the thing is, Harry. The thing is. I can't remember. I can't remember the thing I should remember. I can't tell you what it was like when she died. I can't say. It's not there. I try to remember and all I see is the mountain and the signs of us driving upwards. That's all. Mountain and light.'

He nodded slowly, waiting on his thought. 'So, how was he disguising her? Is that something we do?'

'When you start speaking, Harry, any of us – when you start speaking something happens. Something is blocked. Don't you think? You start talking and the heart of the matter is rushed. You talk over it. It's trying to speak, but you're talking over it. Leaning in. It's breath. As soon as you start to describe anything, it hides. It's replaced by something, something that wasn't there previously. I blamed him like this: I said all his talk, all his war talk and his intimacy with all his war talk, I said it was all to disguise the fact of her. He should have stayed silent, that's what I said.'

'That's not a disguise. That's life,' Harry said. 'The key fault of life.'

'Fault. You say it's a fault.'

'Life's faulty. But that's not an excuse. I listened to you. I listened to your story. I listened as that woman drove and you spoke and you went on. I listened and I was, what? Revolted, that's the word. You know that, mate? Revolted. Revulsion. That's a word, if you want a word. At what point does it become okay to say such things? That kind of language. The talk of war, blood and how blood will out: it's cheap, it's penny a pound stuff, mate. Take it back and forget it.'

'How?'

'It's titty pictures. A peep show.'

'How do I take it back?'

'Titties and leery faces. That's what you sounded like. You don't take it back. Mate, I shrug. I feel my shoulders shrugging. Get in a boat, get on the water, head home. You both killed her, if you want to know. If you want an answer. You both killed her. Go home.'

And I am running on mere air. Celia had said my body would disappear. I would become the vapour through which others would ride, she said that. She was utterly right. There is little between my bones and the skin that houses them. I am the air and the water I put to my lips. I see birds squabbling in the earth. I taste the dust thrown up by living things. I'm riding away from her. Towards Thomas I ride and I ride away from her and whatever illness she has prescribed for me. I ride through long lines of fields and past gates, each endlessly repeated since the start. Pasture, animals, stock and trees. Over and over, everything green or rock.

A car closes, a honk of horns. I swear in return, shout out. One leans from the window and stares down at me the

entire length of the road until they are out of sight. I shout, 'Fuckers!' It's a good word to shout, sounding out like a mis-struck nail.

Then I ride in their wake. 10 minutes, 20. An empty road but for shadows of plane trees and oak. The physical weight of shouted words inside my head. In my mouth, in the place where things are made memory.

'Give better answers,' Marya had said.

'Don't believe everything you think,' Harry had said.

I fall for sentiments, not because they are true but because they seem true.

The valley opens wider, though logic says it should contract. Hills distant and dim. The only shadows are under the trees and I feel my body lag. I rest under a tree whose roots dangle in the river where the waters part and rejoin so easily. All about me the pain draws away the ether effect and asserts itself. Pain deep against the bone.

I gather Celia's things together and prepare. I wash the syringe in water. The powder I boil in the spoon over a candle. The water bubbles and the powder dissolves and conjoins into a new liquid. It cools. I draw it into the syringe through the needle resting on a cotton swab torn from a pillowcase in another hotel room in another town in an era before this new time. The stand of trees is shaped as if in the reflection from doorknobs polished and round. There is a small amount of blood in the tube as I jack the plunger back. It swims a snake's curling head before diffusing and sending the liquid to a light cherry. My teeth release and let go my belt strapped about my bicep. A taste of salty leather in my mouth. Quickly the blood dives back under my skin to the vein from which it came. Instantly, I diminish.

The sound of water, of leaves and sky and air.

I sleep. In my dream, cars rustle along a road made of paper, a chart thrown across a great table in the room full of maps deep in the chambers of a mountaintop fortress I dare to imagine in a granite so dense no one can state its age. I dream of faces about the table. Expressionless, concentrated. I see the shape of men's faces pushing up from beneath the paper to make hillock and mountain in the cartography. Noses and foreheads and chins. I dream their mouths are lakes, their eyes pools of blue water populated by shark and whale. No yachts sail them for humanity hasn't yet invented itself. I dream the places where people will congregate to make cities and civilisations, watch them come forth from the hands that appear at the verges where they try to tear the whole of the surface from the heavy oak table on which it sits. Bodies writhe, countries divide and the earth becomes filthy with the sweating limbs of fucking hills. Riders. Some are looking over the shoulders of the map room's chiefs. Louvière is absent from the room. Of course he is. A man who was never there, not in the sense that he made any choice to be there in my dreams. In this room, it's only me and Celia. She isn't smiling for anyone. I brush hair away from her face and she displays the root of her corrupted temper. Her face unwilling to soften. How much of her amusement at my lies has transformed into anger? She's younger, and she's whispering. She tells me I must ride. I ask from what and she is yelling, her foot prodding me to rise or fall and I am up and riding once more through hanging branches and shadows and sun.

Branches against my face and blood ripples on my skin. I'm riding hard. My head brimming with the blood of effort. I haven't seen a car since I exchanged pleasantries with those men. I've seen a cart with a woman on the bench, a man walking beside the horse, the straps in his hand. Flies buzzing around the nag's eyes and ears, pieces of leather

which twitch and listen. I have seen a fisherman with his line in the water, the small ripples where it disappears on the surface. I'm riding and I can barely feel my legs. I've seen a boy, shirtless and singing to himself. Nobody recognises me, I am a rider in a valley.

Here a river, once near a glacier: hear the way it all carries mountains to the sea.

I am slowing for I have to climb the ridge rising above the valley. I have reached the point at which it narrows and the river becomes quick as it drives through two precipices of rock that were once a colossal boulder that tumbled from the mountains, dragged by glacier and placed here and split by time and water. I climb hundreds of feet. Soon the road evens and I ride above the rushing spew and it howls and pleads for the motion to stop and rest its head as it thrashes itself on the rocks. Water rises skyward. I feel it on my face, it is a face that needs the moisture and I shine momentarily. I catch flashes of yellow in my periphery as I chase tightening corners where this road has begun to wind. As if a dream has once more awakened and taken me to those fields where the sunflowers stare across a sea of themselves.

I slip through shadows. Each a cool pool as I slip out of the sun. And as I rise out of a valley into a series of corners cut out of rock I think of the south where these nightmares began, a return to the south – but there are no moments to think because now they come at me. They have returned, an hour, 80, 90 minutes, they've returned. They circle around in the dust and ride alongside me. They swear, they spit at me. I do the same. If this is a race they want – I will spit, I will swear. And I stare, my top lip like a scar. I stand on my pedals and race. Soon their bumper is inches from my rear wheel. They tease it, bumping it, but I go on.

And soon it's the case that I am heading downhill, rapidly now, descending to the valley once more where fields of

clover seem to glisten in this summer air. I pedal and get some speed but they are barely five yards from my rear wheel. I take the corners at speed, I take them so my knees barely miss the gravel as they come around and I'm in a slide I can barely control and I know a car cannot match this kind of madness because a car is not so intimately human. I hear its tyres gliding across the gravel sending clouds to the sky and great handfuls of shingle into the valley as the machine threatens to murder its passengers, whatever madmen they be. I throw myself into corners on whichever side of the road summons me. A red Lagonda coming the other way stammers at the sight of me and seems to stall its eight pistons. My left pedal gouges the paint work and someone will be regretting the lure of this valley's peaceful summons. I lose my pursuer as they pause to squeeze past the car with the shape of my skin almost impaled against its body. I sprint, but it's not a sprint. I measure my speed by the blur on the side of the road, by the gasp in my lungs as I hurtle at the straight ahead. I search inside my top pocket for the phial as the road straightens. It is gone, vanished. I feel the bike slow as the pitch decreases until I am riding once more on the flat of the valley, the ancient boulders behind me, only the shallow rise of the river to the distant hills arching into a heavy blue sky where the morning clouds are slowly burning off, shrinking against the sun. My hands shake.

They come.

I try to imagine dodging, pulling the handlebars this way and that. It seems foolish and I look for other options in the rushes by the slow waters when the bang of the engine comes to my ears as they range up out of the hills behind me and plant a foot on the accelerator and tear more gravel from its purchase in the dust. I follow the road to the left as it circles a field where, if it were in the proximity of the city, it would surely be full of picnicking men and women

eager for the sun. The car is merely feet away and I have not the nerve to try theirs as I believe they are happy to run me off the road. I head into the rough and over a patch of thick grass. I should be thrown from the bicycle, but it goes on and I find the bed of a creek dried and smooth. I glance and see their faces for the first time. I have nothing to tell me who they are, only fear. They shout things. I have no idea what language they are using for it is full of anger. One has a bottle and he attempts to throw it at me, or my bike, I can't say which — though we are one and the same to them. It disappears into the grasses behind me.

One of them shouts my name but I don't believe he knows my name.

Ahead a hundred yards the field diminishes and the road and river join once more. The car is ahead of me. Faces staring at me. A grove of trees, and I head into the grass away from the creek. I'm thrown from the ride, my feet catch in the toe clips and the machine topples with me. I feel for my limbs and I suspect one thing is broken, but I'm not sure where. It is the signals that have been sent to my head, they are rapid and dense and I don't know what they mean. I throw the bike from my body, and stand. The car is slowing in the gravel and I see a door open. I think I see guns but perhaps not. I can't say because I am running. I haven't run at this speed for a long time, a rider's legs don't run, they ride, but now I am running and I head for the river and the dark tunnel of trees. The men are shouting. They each wear hats but discard them as they begin sprinting towards me. It's my right arm. That's the broken limb, the forearm. I pull it in close and hold it with my left as I try to sprint. I gallop in some strange rotation of arms and legs. Soon I find myself in the constricting light of the trees and I take a glance back behind me. They are coming closer. I look amongst them for her, for Celia, for surely she is there, surely this is her

doing. I reach and stretch to see. I only see that one has a stick and I realise they aren't armed with weapons that shoot and fire. I almost stop.

Instead I run over old logs and they crack, a fox runs forth into the underbrush where it hides waiting for my passing. I shout. I swear because the arm's broken bone is pushing through muscle and through the adrenaline thumping through my body with each fist of a heart beat that threatens to break ribs.

'Look at me,' I shout. 'Look at me!' I don't have a reason to say these words but they come out. 'Look at me!' I'm running as hard as my legs let and I find myself in the shallows of the river where the water runs easy into the trees. I decide the water can take me. Take me like old memory flushed to the sea. I lunge into the rush and feel myself collapse onto my knees. The men at the shore. I push myself up and almost faint and fall into the water once more. I shout to myself and I'm up.

One throws a stone. I look back at them. He is 30, 40 yards away. A man in a driver's uniform, buttons picked out by light. The stone misses by some distance, making a wet clunking sound as it takes the water. I think to do the same but it's my throwing arm which has been cracked and is now making my body shake as if it weren't summer but the dark centre of a winter whose wind hacks at your body as if it were a woodsman's tool thrown again and again at the trees until something snaps and timber splinters. I swear and feel the curse straighten my muscles. I run into the water and let it surround me, I think to float down river, float to the rocks below and somehow remove myself there and find help. But help from whom I don't know. I look amongst them once more for the sight of her eyes, shaken, bloodshot. They must be from her, these men. From Discuter, from the hardest part of her mind she summoned these men to follow

me here. The punishment, an inevitable recompense for my failure as a host for my brother, for Louvière and all this damaged history. I shout her name, just to hear her named. Nothing returns.

I stumble and try to find depth in the river's centre, but there is none, just rocks that crack on my tailbone. And then another sensation. It's my head, something had cracked on my head. I put my hand up. I feel there and blood is in my hair. A small detonation in the water. The river splash and water rising in a strange way and then my shoulder. I look back at them. They are 15 yards away, their mouths are moving but I hear little because blood seems to have made its way into my ear. I stand but stagger. There are five of them and they are each in the motion of throwing a rock towards me or picking another from the riverbed. I look at their faces but not one pair of eyes I recognise. A rock catches my ear, tearing the cartilage. I put up an arm. It is my right arm, it falls at my side. I go down on one knee into the water and slip on the wet boulders. Another rock clacks into the back of my head, it stuns and I look back at them. My ears full of dull, muted sound. They stop and look, they see the blood now. Six eyes watching me, eight eyes. Ten eyes watching me. Two men standing still with stones in their hands, smooth rock and they seem to be weighing them as if someone is about to open their mouth, as if someone is about to open their mouth and finally say what they have been wanting to say since we arrived here, here at this river under an evaporating sky. I look, but she is nowhere. I look, and there's only the silence of water, broken by stone.

Author's note

While this novel is primarily a work of fiction, I have attempted to utilise historical data as much as possible, stepping outside or shifting the framework when need be. When it says it was raining, it was most probably raining. When the team are mown down by motor vehicles, they were indeed hit by cars or motorbikes. Where they place in the various stages, their times and so forth, are real. Historical records don't always agree, hence I have used my imagination when information conflicts. Although the Belgians, Celia, Louvière, the Spaniard, the Discuter team, our narrator and their narratives are most definitely fictions, the other named characters (in the main) are based on real people running about in fictionalisations of – for the most part – actual events. Australians Hubert Opperman, Ernie Bainbridge, Percy Osborne and New Zealand's Harry Watson were indeed the first English-speaking team to ride in the Tour. All the words they speak are from my mind, all voices fictions. However, for details about these men and the race itself I am indebted to numerous books, websites, documentaries and institutions.

The Kennett Brothers' biographies of Watson and O'Shea – *Harry Watson: The Mile Eater* by Jonathan Kennett, Bronwen Wall and Ian Gray, and *Phil O'Shea: Wizard on Wheels* by

Jonathan Kennett and Bronwen Wall – were an essential starting point for this novel. *The Unknown Tour de France* by Les Woodland and *The Yellow Jersey Companion to the Tour de France* (edited by the same), *Tour Climbs* and *A Race for Madmen* by Chris Sidwells, Geoffrey Wheatcroft's *Le Tour* and Ellis Bacon's *Mapping the Tour* were vital for understanding the history of the race, its many heroes and anti-heroes, the geography and roads, its place in French society and its mythology. *ANZACs on the Western Front (The Australian War Memorial Guide)* by Peter Pedersen, *Shattered Glory and Kiwi Air Power* by Matthew Wright, Channel 4's documentary series *The First World War*, Lyn MacDonald's *Somme* and many other documents were vital to the construction of Celia's, Thomas's and Louvière's narratives. *In Europe* by Gert Mak provided context, faces and the tale of the eagle in the Pyrenees. Leo McKern's 1976 narration of the documentary *Somme* supplied a sense of the occasion for when the characters visited the battlefield. Australian newspaper archive *Trove* and the National Library of Australia's collections were extremely useful in my quest to learn more about the riders themselves; indeed so were the unnamed contributors to amateur websites around the world.

Immense thanks to Andy Kifer, Rebecca Gardener and Will Roberts at The Gernert Company; Caspian Dennis at Abner Stein; Paul Baggaley, Nuzha Nuseibeh and Kate Green at Picador UK; Fergus Barrowman, Ashleigh Young and Kirsten McDougall at VUP in NZ; Damien Wilkins at IIML; my MA class; Carl Shuker for encouragement, support, advice and attitude; my family, Simon (for some early, blunt advice), Adi, Anna, Rosalyn, Francie, Henry and Jim; my readers Cate Palmer, Hannah Uprichard, Amy Head, Patrick Fitzsimons, Laura Southgate and Hamish Clayton. I must also thank

Hamish for all the priceless conversations, ideas, advice and advocacy – everything appreciated. Final gratitude is reserved for Laura. You pored through, edited, read the thing aloud when I wasn't able, made suggestions, laughed, shook your head, and let me know when I got it right. This is for you.

DHHC, March 2016